Ac...

THE BARRENS

"Consuming creative passions. . . . Astonishing insights. . . . [Oates] really gets you thinking about the perilous work of making art."

Review

"Oate...   Smith
novel   h the
autho   re of
huma   *Ierald*

"*The*   e first
page.   ness."
                                                                        Press

"Oat   e you
think   spense
nove
                                                                        Mail

"*The*   ursion
into   incing
read
                                                                        ibune

"Jo   nding,
hea   lar art
of
                                                                        urnal

"I   like a
tru
                                                                        Ledger

	DATE DUE		

THE
BARRENS

JOYCE CAROL OATES

WRITING AS

ROSAMOND SMITH

An Otto Penzler Book
———

CARROLL & GRAF PUBLISHERS
NEW YORK

THE BARRENS

Carroll & Graf Publishers
An Otto Penzler Book
An Imprint of Avalon Publishing Group Incorporated
161 William Street, 16th Floor
New York, NY 10038

First Carroll & Graf cloth edition 2001
First Carroll & Graf trade paperback edition 2002

Library of Congress Cataloging-in-Publication Data is available.

ISBN: 0-7867-1038-1

Printed in the United States of America
Distributed by Publishers Group West

Ultimately one loves one's desire, not the desired object.

—Frederich Nietzsche, *Beyond Good and Evil*

Contents

I

The Haunting

1

Where she'd died wasn't where she would be found. That was one of the few facts they would learn.

A coastal marsh near the south Jersey shore, at the edge of the Pine Barrens. Where the incoming tide lifts the body, buoys it up then surrenders it by degrees back to the marsh. Like sleeping it must seem. To the dead girl. This slow rhythmic rising and ebbing, rising and ebbing of the tide. Like breathing. A stinging northeast wind off the Atlantic pushing through cattails, seagrass. By night, by day. Dusk, dawn. A ceaseless wind. A rain-swollen sky. Even by day the swamp is shadows. When the tide returns the body seems to awaken, floating again in shallow brackish water that has frozen on its surface, and now thaws, a dark glitter thin as the thinnest glass. A stippled surface in which filaments of cloud are reflected dimly. By night, a glaring full moon. High-scudding broken clouds. As if part of the sky had been dislodged and was being blown from one pole to the other. Always the wind, always the tide! While the naked, broken body lies on its back in the posture of sleep. Head turned too sharply to one side. The mouth is opened in a mute scream. A paralyzed scream. The mouth is a hole ridged in blood. The nose has been smashed, the jaws broken. The eyes are open in their blackened sockets, sightless. Long tangled hair rippling like seaweed when the coastal water returns. Always the tide returns, twice daily, in a quickened current, in gushes. The sun burns through the mist, the body is exposed. A dead body is a broken thing. Among so many broken things. Stumps of dead trees, dead vines. The naked, broken body is stirred by the incoming tide as if waking, returning to life. But scummy with coagulated blood. Dark patches defacing the body like swaths of tar. Bony wrists and ankles bound by wire. The lacerated throat bound by wire cutting so deep into the flesh the wire isn't visible. Gulls swooping overhead, darting, stabbing with their sharp curved beaks. Their high, excited cries. Who would love this body now, who would dream of this body now?

Who would touch this body, now?

2 He was reaching out, stooping—trying to reach her.
Just to touch her! To awaken her.
To let her know *Hey I'm here, someone is here.*

Twenty-one years ago. November 1976.

In Burlington Township in a marshy, desolate area of the Deer Isle Wildlife Sanctuary at the edge of the Pine Barrens. About twenty miles northwest of Atlantic City though there was no direct route there.

Nor was there a direct route there from the girl's hometown, Forked River, on the coast, north of Atlantic City.

Twenty-one years!

Why am I thinking of this now, why now?—he did not know and did not want to know.

For he was another person now, an adult and not a distraught adolescent. He was a husband and a father of two young sons. And the girl long dead. And buried. In a churchyard in Forked River he'd visited in secret, but not for a long time. She had no spell over him now. He'd forgotten her name.

Of course he hadn't forgotten her name. *Marcey Mason.* It was more deeply imprinted upon his memory than his own name. A cheerleader's name, the name of a popular, smiling girl. *Never would he forget that name.*

The *missing girl* from Forked River, New Jersey.

At first, she'd seemed to have vanished. "Into thin air."

She'd been last seen leaving school. A weekday, early November, already dusk at four-thirty. The *missing girl* she would be called in the media. The *missing girl* she would be called by people who had not known her or her family. Those sixteen days the search was on for her. Along the Jersey coast from Breton Woods south to Cape May. Someone had phoned in an anonymous tip to police that the *missing girl* was being punished for "bad behavior" and would be found in or near water. Another tip sent search parties inland into the Pine Barren marshes and cranberry bogs along the Batsto River. The Pine Barren natives were resentful of so many strangers. Law enforcement officials. If a town girl had been kidnapped it had nothing to do with them. Though tales were told of bodies lost in the barrens, dumped and never discovered. Though local legend was, you could vanish in the barrens as if you'd never existed.

Marcey Mason was discovered sixteen days after her disappearance by hikers in the wildlife sanctuary. The *missing girl from Forked River* almost unrecognizable now.

In his dreams he'd been the one to find her. *Marcey? Marcey!* As in life he'd never spoken her name. Scarcely knew her. Yet in this fantasy Matt McBride, fifteen, was the one of how many hundreds of searchers to find the *missing girl.*

He hadn't imagined her dead, though. Her body mysteriously mutilated. Wrists and ankles bound in wire tight and brutal as you'd secure debris for dumping.

He'd imagined her alive, of course. She would have been bound, with rope; a gag in her mouth to prevent screaming. She would have been—where?—a hunter's cabin, maybe. He would push the door open, and there she'd be.

The one thing he'd been right about was the Pine Barrens.

Marcey? You're safe now. I'm here.

I'm Matt McBride. I'm here!

Her eyes had filled with tears of gratitude.

Her eyes had filled with tears of love.

The *missing girl from Forked River* was seventeen years old and a senior at Forked River High School when she was taken from the life she'd known to be sexually assaulted, tortured, and finally garroted. And left like debris in the swamp. So it happened that the *missing girl* would be forever a girl, while her classmates were doomed to grow up. Her smiling face, her freckled face. Radiantly pretty. "Innocent."

That face smiling up from newspapers, fliers, posters. Every time you turned on the TV.

The cruel thought came to Matt McBride, staring at the girl's smiling face before her body was found *I bet you aren't smiling now.*

She would be found naked. A final humiliation.

Her clothes partly burned a few yards away, on solid ground.

Immediately there was a rumor that *something was missing from the girl's body, surgically removed.*

The rumor was general in Forked River, yet no one seemed to know any facts. No one Matt McBride knew, knew.

Waking how many times sweating and excited in his bed wondering *Had he done it with a knife? Removed it with a knife? And what had he done with it—afterward?*

Even the crudest guys didn't joke about it, exactly. That part of Marcey Mason that was *missing.*

The girls pretended not to have heard the rumor. At least, in the presence of guys.

The *missing girl from Forked River.* Matt McBride hadn't thought of her in years. He was certain.

As he rarely thought now of Forked River, his past. His childhood, boyhood. Now that the old house had been sold and his father had died and his mother and sister moved to Florida and his brothers drifted from him. He'd never known Marcey Mason. He'd never spoken to her. She'd been two years older than Matt which is another generation in high school, nearly. And what an abyss between one of the most popular senior girls, cheerleader and star soprano, and a fifteen-year-old sophomore boy with acne-riddled cheeks and a cracking voice.

Within two years Matt would grow into a lanky, muscled, sports-minded good-looking American guy with a certain confidence and swagger a girl like Marcey Mason might have noticed, but of course there hadn't been time. He'd been too young.

She'd died too young.

And whoever her killer was, he'd never been found.

3 "Matt?—wake up. You're having a nightmare."

He woke. In a heartbeat. His mother's clawed hand had been grabbing at his shoulder but in fact it was his wife's hand, and it was his wife's voice warm and urgent in his ear. "Matt? Come on."

Yet how was it his nightmare, he wasn't a man who had nightmares. It belonged to the marsh, and it belonged to years ago.

He believed he was awake but the confusion continued. His heart pumping with adrenaline. He hadn't been asleep at all—had he? He'd only just gone to bed. He was insomniac, and a prowler of the house at night as his father had been, yearning for the open road. He'd seen the *missing girl* in a closeup. He'd photographed her himself. As if he'd been there in the marsh himself. His head ached from the effort. He'd wanted to save her, but he'd found her already dead. A broken body and bloodied face no longer recognizable as Marcey Mason the soprano soloist and varsity cheerleader who'd smiled at everyone, friends and mere classmates and strangers. He'd have liked to explain to Tess—or to someone—his father?—but his father wasn't living any longer—that he'd never seen the girl in death.

Nor could Matt McBride have seen such graphic photographs of the corpse for these would not have been made public, still less printed in newspapers or broadcast over TV. Not twenty-one years ago in south Jersey.

"Matt? Let me turn on this light."

Tess switched on the bedside lamp and Matt shielded his eyes, annoyed. The white T-shirt and undershorts in which he slept were soaked in clammy sweat, embarrassing to him. He saw Tess regarding him with worried eyes. As if accusing him of having secrets from her. When she smoothed his damp hair off his forehead he pushed her hand away, such close scrutiny made him uncomfortable. "Matt, you've been restless for hours. Grinding your teeth as if you're trying to say something. Maybe you have a fever? Maybe you picked something up in Florida?" Tess was anxious, and in her anxiety intrusive. Matt mumbled an apology, "Sorry to wake you up, Tess. My mind's been racing, I guess. I don't think I was asleep, exactly . . ." It was almost 4 A.M. He'd gone to bed at midnight, his usual time, and Tess had gone to bed earlier. He'd been thinking about—what? The Everglades. Where he'd been taking photographs for three days. But he hadn't had a nightmare, he was certain.

Matt swung his legs over the edge of the bed. Nervy as a spooked horse. What was it, what was wrong? He knew that Tess meant well, always, in her intrusiveness, which bordered upon wifely reproach of Matt's tendency to keep his deepest thoughts to himself. Tess meant well, so he endured her hands on him now, her hands clutching at his to stop him from scratching his head, hard, a bad habit of Matt's—"Matt, please."

"O.K., honey. I'm fine."

"You were trying to say something. What?"

He was thirty-six years old. He'd been married for nine years. He loved Tess and he loved their sons but there were times, and these times came more and more frequently, when he hated the intimacy of marriage; the curious claim of another to know his private thoughts. Maybe he wasn't a man to have married, at all. Maybe the fault was his. Guiltily he said, "Tess, I don't know. I doubt that it was anything, just nerves. Go back to sleep, why don't you?"

"How can I sleep, Matt? It's as if—" Tess paused, seeking a dramatic turn of phrase, "—something is in the room with us. Somebody else."

"Don't be absurd, Tess. It's nothing."

He would take a shower, change into dry clothes and try to salvage a few hours' sleep—he assured Tess he was fine, and apologized again for disturbing her. Telling himself *Hey look: this is marriage. You know that.*

*   *   *

Never had Matt told anyone in his adult life about the *missing girl* from his hometown. Certainly he would not have told Tess.

Marcey Mason. Buried in the Lutheran cemetery in Forked River, her "remains" put to rest.

Except: her killer hadn't ever been caught, how could she be *at rest?*

It had infuriated Matt that people wanted to believe Marcey Mason was in heaven. She was *at rest, at peace.* She'd entered into *eternal life.*

That bit about *forgiveness of sins,* too.

He'd been a hotheaded adolescent, maybe he was a hotheaded adolescent still. Injustice roused him to anger. He wasn't a guy who could shrug off outrageous news that didn't touch him personally, and he wasn't of the temperament to become cynical, depressed, immured. *He wanted action.* And yet: how?

(Rumors of what had "been done" to Marcey. What was "done" to girls who were abducted, who disappeared. As a boy he'd been guiltily preoccupied with the technical meanings of such adult, clinical terms as "assault"—"rape"—"sexual mutilation.")

Suddenly, in the shower, lifting his face to streaming water, Matt thought he knew why he'd had the dream of Marcey Mason: he'd been in the Florida Everglades taking photographs, for several days; he'd been alone, as usual; hiking for hours photographing that vivid yet dreamlike landscape, those foreshortened waterways where he'd seen logs in the glittering water that turned into alligators; the jungle of trees, dead tree stumps and snaky vines and the flash of brightly colored, noisy birds. And indistinct shapes in the shadowy interior that might be (he knew could not be) human figures, poised motion-less; or corpses, floating amid clots of vegetation. He'd been reminded of the remote Pine Barrens of his boyhood, that region of desolation that was beauty, thrilling to explore on foot.

The Barrens. The *missing girl.* He'd loved.

Not very likely he'd tell Tess these things. Or anyone.

The early years of Matt's marriage had been emotionally turbulent.

There were quarrels that flared up quickly, like a lighted match touched to flammable material; the sexual attraction between him and Tess was so strong, maybe they'd mistaken it for something deeper and more abiding. They'd quarrel passionately, Matt might storm out of the room, out of the house, he'd sometimes slept apart from Tess on a sofa, on a floor, even outdoors. . . . Difficult now to recall what they'd quarreled about. And usually they made up within a few hours, repentant, apologetic, self-berating; they made up, and made love, and forgave each other. For the time being.

Now they were older. Years older. The fever pitch of their early passion had subsided. Matt instructed himself: *You're not a kid, you're an adult. Got it?* "Mathias" was his baptismal name—"Mathias" sounded impressive, like a name carved into a tombstone. He was a husband, and he was a father. He was a responsible citizen of Weymouth, New Jersey. Far from the small town insularity and dead-end prospects of Forked River. Right? Far from the romantic desolation of the Pine Barrens. Absolutely. He was a junior associate in the most aggressive—and the most successful—real estate brokerage firm in central New Jersey and no longer an itinerant photographer bumming his way around the continent, to Alaska and back, being befriended by strangers, including women, numerous congenial women, as he'd done in his early twenties. No more!

He'd married Tess because she'd seemed to love him in a way that other women hadn't. And because she was pregnant by him. And because he, Matt McBride, in his guilty pride and vanity, was not a man to refuse her; nor to insist upon an abortion in the face of Tess's desperation though he'd sensed, at the time, it was a feigned desperation, the expression of a will adamant as his own. He did not think *She has tricked me, trapped me.* He did not think *What is marriage, why is this happening to us?* He'd ceased thinking such thoughts because he'd made his decision, and he believed it was a wise, mature decision. To protect a woman, shield a woman. He would marry Tess, and invent himself as a young husband and father.

He'd tried. And he wasn't going to give up.

*   *   *

It was nearly 4:30 A.M. when Matt, his mind still restless, returned to the bedroom. Tess had fallen asleep as he'd hoped she would, yet, perversely, to martyr herself for his benefit, she'd left the bedside lamp on. Her face, in sleep, looked masklike; the corners of her mouth turned downward. Matt switched off the lamp; he could see well enough in the dimly moonlit room. He went to a window to look out. The night sky, illuminated by the moon, but muffled by strands of cloud, like looking into a cavern that opened into infinity. It was a cold January night. A good night to be inside, and warm. Far from Forked River and the ocean, and farther from the Pine Barrens where, on such a night, the wind would shake the Atlantic white cedars into a frenzy. Six hundred fifty thousand acres of pineland, cranberry bogs, coarse sandy soil. Matt had tried to cajole Tess into taking the kids there for a few days, staying at a motel and exploring the Barrens, but Tess had some objection, she'd worried about ticks bearing Lyme disease, or infected mosquitoes, poisonous snakes . . . "It's a kind of lost, empty place, isn't it? The kids would be bored."

Tess meant she'd be bored. And that was likely.

This far inland, in Weymouth, you could not hear the ceaseless melancholy slap-slapping of the surf. You could not smell the stinging-wet odor of the ocean. In summer a faint, or not so faint, smell of decaying things on the beach. The Forked River municipal beach where Matt and his friends had swum, even when the water was declared "unsafe" for swimming, was nothing like the scrupulously tended tourist beaches of Seaside Heights, Barnegat Light, Atlantic City. Matt liked to think how far he'd come, to live in Weymouth. Sometimes he felt a thrill of pride, even aggression. In Weymouth where everyone had money. *I got here. And I'm here to stay.* At other times he felt guilty, uneasy. As if, not belonging in Weymouth, he might be found out. Or would expose himself, one day.

Tess didn't trust him on the trips he took without her, on business or for purposes of photography. She hadn't trusted him even before she might have had reasons not to trust him. He knew she searched through his things, his computer files if she could retrieve them, she checked his calendar, his address book stuffed with slips of paper and cards; sifted through the papers in his desk drawers, the pockets in his weathered duffel bag and the very lining of his suitcases. He knew, and could not confront her. It was an embarrassment to him. He didn't want to embarrass Tess, too.

You think I've been unfaithful to you?

If she'd asked outright, he might have admitted, yes. A few times. Sometimes. That was his nature, his temperament. He was susceptible to women, he was sexually attracted to women, and frankly he liked women, and marriage hadn't changed that. But Tess would not ask.

Matt's father had advised, in his bluff, hearty man-to-man way *Don't confide in any woman you have to live with.* And, sagely *A woman you live with isn't your friend.*

Matt slipped into bed without waking Tess. He didn't want to resent her: he loved her. He resolved to love her. And he wasn't going to think of—that. The *missing girl*. The Barrens. That part of his lost life he didn't understand, and had grown beyond. He should think instead of the next morning. Matt McBride at Krell Associates where his boss seemed to like him. Where he had a talent for making money. He was happy, wasn't he? Yes. Very happy. For what ease in this, lying in bed beside a sleeping woman, an attractive woman, and in your own house. Safe. As a kid obsessed with sex you fantasize sleeping with a woman but can't fantasize intimacy. For it was intimacy that was the painful matter, and not sex. And this was intimacy. This, now. Some nights with Tess, after love, he'd felt that plunging into the unknown life of another, giving yourself up in the wordless intimacy of flesh, was the true significance of life, and all else was trivial. He'd felt he did love Tess and that this, marriage, was not a trap but the great adventure of adult life. He knew it was possible.

4 Next morning, which was the first Monday morning of the New Year, after the visit from the Weymouth detectives leaving him stunned as if he'd been hit over the head with a sledgehammer, he would realize *This was why. The dream. The missing girl.*

The dream had been an eerie premonition. If you believed in premonitions.

The *missing girl* from Forked River, and now the *missing girl* from Lismore, six miles away. Matt McBride had dreamt of one because the other was imminent in his life. Because he was to be questioned about the other. Drawn into the other. His life abruptly altered because of the other.

He wasn't a superstitious man, yet there it was. Superstition is a kind of primitive faith and Matt McBride was too skeptical for faith. He'd been baptized Lutheran, like Marcey Mason, but he hadn't known her from church because he'd avoided church as a kid believing that religion was for women and weak men.

If Matt had any belief about life it was something his father had told him. *What you see is what you get, kid. Or what you'd get if you could get it.*

5 " 'Mathias McBride'?"—the name was spoken courteously, yet with an air of doubt, as if the speaker, a Weymouth Township detective, had to wonder if it belonged to Matt. "We'd just like to speak with you for a few minutes. Do you mind?"

Just like to speak with you. Do you mind.

Matt would recall these innocent-sounding words for a long time.

There were two Weymouth Township detectives. Of course they'd introduced themselves, they'd even shown their badges, maybe. But in the confusion of the moment, Matt just stood there, behind his desk, smiling, bewildered. The elder of the two detectives was a man in his late fifties who wore glasses with black plastic frames of the kind Matt's high school algebra teacher had worn, years ago. You wanted to think *This isn't a man to take seriously.*

It was shortly after 9 A.M. the first Monday of the New Year. Matt had been back in Weymouth hardly twelve hours and he'd been in his office at Krell for hardly a half-hour and now Weymouth Township detectives had come to speak with him, on what matter he could not imagine.

That inevitable stab of guilt. *What have I done.*

Matt was genial, friendly. Matt shook hands. One of Krell Associates' most promising junior associates. And everyone in Weymouth Township knew multimillionaire Sidney Krell. If the detectives resented Mathias McBride's position, his private office furnished in expensive walnut, sleek black leather and flawless chrome, plush carpeting and that ceiling-high thermal-pane window flooded with winter sunshine, they were too shrewd to reveal it.

Matt invited the detectives to sit down. Showing his willingness to cooperate, he dragged a chair across his carpet for the younger, more taciturn of the two men, who was regarding him with a terse part-smile. As if to say *Think you're bullshitting me? I know you.*

The elder detective asked Matt to tell his secretary not to interrupt their conversation, and Matt did so, feeling his face burn. He wasn't scared. (Was he?) He had nothing to hide. (Had he?) He was wishing he hadn't removed his coat just before the detectives arrived. In his shirtsleeves and flashy suspenders he felt exposed, vulnerable. In his Italian silk tie. What was Matt but a South Jersey kid, an imposter here in Weymouth. These detectives saw through him. He'd been the kind of restless, rebellious kid who'd gotten into trouble in school, fighting in the cafeteria, "mouthing off" as it was called to teachers who pushed him too far. With some of his friends Matt had been suspended for a week from Forked River High in his junior year, only just defending themselves in a brawl in the parking lot. Unfairly, Matt's father gave him hell, walloping him on the head and shoulders with his fist the way you'd beat, not hard but with exasperation and disgust, a badly behaved dog. *Somebody's gonna beat the shit out of you, one of these days.*

The older detective was asking Matt about a young woman named Duana Zwoll.

" 'Duana Zwoll.' " Matt repeated the name cautiously. "I—know the name. Yes."

"The name, or the woman?"

"Both." Matt swallowed hard. The detectives were civil, smooth But he understood how easily that might change.

"Young woman, attractive. Twenty-six. Resident of Lismore, New Jersey. Artist and freelance graphics designer, she's done work for a Weymouth company called VisionView Graphics. You're acquainted with this individual, Mr. McBride?"

Carefully Matt said, not knowing where this was taking him, "I've met Duana Zwolle, I wouldn't say I know her. Has something happened to her?" And this was innocently asked.

Of course something has happened to her. Why else would these men be here.

"*Has* something happened to her, Mr. McBride? We're wondering if you have any information."

Matt's throat went thick. "Why—are you asking *me*?"

He knew it was a mistake to get excited. To appear emotional. He'd had encounters with police, years ago. Of course, at the time he hadn't been a resident of Weymouth, New Jersey. He hadn't been an employee of Krell Associates. Men like these two in their off-the-rack suits and bargain neckties seated in his chairs, on his carpet, regarding him calmly, were cops, naturally suspicious, wanting to be given good reason to be suspicious. He had to realize, too, that they were packing guns.

Matt told them he'd met Duana Zwolle once or twice. Possibly three times. He'd met her locally, at an art gallery in Weymouth. "My wife and I are interested in art, we'd been invited to an opening of her sculpture exhibit. . . . I think." Why was he saying *my wife*? He heard this as the detectives were hearing it. Though he spoke sincerely, truthfully, yet his voice sounded like the voice of a guilty man; a man who knows more than he's acknowledging. And he'd begun to sweat. "Has something happened to—the woman?"

It was difficult for Matt to pronounce the name "Duana Zwoll."

This was the second time Matt had asked the question, but the detectives chose to ignore it. The elder was removing from his briefcase a photograph for Matt to examine. It was a black-and-white glossy, five inches by eight. Matt steeled himself for something ugly but saw only a smiling photo of the young woman, one he'd never seen before.

He had a premonition. She was the *missing girl*. In his pessimistic heart, Matt knew.

The detectives were watching Matt closely. He stared at the likeness of the dark girl in a loose-fitting T-shirt and paint-splattered jeans standing self-consciously beside one of her curious artworks: a collage-canvas of crowded, sculpted shapes. Zwolle was smiling shyly, like one who dreads the camera. It was a smile that seemed to hurt her somber face. Her eyes were large, dark, what you might call luminous. Beautiful. "Mystic" eyes. (Who knows, maybe she was high on a drug? Possibly she was manic?) Matt didn't want to look into those eyes, those were eyes to be avoided.

She appeared to be an intense, serious young artist, in her soiled clothes. She was barefoot; her arms were slender but sinewy with muscle. She stood in a posture of vigilance, steeling herself against the camera's flash. Her thick eyebrows nearly met at the bridge of her narrow, delicate nose; even as she smiled, or tried to smile, her manner was brooding, distracted. Matt had wondered, seeing her in Weymouth, if she had East Indian blood. Moroccan? Possibly she was part-Iranian. Certainly she appeared exotic, though it may have been a quirk of personality. That hungry searching look, that made a man uneasy.

Her hair coarse and crimped like a horse's mane falling past her shoulders. That slightly rank, oily odor.

"Yes. This is Duana Zwolle."

"You're aware that this young woman is missing?"

"Missing? No."

The younger of the detectives told Matt that Duana Zwolle had been reported missing since approximately 6 P.M., December 28. Her place of residence had been left unlocked, lights on, and her car was found in the Delaware Water Gap the next day, keys in the ignition. Zwolle was supposed to visit her family in Maine at Christmas, they said, but she hadn't turned up. People who knew her said it wasn't like her to go away without informing anyone. She'd left food on a kitchen counter as if she'd been interrupted preparing a meal. And there were other facts inconsistent with Zwolle having gone away voluntarily. "We have reason to think you might know something about her, Mr. McBride?"

"Me? But why?"

The detectives looked at Matt, calmly. As if they knew something Matt didn't know, or had forgotten.

Matt said, awkwardly, "I've been away myself. In fact, I left on the morning of . . . I guess it was December 29. I've been traveling in Florida, mostly the Everglades. Taking photographs. I just got home last night. I didn't know about any of this. I hope—"

Matt's words trailed off into silence.

"You don't have any idea where Zwolle might have gone, Mr. McBride? Try to think."

Matt said, stung, "Of course not. How could I know? I'm not a friend of hers."

"But we have reason to think that you are a friend of Zwolle's. Mr. McBride."

"I told you, *I am not.*"

Now Matt recalled: the last time he'd spoken with Tess, from Florida, she'd mentioned having heard that there was a young woman in the area believed to be missing; that young woman artist they'd met with the strange name, Tess couldn't remember. But Matt had had other things, more urgent matters to speak about with Tess and the subject was dropped.

Matt said, swallowing hard, for he understood now the nature of the detectives' interest in him, and wanted to set them straight, "As I've said, I didn't know her. 'Duana Zwolle'—I'd assumed it was an invented name. She was—is—one of a number of artists who'd moved here from Manhattan in the mid-1990's, to live in old farmhouses and converted millworkers' rowhouses on the Weymouth River, in the country. Brockden Mills, Fall Creek, Lismore—picturesque little villages. I think Zwolle lived in one of the converted mills on the river." Matt paused, not liking the way the detectives were letting him speak, asking no questions. "I've never seen her loft. I mean, I'd heard it was a loft. Is a loft. I'd never been invited inside and . . ." *I wouldn't have gone inside if I had been invited.*

Matt's face was burning painfully.

(What did the detectives know? What were they assuming?)

Matt wasn't going to suggest to the detectives, as Tess would probably have suggested, that the local artists, these emigrant Manhattanites, lived very different lives from the rest of Weymouth. There were the usual rumors of sexual promiscuity, homosexuality, drug use. Cocaine, heroin. Matt had always dismissed the rumors as purely spiteful, envious. The fear and loathing of the bourgeoisie for those individuals, most of them younger, who refused to lead conventional lives: marriage, mortgaged houses, children. And high-paying high-stress jobs like those at Krell Associates.

Matt said uneasily, "I've assumed you've asked Duana Zwoll's friends, the people she's worked with . . ."

"We've asked, Mr. McBride." The younger detective was smiling, in a way Matt didn't like.

The older detective said, affably, "We've asked. And one of the men cited as being seen with Miss Zwolle locally, Mr. McBride, is *you*."

"But that's not possible . . ."

Suddenly the tone of the conversation shifted. In fact it wasn't a conversation, but an interrogation. The detectives' civility had worn thin. "O.K., Mr. McB.," the older detective said, his mouth twisting on *Mr. McB.*, as if he tasted something repugnant, "we have evidence you've been involved with this young woman now missing. So tell us how long you and Miss Zwolle were—involved?"

"But I haven't been 'involved' with her. I've never—seen her privately."

Was this true? Matt tried to remember.

"If you know something about where she is, what's happened to her, any information, Mr. McB., now's the time to tell us. It will go much easier for you."

Matt protested, "But I don't know anything about her. This. I'd only met her a few times . . ."

"Never been alone with her, you're claiming?"

"I . . . might have given her a ride home, once. A few weeks ago. November. She'd asked me if . . ."

"October."

"Was it . . . October?" Matt stared at the younger detective, who'd supplied this information. He didn't want to think how the man had known.

"October 25, to be exact."

Matt's mind worked rapidly. Was this a game? But why him? Did they believe he, Matt McBride, was more vulnerable than another Weymouth man? Did they know something about him, his past, he didn't know himself? Had they been talking to people about him? He felt dazed, sickened. He'd read of cases in which police, prosecutors, lying witnesses and informants can railroad an innocent person into prison; but these innocent persons were usually poor, powerless blacks and other ethnic minorities, not citizens of Weymouth, New Jersey.

"If there are other dates you'd seen Zwolle, you can tell us now," the older detective was saying, in his affable, chilling way, nudging the black plastic glasses against the bridge of his nose, and pretending to regard Matt McBride with a modicum of respect, and not outright suspicion. "The more you can cooperate, the better."

Matt said, quickly, "If someone happened to see me with Duana Zwolle on that date, or whenever, it was—just that once, and really a kind of accident. I know, under the circumstances, it sounds unlikely, but . . ." Matt was beginning to sweat visibly. Like a scene in a nearly forgotten movie it came to him; a scene of virtually no consequence in Matt's life. (For how could he tell these men, these unsympathetic strangers, that, the previous fall, he'd had a brief affair with a local woman; a woman he had not loved, and who had not loved him; and Tess knew nothing of it, suspected nothing; and now the affair was over, and done. How could he tell these men that in the context of his emotional life at that time, the strange young woman Duana Zwolle had meant little to him? *He could not.*) "She needed a ride back to Lismore, she said. Sometimes she rode her bicycle into Weymouth, and she'd had an accident with the bicycle and it was being repaired and she ran into me on the street, only just by chance, and—she asked me if I could drive her home."

That was it. That was all it was. Surely they would believe him?

The memory came to him: the girl in her clothes that looked as if she'd been sleeping in them, paint-splattered, wrinkled; her hair long, coarse, uncombed, unkempt; young-looking, like a high school girl and not a mature woman in her mid-twenties. *Excuse me? I think we've met? Your name is—Matt?* She'd surprised Matt, smiling at him, approaching him on the sidewalk. In front of the library. Out of nowhere she'd stepped. Weymouth was a small, friendly village, residents said hello to one another, smiled and exchanged greetings, so this wasn't unusual, or shouldn't have seemed unusual; except Matt had been taken by surprise, for the girl, Duana Zwolle, who'd reintroduced herself and shook Matt's hand, seemed oddly excited. She was clearly shy, yet aggressive; in that way in which shy individuals can be aggressive, pushing themselves into actions for which they aren't suited. Almost, Matt had felt accosted. Another Weymouth woman, knowing Matt McBride from a distance, might have addressed him much more easily, and subtly; Duana Zwolle seemed lacking in such social graces, or subterfuge. Matt was left wondering if possibly this was a sexual advance? Or was he (he wanted to think, yes he was) imagining it? *My bicycle's in the repair shop. I wonder—if you could give me a ride home? If it isn't too much trouble.* Of course, Matt had said yes immediately. He'd been flattered, in a way. It was an awkward encounter, he wasn't attracted to this odd girl, she wasn't his type, but certainly he'd be happy to drive her home. Weymouth was a place, and a state of being, in which friends and neighbors rarely asked one another for favors, as people had done in Forked River, where no one had money. So Matt said yes, sure.

October 25, evidently. Someone had recorded the date.

In Matt's car he'd smelled her: the hair. Yes, possibly he'd felt a sexual stirring. That long crimped hair. Her slender body, small breasts and narrow hips. A fragrance about her that was waxy, feral, yearning. *She wants me. This isn't an accident.*

But Matt wasn't going to tell the Weymouth Township detectives any of this. It was too bizarre. It would only make them more suspicious. He was too much of a gentleman. He felt protective of the girl, who had to be in trouble. He wasn't a man who spoke cruelly or even critically about women.

And he couldn't tell the detectives about the other woman, with whom he'd had an affair. A locally well-known woman, wife of a well-to-do businessman. The detectives would know the name. Matt would protect that name, too.

No wonder he was sweating, squirming.

"So I, I told her yes. I'd drive her home. She seemed so—forlorn. I felt sorry for her, riding a bicycle. Wanting to save money on gas, I suppose. Maybe she didn't even have a car. I guess she didn't make much with her art and I felt sorry for her and—" Matt paused. The detectives regarded him with their deadpan irony. Clearly they were in possession of some information, it may have been erroneous information, that Matt knew nothing of. "Look, I didn't go inside her place with her. That single time. I drove her home. As a favor. It wasn't— personal."

The older detective said, "It was what, then?—'impersonal'?"

The younger detective muttered something to his companion, out of Matt's earshot. A play upon the words *personal, impersonal.* A joke, and probably a dirty joke. Matt's excessive innocence was beginning to grate.

Both detectives laughed. Matt was shocked, angry. He saw that in their relationship the younger was the one to make the older laugh at strategic times. The younger was the feisty bulldog that might take a sudden bite out of some poor bastard's ankle, while his master looked on indulgently. And Matt had been halfway thinking, during this conversation, that the younger detective, who was about his age and height, might be feeling sympathy for him.

Sympathy! They hated Matt McBride's guts.

Knowing he might be a kid from South Jersey, here in Krell Associates in red-checked suspenders and dark silk Italian tie and expensive leather shoes, they hated his guts all the more.

"Maybe," Matt said, feeling a drowning sensation, "—I should call a lawyer."

(Or should he have said: *my lawyer.*)

Now the detectives looked at him with outright scorn. "Whatever you wish, Mr. McB. If you think it's necessary."

"You seem to be accusing me of—something. And you have no evidence, no right—"

"We're just inquiring what you know of Duana Zwolle who's been reported missing," the older detective said evenly. "We have reason to think you know where she is, and what's happened to her."

Matt said, "I've been away! I've been in Florida. I—I have airline receipts, hotel receipts—I'm sure I've kept them."

The younger detective said, "Right. We're sure you kept them, too."

The older said, "You left Weymouth on the morning of December 29, Mr. McB. But the young woman disappeared on the 28th, in the evening. You had time."

"Time for what?"

The detectives stared at Matt calmly.

Matt said, nervously, "I was home that evening. The 28th. I was packing for the trip. I was with my family. Some friends came over for drinks. Ask them." (But maybe that had been the evening before? Matt wasn't certain.)

"Mr. McB., does your wife know about Duana Zwolle?"

"Why the hell are you calling me 'Mr. McB.'? Is my name some kind of joke or something?"

" 'Mr. McBride'—you'd prefer?"

Matt. My name is Matt. I want you to like me.

"Yes. I'd prefer."

" 'Mr. McBride.' Does your wife, Mrs. McBride, know about Duana Zwolle?"

"Know what? What's to know?"

"Your relationship with Zwolle, Mr. McBride?"

"I told you: I had no relationship with Zwolle. There was nothing between us."

The detectives exchanged a glance. Matt couldn't decipher it. A look of exquisite satisfaction, like men who've just learned their long-shot bet has come in? The older detective said, "Nothing between the two of you, Mr. McBride."

"Yes."

"So you can't help us in our investigation. That's your statement?"

"I can't help you any more than I already have."

Matt might have thought this was the end of it, but the older detective continued without missing a beat. "O.K. When's the last time you saw Duana Zwolle?"

"I have no idea." A pulse was beating in Matt's brain. He want to hurt both these men, with his fists. "Any more than you could tell me, asked such a question. If I knew—I'd help you. But I can't."

"What about December 20, Mr. McB.?"

"December 20?"

"Didn't you see Miss Zwolle that evening? Think carefully."

Despairingly Matt ran his hands through his hair. He couldn't think, couldn't remember. Was it possible that Duana Zwolle had been a guest at one of the several pre-Christmas parties he'd gone to? Dimly he recalled some of the young artists to whose circle she belonged at Sidney Krell's reception in the Weymouth Country Club. As many as two hundred people must have attended. He'd been drinking, and he'd had a good time, and his good times blended into one another, blurred as faces in a crowd. "I don't know. I don't think so."

"That night, you didn't drive Miss Zwolle home?"

"I did not."

"And December 24, Christmas Eve?"

"Christmas Eve? Certainly not!"

"You claim you didn't visit Duana Zwolle at her place in Lismore, you didn't bring her a gift? A white cashmere shawl? Think carefully."

"No, I did not. I was with my family. Where the hell are you getting this from? A white cashmere shawl—?"

The detectives glanced at each other. The elder said, wrinkling his nose, "Miss Zwolle's diary."

"Her *diary*?"

"Didn't know the young lady was keeping a diary, Mr. McBride, eh? But you should have. Lots of them do."

Matt protested, "But—how can I be in her diary? I never had anything to do with her."

"No? That's not what you'd guess from what Miss Zwolle has written."

"Look, please! There's got to be a mistake here, officers. A misunderstanding—"

" 'Detectives.' Not 'officers.' "

"We're detectives, Mr. McBride."

"—'Detectives'! What did she write about me? She hardly knows me. Can I see this—diary?"

The elder detective said, "Miss Zwolle's diary is not for your perusal at this time."

"Then how do I know you're telling the truth?"

"If there's an arrest, a formal booking, you'll know. Your lawyer can help you out then."

"An arrest? But—"

Again Matt felt as if he was drowning. As if his brain wasn't getting sufficient oxygen. It was a TV scene, this sort of cruel yet casual interrogation, the detectives had their scripts memorized but he, McBride, poor bastard, didn't have a clue. He felt like a boxer who's been worked over in the ring by an expert. Not a part of him that wasn't bruised, aching, leaking blood. Christ, the very hairs on his head hurt. His mouth tasted of bile. As soon as these guys left—and they were on their feet now, preparing to leave—he'd rush to the lavatory and puke. His hands would be shaking through the day, he'd be distracted and miserable. (What had been planned for Matt McBride's day? Numerous telephone calls. And a luncheon at the Saddlebrook Country Club with a client.)

Matt said, desperately, as the detectives moved to the door of his office, "I guess—you looked in the Water Gap? In the river? If—"

The detectives smiled at Matt, as you'd smile at a clumsy dog on its hindlegs, executing a trick of frantic pathos. "Right. We did."

"She might have just gone away. By herself. Voluntarily. She—I think Zwolle might've been married, at one time. Or—involved with some man, another artist. What I mean to say," Matt wasn't sure what he meant to say, only that, now that the detectives were about to leave, he didn't want them to, "—is that her life, her personal life, might be—complicated."

Matt was informed that, though he wasn't under arrest, he was advised not to leave Weymouth without informing them. If he did, a warrant might be issued for his arrest. "At the least"—as the older detective phrased it—he was a witness in a criminal investigation, thus he was obliged to tell them everything he knew or had reason to suspect, or he would risk being charged with obstruction of a criminal investigation. He should provide them with the receipts he'd mentioned and all paperwork involving his whereabouts for the past week. This would include the names and addresses of people who'd seen him. He was "strongly advised" to make an account of his itinerary, everything he'd done since the afternoon of December 28 when Duana Zwolle was last seen by a Lismore neighbor. He was "strongly advised" to make a written statement of his version of the relationship between Zwolle and himself. And anything he might know of where she might be if she'd gone away voluntarily—"In a missing-person case like this, we never rule that out." Or who might have taken her away, or why.

Matt said, numbly, "She's been abducted. That's the word, isn't it— 'abducted.'" It had a tabloid ring, a fate to make you wince.

The detectives were presenting Matt with their cards. Plain white cards with plain black print. Weymouth Township Police. These men, Matt had to know, were county employees: agents of local government. Their salaries were well below Matt McBride's. He felt the injustice of it, and sympathized with their resentment of him. Long-time residents of this part of north-central New Jersey had a right to resent the swarm of new, moneyed residents who were moving into their hometown areas, driving up property prices and taxes, transforming the countryside. Matt stared at the cards: Phelan, Ricci. The elder was obviously Phelan, the younger Ricci. A team. He was work to them, a morning's work. They would write up their reports on Mathias McBride. Detective Phelan, whose first name happened to be Matthew, was telling Matt that he'd be hearing from them soon. As if to cheer Matt up, since he'd virtually crushed his balls, Phelan said, with a small measured smile, "Mr. McBride, it's possible that you know more than you think. In these investigations, we find that people surprise themselves. They always know more than they think they know."

This struck Matt, in his dazed state, as a revelation of surpassing beauty.

" 'People always know more than they think they know.' I'll remember that."

It was then that the younger detective Ricci, the one Matt had hoped, had fantasized, might be on his side, said something unexpected. The husky youngish man was winding a blue woollen muffler around his neck, one of those items of masculine attire that signals a woman's touch, a gift of affection and esteem, causing the world to perceive him at a slightly altered perspective, as Matt was perceiving him, and feeling again a pang of dismay, of loss, that the two of them were so separated, defined as adversaries, and suddenly Ricci pointed to a photograph on Matt's office wall, and said, "I like that."

I like that. Matt smiled, confused. As if he'd been passed a basketball by a star teammate, now what? He'd have to be equal to the gesture.

Matt said, "I—I took that, myself. It's one of—mine."

The photograph was minimally framed, under glass. At first it appeared abstract in design, but if you looked closely you saw it was an action show of an expressway (in fact, the Jersey Turnpike) at night, in driving rain; in the foreground a giant diesel truck was speeding by in a blur of spray and mist, in the background, on the far side of the median, was an accident scene. Here there were smoldering wreckage, strewn glass, flares. Here were medical emergency vehicles, police cars and vans. There was a festive look to this scene of horror. Or you could say that there was a horrific undertone to what appeared to be a scene of garish motion, bright streaming lights. And now, seeing the scene from the detectives' perspective, Matt had to realize it was a work-scene, too. Many of his—Nighthawk's—photos recorded work-scenes, in the guise of compositions of arresting idiosyncrasy and beauty.

"It was a lucky shot," Matt said. "I mean, for me. When I'd first moved to New Jersey, driving back from Manhattan on the Turnpike." He wanted to say more, to speak excitedly of the experience of the event itself, daring to park his car on the shoulder of the Turnpike, climbing out of his car in the rain, trucks rushing by, the urgency of the moment as he gripped his camera in his hands.

Ricci said, "I like how it catches the eye, y'know?—draws you in. Regular art, I don't get much out of, but a photograph like this, of something real, it makes you think."

The older detective Phelan was staring at the photograph, pushing doubtfully at his glasses.

Ricci said to Matt, "You take these photographs as 'Nighthawk,' right? That's like your—pseudo-name?"

Matt said, " 'Pseudonym'? Not really. I mean, Nighthawk isn't a secret. It isn't that big a deal. It's just a name I use. For professional reasons."

He would think afterward that Phelan and Ricci had done their homework, investigating Matt McBride. They knew about his photography. They knew about Nighthawk.

Ricci said, " 'Nighthawk.' The photos are in the *Star Ledger*, right? *Jersey Monthly*. I see them, I always like them. There's always something in them to make you think."

There were other Nighthawk photos on Matt's walls. He'd had them framed, he'd hung them himself. McBride's vanity. But, well—he was proud of his photography, too. Few clients ever so much as glanced at the photographs and if they did, they made no comment.

Matt said, as the detectives left, impulsively, "I—I'm very anxious about this visit. I wish I could help you. Her. 'Duana Zwolle.' But—"

He would recall afterward to his chagrin, and hurt, that neither of the detectives had shaken his hand in parting. Not even Ricci.

6 *But I had nothing to do with her. Nothing!*
I never touched her, I scarcely know her.
There was nothing between us, please believe me.
If she has been hurt, if she has been killed—I know noth-
ing *about it. God help me.*

Even as Phelan and Ricci were departing in their unmarked police car Matt was in the men's lavatory and subsequently he would work through lunch to catch up on the calls he'd missed, even as new calls came in. He would log in a productive ten-hour day which would include an unexpected on-the-site sale of a $850,000 custom-built contemporary "junior estate" in the Fox Hollow Hills subdivision to a young professional couple moving to Weymouth from Montclair. The commission for Krell Associates on this sale was 6% which included a 1% bonus for Matt McBride—$8,500 for approximately three hours' work. So that Matt could tell Tess that evening in response to her query that his first Monday of the New Year 1998 had been a good day, a very good day.

Maybe he wouldn't need to tell her about the detectives? The diary? Maybe he wouldn't have to upset her, and jeopardize the happiness of their family? Vulnerable as a candle flame it seemed to him suddenly, that happiness. Any harsh random wind might snuff it out.

7 *The wrath of the world.* That night after Tess and the boys were safely asleep and he had the house to himself he sat in a downstairs room darkened except for a single lamp burning on the table before him and like a man in a trance began to set down, at first hurriedly and disjointedly, then with more control, his "itinerary" of the past week and an account of his "relationship" with the missing Duana Zwolle. Handwritten notes these were, with a classy black-and-gilt ballpoint pen embossed with **Krell Associates**. He'd spread the Florida receipts out before him, the itemized hotel print-outs, the flight schedule his travel agent had drawn up for him. Newark to Miami, his Miami Beach hotel, a succession of motels east to west through the Everglades region, the Hilton at Pavilion Key on the west coast. A car rental service, Miami to Sarasota. Airflight from Sarasota to Newark. *My alibi* he was thinking.

How goddamned degrading, demeaning. To be required to explain himself to strangers. To prove he hadn't been in sufficient proximity to Duana Zwolle's residence in Lismore, New Jersey, to make it likely he'd been the one to abduct a young woman by force.

To abduct, and to murder. Possibly rape and murder. For surely that was Duana Zwolle's fate if she'd been missing a week.

The wrath of the world. He'd never believed in Hell, they hadn't been able to scare him as a kid with Hell, but yes he surely believed in the wrath of the world.

He'd been baptized Lutheran, despite his Irish name and his Irish-descended father. His mother had been a serious Christian, possibly, after the age of forty, a little unhinged ("unhinged" was his father's casual term and the consensus in the McBride family) who'd prayed devoutly for the salvation of his soul. She'd taken him to church with the other, younger children until he was eleven, when he'd rebelled. It had been a violent scene, abrupt and unexpected: his mother had slapped and shaken him so he hadn't any choice but to desperately shove her from him, and she'd stumbled backward like a woman in a TV comedy to collide with the kitchen stove, crying out in pain and outrage—"*You!* Little Satan!"

Still, Matt had loved his mother. He'd wanted to make her happy but hadn't known how except to accompany her to church and pray with her, and that was out of the question. He'd felt sorry for her and was deeply embarrassed by her and he'd known to steer clear of her, the wild singing moods as well as the daring raging moods, and as soon as he was old enough, by the age of thirteen, he had after-school jobs and in summer full-time jobs that kept him out of the house for long hours and provided him with money and a certain adult independence. He had two younger brothers and a mildly retarded younger sister and he'd liked growing up fast to put distance between himself and them.

You! Little Satan.

How could it be true, there were too many things that scared him.

His father hadn't believed in Hell—or Heaven—or any of that "ghost world" as he called it disdainfully. But then his father, who'd left the family a number of times while Matt was growing up, drifting away from Forked River, drifting back, hadn't believed in much of anything. *The wrath of the world* was something you could assume, it didn't require any supernatural assistance. *You have to make the first strike, kid. You don't provide just a target.* Through much of Matt's childhood his father worked as a trucker for a long-distance van company that kept him continuously on the move. He belonged to the Teamsters Union and made a good salary. Most of the time he sent a good portion of his salary home. In his own way he was a responsible family man; he loved his children. To prove he loved them he sometimes had to "beat the shit out of them"—though in fact he never hurt them, much. Matt, the oldest, was the most in need of discipline but his father's favorite because the most like his father. Their names were both "Mathias"—but no one ever called them "Mathias." Matt

liked it that his name was the same as his father's but he refused to
be known as "junior."

What he'd known of his big, burly, gray-haired father, he'd admired. Though you needed to be cautious around the man. But then,
Matt's father was rarely home and when he was on the road he rarely
called and when he did call it was likely to be late at night and he
was likely to be drunk, though genially, sentimentally drunk so that
you could love him at a distance, nine hundred miles away in Ala-
bama, three hundred miles away in Connecticut, twelve hundred
miles away in California. You could feel your throat choke up hearing
at the other end of the line that hoarse cheerful voice. *Hey kid, how's
it going? Taking care of your mom, are you? How's the weather there?
Saw this program on TV, the Atlantic coast is washing away! Good
thing we don't live in some millionaire's place on a barrier island,
right?* Twenty years later in the affluent Village of Weymouth in central New Jersey Matt would recall those long summer evenings in
Forked River when his father was home, drinking ale and tossing a
softball around with Matt and his brothers, and those impromptu Sunday drives down the coast to Atlantic City for salt-water taffy, hotdogs
on the Boardwalk, a couple of intense hours at the slot machines in
the casinos—"Your mom won't even know we're gone." Thrilling to
be taken on such breathless outings, an eighty-mile round trip but
Matt figured that was nothing to a trucker used to driving hundreds
of miles in a single day keeping awake on coffee and No-Doz and
something called "ice"—"crystal"—that Matt's father could lick off
his fingers.

Happiest in motion Matt's father had been. Matt couldn't blame
him.

It happened that Matt's father knew the father of the *missing girl.*
They'd gone to grade school together. The case outraged and disgusted
him and for a long time, when he was home, he could talk of little
else. Drunk or sober. He was convinced that the police knew more
than they revealed. He was convinced it was some guy from the neighborhood who'd known Marcey, and she'd known him—"She wouldn't
have gone away with any stranger, right?" Generally, it was believed

in Forked River that a stranger had taken her. There was a steady
stream of traffic through Forked River coming and going from Atlantic
City. At the time of Marcey Mason's disappearance when hundreds
of people were searching for her in the vicinity of Forked River, including volunteers from the high school, including Matt, Matt's father
was on the road but telephoned home every other night to see whether
"that poor girl" had been found yet. It's times like these, Matt's father
told him, when you wished there was a God. Somebody to pray to.
And you wished there was a Hell so the filthy son of a bitch who'd
done this, whoever he was, could suffer for eternity. *Just killing him,
just an execution, if they even catch the piece of shit, isn't going to be
enough.*

8 NAME UNKNOWN. In dreams the visions came to him. That is how he understands they are pure. And not of mere earth.

What do you know of Duana Zwolle they asked of him and he told them he knew nothing but had heard of her disappearance and would pray for her. *I believe in prayer* he said seriously. Stroking his beard he knew they smiled to see, a wisp of a beard springing from the edge of his chin. A beard of silvery blond that did not seem to match the darker sand-color of his hair. *The power of prayer* he said.

He knew they smiled at him in secret. He knew their thoughts of him in secret. He'd known *the girl's* thoughts of him in secret.

He who desires but acts not, breeds pestilence. These words of William Blake he would have liked to inform them but he was too shrewd to utter such. For they were detectives in search of *the girl* and he must remain innocent and not provoke them.

NAME UNKNOWN. His simplicity of heart. He'd spread crusts of bread on the water for the waterfowl squatting on the edge of the river bank knowing her eyes watched him from the high window of her loft. And she would remark to friends *What a good man he is. A simple man. And not like us.* And her friends would tell others, and so the word would spread.

They would not be the first to misinterpret NAME UNKNOWN. To condescend. They would not be the last.

In his trailer in Clinton Falls they came to him. Quickly walking up the snowy rutted drive. Their breaths steamed, they were bare-headed. He knew their car was a police car though unmarked and they were police officers though not in uniform. It was just into the New Year and he'd been expecting them. Or others in their place. So he was prepared. NAME UNKNOWN was never not prepared.

What do you know of Duana Zwolle they asked of him and he did not laugh in their faces saying *I know what you don't know of Duana Zwolle* but instead gravely told them nothing, he knew nothing and her disappearance did not surprise him. And they asked why. And he said with his air of sorrow like Christ who both loved and pitied humankind *Because she once told me, she might have to escape to the West if there was danger from that man.* And they asked what man. And he said simply he did not know. *Her former husband* they asked and he shook his head not knowing. *Or another man* they asked. And he shook his head not knowing.

They asked what is that barn and he explained it was his work studio. He was a sculptor. *Come and I'll show you!* Eagerly he led them to the weatherworn barn not taking time to put on a jacket, his breath steaming and wisps of hair and beard flying in the cold wind and in the studio as in a sacred space they contemplated in silence the life's work of NAME UNKNOWN he wished to retain. His *Marriage of Heaven and Hell* as he called it. Five life-sized female figures with plain painted manikin-faces. Modest and perfect to his eye unlike the brazenness and dirt of actual females. These were made of scrap metal from his various workplaces, yet beautifully polished, and molded wax, and a sand-clay mixture and carved wood and rag-cloth and lifelike glass eyes made of children's marbles. He explained his art to them. And may have spoken too loud and eagerly. For not many visitors had come to this new studio since he'd moved to Clinton Falls the previous winter. There was the Brough woman who loved him and who came to cook for him and clean for him but she was ignorant of art and adored anything by his hand. As she adored his beard and his cock unquestioned. The elder of the detectives interrupted to ask *Do you sell many of these, Mr. Gavin?* and he laughed to hide his fury explaining he would only consent to sell *The Marriage of Heaven and Hell* to a museum as an entirety. *How do you make your living, Mr. Gavin?* the detective asked and he said quietly he did sell certain works of art sometimes, smaller figures, carvings of animals and birds sold for him in a gallery in Weymouth and in another in New Hope. And he was a welder. The younger of the detectives with a sky-blue muffler around his neck of the very hue of the eyes of the oldest figure was prowling about pretending to admire the figures (while in fact his pebble-colored eyes were glancing rapidly about into every corner and crevice of the studio within view and he managed even to step as if by accident on one end of a cardboard carton flattening it) and he said *These statues—is that what you call them?—must be a lot of work, take a lot of time. Where do you get your ideas, Mr. Gavin?* And humbly he uttered the simple truth *In dreams, visions come to us all. An artist is one who remembers.*

And so they went away. As he willed they would.

Watching smiling from inside the trailer. Stroked his wispy beard, and laughed. The ignorant fools believed him of course. Like the other times. They would check out his account of where he'd been on the night of *the disappearance* but the Brough woman who adored NAME UNKNOWN knew what to say. And how to say it. Not smoothly as if memorized. And the boy Randy who was slow-witted but stubborn. They would remember the TV of that night. Which all had watched together and enjoyed. In the woman's place, in Lismore. Yes he had stayed the night with her for often he did. There was no shame to it, they were to be married soon.

At least, the Brough woman so believed.

The detectives went away at last. They had not searched the trailer. They had no warrant to search the trailer. There was no reason to search the trailer. They would have found nothing if they had searched the trailer. Or his twelve-year-old Ford pickup in the drive. Or the barn. He was not a suspect really. If he'd been questioned by them it was not as a suspect really. Only twice in twenty-one years prior to this, in Mountainhome, PA, & in Salem, Del., had he been questioned by police but both times on his own premises, not at a police station. And he had not been booked, there would be no record of *Joseph Gavin* in their computer. For his answers were always simple and direct. His accountability for the times the females had been taken had satisfied them it seemed and he had never been a serious suspect. He was certain.

Never arrested in his lifetime. Nearly forty years, in calendar time. And never would be arrested *for God would send a blazing ball of fire to claim him.*

God have mercy on you, Joseph! she whispered when he removed the gag and she was able to breathe & speak. *O God have mercy on us both.*

But God had only half granted the female's prayer.

9 *How guilt rises like bile at the back of the mouth.*
Even if you are innocent. Blameless.

"There's nothing to this, Matt, is there, eh? The girl."

Sidney Krell put the question to Matt McBride in his blunt, no-bullshit manner. Without inviting Matt to sit down.

"No. There is not."

But how the hell do you know about it? So soon.

In stubborn silence, nursing his hurt and his anger, Matt let Sidney Krell ponder his words. Since he was telling the truth, why should he explain further? Goddamned if he would. He was shocked that Krell knew about his alleged involvement with *the girl* but he wasn't going to show that, either. Matt McBride was blunt and no-bullshit too; that was one of the reasons he and his employer got on so well.

It was near noon of January 6. The Tuesday following the Monday of this terrible new year. Matt hadn't told Tess yet about the detectives' visit and he'd spent much of the night composing a document for them and his head rang with questions and protests and denials and he'd anticipated a day at Krell Associates of intense, concentrated work to keep his mind off the other and now Sidney Krell who was as close to Matt McBride as any living person (since the death of Matt's father) had summoned him into his office an hour before the two men were scheduled to depart for a luncheon meeting at the Weymouth Country Club with several investors, under a pretext of wanting to prep Matt for the meeting, as he often did in such circumstances; and instead he'd confronted Matt with this insulting question.

Unless, Matt thought, it was a reasonable question.

Krell was looking at him with shrewd, watery eyes. *You wouldn't lie to me, son?* A light flashed on Krell's phone indicating a call waiting, but Krell ignored it. His eyes were webbed with broken capillaries, like his goiterous nose; in a rumpled thousand-dollar suit tailormade in Hong Kong he sat hunched forward at his massive desk in his habitual buzzard posture, sucking at his lips. His raspy breathing sounded as if he'd been running upstairs. He said, "I didn't think so, son. Just wanted to hear it from you."

"Well, you heard, Sidney."

It was disturbing to Matt that Sid Krell already knew—whatever it was he knew. The *missing girl*, the *diary*. Probably he knew about the detectives' surprise visit, too. *Nothing gets past Sid Krell in Weymouth* was his boast. Once when he'd invited Matt out for drinks he'd told him you could think of Sid Krell as a fat old dimpled spider at the center of an enormous web, plump at the heart of Weymouth Township. Every quiver of this web registered with him. Every real estate sale, every sizable contract, loan, partnership, lawsuit, bankruptcy, success story, betrayal registered with him. Every living creature that flew into the web—flew and stuck—was known to him.

In his gruff-kindly voice Krell said, "Sit down, Matt. Let's talk."

Hardly twenty-four hours had passed since Phelan and Ricci had come to question Matt McBride. But a far longer period of time had passed in his interior life. *Nothing will be the same now, ever. Her revenge.*

"Maybe you don't want advice from me, Matt. That's your business. But in any sticky situation like this, where there's cops investigating—I'd recommend Jules Cliffe. Y'know Jules, yes?—I introduced you once, I think, on the golf course." Krell hadn't introduced Matt to the lawyer, but let that pass. Matt was well aware of Cliffe, of course; like Sidney Krell, Jules Cliffe was locally renowned, controversial and expensive. "He's expensive, I admit that," Krell said with a shrug, "but he's worth it. And I could help out, y'know. If it came to that."

If it came to that.

Matt had pulled a hefty chrome-and-leather chair up close to Krell's desk as he usually did during their prepping consultations. The acid-black bile taste at the back of his mouth was stronger now, he'd been compulsively swallowing since he'd stepped into Krell's enormous office. He wanted to think that Sid Krell only wanted to help, he'd been generous to Matt in the past as to other younger associates, but with Krell there was often another motive, a deeper and more elliptical motive that wouldn't surface of its own accord.

Politely Matt said, "Thanks, Sid. But I don't need a lawyer."

Krell snorted, flaring his distended nostrils. "Don't need, or don't want? Think carefully, son."

Who else was it who'd recently told Matt to *think carefully*?

He could feel his blood temperature rise.

In his slangy tough-guy manner, acquired from TV or movies to disguise the fact of his intelligence, cunning and instinctive good taste, Krell was saying, "You retain a lawyer like Cliffe and the cops back off fast. The D.A.—y'know, he's an old pal of mine from our days together on the county executive board—he'll back off too, not exactly eager to be made an asshole of in public. Because what these guys do for strategy in law enforcement, and you can't blame the bastards, they're hustling like the rest of America, is to squeeze the balls of some decent upright kind-of naive guy they know is innocent, like you, but they figure they can extract some information from him he wouldn't otherwise provide. It's a game. It's shitty but it's a game. Either you know how to play, or you don't. *You* don't, Mattie. It fucks me up they're screwing with you, who's *my* guy! That's a personal insult, goddamn it." This was a new tact, and Krell stayed with it, his face reddening, jowls shaking as he cursed, until Matt felt an impulse to lay a comforting hand on the elder man's shoulder, to apologize for his own bad luck. Krell said indignantly, "God-damn those cops obviously know Matt McBride isn't their man!—if anybody even took the girl away and she didn't run off by herself—or fake suicide like some of 'em do—they know you're not a true suspect but if they can scare you enough, and blackmail you with threatening to leak their 'evidence' to the media—"

"Evidence? What evidence?"

Krell's gestures were extravagant but vague. "This diary. The girl was allegedly keeping."

The girl. Krell alluded to *the girl* as if she had no name.

And Matt concurred. *The girl, the girl.*

The adversary, and not an equal.

This, Matt would remember later. The coded language between them as men.

Matt tried to speak calmly. A pulse beat in his brain but he heard himself explaining patiently, as if for the first time: there could not be any diary involving him because *he wasn't involved with the girl.* He wasn't even a friend of hers. If there was anything about him in the diary (which he doubted) it would have to be fabricated, and he didn't know why this would be, and he didn't know what to do about it. "It's like a nightmare. And I feel it's only just beginning," Matt said.

How like a frightened, guilty son he was sounding, baring his soul to Sid Krell. The buzzard-father, greedily eating Matt up with his bloodshot drinker's eyes. This was the father who out of his own magnanimity, not out of a sense of justice, would forgive his son even if he didn't believe him. *It's us against them, Matt. It's a Weymouth power thing. Trust me.*

Already it was noon. They were scheduled to depart for the country club at 1 P.M. in Krell's chauffeur-driven Lincoln Town Car. Matt hoped to hell that, by then, he'd be in better shape.

Krell had heaved himself out of his swivel chair like a fat porpoise breaking the surface of the water, puffing and drawing all eyes. As the old man did during staff meetings he was pacing on his carpet, gesturing extravagantly as he spoke. You could see that Krell was morbidly thrilled by Matt's predicament. Matt's anxiety. And the something sexual in the girl's disappearance that had attached itself to Matt despite his innocence. (Surely Krell knew that Matt was innocent?)

Sidney Krell had long ago created himself as a mythic character, a reformed juvenile delinquent (by his own account), a romancer of women (others would attest to this, too), and an "autodidact" of finance (though Matt had heard that Krell had inherited millions of dollars in trust from a grandfather). Krell liked to boast that he'd pioneered in residential and commercial development in hilly rural central Jersey, fighting citizens' zoning boards, township councils and in recent years state and federal environment protection agencies; he'd managed to win more often than he lost, while amassing enemies in the process. "If I had a buck for everybody who hates my guts, I'd be a millionaire." (This was a familiar Krell remark; the joke was that Krell was a multimillionaire in any case.) He'd been sued so often he had a team of lawyers on permanent retainer and he boasted he'd sent their kids through Ivy League universities and law schools. He'd been married twice and divorced twice and was now married to a much younger woman, a former model who was often in their Manhattan apartment or "traveling with friends" as Krell explained with a hurt, brave shrug. Now in his mid-sixties, he had the air of a much younger, antic man. He played competitive golf, tennis, racquetball with younger men like Matt McBride, and made them work to beat him. He had a large, bald, gleaming bulb of a head and thick-tufted eyebrows and a hard little paunch carried like a basketball above his belt. Once, when they were drinking together after the office had closed, and everyone else had gone home, Krell showed Matt his "private protection"—a wicked-looking Smith & Wesson .35-caliber revolver with a polished walnut grip he kept locked in his desk drawer. Sometimes, Krell boasted, he carried the gun inside his coat; he'd had threats against his life, and had acquired a permit for a "concealed weapon." He'd invited Matt to hold the gun, examine it—"Just to get a feel of it, son." But Matt only laughed uneasily and declined. Krell also owned shotguns and rifles. He belonged to the National Rifle Association. He called himself a "natural-born hunter"—though he hadn't much time any longer for the sport. As he was a connoisseur of women though he hadn't much time any longer for women—"Except if one sort of tumbles in my lap, y'know, Mattie? Must happen to a good-looking guy like you all the time."

It had been with typical flamboyance that Krell had hired Matt McBride, exactly doubling his salary to lure him away from an investment company in Bloomfield, New Jersey solely on the basis of an intense conversation the two had had, meeting by chance in an airport cocktail lounge in Atlanta while waiting for a delayed flight to bring them home. (Krell insisted upon upping Matt's coach-class ticket to first class so they could continue their conversation on the plane.) Krell admired Tess as a woman of "high quality" as well as beauty and he even admired Matt's "Nighthawk" photographs and had hung several prominently in the foyer of Krell Associates amid potted trees and stylish inlaid tile. He told Matt he'd wanted to be an artist himself but he'd needed to hustle instead. He'd had to grow up young. He'd made his first million when a million dollars was still a million dollars, by the age of twenty-seven. To Matt's embarrassment he was in the habit of telling Matt he liked his style—"Whatever 'style' is, y'know? You and me, we understand each other."

Krell had stepchildren, more than he wanted. But he hadn't any children. Matt guessed that that had a lot to do with the old man's fixation on him.

Krell was assuring Matt that no one knew about the alleged diary except a few individuals—"Of whom I happen to be one. Never mind how, or why. It's top secret for the time being. Cops keep things like this confidential. There's other things about the investigation I know." Krell was sitting on the edge of his desk, his breath wheezing, looming over Matt like an ominous moon. He'd been a handsome man once, Matt knew from photographs, and you could make out his youthful cocky good looks inside his jowly flushed face with its thin, curiously flaking skin like a peeling wall. "This is confidential, Matt: the girl had a pitiful savings account, less than one thousand dollars, at Midland, and forty dollars in a checking account. Forty dollars! And there's a rumor she owed individuals money, too." Krell paused to let this sink in: Matt guessed Krell was one of those individuals. "Both the accounts hadn't been touched—which doesn't prove, to me, she might not have gone off by herself, faking a kidnapping or a suicide. Though maybe she did commit suicide and didn't want the family to know. She always looked kind of dark to me, foreign, like she has Indian blood, Hindu I mean, and maybe there's shame in suicide in that culture, like with Catholics? *I* don't know. Also, her Visa card is missing and nobody's tried to use it. Sylvia was saying—" Sylvia was the elusive Mrs. Krell—"she'd heard a rumor the girl was a coke user

and hung out with some black guys in Newark who deal in coke but
I wouldn't know, and that isn't in the police report, that I've heard.
She was mixed up with some homeless organization in Newark, I know
that. But the main thing they're keeping secret from the media and
what I've got to swear you to secrecy about, Matt, is—" Krell's voice
lowered dramatically, and he leaned close to Matt so Matt had a
sudden whiff of something sweetish and fumey—whiskey?—so early
in the day?—"In this place she was living in, a renovated old textile
mill in Lismore, on the river, the cops found what they're describing
as an 'obscene drawing or cartoon' of a naked female meant possibly
to be her. A 'hateful' thing. It was left on her bed where it couldn't
be missed." Krell paused, breathing hard.

Matt was amazed. "Sid, how do you know these things?"

"I know, Mattie. Old Sid has his sources."

"And the diary—have you seen that?"

"No. I have not."

"But—what do you know about it?"

"Only that it involves Matt McBride. In some way."

"But that's impossible."

"Well."

"Sid, it *is* impossible. I didn't know her."

Matt's voice was raw, pleading. He hadn't meant to sound like this
but there it was.

Krell said, with an embarrassed shrug, "If you're lucky, Matt,
maybe you won't need to tell Tess about it. Maybe it will—" He made
a vague gesture as if waving away a bad odor. "If you get Cliffe on
their asses, they'll have to turn it over to you. He'll talk to the D.A.
Maybe they won't pursue it. Maybe she'll show up—alive. I wouldn't
put it past a person like that, she's said to be pretty unstable, who
knows? And this drawing or cartoon, they're going to have to show it
to some art expert, I'd guess, to help identify who might've done it. *I*
haven't seen it." Krell went on to tell Matt there'd been fresh footprints
in the girl's loft made by some sort of boot with a distinctive rubber
sole and there was sand they think came from the south Jersey shore
and the place was torn up as if someone had been searching for

something and angry he couldn't find it. "And her artwork—'collages' I guess is the technical term—he'd ripped into with a knife, like he didn't think much of her avant-garde style." Krell's fleshy lips curled in disdain and Matt was thinking uncomfortably there was something wrong here: it wasn't like Sid Krell to be so mean. He could be malicious and funny, but he'd never been purely malicious in Matt's experience, and in recounting tales of others' misfortunes he'd usually shake his head pityingly. Truly bad luck, illness, and death impressed him. There was something out of character here, and ugly.

He's maligning her. Why?

Krell was energetically warning Matt not to breathe a word of what he'd told him to anyone. "My ass will be burned if any of this goes out of the room. I'm taking a big risk for you, my friend." Matt tried to smile. *My friend* was good to hear. (Or was it?) There were numerous Weymouth men of influence to whom Krell was connected, including Republican county officials, and members of the township council, and the chief of police himself, and any of these, Matt guessed, might be Krell's confidante. They might be in business together. Who knew? Quite possibly Krell even knew the detectives. It was like Sid Krell to betray another man's trust even as he made a show of swearing Matt to secrecy. He even chided Matt for having tempted him to disclose secrets: "It's just that I don't want you to anguish over this any more than you need to. See? If there's a diary—I mean, there *is* a diary—and there's some embarrassing stuff in it—maybe even involving me. Hell, sure, I'd guess I'm in it, too. Women get their revenge, eh?" Krell laughed like a man in pain, wiping at his eyes.

Matt said quickly, "Sid, I didn't tell the police I'd met Duana Zwolle through you. I mean—I didn't even think of it. That time after work? When I was leaving, and you were coming in, and—"

Matt paused, realizing that, on that occasion, Krell hadn't introduced the girl to him. He'd had no idea who she was. It had been the briefest of encounters.

Krell interrupted, "I don't know what the hell you're talking about, Mattie. Take care."

Matt's face burned. He knew himself rebuked, like a favored dog who's been suddenly kicked. "I told the police I'd met Duana Zwolle at her gallery. And that was it."

It has nothing to do with you, Sid. Don't worry.

Coolly Krell said, "Sure, kid. That was it. Just tell the suckers the truth. Nobody's taking any oaths here, and nobody's up for perjury. See you later."

So Matt was dismissed, and returned to his office not knowing what Krell's final words meant. Possibly Krell himself didn't know. *Life is mainly making things up on the spot, what's it called—improvising. You don't know what the hell you're going to do until you do it. And nobody else does, either.* Matt's father had told him and his brothers such practical wisdom, in his beery philosophical moods, driving at eighty miles an hour on the Atlantic City Expressway. The old man had seemed to think that these words were optimistic, and maybe that was so.

It was nearly 12:30 P.M. Krell's sleek black Lincoln Town Car would be leaving for the Weymouth Country Club soon, promptly at 1 P.M., as Krell's cars always left on time; so Matt returned to his desk, his desk that was a maze of work to be navigated as a rat learns to navigate a maze in a psychological experiment, excited, not nervous so much as excited, wanting to think that instinctively he'd said just the right thing to Sid Krell, to assure him and to calm him. Krell was a good person at heart. (You wanted to think that.) At any rate, Krell wasn't evil. (Definitely, you wanted to think this.) And obviously Krell had been anxious about—what?—whatever threat it was the *missing girl* represented. *Sid's in the diary, too? Sid's a suspect, too?*

No wonder, the smell of Seagram's on Krell's breath at this early hour of the day.

Matt knew that Sidney Krell spoke of certain kinds of women carelessly and boastfully and he expected other men to tease him (and admire him) as a randy old goat, but such allusions could never be specific, only general. You'd never allude to "Oriana," for instance. Whether there'd been anything between Krell and the woman, or not. Had it been a mistake, then, for Matt to speak so frankly to his employer? He'd only just told the truth after all. The truth he'd told, or hadn't told, the detectives. *Nobody's up for perjury.* But what did that mean?

In Weymouth, in Krell's circle of highly successful yet chronically restless men, it wasn't uncommon that a man, married or not, might be involved in one way or another with a younger woman. Some of these were what you'd call romantic friendships. Some were probably sexual. There was a loose, shifting class, or caste, of attractive young professional women, office workers, public relations and media girls, commercial artists and "real" artists like Oriana and her younger friend Duana Zwolle who might be hired for short-term projects by local companies, or offered commissions; the fees Sidney Krell offered must have been difficult to resist. These artists sold their serious work infrequently and couldn't make a living from it any more than "Nighthawk" could make a living from photography.

In Matt's car, driving Duana Zwolle back to Lismore, maybe they'd talked about this, briefly? And Duana Zwolle had murmured almost inaudibly she wasn't that kind of artist, and Matt had said what in reply?—he couldn't remember. Even if he'd replied, at all. *She asked would I drive her home. I said all right. Though in fact I was busy that afternoon and pressed for time. But I drove her to Lismore and that was it. I don't recall any significant conversation passing between us.*

So he'd written down, for Phelan and Ricci. It was true!

Still, Matt was troubled. After luncheon with the investors—the project was a proposed $150 million medical office complex on a vast tract of land north of the Village of Weymouth, a project Krell had had in mind for at least a decade—he'd take Sid aside and apologize if he'd spoken out of turn. He didn't think he had, but if Krell thought so, that was all that mattered. *Sid, I didn't mean to imply you'd wanted me to—lie, or anything. Because I didn't.* And Krell would slap his meaty hand onto Matt's shoulder and say *For Christ's sake, Matt. Don't give it a thought.*

Yet there was this doubleness to Krell. He wanted you to trust him absolutely but if you knew him, his sly side, his shadow-side, you'd have to be a complete fool to trust him. Yet, if you were clever like Matt McBride and a few other associates at the company, you couldn't ever hint that you knew this: that would be "disloyalty" in Krell's book.

The last time Krell had invited Matt over to his palatial split-level home, without Tess, he'd arrived to discover just Krell's wife Sylvia there, smiling and provocative, with an excuse that Sid had been called suddenly out of town, and Matt was shocked and embarrassed to be thinking *He wants to fix us up together, that's it?* He'd had a single drink with Sylvia and departed and he had the uneasy idea she'd laughed at him kissing her on the cheek at the door and saying, "Another time, eh, Matt?" A few years before, Krell had sponsored Matt for the Stony Brook Tennis & Racquet Club without telling Matt beforehand—and damned if Matt McBride hadn't received an invitation by certified mail to join. To celebrate, Krell took Matt and Tess out to the club for dinner, crowing midway in their expensive meal, "What'd I predict, Tessie? I practically built this fucking place with my own hands." Zestfully, he cracked his knuckles and the three of them stared at his big-knuckled hands as if he'd worked an actual miracle with them. Krell seemed not to know, or was pretending not to know, the import of his words: that Matt McBride had been invited to join the Stony Brook Tennis & Racquet Club not because the membership had wanted him but because of his sponsor's clout; and that Krell had exercised his clout primarily to impress Tess, who'd known of the sponsorship.

Matt had laughed uneasily. "Sid, thanks for all this. But I can't."

Krell's smile rapidly faded. "Can't what?"

"Can't join."

"Why the hell not?"

"Because—" Matt tried to think of a reasonable excuse, other than the self-evident, "I'm not the type."

"Certainly you're the type. *You're my type.*"

Matt said, "That's flattering as all hell, Sid, but—"

Sid interrupted impatiently, "Don't you condescend to me, my friend. You're invited in this place, you're *in*." He turned to Tess, with softer eyes. Placed a hand on Tess's bare arm. "Talk some sense into this guy, Tess. This is your background, you'll be comfortable here, and so will Matt—eventually."

So Krell had talked them into it. Though the induction fee was high—$6,000. And the monthly dues were high. And the charges, and surcharges. Matt had to admit he enjoyed being a member of a prestigious private club to which no other associate at Krell Associates belonged. Playing tennis, racquet ball, squash with a client and taking him to lunch and signing his tab instead of paying. *Makes you feel like you really belong, McBride. But to what?* This spring, Krell intended to sponsor Matt McBride for membership in the even more prestigious Weymouth Country Club. Tess was hopeful this would work out, too.

Thinking these thoughts, Matt lost track of time. When he checked his watch, he'd discovered it was 1:12 P.M.

He's gone without me. That's it?

10 And then as he'd seemed to know he would, though he was more frightened than he'd ever been in his life, and his very life close to extinction, he found the *missing girl*.

He, Matt McBride! He was the one, after all.

She was floating underwater and he'd dived into the water or possibly he was already in the water and he'd opened his eyes. As you open your eyes sometimes into a dream and immediately you're there. The water was murky-green. There was the girl's long, beautiful hair streaming about her head, lifting and floating and tangling with seaweed. And her eyes fixed on his. *Help! help me!*—her voice was so soft, he almost couldn't hear it. He felt the words as vibrations like an electric current along his nerves. Yes he would help her, of course he would help her, yet in fact he resented her, for he wanted to live, and helping her was dangerous for she would grasp at his arm, and her fingers were slender but strong, he knew, he knew those fingers, she would pull him down with her to drown yet he hadn't any choice but must try to save her for his father was watching and urging him on. *Can't just let her die. You're a man now, not a kid. Call yourself Nighthawk!*

So Matt pushed toward the girl. Through the dense, murky-green water. His heart pounding nearly bursting with the effort. This water like liquid plastic. He was choking, he couldn't breathe. And his legs were caught in clotted seaweed. Black muck. But he was able finally to grab her snaky streaming hair, both his hands closing into fists, and *pull! pull!* and there he lay on the bank of the pond, heaving and gasping. *Where was the girl?*—he didn't know, and didn't dare look.

11

People know more than they think they know.
But, he was God-damned sure, he didn't.

Neither Detective Michael Phelan nor Detective Arturo Ricci was at Weymouth Township Police Headquarters when Matt McBride brought over a manila envelope containing photocopies of receipts and his scrupulously itemized "itinerary" and his account, brief but scrupulous as well, of his "relationship" with the missing Duana Zwolle. He left the material with a secretary explaining it was an important document relevant to the Duana Zwolle case. And quickly departed the modern glass-and-brick building and in the parking lot approaching his car he saw peculiar blister-blotches against snow, icy pavement, dreary pine trees and cloud-massed winter sky as if these were being blackened by the action of something like flame pressed against them on a reverse side, the way paper is blackened by a lighted match in the instant before it bursts into fire, and for a confused moment he wondered if this might be an unanticipated eclipse before he realized he was faint-headed, swaying on his feet like a drunk.

But he didn't pass out. He'd been terrified they would arrest him when he'd stepped into the building, maybe that was it?—he'd been thinking, or half-thinking, it was a cop trick to get him to headquarters, of his own volition and without a lawyer? But he hadn't been arrested, and he hadn't passed out. He got into his car, he drove away a free man. His heart expanded like a balloon being rapidly blown up. Maybe the police would let him alone from now on?

He hadn't told Tess about the diary, yet. Days had passed and her behavior toward him indicated she knew nothing, suspected nothing, no one had told her anything, maybe there would be nothing to tell?

Tenderly they'd made love each of the days since Matt had returned from Florida, half-sobbing Matt whispered, "I love you, Tess—I love you," desperate to keep his concentration on Tess, on his wife, on this woman he'd married, this woman who was alive and warm and responsive and grateful in his arms, this woman who loved him in turn and was the mother of his sons he adored, this woman who whispered in turn, "I love you, Matt," and not the other, the *missing girl*, the *drowned girl*, the *lost girl* who clutched at him with her thin fingers, her stark staring eyes and hungry mouth and the tugging-grasping rhythm of her vagina teasing him to a frenzy.

At Krell Associates the daily pace was frantic and bracing as always and Matt McBride was so busy, he'd made no special effort to determine if his eccentric employer was avoiding him or whether (and this was likely given Krell's own frantic schedule) he was out of the office much of the time, possibly out of town. (Matt called Sid's home, unlisted number several times, just to check, and the answering service clicked on, Krell's hoarse voice announcing there was no one to come to the phone right now but if you would like to leave a message giving your name and the time of your call . . . Which left the matter irresolute.) *At least I'm not fired*, Matt thought cheerfully.

At Krell Associates, you were fired within hours of crossing the old man or "disappointing" him, or you weren't fired.

A day, and a night. And another day. And the detectives didn't call, and Matt began to breathe more easily, yet guiltily, like one who has slipped through a net.

12

LISMORE, N.J. RESIDENT MISSING,
10th DAY
POLICE CONTINUE SEARCH FOR
DUANA ZWOLLE, 26
Free-Lance Artist Disappeared Dec. 28

WOMAN ARTIST, 26, MISSING
CENTRAL N.J. RESIDENT
Investigation Broadens in
Probable Abduction Case

JERSEY STATE POLICE CONTINUE SEARCH
FOR MISSING LISMORE RESIDENT, 26
Zwolle Family Offers $50,000 Reward

Several times a day Matt rapidly scanned newspapers, watched TV news and listened to the radio. How many times a day he checked the Internet, typing in DUANA ZWOLLE only to call up, to his intense disappointment, same minimal information, thrown back into his face as if in mockery. Almost, Matt could hear the abductor's taunting words. *None of you will find her, she's mine.*

That had to be it: an abductor, male.

He'd taken her, for what purpose you didn't want to think. The *missing girl* was either alive at the present time, or dead.

Articles about Duana Zwolle in the *Newark Star-Ledger*, the *Philadelphia Inquirer*, the *Trenton Times* were becoming less frequent. Each newspaper had initially published front-page articles, followed by prominent inside features; there were interviews with friends and acquaintances, photographs of the missing woman; the *Weymouth Weekly* had devoted two full pages to the case, including photographs of Zwolle's collage-canvases. But now, articles were buried on inside pages, no more than a paragraph or two in length. *Investigation continues, no new developments. No arrests.*

No mention of an obscene drawing. No mention of the alleged diary. No mention of Mathias McBride.

These were secrets the detectives were purposefully keeping from the media. That made sense, of course. It was only routine police work. Matt had to wonder if there were other secrets about the case, which Sidney Krell didn't know.

Matt had to wonder how long "Mathias McBride" would be protected.

He dreaded the public exposure, the humiliation. He knew that if his name were linked with Duana Zwolle, and Zwolle's abductor was never found, he'd be forever assumed to be that abductor. That murderer.

(Had Sidney Krell been questioned? Matt had reason to think, yes. But Krell was tight-mouthed, and if any of the Krell Associates staff knew, they would never tell.)

Detectives Phelan and Ricci had "appealed to the public" via New Jersey Network, asking for information about Duana Zwolle, but they'd declined to comment extensively on the progress of the case. They'd interviewed a "considerable number" of people, all known friends, acquaintances, neighbors, associates of the missing woman. If they had suspects whom they were investigating, against whom they were building cases that might justify arrest warrants, naturally this wasn't public information. Matt stared at Phelan and Ricci on the TV screen, willing them to speak more articulately, with more animation, zest. Phelan, shoving his old-fashioned black-rimmed glasses against the bridge of his nose!—he looked no more competent than a middle-aged CPA, dazzled by an excess of information. And Ricci, for whom Matt felt, still, an unreasoned brotherly regard, looked ill-at-ease before the camera, speaking stiffly as if he were uttering prepared words. *No. Yes. We can't comment on that. Our number is . . .*

In Weymouth, it was generally assumed that Duana Zwolle would be found, eventually. "Found dead. Poor thing. What else? These things happen all the time." Matt overheard others speaking of the case familiarly, and he resented their mock concern. Especially, women talked about the *missing girl* as if she'd been taken in their place. A kind of sacrifice. "This terrible thing, so close to *us*. Only a few miles away." Tess was frequently on the phone, speaking, Matt assumed, with women friends. Or maybe with relatives, her sister in San Diego who seemed particularly eager to hear the latest Weymouth news, when the news was bad. "No, I didn't know Duana Zwolle, certainly not. We didn't belong to the same social circle. Hardly! But I admired her art, to a degree. And I keep thinking about her, seeing her face. Those eyes . . ." Tess's voice quavered. Matt wanted to wrench the damned phone receiver from her hand, in disgust.

He didn't, though. He tried not to speak with Tess about the *missing girl* at all.

Driving to Krell Associates, each morning Matt listened to local and state news, restless, bored, anxious, impatient. The drive was a twenty-minute commute but sometimes Matt turned off the highway and onto a side road to delay his arrival, cruising through hillsides newly gouged out for the foundations of houses and office buildings as in an anteroom of Hell, if Hell was a honeycomb of "development" without end. Matt awaited the "flash! news bulletin" that would end the case, Duana Zwolle's body discovered in the Delaware River, in a shallow grave beside the river, by the side of the Turnpike, in the Pine Barrens . . . but the only news bulletins were of traffic accidents, multialarm fires, miscellaneous violent deaths. It was not going to happen, Matt thought, panicked. They would never know.

None of you will find her. She's mine.

One morning, parking at Krell Associates, Matt saw Sidney Krell in his gleaming Mercedes in the space reserved for *Mr. Krell*, head bent with listening to his car radio, his face in profile creased in sobriety like the face of an ancient turtle.

The old man was listening to the same worthless news Matt was listening to, and Matt could guess why.

He had to wonder: had Sid Krell been in love with Duana Zwolle?

He had to wonder: did Krell know more than he'd let on, about what had happened to her?

Matt had risked getting into serious trouble, if Krell had found out, but he'd done some casual querying among his colleagues and learned that, yes, in fact Krell had offered Duana Zwolle a "commission" for a mural. How much the commission was, no one seemed to know exactly. Five thousand, ten thousand, twenty thousand? The sum was an initial payment for an original mural in Zwolle's collage-style, to be executed on the site of one of Krell's office complexes. Krell had hoped, it was reported, that Zwolle's art would be controversial enough to get him a little publicity, maybe in the *New York Times*. But Duana Zwolle, for whatever reason, had declined.

Interesting, Matt thought. Zwolle must have needed the money, yet she'd declined. Matt wondered: what had Zwolle said to Krell?

And what had Krell said to Zwolle, in turn?

It would have depended upon how close the two had been. How intimate.

The female office workers at Krell Associates were intrigued by the Zwolle case. Morbidly fascinated by it, you might say. Often Matt overheard them avidly discussing it during their frequent coffee breaks. Sometimes they spoke in excited whispers. They passed the tabloid *Jersey Citizen* among themselves, one of the few papers faithful to the Zwolle case though there was no new news, only a rehashing of the old. Matt's secretary lived near Lismore and claimed to have known Duana Zwolle—"Not well. You couldn't get to know anyone like that. So strange, like in another world. And that 'art' she did, that some people claim to like, I don't get. Do you? It's weird, isn't it? Definitely that girl had a secret life but I feel sorry for her, she's paid for it now."

On the flight home from Sarasota he'd read in *Scientific American* how in a corpse blood sinks with gravity, and this helps a pathologist determine how long the body has been dead. You slice into the flesh, and no blood runs out. You poke the flesh and it will darken at the point of contact and remain that way. As the body stiffens in rigor mortis parts fill with blood seeking the lowest level. *The longer death, the more dense and clotted the blood.*

Of Nighthawk's several hundred photographs, of those hundreds more he'd taken since the age of twenty but had discarded, there were only four of human corpses. Three were accident victims, snapped by the roadside within minutes of the accident: not close-ups of death but from a distance, so that the motionless human shape in its pool of dark blood was but a single abstract shape amid others in a composition of stark, neutral shades. These photographs were tasteful enough to have been published in the *Newark Star-Ledger*, the state's premier newspaper. The fourth corpse, photographed in glaring whites, grays and blacks on a mortician's table, draped with a white cloth, only its thick-haired head showing, and a face taut yet creased as a ravaged old football, had been Mathias McBride, Senior who'd died, aged fifty-four, in 1985, of lung cancer in a Philadelphia hospital. This, Matt kept in his portfolio, unpublished. He'd never showed it to anyone. Not Tess: she'd have flinched from it, and asked him why he had to be so morbid?

Why Nighthawk, and why so morbid?

He'd learned that "Duana Zwolle," which he had thought an invented name, was legitimate. There was a Zwolle family, parents in their mid-sixties, living in Bangor, Maine, where Duana and a twin sister had been born. The father was a self-employed cabinetmaker, said to be very skilled; the mother, a former elementary schoolteacher. There was an older brother who taught high school in Vermont, and there was an older married sister who lived in Lake Placid, New York; the twin sister, named Rue, or Ruellen, was a graphics artist currently living in Santa Monica, California. As soon as they learned of Duana's disappearance the Zwolles came to New Jersey to "cooperate" with police. They'd been interviewed frequently by the local media. The parents were youthful for their age, the father had Duana's dark complexion and serious, shadowed eyes. Matt felt something of the Zwolles' loss, watching these earnest interviews, which presented Mr. and

Mrs. Zwolle as the "anxious" parents of the *missing girl* who were yet "hopeful"—"trusting to prayer and the good will of others." There was something so familiar about the Zwolles' pretense of hope, contrasting sharply with the sick, frightened expressions in their faces, that Matt felt, for the first time, the futility of the search. *He has her, he won't give her up. Except as a body he has discarded.*

How did Matt McBride know such an ugly truth? He knew.

The Zwolles, who clearly had not much money, were bravely offering $25,000 for information leading to the "safe return" of their daughter. This reward, perhaps perceived in affluent north-central New Jersey as inadequate, was generously upped to $50,000 by the intervention of a Weymouth resident who wished to remain anonymous. (It was an open secret that the donor was Sidney Krell.)

Now attractive eye-catching posters bearing the likeness of DUANA ZWOLLE, MISSING were seen everywhere. They were striking black-and-white compositions designed by Zwolle's artist-friend Oriana. Matt counted eleven of these posters during a five-minute walk from the Weymouth Village post office to his bank, Midland Trust on Main Street. Each snatched at his eye like a call for help. The *missing girl* he was certain he'd hardly known and whose presence in Weymouth had been to him, if he wished to admit it, which of course he never would, something of an irritant, now so vivid a part of the environment it tended to erase the environment itself. For how could you glance innocently into a store window where the poster had been conspicuously placed, how could you look into the window and not, instead, at the poster, the girl's dark, widened eyes, her slightly parted lips and delicate features, the mane of bushy, unkempt hair framing the face, the *missing girl* who seemed to be staring out of a cruelly confining space, a cell, a box, a coffin, begging for help, appealing to *you*? Matt found himself standing on Main Street in a biting wind gazing at the face of the *missing girl* in the window of Reinhart Stationery & Office Supplies until peals of impudent laughter, girlish laughter, from a group of teenaged girls pushing by on the sidewalk, wakened him.

I didn't. I don't know. I'm not the one.

No one knew about the diary yet. If there was a diary.

Except: the Zwolle family must know about the diary. As Duana's next-of-kin, they would be in possession of her property.

January 10. On the 7 P.M. Newark news, it was announced that state police were acting on an anonymous tip in the Duana Zwolle missing-person investigation, this time searching the Delaware River more extensively in the area of the Water Gap. "An anonymous caller to the *Jersey Citizen* claimed that the young woman was being punished for her 'bad behavior' and would be found in, or near, water." The news anchor spoke with an air of barely contained excitement, eyes fixed to the teleprompter.

Bad behavior? Matt had heard this before.

Bad behavior? Hadn't Marcey Mason been punished for the same thing?

And her broken, mutilated body found in water.

Matt couldn't sit still, Matt couldn't hope to sleep, Matt believed himself in possession of a crucial truth.

Was there a connection between the two abductions, yes there must be a connection, yet possibly he was remembering inaccurately, he wasn't thinking coherently, nerves strung tight and mind racing, distracted at work yet more distracted at home, listening with difficulty to Tess when she spoke to him, listening with difficulty to Davey and Graeme who chattered to Daddy excitedly of their adventures at school, even his hugs and kisses were vague, his mind flew elsewhere, he was thinking of Marcey Mason and he was thinking of Duana Zwolle and of *bad behavior* (which could only mean sexual behavior) and of a girl's body found *in or near water* (which could only mean that Duana Zwolle was dead), he knew he should contact Phelan or Ricci, he had their cards in a secret compartment in his wallet (for he dreaded Tess discovering them), should drive to police headquarters, no, just telephone, just leave a message, yes but his call would be taped, probably that was routine and did he want to identify himself?—why draw the attention of police to Mathias McBride another time?—for Mathias McBride was still a suspect in the case, why invite more scrutiny from the detectives those sons of bitches who'd crudely accused him to his face of having had a sexual relationship with Duana Zwolle, regarded him as if he was an upright piece of shit so why risk activating their interest in him?—why when he'd managed for weeks like a man who has been holding his breath in poisonous air to escape public exposure and humiliation not to mention the collapse of his marriage and the prospect of paying a hot-shot lawyer whose guts he frankly hated a minimum of $350 an hour to prove the innocence that was his by right?

He'd have to be crazy, and Matt McBride wasn't crazy yet.

He would provide the police with an anonymous tip of his own.

On an office computer, not his own, at Krell Associates, Matt typed out the terse information:

In November 1976, "bad behavior" was given as a reason for the rape-murder of a high school girl in Forked River, N.J. Her body was found in Deer Isle Wildlife Sanctuary. Her murderer was never found.

This Matt printed out and mailed in a plain envelope to WEYMOUTH POLICE from a mailbox on Main Street. He wore gloves. Fantasizing DNA tracing, he didn't lick the stamp. How could they trace him?

Maybe that was risky. But it was done.

Next thing, it *was* risky, but he did it anyway, drove to Lismore with Nighthawk's camera.

Along the potholed gravel road, Mill Row, beside the Weymouth River. No one seemed to be watching as he photographed the crude stone facade of what had been a textile mill until 1957, now converted for private commercial and residential use. A dozen times he'd seen this building in TV news footage, the same footage played and re-played showing, at the farther end of the long, graceless, two-storey building, the exterior of the *missing girl's* rented "loft." There was little to see: cameras couldn't penetrate the building or the shuttered windows. There was an outdoor wooden stairs that looked in need of repair. Beyond the building was an overgrown field and beyond that a woods. A no-man's-land, no longer rural yet hardly residential. Two hundred yards above Mill Row was the state highway.

When Matt drove Duana Zwolle home he'd let her out on the gravel drive in front of her residence. Quickly she'd ascended the stairs, not looking back at him. *Her pride. She's hurt. I can't help that.* He hadn't watched (had he?) her unlock the door painted an inappropriate red, he hadn't watched her disappear inside. He'd driven to the end of Mill Row, a cul-de-sac, to turn his car around.

Look, I didn't go inside with her.

I was not her lover.

It was rare that Nighthawk worked by day. Tramping in the icy grass taking photographs, happy in his Nighthawk-trance. This midwinter morning more resembled twilight than day. The bleak sun was hidden by masses of clouds like a blinded eye. The Weymouth River, invariably described as picturesque, was shrouded in mist and of the spiritless hue of molten lead. Matt used up a roll of film, and began on another. How could he be happy at such a time, taking such photographs, absorbed in technique, though knowing that Duana Zwolle had been "taken or led" from her residence down these very stairs sometime in the evening of December 28, and that she and her abductor or abductors had driven away in Zwolle's car and no one had seen them.

And she'd never been seen again.

And probably now was dead. *In or near water.*

It looked as if Mill Row, as the converted mill was called, wasn't a success as a rental property. Most of its space was empty and some of it looked unimproved. Maybe the developer had run out of money. From news reports Matt knew that, in addition to Duana Zwolle, only three residents lived in the building, and they lived at the end near the entrance. Duana Zwolle's second-floor loft was above a studio shop called The Potter and beside an "antique" shop, The Attic. When Matt had driven Duana Zwolle home he'd thought the place, the setting, the isolation, the crudely quaint old mill exuded an air of romance. He'd thought *Nighthawk could live here.* Now, the place seemed to him almost unbearably lonely.

He was photographing the exterior of Duana Zwolle's residence as seen from the perspective of the ground below, and from midway up the rickety stairs, and from the landing at the top of the stairs. He took several close-ups of the door, which had been painted a bright, brave lacquered red, probably by Duana Zwolle herself. *A bull's-eye of a door.* Risking a fall, he leaned over the stair railing to photograph the front window of her loft, which was a broad plate glass window overlooking the river, and shuttered from inside. (Matt knew from news reports that the Zwolle family had shuttered it to prevent TV camera crews from using zoom lenses to get inside.)

He photographed the river: a sight Duana Zwolle must have seen often, repeatedly, maybe dreamily, looking out her window into a kind of suspended space. An eerie timelessness. On the river's opposite shore was more uncultivated land and vehicles passing on the narrow river road were hidden from sight.

Again thinking *Nighthawk would be happy here!*

Maybe it was a stupid thing to do, sure he was a "suspect" in the case, but fuck it, he didn't care, he decided not to care, as Nighthawk he was impulsive and willful and determined to do what he wanted to do and not what others wanted him to do nor even what might be wise for him to do, and to refrain from doing. He tramped around the property taking photographs, from the rear of the building, from the side, reckless as a kid in his twenties. *What's a camera but an eye of God? You don't even need to believe in God.*

It was a fact: he hadn't felt so good, so free and so guiltless since the start of the new year.

13

NAME UNKNOWN. In such blinding dreams the visions fell upon him! Blasts of lightning. Erupting the night sky, tearing the silence in two. Striking earth.

He'd instructed the woman to make the call. He'd written the words out for her and destroyed them afterward. He didn't trust her to remember. Not that she was slow-witted like her little boy but so excited and eager to please him, it's the state in which errors can be made. *Never tell them too much. They are the enemy. Anybody comes snooping around here asking you questions about me just say you don't know. Tell them to come to me.*

There is the Joseph Gavin life. It was Joseph Gavin the detectives came to see. It was Joseph Gavin who is required to pay taxes to the state and renew his New Jersey driver's license every few years. In his Joseph Gavin life he is a welder. He has been a welder since graduating from high school. Class of 1976. Forked River High School. Vocational arts, his major. Where he passed invisible among his classmates. *Yet now you see me & in a little while, you will not.*

Joseph Gavin doesn't work regularly. He does not work routinely. Yet he is proud of his skill which was the skill of his father and grandfather before him. His employers praise him. They wonder at his silence. Almost you would think *is he mute?* Ashy brown hair flowing like Christ's to his shoulders, and his thin curly beard like woodshavings. In T-shirt sweated through you could see his hard ropey muscles, shoulders and arms. His legs are short in proportion to his torso and his eyes are meek and glaring in his face. His skin slightly pitted. His mouth moving, sucking in silent thought. *A weirdo!* He's heard some of them laugh behind his back. *But he does pretty good work.*

Joseph Gavin isn't hired regularly because he is NAME UNKNOWN and scorns a telephone. He scorns joining a trade union. It's goddamned difficult to reach him. He moves every few months sometimes. He will remain in Clinton Falls for the detectives are watching him. They are watching other men (he knows) & they are watching NAME UNKNOWN. He has lived in many places.

Each time he creates one of his figures of *The Marriage of Heaven and Hell* he will leave that place and move on.

Though not so long as his enemies observe him.

His angry boyhood in Forked River. Where the stink of rotting things from the beach (fish, shellfish, jellyfish, slimy snaky seaweed) permeated his sleep. Where his throat choked sometimes so he could not speak & veins emerged like trembling worms in his forehead & neck. To Mountainhome, Pennsylvania, in the Poconos where he sought beauty. He was twenty years old then & for a while happy. There, a vision of *The Marriage of Heaven and Hell* came to him. Where the sacrifice of the dancer L R was determined. He had not intended it when coming to the mountains to live yet had known when the vision like a fireball swept over him it was not to be denied.

He had brought no power tools with him. He had used a fish-gutting knife which had lacked fineness. He had no idea what were *tendons* and what mere muscle, or flesh. There were other reasons for his failure but he did not dwell upon them.

Then to Salem, Delaware where he first began making animal & bird wood carvings to sell to gift shops and made $1,100 in that year alone. Then to Catonsville, Maryland where a vision directed him, he had to trust there was a purpose to it and in time, there was. And then to Aberdeen, Maryland. And a return to New Jersey in his thirtieth year. He understood there was purpose to this, that NAME UNKNOWN could make no errors if he trusted the guidance given him. This house trailer of his purchased in Cherry Valley where he lived for eighteen months, a welder and a sculptor. Then East Orange where no vision came and at last Clinton Falls which is fifty miles from Lismore along the Weymouth River.

In each of these sites NAME UNKNOWN has made a sacrifice. He has made a sacred figure.

His semen and their blood commingled. A precious fluid. Brimming with life he can observe with his naked eyes. Mixed then with sand and clay and shaped with his deft fingers and fired in a kiln. In his sculpted forms. In molten metal to be welded and in wax shaped by hand lovingly caressed and kneaded. (What a shock to NAME UNKNOWN to walk into the Weymouth gallery to see that another artist had stolen certain of his ideas, of hand-kneaded wax. And his symbols of crosses and eagles. In her ugly "collages." Which she would never confess even as she pretended to admire him and to "want to be his friend.")

That gritty glittering sand of the Pine Barrens mixed with a commercial clay the hue of oxblood and with her blood and the secret fluid of NAME UNKNOWN. So his art figures outlive all merely mortal flesh. And even that cruel bitch Oriana who laughed at NAME UNKNOWN almost in his face had to admit the radiance & mystery of his work.

Yet it has been promised to NAME UNKNOWN in a vision that he will one day achieve even more. To stitch a pair of LIVING EYES to a sculpted face of copper for instance or treated hide, and wax. The genius of NAME UN-KNOWN. Someday he will be acclaimed. It is a question of when, and he can be patient. Since the age of nineteen when the first vision fell upon him blinding and paralyzing so he could not speak for days, he knew he must fulfill his destiny *even before he knew clearly what that destiny would be.*

Forked River. When he was not yet NAME UNKNOWN. In the high school where at lunchtime he stuffed his face & gut with macaroni & cheese in mute rage. & his grades low C's & his teachers scornful of him or pitying, which was worse. & pimples on his face, back and ass which he picked with his angry nails to bleed. & for years passing invisible through their eyes who did not see Joseph Gavin who'd been their classmate through the years. His smudged charcoal drawings in ninth grade they laughed at behind their hands. His stumpy clay figures in art class. The papier-mâché project they were assigned, & he was so anxious & sweaty he kept starting over, and over, repairing his mistakes until the thing was stained with paste, & worthless & contemptible in his own eyes though he had meant it to be the Archangel Gabriel & he smashed it with his fists & ran out of the room & they were too surprised to laugh & maybe they were afraid & even the teacher so scornful of him did not report him & he was allowed to major in "industrial arts"—which his father had wished for him.

He needs a trade he'd overheard his father say to his mother. *Once they see what he can do, he's reliable. He'll be O.K.*

& so it would be, in time.

The Easter concert assembly of April 1976 he would remember through his life! Of so many days endured & despised & as forgotten as shit, squeezed from the anus in revulsion & relief, is forgotten. Joseph Gavin did not wish to attend—but had no choice. For while you are in school you are trapped & have no choice. Dozing through assembly, his head lolling on his shoulders so some of the guys poked him. Spittle dangling from his lower lip. But this assembly, he didn't doze. The chorus of girl singers in their white silk robes with gold trim. And the soprano solo—"Ave Maria." The chorus humming behind. A voice like an angel's & her face he could not believe SO BEAUTIFUL. Almost he could not recall, staring at the lighted stage from his seat many rows away who the girl was. Though living in his neighborhood, on a parallel street running to the ocean's edge like his, & her father a factory worker like his, & she was a year behind him in school, & younger, & yet she did not seem younger to him now but a grown woman in her beauty & pride in her voice. & the applause & cheers like a waterfall— so thunderous! He did not then think *Not one of them would clap for me like this. Not one of them would clap for me at all.* For he too was clapping & must have been noisy for some of the guys poked him to shut him up. & after that hour, in April 1976, he knew.

Yet it was six months before the certainty came to him. For he did not know *what it would be*, only that that girl would be the one. He did not think *I love her* for there were no words for what was so fierce in him & unwavering. & he graduated, & left school, & became an apprentice welder, & seeing her on the street he would cast his eyes quickly away from her not wishing her to see & to know & she was of those pretty popular girls who smile & call out *Hello!* to all, even misfits & losers. Even Joseph Gavin who was fattish then & his hair the color of dirty sand & crew cut & often a two-day beard on his jaws like something smudged & walking with his head down, & fast. & he would discover that the girl (he could not keep her name out of his thoughts: Marcey Mason) had boyfriends & one boy in particular & watching the couple even on the street together in plain sight you could judge their behavior when alone. & so he perceived the angel was soiled in her soul. As surely in her underwear. & the beauty of her soprano voice betrayed. & the need for her to be punished for such bad behavior ached in him like a decayed tooth & so out of sleepless nights permeated by the stink of the beach which is the stink of the ocean's death washed upon the shore for all to behold he understood what he must do.

SING FOR ME he bade her. & she was terrified & trembling & could not sing. SING FOR ME he bade her & she knelt in prayer & he told her he would pray with her, from behind standing above her & he had no fear she might run, for her ankles were bound with wire, & her wrists, & in any case he could catch her as easily as a dog catching a fleeing rabbit in its jaws.

Because he had the keys to his employer's delivery van & no one would know. & gone for hours & yet his mother would believe he had not been gone at all & spoke truth as she believed it, & could not be shaken when police questioned her, & questioned him & his answers were brief & scared as a boy would be scared & confused as a boy would be confused. & he was a welder & a reliable worker. & there were so many others, boys & men, & the girl's own boyfriend, to be questioned. & the strong belief was, it had been a man from out of town. A stranger driving through. For no one in Forked River would wish to harm this girl so popular & pretty & her family well liked. & days passed while they waited for a ransom note & there were many telephone calls including those who claimed they knew where the girl was & asked for a reward. & he would call, too—to explain why the girl had been taken that it was not for ransom purposes which he would scorn! & all this passed by his head like a rushing torrent. Like a movie seen up too close & the sound deafening. & within this, he had no difficulty continuing his life as always. For he was working eight hours, five days a week & making a good salary for age nineteen. & living at home, & a quiet life. & it was his secret vision of how she had sung for him at last. He had promised her he would release her & she had promised she would not tell anyone about it (for she knew him of course, that was why she had come to him when he'd called out for her to help him in a voice of hurt & surprise) & she did sing for him, or tried to—"Ave Maria." It was not the pure soprano voice of his memory but a breathy thin voice, a girl's voice frightened & not true music. SING FOR ME he bade her & molten flame passed over his brain as

she sang & standing behind her he looped the wire around her hair & head
& pale neck & his strong fingers squeezed, squeezed.

   & SO IT CAME TO PASS, WHICH WAS ORDAINED.

   & HE WAS NEVER SO HAPPY IN HIS LIFE TILL THEN NOR HAD ANY PROMISE
OF WHAT HAPPINESS MIGHT BE.

14

". . . Matt, aren't you listening? Damn you, I've been talking to you."

"Honey, of course. What?"

Tess stared at him. He saw her mouth tremble, with the wish to say something wounding, hurtful. She was a jealous woman uncertain of the object of her jealousy: not the *missing girl*, surely?

They'd been watching the eleven o'clock news out of Newark. A female reporter with a microphone in her hand, her russet-red hair blowing stiffly in the wind, was on camera in a wintery location, ice-streaked boulders behind her, dark rushing waters of the Delaware River behind her. This was the windblown site, approximately one mile south of the Water Gap, where a torn, bloodstained white cashmer shawl believed to belong to Duana Zwolle had been discovered partly hidden between ice chunks on the Jersey bank of the river. It was the first new lead in some time, and the local news media were playing it up extravagantly. The shawl wasn't shown, of course. The police crew was shown, at a distance. This film footage had been taken hours after the discovery, when the action was long over; the camera panned out onto the broad, glittering river, frozen at its shores, which sounded in its passage like a waterfall of brittle, breaking ice. Matt stared, and shuddered.

Tess persisted, "Is there another woman? You can tell me."

"No, Tess. There is not."

Matt's face burned, as if Tess had slapped him. He saw the resentment in his wife's eyes, that she'd given in to such a demeaning question, like a willful child who can't resist behaving in a way to hurt both herself and another.

She said, "You're never with me, any longer. Your mind is elsewhere."

Your heart, she might have said.

Matt couldn't think how to reply. He couldn't trust himself to reply.

Frustrated with each other, they turned their attention back to the TV news. A "new, crucial lead" in the case of the missing Lismore resident Duana Zwolle, twenty-six, a free-lance artist who'd disappeared. . . . Weymouth County detectives were working with New Jersey police in investigating this new lead, as the reporter told the TV audience in a thrilled voice—"But they are unable to discuss their progress at the present time."

Tess said, "Why don't they come out and say it: she's probably dead. A shawl, covered in blood. What else do they want?"

Matt felt a stab of hatred, hearing Tess speak this way. Though surely she was right.

"They don't want to give up hope. It's only natural. The girl has a family, Tess. Think how you would feel if . . ."

"But it's worse this way! It's sadistic."

The discovery of the bloody shawl had been made within thirty-six hours of Matt's anonymous note to the Weymouth police. He had to wonder if there was some connection. It was a grim discovery in any case. Tess was right, the *missing girl* had to be dead. If her body had been dumped into the Delaware just below the Water Gap, the current would have carried it miles downstream.

Possibly the body had been weighed down, and had sunk deep beneath the waves. Never would it be found in that vast expanse of dark rushing water.

Unlike Marcey Mason. Whoever had killed Marcey had wanted her broken body to be discovered for it had been carelessly hidden, near a hiking trail.

Tess rose suddenly from the sofa, and went upstairs to bed. Matt lingered, switching through the stations. Network, cable. . . . As if, somewhere in the night, there was more news of Duana Zwolle, to put his mind at rest so he might sleep.

Next morning, driving to work, fumbling with the radio news station, Matt learned that the shawl had been identified by a woman friend of

Duana Zwolle's as a gift the young woman had recently received for Christmas. "From a lover of Duana's, but she wouldn't tell me his name."

Matt thought calmly, They will arrest me now.

And yet they never did.

Intermittently through his life as an adolescent and an adult Matt had been insomniac. As a younger man he'd hardly noticed, for staying up late, drinking, talking with friends, had been an integral part of his life. Now, he was too restless to sleep even when he was exhausted. Days spent impersonating an ambitious young associate at Krell Associates, drawn to subterranean thoughts of the *missing girl* he believed he ought to find, yet could not, left him exhausted yet unable to sleep. In the past he'd used the time to work in his darkroom at the rear of the house, developing Nighthawk prints. Always a nocturnal preoccupation, as if the photograph negatives emerged out of night, and not day. But since returning from Florida, since Zwolle's disappearance, Matt had fallen into the habit of watching TV into the early hours of the morning, searching for—what?

You won't find her, she's mine. Not until I abandon her will you find her.

Almost at such times Matt could "hear"—could "see"—his adversary. His fingers flexed, his fists clenched, with the desire to do violence.

"If only, back in October, I'd gone inside with her . . ."

Duana Zwolle had wanted him, and Matt in his cowardice had drawn back from her. It was as simple and blunt as that.

Sometimes on late-night TV, on a Jersey cable channel, Matt discovered a feature on Duana Zwolle. Nothing new, of course; very likely he'd seen it already, more than once. Yet he sat staring, fascinated. The life we continue to lead on film, in others' imaginations, even after we've died. It intrigued Matt to see footage of Lismore, of the facade of Zwolle's loft, since he'd developed his own photographs. Two rolls of film, twenty-four shots. He hadn't told Tess about these, and didn't intend to. Of the lot, several seemed to him outstanding.

One was of Zwolle's front door and, from an angle, the shuttered front window in whose glass images of sky, river, trees were reflected as in a dream of impending disintegration. Another was a stark shot of the badly weatherworn exterior stairs seen from below, a photograph that was a puzzle until you had the key: *stairs*.

The stairs the *missing girl* had been forced down, or dragged down, by her unknown abductor.

All but one of the new Nighthawk photos Matt had hidden, for the time being, amid his IRS files in his home office. It would have been too difficult to explain them to Tess, or to anyone.

Nor did Matt want to share them with anyone.

15

Nighthawk had never photographed the girl in the marsh. At that time, twenty-one years ago, Nighthawk hadn't existed.

He'd never seen photographs of the girl in the marsh. There must have been police photos, coroner's photos, but of course he'd never seen them.

Matt McBride had begun taking photos in high school, though not very seriously. He'd been too involved in other activities, football and the swim team and his after-school jobs. To be a good photographer you have to have an eye. To have an eye you have to know how to be alone. Even in the midst of others, you have to know how to be alone. *The eye of God. No desire and no pity. Looking upon all things, in heaven and in hell, with equanimity.*

One of his assignments for the school newspaper was to take group photos. He was allowed the use of a weighty Nikon flash camera, property of the journalism club. He'd taken a photo of Girls' Chorus for the paper. He hadn't had much awareness of Marcey Mason in the chorus, at the time. This was twelve days before she would be taken away, mutilated and killed. Before newspaper and TV closeups of the *missing girl* would supplant all other images of her.

But there she'd been: in the first row of smiling girls, near the center of the group. Twenty-two girls on three rows of risers. For the occasion they were wearing white blouses and dark skirts. Marcey Mason was smiling trustingly into the camera's flash knowing it would treat her kindly. Glossy shoulder-length hair, a heart-shaped face. The *missing girl* before fate overtook her.

If Matt McBride, a sophomore at the time, had noticed Marcey Mason, she would have been to him another of the radiantly pretty, popular senior girls at Forked River High. As distant to him and as unobtainable an object of desire as any adult woman.

16

Matt would think afterward *This was luck.*

That his sons were spared the sight of seeing their home invaded by Weymouth Township police. Spared the sight of seeing their Daddy they adored so unmanned, humiliated.

The warrant was served at last. Matt had been waiting, and it had not happened; and one Saturday morning, when he hadn't been thinking of the *missing girl*, but of his sons Davey and Graeme whom he'd driven across town to visit with friends of theirs (two brothers their ages, seven and five, whose attractive, sociable parents were also friends of the McBrides from the Stony Brook Tennis Club), the warrant was served.

It was a blindingly sunny winter day. Matt McBride was wearing dark glasses, a sheepskin windbreaker, hiker's boots. A sporty-suburban guy, looking young for his age. Driving the kids to the Holtzmanns', he hadn't switched on the radio. It was Saturday morning, a time of family errands, innocence. He'd give himself a break from his guilty obsession with the news. Davey beside him, Graeme in the backseat, his sons, his sons he knew he didn't deserve, the three of them talking and laughing, he'd felt good; he'd felt blessed. Sometimes, love for his sons came so strong it left him almost dazed, as if he'd been staring too long into the sun.

His marriage with Tess was troubled, he knew. But not his love for these children.

Driving back home, Matt was tempted to switch on the radio. . . . Like the temptation to smoke if you've quit: an almost physical yearning. He'd been thinking of—dreaming of?—that white cashmere shawl. He saw it smeared, stiffened, with blood. Never in fact had Matt seen this shawl and yet there it was vivid in his mind's eye, a patch of white glaring out of the shadows of ice-locked boulders. Along that stretch of the Delaware River, steep cliffs dropped to the river; the banks were shaded for much of the day, especially in winter. Almost, Matt might have believed he'd been there . . .

Is there another woman? You can tell me.

Of course Matt couldn't tell her. Not his wife, not Tess. She would have been devastated with hurt, chagrin, rage. She could not possibly have understood.

You're never with me, any longer. Your mind is . . .

Matt was becoming restless, thinking these thoughts. No: he would not switch on the radio. He knew that his obsession with the *missing girl* was morbid, he wouldn't give into it any longer. He was driving through the village of Weymouth, having forgotten to take a back route. Saturday-morning traffic clogging Main Street where shoppers descended upon the Weymouth Food Mart, The English Shoppe, the Village Pharmacy, Boutique Du Jour, Seabury's Women's Shop, The Pantry, Jameson Gallery, Swank's, Reinhart Stationery & Office Supplies, Peck's Shoes, Ann Taylor, Gap, Banana Republic, Starbucks, Country Kitchen Gourmet Foods & Gifts. The secret music of Weymouth was the sound of cascading gold coins, a Niagara Falls of riches. And what you could see was only the tip of the money-iceberg, as Sidney Krell liked to say.

"I hate this place. I don't have a fucking idea why I'm here."

They'd moved to Weymouth because Tess had fallen in love with the area, but it was unfair to blame Tess, for Matt had been enthusiastic, too. At first. They'd bought a house in the "exclusive residential community" called Weymouth West Villas; they'd paid a lot, and already the worth of the house had risen considerably. The population of Weymouth Township had doubled within a few years. It would double again, perhaps more rapidly. This part of the Garden State, Krell said, was still green, and ready to harvest. Krell had a habit of rubbing his hands briskly, gleefully. Yet there was an air of regret when he spoke more thoughtfully. "Sure, it makes me sad to see what we're doing. I live here, too. I remember what it used to be like. But I'm no fool: if I don't develop the land here, some other unconscionable bastard will." And Krell laughed, showing his gums. The cruel thing about Krell was, having drawn you into sympathizing with him, he'd laugh heartily in your face.

Krell set me up to meet her. Like he set me up with his wife. Is that it?

Krell. The fat dimpled spider at the cobweb-heart of Weymouth.

Matt would've liked to hate the guy, but it wasn't that easy.

Krell liked to boast that he knew everything that was going on in Weymouth, but he hadn't known about Matt's involvement with a local woman. A woman well known to Krell, the wife of a prominent Weymouth investment banker. A golf friend of Krell's, in fact.

Outside the village, in the hilly area west of town, Matt passed a winding gravel road, Fox Hollow Lane, and thought of that woman. He felt an immediate sexual unease, a stab of regret. Though not guilt. *Tess never knew, never guessed. It meant nothing.*

Sure, Matt had been flattered sexually. Any man would be. A kind of adolescent radiance had shone, for an intense five-month interim, upon him. So long as Tess never knew, he reasoned she couldn't be hurt; if she wasn't hurt, what did it matter what he did? All husbands must live private lives, sexual lives, to which their wives have no access. The affair hadn't seemed to Matt *adulterous*, in the old, Biblical sense of the word. It had been too casual to be sinful. Just an affair. Better yet, a series of incidents. Sexual encounters. Not much conversation. Matt had never believed that the woman had loved him, or that he was expected to love her. She wasn't the wife of a friend of his, so he wasn't betraying a friend. (That, Matt vowed, he'd never do. Tess maybe, but not a friend!) There'd been a dreamlike aura to the interlude for the affair had begun abruptly, a maneuver on the woman's part, drawing her hand along Matt's arm slowly, suggestively, at a cocktail gathering, fixing her expertly made-up gaze upon his for a long, unmistakable moment—" 'Nighthawk.' You're the one." The affair had ended abruptly, too: the woman went to visit wealthy relatives in San Diego and hadn't returned for ten weeks, not calling Matt before she'd left, or while she was away. When finally Matt was able to speak with her he'd said, trying to sound only casually critical, "That's a kind of shitty way to treat a friend, isn't it?" The woman had said, startled, but otherwise unmoved, "Is it? I'm sorry."

Because of this woman, Matt hadn't been in any state of mind to relate to Duana Zwolle. When she'd spoken to him, made her request of him. Those eyes of hers had sought Matt's and like a fool he'd turned away, embarrassed.

No. You can't exist for me, Duana.

There was nothing he regretted more, now. That he'd been so blinded, so deluded. He'd had a chance to save Duana Zwolle from the terrible thing that had happened to her, and he'd failed.

Matt wished he knew Ricci well enough to talk to him man-to-man. Off the record. Ricci was a good-looking guy, Italian, women must be attracted to him, too; Matt had noticed a wedding band on Ricci's hand, he was married. A family man, like Matt. All he'd need to tell Ricci was the truth: At the time Matt was suspected of being Zwolle's lover, Matt was involved with another Weymouth woman. *I'm not proud but it did no one harm. But I can't talk about it, see?*

Ricci would understand, wouldn't he? Off the record?

There was Matt McBride's expensive, mortgaged house: white-brick "contemporary," glass and stucco and redwood trim, on a tastefully landscaped knoll amid the wooded two-acre lots of West Weymouth Villas. It was a house that would have seemed like a castle in Forked River but wasn't much distinguished in Weymouth. Matt never saw it without feeling pride and panic conjoined. Turning into the driveway, Matt saw a sight that was sheerly panic: three Weymouth Township police cars parked in front of his garage.

It had happened. They'd come. They had a warrant.

The front door was open. Matt entered, like a man entering a burning house. Tess ran into his arms, grabbing at him. Her face was pale and her eyes brimmed with tears of fear and indignation. "Matt, they say they have a search warrant! Matt, make them stop!"

There were six or seven officers. Who was in charge? The older

detective, Phelan, with the black plastic-rimmed glasses, informing
Matt in his coolly courteous way that they had a warrant—"Read it
through, Mr. McBride. And don't try to interfere with the officers."

Matt stared at the document, uncomprehending. What was he expected to do? "I have nothing to hide, I could have shown you myself.
This isn't necessary . . ." No one listened. Tess was sobbing. Phelan
had turned away and was aiding in the search, as if Matt weren't
present. *The wrath of the world* Matt thought. You expect it all your
life, but when it arrives you're disbelieving.

"Matt, I don't understand! Matt, why are they here! What has this
Zwolle woman to do with *you!*"

Matt tried to comfort Tess, as you might comfort an accident victim.
He stood in the doorway watching strangers rummaging expertly
through his house. Drawers, cupboards, closets. His computer files
were "confiscated"—not to worry, Matt was assured, he'd be given a
receipt. It might've been comic, even the interiors of the refrigerator,
the oven, the microwave were examined. Sofa cushions were lifted
and examined, the crevices and cracks of furniture. Expensive carpets
were rudely flopped over, showing lines of dust and even grime. Tess
sobbed louder. "What are you doing! Stop! God damn you!" Matt
would recall afterward the righteousness of Tess's indignation, set
beside his own more subdued reaction: guilt, shame.

Beautiful expensive furniture Tess had chosen with exquisite care
was yanked unceremoniously away from walls. The backs of mirrors
and paintings were examined, left to hang crooked on the walls. Mat-
tresses were lifted from boxsprings, even in the boys' room. The rooms.
The boys' room! Matt's face burned with shame. His fingers flexed. If
Davey and Graeme were witnesses to this. . . . "Can't you at least let
this room alone? Have you no *decency?*" Tess raged. There were two
female officers, no less briskly efficient and unapologetic than the
male officers. They were like a force of nature, not to be stopped. Matt
envisioned himself, a hot-headed kid in his twenties, fighting with the
officers, grappling and being forcibly subdued, cuffed. Maybe they
were waiting for him to make a rush at them, now: maybe they were
watching him, hoping. But no, you had to see that these officers were

doing their job; in other circumstances Matt might have admired them; Nighthawk might have photographed them.

No part of the McBrides' elegant house and attached three-car garage would be spared. The gardening shed. The boys' outdoor gym, swings. The boys' toys. The basement, the attic. Several bathrooms including the sparkling guest bathroom on the first floor with its hand-stitched Irish linens and lemon-scented soap and gleaming onyx tiles: medicine cabinets were invaded, the very toilet tanks. Matt was conscious of how restrained the Weymouth cops were: if this were a black household in the ghetto, if these were city cops, they'd be leaving devastation behind. As it was, it looked as if a strong wind had blown through the house, setting things awry, off-balance. What was most confusing was that the search was being conducted simultaneously in numerous rooms, so that Matt rushed from one to another, like a hapless character in a farce. "No! Wait. I can open that for you"—"Hey: there's nothing in there, I swear." He was desperate to protect Nighthawk's darkroom where strangers were mechanically rummaging through drawers, his storage closet, examining his camera equipment as if it were bomb-making materials, sliding stacks of Nighthawk prints, contact sheets and negatives into cartons stamped WEYMOUTH TOWNSHIP P.D. Phelan was telling Matt that everything would be "tagged" and "returned" to him; nothing would be lost; they were experts at this, don't worry. "The search is for evidence pertaining to Duana Zwolle, no one and nothing else. See?" Maybe Phelan meant to comfort Matt? If he'd been cheating on his income tax, for instance. If he was running a scam here in his darkroom, under the alias Nighthawk.

"I wish you could have talked to me first," Matt said angrily. "I'd have liked my wife spared. She has nothing to do with any of this."

Phelan shrugged. As if to say *Sure she has, she's your wife*.

In Matt's office there was that bastard Ricci and another cop dropping papers, folders, the McBrides' IRS records into cartons. Matt's heart was pounding dangerously. He would never forget this humiliation. The expensive Moroccan carpet overturned, the contents of Matt's wastebasket, the undersides of his chairs, table and desk. . . .

At headquarters, they would discover the Nighthawk photos Matt had hidden amid the IRS files. Those secret photos Matt had taken of Zwolle's residence. He hadn't wanted Tess to see and now the police would see and seize as evidence. *But they mean nothing. I'm not a guilty man.* Ricci glanced at Matt coolly, only the smallest hint of recognition, this man who'd said he admired Nighthawk's photos. Betraying Matt like an evil brother. One moment Matt was staring at the detective, a fierce smile distorting his face, the next moment Matt stepped forward, to take a file from Ricci's hand, and swift as a door being shut in his face Matt was being led away, arms expertly pinioned behind his back. "Mr. McBride, through here. Wait in here, please." He struggled, he was groaning and cursing in pain. Pulses beat in his forehead close to bursting. He would feel the physical effect of the attack for days afterward, in the muscles of his upper arms, and his shoulders. As if he'd been gripped by an eagle's talons. Lifted high, and let drop. As his wife looked on in horror.

Ricci was saying, "Go talk to Mrs. McBride, OK? Take care of her."

Matt took Tess aside, into an alcove of the kitchen. She was hysterical, which made him calm; anyway, calmer. Nothing like a physical workout to render a man calm. Humble. "Look, Tess. They think I might have something to do with the—missing woman. Zwolle. That's what this is, honey." Tess said, "They were saying—'Zwolle.' But we don't know her, I told them. Matt, I told them." Matt said, gripping Tess's shoulders, "I know, honey. But they think I was— involved with her." Tess said, blinking, "Involved with—? How?"

There was a moment of temptation, strong as a physical urge, when Matt might have lied. For Tess, staring into his face out of her teary eyes, wanted to be lied to.

Matt told Tess, quickly and disjointedly, all the while stroking her arms, what he knew. About the "alleged diary." About the shawl. An eyewitness claiming he—or she—had seen them together. And what Sid Krell had told Matt.

Matt insisted, "There wasn't anything between us, Tess. Really. I hardly knew the woman. I don't understand why I've been drawn into this case. Please believe me."

Tess hesitated only a moment. She would believe, she would decide to believe her guilty-sounding husband. Matt saw her face tighten with resolve. He felt the steely pride of her soul. Gripping his hands tight she said, "We'll call Sid. He can recommend a lawyer."

Matt said, "He already has."

Yet the seige wasn't ended. The detectives had a warrant to search Matt's office at Krell Associates as well.

Quickly Matt said, "I'll take you. I'll cooperate. I have nothing to hide."

He was driven in the back of one of the squad cars, Ricci at the wheel and Phelan in the passenger's seat. He had an impulse to cover his face with his hands: What if a neighbor saw him? The exterior world passed in a blur. He was numb, battered. The adrenaline rush had subsided and the pain in his upper body throbbed. He would remember this humiliation for a long time.

The look in Tess's eyes. That moment of recognition. *You've betrayed me. I will never forgive you.*

Sometimes on weekends, out of industry or terror, Krell employees came to the office to "catch up" on their work. Sometimes Sid Krell showed up himself. A self-confessed workaholic, Krell encouraged his younger associates: "You don't have to be crazy to be a success in our field, but it helps." Matt, who'd been falling behind in his work, had planned to drop by the office that afternoon. Since January he'd resented the time he had to spend at Krell Associates, and at the same time he was anxious to increase it, to demonstrate to Sid Krell that his faith in Matt McBride wasn't misplaced. Yet he felt the sick, sinking feeling of being left behind, like a failing swimmer.

"Excuse me, detectives? Is it legal to enter Krell Associates? This isn't my property, you know. Sid Krell might sue you." He spoke politely, he'd regained his breath. In the rearview mirror Ricci's eyes shifted to observe him.

"It's legal, Mr. McBride. Warrant signed by a judge."

Phelan added, "Let us worry about that, Mr. McB. You just provide the keys."

The parking lot at Krell Associates was empty. A relief.

Matt unlocked a door at the rear of the building and led the detectives inside and along a corridor to his office. How unnaturally quiet it was in this building, at this time. He fumbled with his key, opening his office. He dreaded one of the detectives taking the key from him. He'd gathered that only the detectives were going to search his office, not the others, which was possibly a good sign. (How Matt grasped at "good signs." You want so badly to believe that people like you, trust you.) Inside, Matt opened his desk drawers, pulled out the sliding drawers of his filing cabinet, identifying documents, contracts, correspondence, computer disks. He switched on his computer, logged in. He was trembling with rage and hatred of these men, and of the authority they represented, but you wouldn't guess that seeing him "cooperate."

Phelan and Ricci took away relatively little from Matt's office, mainly computer disks and handwritten notes on yellow legal-pad sheets. "Love letters, you think?" Matt asked. But the detectives declined to answer. They were methodical, just doing their jobs. Matt had to acknowledge they knew what they were doing: those ingenious places you'd think to hide something, a packet of love letters or photos, for instance, inside a portfolio of legal documents and contracts, or taped up against the underside of a drawer, or beneath the filing cabinet, they deftly searched out. With Matt's help, they lifted the heavy carpet and examined its bland underside. Determined to replace things as accurately as possible, so that no sign of this search would remain, Matt helped the detectives remove shelves of real estate reference books, law books, New Jersey maps and Township printouts. These items were shaken in turn and not one note, not one memo, not one snapshot fell out to incriminate Matt McBride. Matt heard himself say, "If an individual who has abducted a woman, and possibly murdered her, is smart enough not to get caught, why would he hide incriminating evidence in a place sure to be searched?" The question hung in the air, a taunt, but the detectives continued their search. It may have been that Ricci's face flushed, just perceptibly. Matt said, "Of course, you're just doing your job. You're 'investigating' a probable crime. I should be grateful, as a citizen. You might do as much for me, one day. If I were a 'victim' of a crime."

The telephone on Matt's desk began to ring. That would be Tess. Matt felt a stab of guilt, but didn't move.

"You want to answer that, Mr. McB.? Your wife probably."

Mr. McB.! He'd have liked to punch the smug older detective in the face.

"No."

The phone rang four more times. If Tess left a message, it would be on Matt's voice mail.

Matt said, "Nothing will make it right again. In my marriage."

To this, the detectives didn't reply.

"There's an infinity of places to hide something, you know. Why'd I hide anything *here*? I'd choose some desolate place in the country, in Hunterdon County, or better yet down in the Pine Barrens. I grew up near the Pine Barrens. It was always said that bodies were dumped there, and never found. . . . Of course, sometimes a killer wanted his victim's body to be found, after a while. But you know this, I guess."

Ricci said, "That's where she is? In the Pine Barrens?"

"I was speaking speculatively. I was asking a question."

"The Pine Barrens is a big place, though. A thorough search would take a long time."

"That's what I mean: there is an infinity of places to hide what you want hidden."

"But we find lots of things, Mr. McBride. You'd be surprised. Right in people's houses, in their bedrooms. In their computer files."

Ricci was removing the Nighthawk photos from the walls, examining these one by one, front and back. Matt dreaded the detective ripping the photos out of the frame; but Ricci was able to ascertain that nothing had been slipped between the photo and the cardboard backing. As he finished with each photo, Matt took it from him quickly, to return to its proper place on his walls. *These too have been demeaned. Defiled.* Ricci was frowning at one of the photos, holding it up. "This wasn't here last time, was it?" Matt was astonished at the detective's shrewd eye. His memory for visual detail. He hadn't asked a question, he'd made a statement. Matt said yes, this was a recent print. "I took it out in Lismore just a few days ago." But the photo had no connection with Duana Zwolle, nothing of Mill Row was in it. The interest of the photo was purely compositional: a distant river shrouded in mist, and an eye-like glare through the mist of an oddly placed sun; this sun was in fact the reflection of the sun in the mirror-like, leaden surface of the water. In the foreground were stark winter trees like slightly deformed human figures. . . . This photo was unlike most of Nighthawk's work, being a still life; Matt had been certain there was nothing in it to link it to Lismore and to the *missing girl.* Why he'd taken it, and why he'd brought it to his office to place on the wall where, when he glanced up from his desk, his eyes drifted immediately to it, Matt could not have explained to anyone, and certainly not to Detective Ricci who was staring at him. Ricci said, "The other photos are dated, but not this one. Why not?"

Matt said, "I didn't get around to it."

"It's taken in Lismore? Where, exactly?"

The riverbank near Zwolle's converted-mill residence. Looking out. A view she'd had seen, often. A way of seeing what Duana Zwolle had seen daily. *The others, in the IRS file, will be discovered too.* Matt said irritably, "Where? You can see where, if you know the location. On the Weymouth River. It's what you call a nature shot. It's generic, it could be anywhere."

"But the interest for Nighthawk is that it isn't anywhere, it's Lismore."

Ricci placed the photo in the carton marked WEYMOUTH TOWNSHIP P.D. Matt felt the impulse again to wrench it from him, and to provoke the physical reaction he knew these men were capable of. The pain they could inflict. Phelan was middle-aged, and fat in the gut, but obviously a tough guy, ham-sized muscles he hadn't had reason to use in a while. And Ricci was a guy who worked out, for sure. Suburban police work must be boring as hell to him, probably hadn't drawn his gun, still less fired it, in years.

The search of Matt's office at Krell Associates was over. Seeing the expression on Matt's face, which may have signaled danger, the older detective said, "You're not under arrest, Mr. McBride. You can speak freely to us at any time, you don't need a lawyer."

"What's that mean—'speak freely'?"

"You can aid in our investigation and what you tell us can't be used against you."

"Until in fact I'm arrested? Then everything changes?"

"Why assume you're going to be arrested? We're just gathering evidence."

Matt laughed, and saw the detectives to the rear door of the building. He'd call Tess to bring him home. Damned if he was going to climb into a Weymouth Township police car another time, unless he was handcuffed, and then he wouldn't go without a struggle. He vowed.

17

The name *Duana Zwolle* would never again pass between Matt and Tess.

Almost, Matt would think that Tess had forgiven him. Passionately she said, "I believe you, darling. I love you. Of course, that girl was lying. She must have been lying."

It was during this time of siege that Tess most surprised Matt. He'd expected a very different reaction from his wife, yet, like the defiant carved figurehead at the prow of an old ship, plunging through a stormy sea, she managed to rise to the occasion, and would maintain her steely resolve. She would be fierce, brave, intransigent. She was the daughter of a Rye, Connecticut surgeon, a well-to-do man accustomed to giving orders and being obeyed, and in this time of marital strain Tess was her father's daughter, keeping all doubt to herself, confident and self-assured in public. Word spread quickly through Weymouth that Matt McBride was "somehow involved" with Duana Zwolle; Tess countered this by saying, calmly and adamantly, that there was "no truth, not the slightest truth" to the rumor. Like the beleaguered wife of a politician threatened by scandal, Tess McBride may even have enjoyed her role. They would present a unified front, the McBrides.

"No one is going to destroy this marriage," Tess told Matt grimly. "Not with insinuations and lies. Not from the grave! Never."

After the detectives left his office, Matt tried to call Tess but the line was always busy. He called a taxi instead, to bring him home, and when he entered his house, that would seem to him forever altered as if smudged with strangers' prints, he heard his wife's raised, urgent voice on the phone. At first he thought she must be speaking with her father; there was the identical tone of intimate pleading, girlish expectation. But it soon became clear that Tess was speaking with Sid Krell in a way surprising to Matt, who'd never heard her address Krell like this. "I don't mean money, of course, Sid! No. We're fine. I mean—we can make our way. I mean emotional support. And your advice. And your help, you know, in explaining the situation to people here, because everyone will be asking *you*. You know what Weymouth is like."

Matt had to wonder: What was Weymouth like? And why should Tess care so much?

"Oh, Sid! Thank you. *Thank you*." Tess's throaty voice caught with emotion. It sounded genuine. If she and Krell were together, she'd have framed the old man's florid face in her hands and kissed him lightly, daringly on the lips. "Matt will be *so grateful*."

Matt pretended he hadn't overheard this exchange. He preferred to have Tess summarize it for him, later.

Already Tess had telephoned Jules Cliffe. She knew Cliffe as the "difficult, temperamental but brilliant" lawyer-husband of a Weymouth woman friend. Matt and Cliffe were to have an emergency meeting that evening at Cliffe's home a few miles away.

"I won't attend with you," Tess said. "So you can speak openly to Jules Cliffe. You can tell him *everything*."

In a frenzy of energy she'd managed to restore much of the searched house to order. Except for the heavier pieces of furniture that had been moved away from the walls, and scattered items in Matt's office and darkroom. Especially, Tess was determined to straighten the boys' bedroom so they would never suspect that strangers had entered it, for whatever purpose. Proudly she led Matt to see the room: "If anything," Tess said, laughing, "it looks *too neat*." She rumpled Davey's bedspread just slightly. The room was wallpapered in a navy blue nautical design with matching corduroy bedspreads; the boys had their own TV set, with shelves of videos. These, Tess had put back neatly, and now she rearranged them slightly. Matt wanted to grab his wife's frantic hands, and hold her tight. She was fevered, exhilarated. He guessed this was a form her hysteria had taken; fortunately for her, and for him. Yet it was unnatural, and could not last. Tess spoke of using the occasion to clean out drawers and closets she'd been meaning to clean for years; throwing out old clothes of hers, "I'll never wear again in this lifetime." Her eyes that were bloodshot from crying now shone, her cheeks were flushed and rosy. She was an attractive woman of early middle age breathless and thrilled as after a vigorous physical workout, swimming, tennis, sex. The kind of sex the McBrides rarely had any longer, since the arrival of their babies.

"Hey: I love you," Matt told Tess. He managed to catch at her flurried hands, and to hold her still, for a moment. "All this will work out, you'll see."

"I will see," Tess said firmly. "That's what I'm doing."

The phone was ringing. Tess pushed from him, and ran to answer it. "Daddy! He*llo*."

Two days later, in the early evening. There was Matt sitting on the family room steps, leading down from the kitchen. The room was semi-darkened. No one was around. Matt in his expensive sporty clothes he'd worn to work that day, necktie loosened. As if he'd been overcome with exhaustion and sat down here, heavily. Where otherwise he'd never sit. Head in his hands like a TV daddy. His eyes were shut tight, for his vision swirled. He hadn't been drinking. He hadn't dared. Krell had offered him a drink in his office, and Matt had quickly declined.

"I can't, Sid. No."

Five-year-old Graeme peeked around the corner at Daddy. Was this a game? Daddy liked games; Daddy was ingenious with games; there were games Daddy'd invented, nobody else's Daddy knew; but you couldn't always tell if Daddy was playing one of his games, or if Daddy was "serious." Graeme crept up behind Daddy to poke him in the shoulder, giggling. (Daddy flinched, and stifled a groan. His arm and shoulder muscles ached like hell from the manhandling of the other day.) "Daddy? Hey!"

Matt turned to grab the little guy, and hugged him. Graeme asked Daddy what was wrong and Daddy said nothing, only just a "bad headache," nothing for Graeme to worry about. But Graeme, who was a worrier, placed his warm little hands over Daddy's eyes and said, in a child's fierce vow, "Daddy, I'll make you *all well*."

Graeme's voice quavered with fear.

18

NAME UNKNOWN. This New Year he would recall. When he began at last to soar of his own volition. Having not always the need to await the vision. An angel of wrath might touch his shoulder with flaming fingertips, he'd turn and see only just the fading shadow. But that was all NAME UNKNOWN required—the fading shadow.

Shrewd in strategy. Carrying the white cashmere shawl stained with the female's blood & dirt to the rocky bank of the Delaware River where it would be found. And reported on TV, and in the papers (he scorned to read except sometimes in the 7-Eleven in town, staring smiling at the crude headlines & repeated photos of D Z).

Because he'd transported this one also to the Pine Barrens as he had M T from Trenton and M M he'd loved long ago in Forked River before he'd known of her deceit. He'd brought them upriver to the juncture of the Batsto River & the Mullica where there was an old sand road leading into the wilderness forming a natural cross with another sand road, and a collapsed ruin of a church with a tarnished cross still partway erect he'd discovered three autumns ago and had not forgotten knowing it would have significance someday. *This vision burnt into his soul.* It was his strategy to place the shawl far away from the sacrificial site to confuse his pursuers. The northern hills of New Jersey were so different from South Jersey. Downriver from the turn off where he'd left her car to be found. Where it was icier, a true winter. With the shawl in his pocket wrapped in cellophane (for if they seized his jacket? examined the pockets? they might find traces of the cashmere wool, even of her blood) he'd climbed down onto the icy rocks panting and shivering and laughing with excitement. One misstep, and he would slip into the freezing black river. In his rubberized boots from Sears the largest-sized boots available & the toes stuffed with rags to fit his stocking feet that were only size nine. That those bastards at Forked River Junior High had laughed at, saying they were a girl's feet.

No one laughed at NAME UNKNOWN now he was an adult, never to his face.

Taking time to position the shawl at the very edge of a rock partly submerged in the water. It must not appear to have been dropped from the riverbank fifteen feet above. For they would know this. It must appear to have snagged on a sharp edge of the rock, rushing past in the water. And taking care the shawl did not loosen and get swept away.

For this too was a work of art. NAME UNKNOWN was an artist of perfection. As the beautiful carved & molded figures of *The Marriage of Heaven and Hell* were the perfected forms of the filth-encrusted & deceitful females in flesh.

The white cashmere shawl. A label boasted of Inverness, Scotland. He'd discovered it in the rear of a car parked behind one of the old factories converted into galleries & shops on the Weymouth River. Guessing that one day it would be needed. When, or how he would wait to discover.

What is now proved was once only imagined.

The white cashmere shawl he'd left for D Z, as a gift. At Christmas. Yet it had been a sign, too. *If she takes it in, if she accepts and wears it.* Carefully he'd wrapped it in Christmas tinsel & hand-lettered a card of stiff white paper FOR DUANA WITH LOVE. Placed outside her door that was painted a bright lacquer-red. She might have wondered at this, which of her lovers would have left such a gift in such a way, yet in her femaleness was flattered as NAME UNKNOWN had anticipated. So taking up the package and inside hurriedly tearing off the tinsel (as he imagined her, seated hidden behind the wheel of his Ford pickup parked on Mill Row in the shadows) Such was her doom! His laughter was not bitter but just. For he had wished to love her. Yet was not loved in turn. *For every female in her crotch is surely a whore, as in her bowels she cannot help but be filth.*

He was not D Z's enemy. He was no man's or woman's enemy.

But she had made herself into his enemy in her brazen theft of NAME UNKNOWN's ideas with no acknowledgment or gratitude. Gilt crosses in her ugly "collages" and the flying silhouettes of wrath-angels she would claim to be hawks & eagles, and hand-molded wax glittering with mica. These framing a myriad of photo-images, glossies & old postcards he believed too were in subtle mockery of *The Marriage of Heaven and Hell* which somehow she had seen though claiming she had not. (For he had not yet exhibited these figures. No gallery wished to display them though they would display his quick-carved birds & animals for easy sales.) Yet smiling. That look of pity. *I want to be your friend, Joseph.* He wondered at her dusky skin that was soiled in certain light. For she was not a pure Caucasian, was she?— and the dark hair sprouting from her head that was a mulatta's. It was from Oriana he learned that D Z was a volunteer each Sunday at a mission for the homeless in Newark, she herself would not speak of it as if embarrassed. In her heart she was meant to be a sister-bride to NAME UNKNOWN. This he knew from his first sight of her in the gallery. Her shining eyes and uplifted face. *She knows me! Does she know me?* Observing her through the summer, and into the fall. At a distance as you might observe a wild creature easily startled. For NAME UNKNOWN had the power of absolute stillness like trance. *Where's your mind, Joey?* his uncle would laugh snapping his fingers in front of his eyes. His aunt chiding as he'd afterward overheard *Joey's simple but good-hearted. He's harmless.* And one night their house would go up in boiling-black clouds of smoke and the Forked River firemen would save only the gutted ruin. So shrewd & sparing in his vigils not one of them took notice except a Negro fishing along the river off Mill Row, seeing NAME UNKNOWN more than once, maybe more than twice or three times squatting on the riverbank tossing crusts of bread to the geese & ducks out of the edge of his eye watching her red-lacquered door until it opened, she descended the shaky wooden steps and got into the Volvo to drive past him, past his bent back, along the bumpy gravel lane not seeing him he was certain, but the Negro (from Trenton, as it came out) smiled & spoke to him & he had no choice but to smile & speak in turn for he was no racist, in his heart he believed all men all equal in the eyes of God if not in the cruel eyes of man. And afterward avoiding that stretch of riverbank. For there was much else to be done, and NAME UNKNOWN would do it.

Yet she would pray for him. Like the others, too, she saw in his face a promise of goodness. She may have believed as certain of the others believed that he was simple of mind as of heart & *harmless.* Though guessing (he would guess) that he was no fool by the care with which he entered her life like a bodiless shadow. For once NAME UNKNOWN had his vision, NAME UNKNOWN could not be stopped. He would surprise her from behind. Who had invited him into her loft out of pity & surprise he would come to her broken in spirit at this holiday time. He would tell her some measure of truth for always there is truth in his speech. About his promise to provide for his mother in her infirmity but his poverty, which he was embarrassed of, for his art did not sell nor did gallery owners wish to display it. D Z would say he must continue to have faith in himself, she was often in doubt herself, of her worth as an artist & her very life, measuring herself against her twin sister (she would show him this girlish face & figure in photos scattered through the collages which he would have believed to be her own likeness) who had not the dark vision of life she herself had from birth though seemingly they were twins in the body's smallest particulars. *Some are born to sweet delight, some are born to endless night*—so NAME UNKNOWN quietly uttered. D Z nodded in smiling acquiescence but did not seem to recognize the source of this truth. Across the quilt that was her bedspread in the next room he saw the white cashmere shawl. He knew then it was the net he would capture her in, as you might surprise & overcome a wild creature trapping its legs or wings in your embrace.

So she should have known. That NAME UNKNOWN was not simple but cunning as God is cunning, & as unexpected. His leather gloves he would not remove in her loft claiming his hands were covered in ugly eczema and required ointment to soak into the affected areas and his tight-fitting leather cap with a visor he did not remove in the loft, his hair coiled up inside so not a strand of it might fall & be detected afterward. And the ugly drawing he would leave on her pillow, in the clumsy style of an artist he'd learned D Z had lived with in New York, whose paintings of obese naked females depicting flaccid breasts and genitalia like a monkey's exposed to the eye were known & applauded by the ignorant art world. While *The Marriage of Heaven and Hell* was neither seen nor known.

So angry did NAME UNKNOWN become when he thought of such injustice, he felt the flame of the wrath-angel consume him. And all he touched was consumed in turn.

Yet daring to pray for him! When she came to life again he wetted her lips that were dried & cracked so quickly and kneeling over her heard in astonishment her whispering *God have mercy on you, Joseph!* Then drawing breath, her eyes dilated in exhaustion & terror *O God have mercy on us both.* For this he blessed her with a kiss of wrath. That she should pray for him: for NAME UNKNOWN! Who believed not in God's mercy but in God's justice. Biting her lips, his teeth sinking into the flesh suddenly biting and tearing. And how delicious that flesh, & how hungry he was without knowing. And a hot spurt of blood as she began to scream and struggle. And his cock filled to bursting with blood & the precious fluid of his groin always so much more powerful than he can recall.

That was at the waning of the old year. Now it was the new year. In the drafty barn warmed by crude space heaters he lost himself in contemplation of the sixth figure of *The Marriage of Heaven and Hell.*

II

The Hunt

19 *At last they were alone together.* In a car he did not recognize speeding along the country highway to Lismore. The landscape was blurred as in a dream. Yet he had an impression of hills, farmlands, cornfields hazy in the waning sun. It was late October. The deciduous trees had turned. Their leaves were russet-red, pale yellow and gold with an ache of melancholy. The girl whose bicycle had broken and who'd come to him to boldly ask him would he drive her home had not spoken for miles. He could smell her hair that was somewhat oily, and a more astringent odor that might be paint or turpentine. He'd noticed her childlike hands, the uneven fingernails that weren't very clean. He'd noticed the knobby thinness of her wrists. That he could encircle with his thumb and forefinger so easily. She was leaning strangely forward in the passenger's seat, elbows on her knees and her fingertips pressed against her eyes. Her long matted hair falling into her face. She wore a shapeless dark jersey and badly faded brown corduroy trousers. On her feet were waterstained running shoes faded to no discernible color. They were the size of a child's shoes, her feet were so small. He was thinking how easily he could cup those small feet in his hands, he could kiss the toes. *I want to love you, believe me! I want to save you from what's to come.* He understood the risk in removing his eyes from the road that rushed beneath the car. He understood he must grip the steering wheel tight with both hands. For it had rained recently, the road was slick with wet leaves. At the horizon the sun was a melting red wax ball. He was a man who behaved frankly, even bluntly—he wasn't a subtle man and sometimes he believed he'd been born without a conscience. Christ knew, he'd hurt his wife and he'd hurt other women and he'd been a violent man sometimes for there was the time in Fairbanks, Alaska, when in a tavern parking lot he'd savagely beaten a guy who'd been insulting and threatening a woman, he'd broken the guy's nose and loosened a few teeth and why nobody'd called the cops to arrest him he wouldn't know, or if they had no cops had showed up. That had been eleven years ago and he wasn't proud of that behavior any longer though possibly he was, just a little; at the slightest pretext he'd tell this girl about it, and she'd shake her head in disapproval of him and he'd say *Well, y'know—I was young, I was a hothead like my old man especially when I was drinking.* And they'd laugh together in contemplation of that hothead kid he'd been, but wasn't any longer.

I want to. I want to try. Please believe me!

Impulsively he put out his hand and grasped the girl's small, chilled hand. At once her fingers gripped his, they were strong fingers. He was shocked at the powerful surge of strength in her soul. She turned to him smiling. Her skin had an olive-dark pallor yet her features were so radiant he couldn't see them clearly. Knowing she was beautiful, the most beautiful woman he'd ever seen. *I can love enough for us both* she said.

20 It was as Sidney Krell in his sinister spider-wisdom had predicted: once you hired a lawyer like Jules Cliffe, the police had no choice but to back off.

"These suburban hick-cops," Cliffe said disdainfully. "They're like those scaly overgrown rats you see prowling around here sometimes at night—'possums. They're dim-witted and near-blind and they operate by smell and some weird radar-sense that half the time doesn't work. But they've got sharp teeth, and probably carry rabies, and you wouldn't want the ugly little bastards biting you. *I'll* get rid of 'em, trust me." Like his friend Sid Krell, Jules Cliffe spoke with a bluff man-to-man swagger and a weakness for slang that dated him as much as his precisely sculpted, very white hair and his dignified if puckish manner. He reminded Matt of an elder statesman in some long-ago president's administration—Eisenhower, maybe. He was in his early sixties and his handsome, finely creased face looked carefully arranged as if he'd molded it with his fingers before inviting Matt into his office.

He'd gotten on the phone and shouted at Weymouth Township authorities. He knew them all, and they knew him. Matt listened in amazement as this patrician-Boston lawyer spoke to the chief of detectives, to the township police captain, and to an assistant district attorney who was a friend of his, demanding to know on what grounds detectives had searched the home and office of his client Mathias McBride; he even called the judge who'd signed the warrant, addressing him as "Hank" and giving him hell.

He'd demanded to be sent a copy of those portions of Duana Zwolle's diary that purportedly involved his client. He'd demanded to be kept informed of the "progress, if any" of the police investigation into her disappearance.

Matt was Jules Cliffe's admiring audience of one. *How we need to perform for one another to know we exist*! But this was a damned good performance.

Matt noted how, though Cliffe was speaking over the phone, he gestured eloquently with the fingers of his right hand, as if he were in a courtroom. His fingers were slender and well-shaped and his nails appeared manicured. Unlike Sid Krell, whose expensive tailor-made suits were invariably rumpled-looking and fitted his frame awkwardly, Cliffe was impeccably well-groomed and his dove-gray woolen pinstripe suit fitted him without fault. He'd turned in his swivel chair so that Matt saw him from the side, a profile on a gold coin.

With a snort of indignation Cliffe hung up the phone. What had been decided? Something crucial? Almost, Matt liked the sensation, like sliding into an anesthetic, of surrendering his responsibility to another, more capable and cunning individual.

In a dramatic gesture, Cliffe turned back in his swivel chair to face Matt, and asked him point blank if he'd "had a thing going" with the missing girl? Matt, who'd already explained carefully how slightly he'd been acquainted with Duana Zwolle, having spoken with her no more than two or three times, was offended. "No, Mr. Cliffe, I did not."

"Son, I believe you," Cliffe protested, smiling and showing broad damply white teeth, even as his zinc-colored eyes regarded Matt coolly. "But tell me about it, just the same. And call me 'Jules.' "

People know more than they think they know. This observation, Matt was beginning to fully appreciate.

Each time he recalled his acquaintance with Duana Zwolle—disjointed, brief as it had been—he was remembering a little more. (Or was he inventing? Imagining?) Like a trauma victim revisiting the scene of nightmare. You want to be free of the nightmare, yet you're drawn to it: fascinated. Matt saw Jules Cliffe glancing at him with interest. Man-to-man.

"She really was a strange one, eh? Too bad I never knew her."

There was a mild emphasis on the word *I*. As if to indicate that he, Jules Cliffe, would have known how best to deal with the mysterious Duana Zwolle.

Matt had given his swaggering attorney a copy of the report he'd typed out for Phelan and Ricci. (The cops had never commented on it. They'd never thanked him for it.) The brevity of the report seemed inadequate, maybe suspicious. *Sometime in late June/early July 1997 I visited a small gallery in Weymouth, on Front Street. It was just chance I saw an exhibit of collage-sculpture (I guess it's called) by a local artist whose name was new to me. While I was there, the manager introduced me to the artist herself—Duana Zwolle who happened to be in the gallery. We might have talked for a few minutes. Probably I told her I liked the collages. I don't think she knew I was a photographer, she said nothing about this. We didn't talk long.* Was this true? In fact, Matt had gone into the Tomato Factory Gallery on June 17 (he'd checked this date) with the deliberate intention of seeing *A Garden of Earthly and Unearthly Delights* by the young artist Duana Zwolle; it hadn't been chance.

(In the local paper, the brief, cool review had judged Zwolle's work "obscure" and "willfully murky" but "dramatic." Matt had wanted to see for himself.) But Matt had actually gone to the exhibit because he'd met the exotic young artist a few weeks before, at Krell Associates. At least, he believed he'd met the young artist; Krell hadn't told him her name. This had been the chance meeting: at about 7 P.M. one weekday when the rest of the staff had gone home, Matt was leaving his office when he encountered Sid Krell in the company of a stranger, a dark-haired girl, ushering her into his office as Matt passed in the corridor. Matt saw, in his employer's creased face, a look of subdued rage. God damn! Seen with this girl, when he'd had reason to believe no one else was in the building. Krell said breezily, to the girl, "This is Matt McBride, number one 'associate,' " in a way both affectionate and condescending. The girl glanced at Matt with a small smile, and did not speak. For a moment their eyes locked, in mutual alliance against the older man; it was sheerly instinct, a residue of adolescence; that mutinous, sexual undercurrent of adolescence. *We're young, he's old: He's a fool!* It was rude of Krell not to introduce the girl, but that was Krell's way. Matt saw that she was beautiful if diminutive, and shy: sloe-eyed, with dark, delicate features, severe eyebrows and long carelessly cut dark hair like a mane; she was wearing bleached jeans, open-toed sandals, an Indian muslin green tunic top; her fingers were paint-stained, and the nails uneven; she stood no more than five feet three, weighed perhaps ninety-five pounds. Matt supposed that this girl was one of Sid Krell's artist friends; mainly women, whom Krell made a point of "patronizing" for his own purposes. Matt would have paused to shake hands with the girl, but clearly Krell didn't want any prolonged encounter. "Working late, eh, Mattie?—good boy."

Matt smiled at his employer, and at the mysterious unnamed girl, and left the building with an airy wave of his hand.

He'd been stung by the old man's rudeness. He'd been intrigued by the unnamed girl.

Now, in Jules Cliffe's office, Matt felt obliged to mention that first meeting. If you could call it a meeting. "It was my impression that Sid was offering this woman a commission to create a mural for one of his building lobbies. You know, Sid likes to support local artists. . . ."

Cliffe laughed as if Matt had said something witty.

"Right! That's our Sid. Philanthropist."

Matt wondered how much Cliffe knew. Maybe these rich powerful old bastards pass girls among them? If they can get the girls to cooperate.

Maybe Krell is the man? The man who's responsible? At least, he might know what happened to Duana.

Krell would never "abduct" any woman, himself. But Krell was the sort to hire others to do his work for him.

Matt was thinking of Krell's gun collection. The revolver he'd shown Matt slyly, daringly, like one boy showing another a forbidden toy. Krell had caressed the barrel, the smooth blue-black metal, explaining that a gun has to be cleaned often, with care. *Don't worry, Mattie, I have a permit for this. To carry on my person.* Matt recalled a sexual thrill in the older man's hoarse voice.

Cliffe was saying sharply, "What is it, Matt? You look like you're seeing a ghost. What're you thinking?"

Matt rubbed his eyes vigorously. "Nothing," he said. "I'm thinking nothing."

"Thinking nothing is a good trick, like an erection. Only just try to maintain it." Cliffe laughed heartily and without mirth.

Matt was subtly shocked by this remark, its casual vulgarity and its irrelevance. What did it mean? Did this bastard think he was lying?

Faltering, Matt continued with his account of how briefly he'd met Duana Zwolle, how little he knew of her. He could hear his voice, usually so composed, in speaking with clients and over the telephone so skillfully modulated, now quavering with indecision, regret, guilt. *Why do I sound like a guilty man? I am not*! He knew that Jules Cliffe couldn't seriously believe that he, Matt McBride, had had anything to do with the disappearance of Duana Zwolle, yet he could see that Cliffe was beginning to be baffled by Matt's testimony. A criminal lawyer would have to decode, from a client's account, not only what might be true and what might be false but what might be convincingly presented as "true"; and this "truth" could only be relative, for a hearing before a single judge would be very different from a trial before a jury. Quickly and not very coherently Matt was passing over the meeting with Duana Zwolle in the art gallery. It was true he'd probably told her he admired her collages for Matt was the kind of person who couldn't resist praising others as you'd praise your own kids, to make them happy, to make them smile—"Great work! Terrific." In fact he'd been shaken by *A Garden of Earthly and Unearthly Delights* and hadn't known what to say to the girl who'd appeared silently beside him in the awkward, low-ceilinged space of the gallery. There was an odor of mildew, of cobwebs; the old canning factory had an ancient stone foundation, and the cellar surely had an earthen floor. The Tomato Factory Gallery, only a few years old, had been painted by its artist-owners in bright, brave primary colors, yellow, blue, green, red, to suggest a childlike simplicity and audacity, and the gallery hoped to be known for its "experimental" work. Yet these collages of Duana Zwolle, each measuring about five feet by three feet, and partly composed of three-dimensional objects, were overpowering in the meager space, and Matt McBride had had an almost visceral response. *Nighthawk! This is Nighthawk in another lifetime.*

Not that the artist "Duana Zwolle"—only a name, and a peculiar name at that point to Matt—had plagiarized any of Nighthawk's images in the snapshots and old photos she'd used in the collages. (Yes, he'd checked. He'd spent forty minutes examining the complex, labyrinthine surfaces of *A Garden of Earthly and Unearthly Delights* seeking Nighthawk traces, or maybe, though knowing the quest absurd, he was seeking his own likeness in the miniature faces of strangers?) And there beside him, out of nowhere, appeared the girl he'd first glimpsed, or believed he'd first glimpsed, with his employer Sidney Krell in an awkward encounter; Matt, frowning at wax shapes molded by hand and affixed to blue ceramic shards of sky, hadn't heard her approach, and became aware of her only when he glanced to the side. She came barely to his shoulder. She was a child, hipless and flat-chested and that mane of untidy, kinky hair with its oily sheen!—his first instinct was to smile in derision. *What do you know about art? You!*

Was she waiting for him to speak? She was silent, yet so tense he could sense her tight-strung nerves like the strings of a musical instrument finely vibrating in anticipation of being touched. And that faint odor lifting from her, that hair, those shapeless clothes, of something yeasty and feral and anxious. Somehow, he'd known who she was. Before the gallery manager called over, flirting and intrusive, "There's the artist right there! Mind what you say." Duana Zwolle shrank away at this remark, turned and walked quickly out the door even as Matt called awkwardly after, "Excuse me?—this is great work. This is terrific, I mean it. Like nothing else I've ever—" His voice trailed off, he felt like a fool.

He'd wanted to break the spell of her intensity. But he hadn't wanted her to escape.

(Amid the collages he'd noticed a face like Duana Zwolle's, repeated a half-dozen times as other faces, human figures and images were repeated in dreamlike asymmetrical patterns. Not for a long time would he learn that that face wasn't in fact Duana Zwolle's but that of her twin sister Rue.)

Now Matt was alone in the gallery with its slanted, warped floor and uncomfortably low ceiling. In this cramped space the six vivid collages of *A Garden of Earthly and Unearthly Delights* pressed upon him like obsessive thoughts; he couldn't step back far enough to see how they were structured. Too much detail, crowding his head. The female gallery owner strolled back to say, "She's a mystery woman, our 'Duana Zwolle.' Hasn't said more than a dozen words to me or my partner, I swear. She looks like she's sixteen, doesn't she? But not *young*. I mean, in her eyes. Did you get a look at her *eyes?*"

The woman seemed eager to talk. Lonely in this gallery so few people visited except on weekends. And she'd recognized Matt when he'd come in, as Tess McBride's husband.

Matt said stiffly, "No. I guess I didn't."

But such details weren't relevant to his testimony for Jules Cliffe, and Matt skipped hurriedly over them. He decided to say nothing about the numerous times he'd seen, or been aware of—without speaking, without acknowledging—Duana Zwolle in Weymouth and vicinity in the following weeks and months; it was only natural in such a small town, that individuals might see one another frequently, at a short distance, without speaking. (Maybe, in retrospect, it was more than a coincidence? A skeptical observer, a police detective for instance, might think so. *But I wasn't following her! I swear.*) Matt told Cliffe in more detail and with more emotion of the single time he'd driven Duana Zwolle in his car to her home in Lismore, months after the meeting in the gallery; on October 25, 1997, this had been; the Weymouth detectives, claiming they'd gotten the date from the girl's diary, insisted it had been October 25, and Matt supposed this must be so. The afternoon had been sunny and almost warm but the cornfields outside town were in tatters and the leaves had changed and he remembered how the wind was rippling on the Weymouth River as he'd descended that long banking hill into Lismore, how the river had looked like late autumn. *Piercing his heart, such beauty. Though he'd hardened his heart against it.*

He remembered the girl close beside him, in his car. The scent of her hair. Her body, inside her clothes. Strange he'd been sexually aroused when he didn't find her attractive. When he'd hardly looked at her. *When he hadn't wanted to look at her.*

This time, too, their meeting happened so strangely, Matt had been taken by surprise. Leaving the Weymouth public library on Main Street and when he emerged there was a figure, he'd thought at first it was a high school kid, approaching him for a handout. In that way shy people can be aggressive. Suddenly there in front of him. In a patch of bright autumn sunshine that made her oily hair glitter and gave color to her pale, olive-dark skin. "Excuse me?"—she'd spoken so softly, Matt wasn't sure he'd heard. She was carrying a badly soiled duffel bag slung over one shoulder and she looked windblown, disheveled. She wore a shapeless dark jersey that fell to her hips and faded brown corduroy trousers and stained running shoes. Her hair was longer and more matted than he remembered and there was an anxious vibrancy about her, a raw, childlike hunger in her eyes, and even before she spoke he was steeling himself. *No, look. I can't. It might've been, but it can't be. I'm not the one. Not now. Leave me alone!* Yet Matt was too polite to pretend he hadn't seen her, and hadn't heard her. Their eyes locked, he couldn't escape. She was speaking rapidly, almost inaudibly, telling him a tale of needing a ride home—to Lismore—she had to be back within the hour and hadn't any transportation—her bicycle had broken down. Her bicycle! Well, Matt had to accept this as true. He supposed it was true, in some way. *Only why me? Why approach me?* Already his car keys were in his hand, his car was parked less than thirty feet away.

So he'd said sure, of course he'd give her a ride home. Never guessing what a mistake this was. *For how could he have guessed?* That this strange, lone woman loved him, wanted *him*?

(And someone had seen them? A sharp-eyed suspicious witness who'd spoken with the police? Duana Zwolle climbing into Matt McBride's car with him, the two alone together in the late afternoon of October 25, 1997? Meeting on Main Street in full view of anyone who chanced to see, a married man and an unmarried "artist-type" woman already on such intimate terms they hadn't any need to go through the social formalities of greetings, shaking hands?)

Once they were in Matt's car, a handsome new-model Acura with bucket seats, a teakwood dashboard and pale beige plush upholstery, once they were alone together in such close quarters, Matt had begun to get nervous. He'd begun to talk, too much. For that was Matt McBride's new style: hiding silence inside words. The more he and Tess chattered at each other, laughed and teased like a loving, just slightly competitive couple, the more he could hide his silence, and guard it. And he'd become one of the most successful salesmen at Krell Associates because he could talk, *he could talk and he could charm.* And so in the presence of this strange, unnerving young woman—this *girl*—he didn't want to recognize as the collage-artist of *A Garden of Earthly and Unearthly Delights* he'd been brooding on for months, but had resisted going back to the gallery to see. *For Duana Zwolle was talented, gifted. Nighthawk rejoiced in her, as one of his own kind.* So he was talking nervously, on the drive to Lismore that October afternoon, and maybe wasn't paying strict attention to what he said, fending off Duana Zwolle's intensity, that frank, raw, wordless hunger in her gaze that seemed to indicate *We are alike, we are fated, you and me. You know this.* Duana Zwolle sat mostly silent. Clearly she was tense, self-conscious; physically ill-at-ease. Unlike the socially poised, chatty women of Weymouth, and Matt's female colleagues at Krell Associates, who were as aggressive and vocal as any of the men. Unlike the women with whom Matt McBride was intimate. At the start of the drive she'd glanced shyly at him, saying softly, "Thank you. This is very kind of you." And later, as they were approaching Lismore, Duana Zwolle murmured that she admired his photographs—"The work you do as Nighthawk." Matt glanced at her in surprise. "You know who I am? Well." He was touched. He was pleased. He was excited. Wanting to ask *How long have you known, how long have you been aware of me?*

Duana Zwolle had seemed to want to say more, but didn't.

Nor could Matt bring himself to ask that question, or others about the young woman artist's opinion of his photographs.

For there he was driving his new, beautifully styled expensive car. He was Mathias McBride: husband and father and successful real estate agent in a notoriously competitive field. His heart was beating more rapidly than it beat when he was on the verge of closing a million-dollar deal, or on the verge of making love with any woman. Maybe he resented this, his own excitement. How like an unwilled dream this afternoon had become, a sudden drive through a hilly, autumnal countryside; through a landscape of harvested fields, rows of dessicated cornstalks, scattered woods. Alone together with a woman, any woman, what might happen? *I don't want this! I didn't invite this.*

He'd had his life of adventure, wandering, wayward encounters, romances flaring up abrupt as struck matches and as abruptly extinguished, when he'd been a younger man; in the West and in Alaska especially, he'd led a wild, self-destructive life, drinking, doing drugs, amphetamines; he'd risked injury, arrest, even death. *How happy I was!* He would have liked to explain this to Duana Zwolle because he knew she'd understand, as he wouldn't have even wished Tess to understand had Tess been capable of such understanding. He would have liked to explain Nighthawk to Duana Zwolle. *But no! No words. And if you touch her, McBride, you'll never be able to retract that touch.*

So Matt, contrite, said nothing further. And Duana Zwolle, sitting stiffly beside him, stared straight ahead, and said nothing further either.

Exactly as he'd told the detectives, and was now telling Jules Cliffe, Matt had driven the young woman artist home to the crudely converted old mill on the river, in Lismore; he'd driven a quarter mile or so along the bumpy gravelled Mill Row, and let her out at the farther end, where, she'd told him, she was renting a "loft-flat" on the second floor of the building. Matt had had only a vague impression of the building: a potter's, an antique shop, a wool shop. Mostly, the place seemed vacant. FOR SALE and FOR RENT signs prominent, listed with a Weymouth realtor, a competitor of Krell Associates. *I don't recall any significant conversation passing between us. She didn't invite me inside, and I would not have accepted the invitation if she had. I never saw her again after that.* He wouldn't mention that he'd absentmindedly noticed her car, a battered-looking Volvo, parked in a weedy gravel lot; nor that he'd deliberately not watched her hurry to the outdoor stairs, duffel bag slung over her shoulder, knowing she wouldn't glance back at him. He'd hurt her pride as a woman, maybe more cruelly he'd hurt her pride as a fellow artist.

Denying her. You self-righteous bastard.

Nor would he mention to Jules Cliffe, though the visual memory was flooding back to him now, how he'd been struck by the lonely, rough-hewn place in which Duana Zwolle lived. An uncultivated field beyond the weatherworn stone building, and beyond that a dense woods of pines and deciduous trees; Mill Row dead-ending, in a quagmire of deep-rutted mud and scattered gravel. In all, Mill Row was about a half-mile long, and not a real road; it had once been a service road linking several commercial buildings to the larger highway. The riverbank along Mill Row was a steep, rocky slope, littered with debris in places, though the view across the river was "scenic." Matt had tried to capture the atmosphere of the setting in his photographs, and he believed he'd succeeded, to a degree. (He hadn't yet mentioned the photographs to Jules Cliffe. Frankly, he wasn't sure how to explain them, not only why he'd taken them at such a difficult time in his life but how he could make his motives sound plausible to Cliffe.) On that afternoon, he'd happened to notice several men fishing from the riverbank, two or three appeared to be black men, and there was a white man, though possibly the white man wasn't fishing, only squatting on the riverbank on his haunches and looking out over the river. Returning to the highway, Matt passed these men a second time, and as he drove past the white man turned to stare at him below the rim of a yellow leather cap. *Do I know him? From where?* It was only a fleeting thought. Matt's fine-tuned Acura was bucking in the pot-holed road, and he had to pay attention to his driving. But he came away with an impression of a strangely ethereal face, a pasty-pale face, partly hidden by the yellow leather cap and straggly silver hair, finespun as a woman's and falling to the man's shoulders; the man had a wispy windblown beard but no moustache so that the beard seemed to be floating away beneath his chin which Matt seemed to know was a weak, receding chin. The man was probably Matt's age, of medium height. An odd character in bib overalls, a grimy red scarf knotted at his throat, who reminded Matt of individuals you might glimpse in the interior of the Pine Barrens, those natives to the region called "pineys." *But he's probably an artist. Affecting the look of a piney.* Matt wondered if Duana Zwolle knew this guy, if he lived in the old mill and had a studio there and if he was insufferably Christly as his appearance suggested. A wave of masculine repugnance swept through Matt but vanished immediately, and he forgot this character immediately, in his brooding over Duana Zwolle.

He wouldn't tell Tess about the encounter. Nor would he tell his lover Abigail.

Cliffe said sharply, "But you didn't go upstairs with her, right? Not that time or any other time."

Matt hesitated. Of course he hadn't, that was the point of this long testimony, but the words, the angry denial, stuck in his throat. Cliffe was staring at him, impatiently tapping a pen against his glass desktop.

Matt said, "No. I did not. But the police are saying, or someone is saying, I did. That we were having a love affair. Apparently it's in her diary. I—"

Cliffe interrupted. "Never mind the damned diary. I'll get hold of it, if it exists. It's only the girl's side of it, in any case. Corroboration would be required to make anything stick, we know how lovesick females fantasize." He laughed harshly, and again without mirth. "I'm asking you man-to-man, and remember we have attorney-client privilege, any secret of yours is absolutely safe with me: You never slept with this 'Duana Zwolle,' never made any sexual overtures to her, were never 'intimate' with her? Yes?"

Matt, rubbing his eyes, was seeing again, suddenly, vividly, the look of longing and appeal in Duana Zwolle's face when she'd approached him in front of the library; when she'd glanced shyly at him telling him she admired his photographs; the stiff, hurt way in which she'd walked from his car, duffel bag slung over her shoulder, to climb the outdoor steps to her loft. That these steps were made of wood, were rickety and rain-rotted, added to Duana Zwolle's humiliation. He'd never wondered what it must have cost her, a shy person, an individual of pride and integrity, to have risked so much, until now. Suddenly he was stricken with self-loathing like nausea. "Look, I'm responsible for what happened to Duana Zwolle. Even if I didn't have anything to do with it I allowed it to happen, Goddamn it I didn't help her when she needed help. And now—"

Jules Cliffe snorted with derision. His commentary was quick and to the point: "Bullshit, friend. Bull-*shit*."

He tossed his expensive black fountain pen down onto his desk. It was the end of that day's interview.

21

NIGHTHAWK. *I can steal, I'm a master thief. I can plunder other lives. But I'm a lover, too.* That was the power Nighthawk wielded, Nighthawk's beautiful camera in his hands that never shook as Matt McBride's hands might shake.

But Nighthawk had never taken Duana Zwolle's photograph, and this failure hurt. It was like an inflammation of the lining of the heart. In his car, that October afternoon, he might have turned off the highway to park along a country lane—one of those lanes leading into a farmer's field—he might have framed her delicate, hopeful face in his hands gently, he might have explained to her *Yes I can love you, Duana—only just not now. Not now, in my life. But someday.* And she would have understood. He knew. Her deep-socketed eyes that were intelligent and unaccusing. *We will be friends, then? Please. I'm so lonely.* She would speak without subterfuge. She would speak her heart. And Matt would say at once *Yes. We will be friends.*

But these words hadn't been said. He hadn't parked his car along a country lane, he hadn't framed her face in his hands, he hadn't opened his heart to her, nor she to him. None of this had happened. And he had no private image of her, smiling at him, to contend with the public image, the tragic *missing girl* of the media and the $50,000 REWARD OFFERED posters.

"So tell us, Mr. McBride. 'Nighthawk.' Exactly why did you take two dozen photographs of Duana Zwolle's residence in Lismore and the area nearby?"

For a long moment Matt sat silent, his head in his hands. You could hear his breathing. That morning he'd shaved quickly and carelessly, a tiny nick in his jaw kept filling damply with blood. Yet he'd come voluntarily, with his expensive lawyer, to be interviewed at Weymouth

Township Police headquarters to aid detectives in their investigation into the disappearance of Duana Zwolle.

It was twenty-eight days since she'd vanished. In his distraught state Matt wondered if that might mean something: twenty-eight. For she'd vanished on December 28.

Each day she's missing, it's more unlikely she'll be found.

Sick with guilt, Matt was seated at a rectangular table in a windowless "interview room" at the police station. Staring at the opened packet of glossy prints, Nighthawk prints, spread on the table before him like incriminating evidence. And there was the framed photograph the detectives had taken from his office at Krell Associates. He tried to concentrate on the question Phelan had put to him. It was distracting, to see Jules Cliffe examining the photographs, seriously staring at each in turn, frowning severely. *Why? Why were the photographs taken? Because Nighthawk had a need to take them.* Matt said quietly, "I'm not sure."

The younger detective Ricci, who'd made it a point to stare at the tiny bleeding cut in Matt's cheek, asked coolly, "And why at that time?—you claim it was two weeks after Duana Zwolle disappeared."

Matt said, "That, I don't know either. One day I had my camera, I was driving along the river, I found myself in—Lismore." He hesitated to point out to the detectives that he'd obviously taken the photographs after Duana Zwolle had disappeared, because there were shutters visible in her front window. He didn't want to seem to be defending himself strenuously, like a guilty man.

The detectives must have noticed the shutters, too. The time of the photographs couldn't be a serious question.

Phelan was asking, with cruel courtesy, "So why did you try to hide them, Mr. McBride? In your IRS files?"

Because I'm stupid, you son of a bitch. I made a mistake.

Jules Cliffe interrupted, as he'd interrupted several times previously, and the questioning was deflected before Matt could reply. Matt had to wonder not why he'd hidden the prints, but why he hadn't hidden them in a better place.

It was strange: Tess hadn't asked Matt about the Lismore photographs. She knew the police had confiscated them because he'd told her; but he'd told her only what he needed to tell. She'd said she believed him that there'd been nothing between him and Zwolle. (Did she believe this? Certainly, Tess wanted to believe.) It was Nighthawk that made Tess uneasy. Nighthawk, Matt's other, nocturnal life. A life that had nothing to do with her. Tess claimed to admire the photographs, or said she did; except why, Tess asked Matt, were the photographic subjects such "ugly" people? such "losers"? It wasn't as if there weren't plenty of attractive people in New Jersey, Tess joked.

She resents Nighthawk. He isn't her husband.

Jules Cliffe and the Weymouth detectives were disagreeing over the employment of "hide"—"hidden." Cliffe objected to the detectives use of it in their questioning, and the detectives defended it. Matt noted how, in the lawyer's presence, his old pals Phelan and Ricci were different, diminished men. Their off-the-rack clothes, their haircuts, their grooming. They cleared their throats more often, they stumbled over words. Their grammar was uncertain. They were like skilled boxers confined in cages: they couldn't strike with their well-practiced, lethal combinations, they couldn't employ their fancy footwork. They were flat-footed, and made to look like provincial Jersey cops. They resented Cliffe whom they knew by reputation and they looked upon him with loathing. It was true, Cliffe seemed to give off a glow. Ten-forty-five of a weekday morning in Weymouth and Cliffe was wearing a thousand-dollar tailor-made suit, a perfect fit. His necktie was Italian silk, his shirt was an item of beauty and he wore monogrammed gold cuff links. White-sculpted hair, Boston-patrician manner. Cliffe was a preening pedigree dog beside whom the Jersey detectives were mongrels. A mongrel can be trained and courgeous and smart as hell but still he's a mongrel and knows it. Matt regarded Phelan and Ricci sympathetically. But he was damned glad that Cliffe was on his side.

Cliff was speaking briskly, addressing the tape machine on the table as if Phelan and Ricci were mere flunkies who'd switched it on. Though Cliffe must have been improvising, a remarkable speech issued from his lips as if it had been prepared: "My client Mathias

McBride, whose professional name is 'Nighthawk,' is a known and much-admired photographer whose work has been appearing in New Jersey publications for the past six years. As 'Nighthawk,' Mr. Mc-Bride has a reputation for artistic integrity. He is not a commercial photographer or a photojournalist. A serious photographer follows his vision like any artist. If Mathias McBride wants to take photographs in Lismore, that's his prerogative. Many photographers have been out to Lismore, TV camera crews and others. You know that. Weymouth police have no grounds for harassing Mathias McBride. You have no evidence linking him to the disappearance of Duana Zwolle and you have no reason to involve him further in your investigation. And when am I going to receive a copy of the young woman's diary? My patience, gentlemen, is being sorely tried."

The interview ended. Matt's Nighthawk photographs, computer disks, letters and other random items seized in the police search were returned to him by a clerk. Each item labeled *McBride*.

Matt felt a stab of shame. How sordid this all was, "evidence" that hadn't panned out.

22 NAME UNKNOWN. In a fierce fiery vision it came to him suddenly *You must return, your enemies will note the absence of NAME UNKNOWN if you stay away longer.* Though he had begun work again as a welder working twenty hours a week in a machine shop in Newark. Where he was *Joseph Gavin*, and was paid by weekly check with deductions for taxes and social security which no American can escape. Needing money to feed himself whom the capitalist society would let starve like a dog if he did not sell himself to industry.

For Art & Beauty are of no value in the marketplace. This was an ugly truth NAME UNKNOWN had understood since the age of nineteen; it held no further surprise or bitterness for him.

Driving then to the Village of Weymouth for the first time since *the day it had happened*: December 28.

This affluent village he detested, for its worship of material things. A false beauty mocking the true.

Yet smiling with boyish excitement seeing the many posters in store windows. Like shouts of pain, alarm, fear.

$50,000 REWARD

DUANA ZWOLLE

LAST SEEN DEC. 28

NAME UNKNOWN ducked his head smiling doubting they would reward *him* with $50,000 if he led them to the *missing girl* away in the snowy Pine Barrens. A *snow-burial* it was. For the earth had been too frozen for digging. After the first thaw, he might return. Or might not. *A dead body revenges not injuries.*

There were only two galleries in Weymouth where NAME UNKNOWN had been decently welcomed as a fellow artist. And even in these he had reason to believe the owners smiled at him behind his back. Today, he had only a single new wood carving to offer, a squirrel with an uplifted plume of a tail, on consignment. This was the only kind of work by NAME UNKNOWN the gallery owners would display. No exhibit of NAME UNKNOWN's major work was ever offered. Yet he took care to disguise his hurt & outrage. Only just smiling as Jesus might smile in the presence of His enemies & mockers. *O ye of little faith, take warning!* Saying yes he understood, life-sized sculptures of THE MARRIAGE OF HEAVEN AND HELL are not for all tastes. Though today it seemed not even his animal carving was welcomed at either gallery. At the Jameson Gallery on Main Street the carving was dismissed as *not quite right for us, sorry* & at the Tomato Factory Gallery the female owner explained sniffing she could not take it for *there was no room*. Also *business was slow after the holidays*. NAME UNKNOWN hid his hands trembling. His strong, steely fingers. His fingers yearning for the good feeling of wire. A loop of wire.

Yet he hid his hurt & outrage. Peering smiling into the very space where the previous summer he had been sickened to discover the ugly collages of D Z on blatant display. *A Garden of Earthly and Unearthly Delights*—the very title stolen from NAME UNKNOWN.

So it was just & ordained, that NAME UNKNOWN must steal from the female in turn. NAME UNKNOWN had wished to appropriate her eyes, so beautiful. But this was a vision not to be executed. Shimmering jelly-eyes he tried to insert into wax sockets of a female angel but saw the futility of the attempt. *For human eyes would rot. For such purposes glass marbles are superior.*

The vocal cords of M M and leg tendons of L R & V J he had tried to use too but had soon abandoned. This was *defeat*.

This brassy-haired female who believed herself an artist did not inquire of NAME UNKNOWN where he had been these five weeks. Did not seem to have missed NAME UNKNOWN. And now her vague forced smile trying to be polite but clearly waiting for him to leave. *& if I return I will burn this place to the ground.*

The phone rang. She wished him to leave. He lingered to overhear.

The female was saying with a laugh of weariness *Since Duana I've been a wreck. I wake up a dozen times a night. I look at the stuff on these walls including my own paintings and I think What the hell? We try so hard, and why? For what? To save our souls?*

NAME UNKNOWN slipped silently away. Cradling his wood carving beneath his arm like a living creature.

Only with the ugly fierce-faced black girl V J in the quarry in Catonsville, MD, where she would never be found & her sweat-stinking clothes burned in gasoline had NAME UNKNOWN been tempted to seek out police to speak with them, & that for his own purposes to test them. (V J was an Olympic runner at the branch of the State College & her photo too many times in the papers.) & now in Weymouth a strange need overcame him to laugh in their faces. Driving carefully past the WEYMOUTH TOWNSHIP POLICE DEPARTMENT building. Eagerly staring. Wondering wouldn't it be natural for him, a friend of the *missing girl* and a fellow artist, to inquire about the investigation? For the detectives had come to his trailer in Clinton Falls to question him. And he had never heard further. In his jacket pocket he carried their cards: *Detective Michael Phelan, Detective Arturo Ricci.* They had asked him to telephone if he had further information of D Z but he had not. (In his place, & following his instructions, the Brough woman had called. But they didn't know that.) Now thinking *But it would be natural, wouldn't it?*

In his rusted Ford pickup driving past the Township building at twenty miles an hour. Frowning & staring with great concentration. If it was meant for him to enter that building he would receive a sign. He turned, & drove past a second time. His heart began to beat harder. *Yes? No? Yes? No? No.* A deep breath suffused him. He was not meant to seek out the Weymouth police, the detectives with their narrow suspicious eyes, not at this time.

Instead, he drove to Lismore.

Oh. Joseph Gavin. Hel-lo.

But the woman's voice, usually so buoyant & insinuating, was flat. Nor did her eyes linger caressingly on him, his fine-spun hair to his shoulders she'd once praised, his beard & his body as in the past. Oriana, hair scraped back from her face as with a trowel, held a crumpled tissue to her nose where the nostrils were inflamed with a severe cold. Surprised, he saw that

Oriana was older than in his memory. He felt a stab of elation that NAME UNKNOWN had such power over these females. For Oriana was the friend of D Z who had been most often interviewed about her on TV, more even than members of the Z family. On TV, Oriana's voice had been strong & assured & her eyes outlined in theatrical black glared with fanatic certainty. *Of course I believe that my dear friend Duana is alive! I refuse to surrender hope!* But that had been in the early days of the search.

Since moving to central New Jersey, NAME UNKNOWN had often visited Oriana in her studio-gallery in Lismore which was called, simply, ORIANA. This was before learning of D Z & knowing what must be done with her. For of the many artists of the region, it was Oriana who knew everyone & welcomed everyone. She who organized the Lismore Art Festival & the River-front Art Fair. She who was a spiritual child of the Sixties as she boasted. Where Oriana was actually from, there were numerous tales. NAME UN-KNOWN perceived the woman to be a liar and took no interest in her delusions & pretenses as he took no interest in her lascivious eyes caressing his limbs. Her eyes were an earthen green and her hair a bleached white-blond dry as straw. He had touched it once, in blessing her; & had all he could do to resist drawing his hand back in revulsion. For there was shamefulness & mockery in Oriana no man could trust; & no artist could trust; though NAME UNKNOWN hid his dislike, for often the woman would feed him as she fed others if he appeared hungry & needy. Her most delicious soup a rich thick lentil soup simmering on her stove for hours.

Oriana lived alone in the Village of Lismore, population 700, in a stable converted to a small dwelling place that doubled also as a studio and a gallery open at certain hours for customers. The old woodframe and stucco building had been painted, by Oriana as she boasted, a bright apple green with red trim. Even in winter, in the beds bordering her front walk there were vivid purple and cream-colored heads of flowering kale. NAME UN-KNOWN parked his Ford pickup at the curb & with downcast eyes knocked at Oriana's door as he entered, jangling the bell. For they would share in common the grief of D Z missing these weeks from their midst.

So glancing over at NAME UNKNOWN, Oriana murmured her flat greeting. He heard no welcome in her voice as he would have expected. Though loathing her, he believed she admired him, & lusted after him. Yet there was no leap in her eyes. No rich delicious odor of soup simmering on the big iron range at the rear. *Well, Joseph. Haven't seen you for a while.* Blowing her nose rudely, her mud-green eyes indifferent on him. There was another person, another female, at the back of the shop sitting on the edge of a work bench. NAME UNKNOWN felt a stab of disgust for these females he knew by instinct to be lesbian, & not natural.

Long he had wondered if D Z had been of their species.

Another reason for D Z to be punished. & her gift of art taken from her who had not been worthy of it.

Maybe it had been an error to come here, & to Lismore itself? Maybe Oriana had not missed him? And seeing him now, would she be suspicious? He would not wish to kill this female, too. He had had no thought of that at all. Saying quickly, plucking at his beard *It was the bad weather, Oriana. The ice that kept me away. And my truck breaking down. And I am working in Newark again.* Oriana seemed scarcely to listen where once she, and D Z had she been present, would have sympathized with him; a fellow artist forced to sell himself in the marketplace. On the walls of Oriana's gallery were large rectangular paintings of fleshy female nudes in gardens amid bulbous fruits & vegetables of the texture of flesh themselves, a lewd art offensive to the purity of NAME UNKNOWN. Though he was generous-hearted as always giving no hint of his revulsion.

Strange, that Oriana had so little to say to him. Clearly waiting for him to depart. Shyly he mentioned to her his newest figure taking shape beneath his fingers would be the sixth in the series THE MARRIAGE OF HEAVEN AND HELL. In all, there would be nine such figures. *In honor of our friend who is missing. Though I began it last summer.* He saw that Oriana winced at these words. He spoke more gently, to hide his mounting anger. *Is there any news of her, Oriana? Any hope?* Oriana rubbed at her inflamed nose & shrugged. She wore a baggy soiled black sweater & soiled jeans too tight for her buttocks. Her gaze drifted to the rear of the cluttered space where her woman friend waited. Possibly Oriana had grown weary of the vigil of D Z, she had helped make posters and pass out flyers and on TV had made an appeal to whoever might know of the *missing girl* & NAME UNKNOWN had reason to believe she had spent time with the Z family as well but possibly now she was beginning to surrender hope. NAME UNKNOWN bit his lip not wanting to laugh in the female's face. This new heaviness in her, a woman in her late thirties at least, & the glisten faded from her skin. She was saying, shuddering *Oh Joseph it's a nightmare, it doesn't end. If she is alive she may be suffering. Almost I pray for her to be found. To put an end to—this horror.* NAME UNKNOWN felt his eyes sting with tears for he was childlike in his sympathies, that was known of him & admired in him. And Oriana noticed, but sighed & said *I guess I don't want to talk about this right now Joseph, please.* So he knew he was expected to leave. Though his stomach growled with hunger there would be no meal for NAME UNKNOWN this evening at Oriana's table.

He would have requested they pray together for D Z but knew Oriana in her selfish mood would not consent. For the woman wanted NAME UN-KNOWN gone, that she might be alone with her female lover.

NAME UNKNOWN had too much pride & self respect to linger. Quickly he left & walking away felt their eyes on his back, & their sneering smiles.

The decision then came to him he would not return to the home of D Z & the Weymouth River. He would not return to the place from which he had carried the female struggling for her contemptible life. For instinct warned him *You have done enough, & maybe you have done more than enough.*

23 For so many days and nights in this new year had Matt McBride been imagining Duana Zwolle's diary, with such anticipation and dread, it was a shock for him to receive from Cliffe's office a packet containing only a few sheets of paper, brought to him by a messenger one afternoon in late February. *Mathias McBride. Confidential. Deliver By Hand.* The pages were photocopies of the diary in which Matt evidently figured; the mysterious, incriminating diary; the diary that had brought Weymouth detectives to him, and altered the course of his life; but most of the pages had been heavily censored so that passages floated in blank space like deranged poetry. All were written in hand, in a beautiful, unusually large script, in black ink with a felt-tip pen.

Duana Zwolle's handwriting, he'd never seen before.

The packet was delivered to Matt one afternoon in early February, in his office at Krell Associates. He signed for it, trying to remain calm. As soon as the messenger left his office he opened the packet, with shaking fingers removed the pages—less than ten?—so few?—and began eagerly to read.

Nighthawk. I am so happy, I could die this hour.

This first entry was dated 17 June 1997, the day Matt had met Duana Zwolle at The Tomato Factory Gallery.

Matt's eyes misted over, he couldn't see. A telephone was ringing at the periphery of consciousness, lacerating his nerves. Abruptly (and recklessly: he was expected to drop by Sidney Krell's office for a brief consultation on a land-surveying contract that was being drawn up, later that afternoon) he decided to take the rest of the day off, to escape Weymouth, drive out into the countryside and read the diary in isolation.

Now I will know! At last.

It was one of the most powerful emotional experiences of Matt Mc-Bride's life. When he returned to Weymouth in the early evening, he would feel himself a changed man. Seeing his house, his family, like a traveler who's been gone a very long time.

His eight-year-old, Davey, hearing Daddy drive his car into the garage, ran into the kitchen to greet him, for Daddy would be entering the house by this rear door. Yet Daddy remained sitting in the car, it seemed, for a while, before getting out, and approaching the steps. Davey had opened the door, waiting impatiently for him. He called, "Daddy? What's wrong?" Matt entered the over-bright kitchen and stooped to kiss his son, swaying just slightly. Or maybe it was the room that swayed.

Davey said, "Daddy, did something happen to your eyes?"

24 Here at last was the diary of the *missing girl.*

Matt read it not knowing if he was fascinated, or revulsed. If Duana Zwolle had been deranged, or simply in love with him: that is, in love with Nighthawk.

One thing he knew: no woman had ever so cared for him, brooded upon him, obsessed over him as Duana Zwolle. Now that it was too late, he was beginning to understand what he'd missed in life.

> I am so happy I could die this hour

And,

> Nighthawk. We will be together
> one day I know.
>
> This side of the grave
> or the other.

The diary was mostly passages like this, poetic in form though explicit in statement. The first entry in the material given to Matt was from June 1997, the last was dated Christmas Eve of that year. Matt had never read another individual's private diary, and found this experience unnerving. "We have no right. None of us. To violate her. Now that she's . . . now that she isn't here to protect herself."

> Nighthawk. Don't turn from me,
> don't laugh at me in scorn.
> Long before our births, our destinies
> were woven together.

Yet in the gallery today you behaved
in ignorance. "Mathias McBride."
In denial of Nighthawk & of our love.

This was true! Matt remembered: that day in the Tomato Factory
Gallery. He'd been looking at Duana Zwolle's collages for a long time,
not thinking so much as lost in contemplation, wonder. And then he'd
turned to discover the artist beside him as if she'd appeared out of
nowhere, summoned by his desire.

He hadn't been equal to the moment.

He hadn't been equal to Duana Zwolle.

He saw her now, clearly, as she'd been on the day of this diary
entry: an intense young woman, small-boned, graceful, dark; of a melancholy temperament, very different from the woman he'd married.
He was struck by her eyes. Her beautiful deep-set eyes. Yet his reaction was uneasiness, resistance. The gallery owner had introduced
them and Matt had only smiled genially, in his practiced public voice,
praising the artist for her "interesting"—"unusual"—work. Duana
Zwolle's gaze on him, her unsmiling response to his bullshit.

Face it: Matt had been afraid of her. That intensity. That remarkable *will*.

The net flung over me, & over you.
The long summer following. Your blindness.
Hiding from me: husband, father.
Coward.

On a page dated August 9, Duana Zwolle analyzed in admiring
detail one of Nighthawk's photographs, titled "Nocturne," that had
been reproduced in *New Jersey Life* that month. It depicted a couple,
not young but glamorous, kissing, laughing together as they kissed,
huddled beneath the awning of a closed liquor store in Hoboken,
waiting for rain to pass; the sidewalk in front of them was puddled
and gleaming, light from a streetlamp fell upon their vividly illuminated faces. It might have been a movie still: the man was handsome,

swarthy; the woman was heavily made up, with darkened lips, like a film actress of the 1940s. Matt had been driving by, seen the lovers and made a quick decision to photograph them, guessing they wouldn't mind, wouldn't even notice. He'd been right.

NOCTURNE. Our love enshrined.

In August, Duana Zwolle noted,

> You disappear from Weymouth.
> I am alone.
>
> Alone not alone.
> I am waiting.

The previous summer, Tess and the boys had spent most of August on Martha's Vineyard, at Tess's parents' shingleboard "cottage" on the ocean; Matt had flown up once or twice for the weekend, and had spent the last weekend of the summer there, with the usual ambivalent feelings he had for such family-oriented vacations. Of course, he loved his family. And he got along well, for the most part, with his in-laws and other relatives of Tess's. Now he wondered: how had his behavior, his role as *husband, father* been perceived by Duana Zwolle? Had it been avoidance of her, had he in fact behaved like a coward?

He thought, I might have called her.

I might have driven to Lismore to see her.

Dated 25 October was a long entry, in Duana Zwolle's small, intense, hurried handwriting:

> Today   another day   the net flung over me!
> Flaming & tearing my flesh
> Like those lethal "radiant garments"
>   given by Medea to Jason's
>   innocent young bride.

This was the day Matt had driven Duana home from Weymouth; the day she'd approached him on the street to ask a favor. Her version of the drive was astonishing to Matt.

> Netting us so close. In your car.
> & the words unspoken between us NIGHTHAWK

> Seeing in your eyes my own

> You were kind, you say "yes"—
> you'd "be happy to drive me home"
> (I laughed. I saw you were frightened of me.)
> (Yet it's true, Matt: my bicycle had broken,
> yet also true I stalked you like a hunter.)

> With your eyes you told me: all that I knew.
> Even your cowardice seemed to me   our destiny
> so how could I blame you   husband, father

It was true, Matt thought. During that drive there had passed between them . . . something. Not words, but . . . something. A palpable tension. Anxiety. Matt had been painfully aware of the young woman beside him in his car, and though he'd certainly not indicated to her anything of what he felt, he'd known he had felt it; and she had known, too. So, strangely, accusingly, she wrote:

> Yes you confessed, Nighthawk   YOU LOVE ME.
> Driving out of Weymouth
> Driving us into the hills
> Driving us into the FUTURE

Was this why the detectives had suspected Matt? They were guessing, they'd meant to bully and intimidate him into confessing, yet in their ignorance they were right. He had confessed to Duana Zwolle, in his way.

Through November and December there were scattered entries. Matt thought he could match them with specific episodes in his life—but he wasn't sure. Duana Zwolle's ardent voice began to hypnotize him in its persistence, its certitude. And maybe this is what love is, Matt thought: the realization of one's soul in another.

> Nighthawk/Matt   you've made me so happy
> here in this place/in this bed
> I hate sharing you with another/others
> yet sometimes I think—
> I am beyond desire
>
> Beyond desire as in the Clear Light of the Void

An entry for 11 December,

> Don't be angry Nighthawk/Matt
> I did keep vigil in our place/in December rain
> I knew you weren't coming/you'd explained
>
> I don't mind being hurt by you/if hurt is love.

Matt tried to remember what had happened on December 11. He'd check his calendar but . . . but of course this entry wasn't literally true.

Yet, how convincing.

Almost, Matt was beginning to believe.

The final entry, 24 December, Christmas Eve. He read it hesitantly, with dread. The final entry of Duana Zwolle's life, probably. And what a surprise it contained:

> This beautiful gift thank you!
> A fineknit white cashmere shawl
> TO DUANA WITH LOVE

(I hope it is not Medea's "radiant garment"
binding us)

But where pain & anguish—our love.

Nighthawk knows.
In the New Year, we'll declare ourselves.
This secrecy will end   consumed like flame

In the New Year—

But the entry broke off unfinished. As if Duana Zwolle had been interrupted. *By him. The abductor. The punisher of bad behavior.*

What was most mysterious about this entry, of course, was that Matt hadn't given Duana Zwolle a white cashmere shawl. He'd never given her any gift. Here, clearly, she'd been mistaken. You could say she'd been deluded, except, evidently, there'd been a cashmere shawl in her possession, which would one day turn up bloodied and torn on a rocky bank of the Delaware River.

Someone else must have given it to her. Who?

The abductor. That faceless nameless Other.

Duana had mistakenly assumed the shawl was from Matt/Nighthawk. That seemed clear. Her delusion was understandable, in the context of these diary entries. Yet the delusion was a fatal one. For if Matt had been the one to give Duana the shawl, very likely she'd be alive now.

25

There was Duana Zwolle's voice, in solitude, in dreams.

There was Tess's voice, and her alert eyes confronting his.

"Matt. Tell me, has something happened?"

"What? No."

"You would tell me—if something has happened?"

"Of course I would, honey. You know that."

It was mid-March. A season of prematurely warm days, a spring thaw come early. Unnatural sunshine and snowdrops, crocuses, even the buds of forsythia on the verge of bloom. The snow and ice of only a week ago, melted.

This wasn't the first time that Tess had confronted Matt, since the infamous police search in January. Since Tess's fervent declaration that she believed Matt, she believed her husband, she loved her husband and would not for a moment consider that he might have been involved with—that *missing girl* whose name she'd never spoken, since the search. What might have provoked her, if there was any single thing, Matt had no idea. He seemed never to be thinking about Tess except when she stood before him demanding his attention, or, in their bed, pressing her warm body against his in accusation as much as in yearning. It was not that he'd forgotten her—for how, after all, could a man forget the woman with whom he lived?—but that, somehow, he no longer thought about her. His manner with her was unfailingly congenial, his smile warm and immediate.

"It's just that you seem—distracted lately. And distant. Even when you're home with us."

Even when you're home with us. There, the accusation.

Matt McBride wasn't a man who liked being accused of anything, as he wasn't a man who liked defending himself. But, knotting a necktie, frowning into the mirror of their bedroom bureau, he said, "That may be, Tess. You must know I have a damned lot on my mind."

"But I'd thought that Jules Cliffe had made a difference, Matt; and that the police weren't harassing you now."

Quickly Matt said, "Right. Cliffe has made a difference. As far as I know, the cops are backing off from 'Mathias McBride.' For the time being at least."

There was a pause. Tess's eyelids quivered. How hard she was trying, to remain neutral, poised. She wasn't a woman accustomed to pleading with any man, not even her husband whom she loved very much, more than pride would have wished, but of whom she'd never been, since the early days of their love, wholly certain. How pride lacerated her, like coarse fabric worn against her sensitive skin, that she might seem to this man to be a jealous, anxious wife interrogating him. *And was she still going through his things, in stealth? Checking his pockets, his calendar, his answering machine tape?*

The photocopied diary pages, in Duana Zwolle's hand, Matt had hidden safely away, in one of his files at Krell Associates.

" 'For the time being'? But why should they bother you at all? I thought we'd been through that."

"We have. We've been through it."

"Is there anything else, anything new that I should know about?"

"No, Tess. There is not."

"You've been neglecting the boys, too. They miss you."

To this, Matt made no reply. He supposed it was true, and he regretted it.

And he meant to make amends. Soon.

Tess was saying, carefully, "From what I've been hearing, the Weymouth police haven't made much progress in their investigation. People think the river should be dragged more thoroughly. Imagine the girl's family. Those poor parents! It just goes on and *on*. This is, what—the third month? If whoever did it is a serial killer, which people think, they seem to be only just waiting for him to strike again. We're all so vulnerable. When you're away, and the boys and I are alone together—" Tess paused, and took another track. "I mean—

wherever she is, whoever took her—whatever happened to her—"
Tess was speaking rapidly now, her eyes seeking out Matt's in the
mirror even as, with impatient, clumsy fingers, Matt unknotted his tie
and tried again, and avoided looking at her. "Oh Matt, what if it's
never solved? I was reading in the *Star-Ledger* about other girls and
women in New Jersey and Pennsylvania, Maryland, Delaware—who
were abducted, some of them never recovered, though it's been years.
There's something unbearable about one of these cases when it isn't
solved. Or maybe I mean injustice—it's so hard to *accept*."

Matt wanted to end the discussion, before he became emotional.
And he wanted to leave the house: he had an appointment. (Not a
business appointment, as he'd led Tess to believe. Though he hadn't
precisely lied to her.) He said, "The fact is, Tess, in a sense all
'mystery' *is* solved. There may be injustice, sure. But somewhere,
someone knows the solution to a 'mystery.' If not us."

26

Matt believed this. That the mystery of what had happened, or was still happening, to Duana Zwolle had a solution. Someone knew. Maybe more than one person knew. And he, Matt McBride, was going to find out.

The first time Matt had driven to Lismore, in January, to visit the studio-gallery of the woman artist who called herself "Oriana," Matt seemed to have arrived only just minutes after she'd posted a CLOSED sign in the front door. "God*damn.*" He knocked, but no one answered. He shaded his eyes to peer inside, believed he saw figures at the rear, but no one answered. Yet it was forty minutes earlier than the the the closing-time of 5 P.M. indicated on a sign beside the door, and he'd just seen, as he'd driven up to park, someone leaving the building, to climb into a battered-looking Ford pickup and drive away.

In his nervy, edgy mood, Matt McBride was noticing things, and people, he'd never have noticed in normal times. Taking note for instance of this vehicle, the faded color of tin, with Jersey plates, driven by a bearded, long-haired man who struck Matt as looking familiar. A visored yellow leather cap on his head, a scruffy windbreaker. A lean narrow putty-pale face. *Who's that? I know him.*

The man he'd seen squatting on the bank of the Weymouth River, a hundred or so feet from Duana Zwolle's residence, the afternoon in October he'd driven her home. The long-haired bearded character Matt supposed to be a local artist, a homegrown eccentric affecting the dress of a "piney." This time, the man hadn't noticed Matt drive up, he'd been walking quickly and jerkily, grimacing to himself, staring into space. As if he'd had a quarrel with someone inside the apple-green gallery called ORIANA.

If, that day, Oriana had answered her door and let Matt in, Matt could have asked her who the bearded man in the yellow leather cap was; but Oriana hadn't answered that door, and Matt had turned away frustrated.

The second time he'd driven to Lismore, in February, it was after he'd received the photocopied pages from Duana Zwolle's diary, and he'd had the idea that possibly Oriana, who'd described herself in interviews as a "sister-artist" and "intimate friend" of Duana Zwolle, had also seen portions of the diary pertaining to her, and would like to compare notes with Matt. Considering Duana Zwolle's interest in Nighthawk, it was possible she'd confided in Oriana about him. Matt had many questions to ask Oriana! But that time, like the first, he'd gone away frustrated: when he arrived at Oriana's studio-gallery, the six-foot, statuesque blond woman was there, but reluctant to see Matt because she had a visitor—"Maybe another time, Mr. McBride? I really can't talk now." Her voice lowered to a thrilled whisper. "I have a visitor—*Nicholas Roche*." Pacing in her gallery, impatiently smoking a cigar, was a pale, petulant-looking man of about Matt's age with dark hair cut in a fashionable buzz-cut, small heavy-lidded rapacious eyes, an air about him that boasted *artist*. He wore an expensive ankle-length leather coat and lizard-skin boots. This time, at the front curb, a classy black Jaguar was parked, bearing New York plates.

Successful artist, Matt thought.

That day, too, he'd driven back to Weymouth. Feeling like a rejected suitor.

Matt recalled the occasions he'd seen Sidney Krell in the company of tall blond Oriana the potter-painter who wore silk kimonos in bright colors, handwoven tunics and caftans and peasant skirts, turbans, head-scarves, shawls and her own handcrafted silver-and-feathered jewelry. Oriana, lavishly made up, was gorgeous as a poster might be gorgeous: you stared, you were blinded, you could only admire. Oriana exuded sexual energy one could virtually feel, like radiant heat. Beside her, Sid Krell was short, aging, overly eager, embarrassing in his attentiveness to a woman not his wife, and so clearly not his type; he declared to friends he was infatuated with Oriana and willing to be made a fool of for her sake—"For the sake of Art!" Yet, being Sid Krell, he was sardonic, sarcastic, nobody's fool. The couple quarreled in public, exchanging profanities and obscenities and even a few blows. They were a local "item"; Krell basked in such attention; then again, sober, hung-over, he was deeply ashamed of himself and repentant. Had there been an actual affair between the two? a sexual relationship, of any kind? Or only just a romantic friendship? Matt wouldn't have been one to know, and would not have wished to know. For he sensed that those younger people who were invited to be Sid Krell's confidantes would later regret it.

It was known that Krell had paid thousands of dollars to Oriana for a number of vases, urns and sculpted figures, and had commissioned a "major work" from her; when they'd ceased being friends, he'd demanded much of this money back and had threatened to sue—"to break"—Oriana. But Oriana hadn't been intimidated in the slightest. She refused to hire a lawyer, she declared, but would appeal to the "court of public opinion—" the media. As an artist, Oriana believed there could be no negative publicity. The goal of the artist is to be seen, so that the artist's work can be seen, and bought.

In the end, Sid Krell had backed away. He'd met his match, he acknowledged. Here was a woman who sought the public eye even more than he, and wasn't fussy about the circumstances of publicity. As apparently the last person to have seen Duana Zwolle on the evening of December 28, except for her abductor, and one of the few persons connected with Duana Zwolle who was tirelessly willing to be interviewed, Oriana had seemed perversely to bloom after her friend's disappearance. For a while, each time Matt switched on the TV, there was Oriana's glowing face. Her Nordic blond hair loose on her shoulders, or gathered in sculpted twists and coils around her head; enormous silver-and-feathered earrings dangling from her ear lobes, long fleshy-muscled arms adorned with rattling bracelets. Oriana had generous hips, generous breasts, a moonshaped face that dominated the TV screen. Even practiced interviewers, good-looking women with TV skills, appeared dwarfed beside her. While the Zwolle family refused requests for all but a few, brief interviews, and the Weymouth police were close-mouthed and uncooperative, there was Oriana to take up the challenge. Matt had several times seen film footage of the woman's studio-gallery in Lismore, her pots, urns and sculpted figures, and her gaudier, large paintings in the faux-primitive style of Rousseau; he was captivated by her husky, seductive voice, her elaborately made-up eyes, and her grave yet exuberant manner. As if the disappearance and possible death of her friend and sister-artist Duana Zwolle were a truly world-shaking event, a mystery gripping not just central New Jersey but the entire nation, and she, Oriana, with no last name, an icon of anxious expectation, keeping a vigil for Duana Zwolle's safe return. Breathlessly Oriana would declare, "Like all artists of genius, Duana Zwolle is one who lives on the edge—of imagination, and of life. I, Oriana, am preparing for a triumphant ending to this nightmare, but, as I am a child of my time and place, I am also preparing for—tragedy."

The interview ended with shots of Oriana's new work, a large, lavishly colored canvas purportedly an "exploration of the metaphysical concept of *suspense*" she was painting while waiting for Duana Zwolle's return.

It was a remarkable interview. Matt had decided halfway through it he couldn't bear this woman, this exploitative, self-aggrandizing and shameless woman, even as, as a man, he was attracted to her, in a way so much more explicit and uncomplicated than a man might be attracted to Duana Zwolle. For the one was primary colors, in a burst of noontide light; the other subtle, uncertain colors, in nocturnal half-light. Still, he'd taped the interview, which had been with a local Newark station. Late at night, now that news of the *missing girl* was rarely broadcast, Matt might replay the Oriana interview, as well as other tapes; late at night when his family was long asleep (at least, Matt assumed that Tess was asleep), and he was gripped by loneliness like ice casing his heart.

We will be together, I know.
This side of the grave. Or the other.

It was on March 18, in the early evening, that Matt McBride finally met the flamboyant woman artist who called herself Oriana, in her studio-gallery in Lismore. He'd made sure Oriana would be available to him: he'd called to make an appointment. Introducing himself over the phone as an "amateur collector of American art" (which was arguably true; Matt had purchased a number of photographic prints over the years and, who knew, he might purchase something of Oriana's too). Yet he didn't intend to deceive: he gave Oriana his real, formal name, "Mathias McBride." He'd mentioned that he had known, slightly, and respected as an artist, Duana Zwolle.

Hearing this, Oriana was silent. Matt felt subtly rebuffed, even over the phone. He wondered if he'd already made a tactical error?

That day, approaching the small town of Lismore, descending the long curving hill to the river, Matt remembered driving here with Duana Zwolle; the tension between them, the passionate unspoken words. He began to feel an uncanny, almost physical tugging of the Acura's steering wheel in the direction of Mill Row and the river. How badly he wanted to drive there, to see another time the stark stone facade of the building in which Duana Zwolle had lived and worked, the shuttered window and the weatherworn outdoor steps! *A hungry ghost wandering in yearning*—was that what he'd become? But he refused to give in to this powerful desire. He was headed for Bank Street, at the village center, and not the river.

He'd brought some of his Nighthawk equipment, though, in the backseat of the car. A serious photographer is never unprepared, like a serious lover.

There, for the third time, he saw Oriana's self-displaying artist's residence, on a narrow backstreet of the historic village. ORIANA proclaimed a cream-colored sign, creaking in the wind. The place appeared to be a converted stable or carriage house: a smallish woodframe building painted a cheery apple-green with red tendril-trim like an illustration in a children's storybook. Beside the old-fashioned flagstone walk was a border of those cabbage-like plants Matt couldn't identify, vivid purple leaves. Like exotic flowers strangely blooming in winter.

The OPEN sign was still prominent in the window. Inside, the gallery was lighted. Matt felt his heartbeat quicken in anticipation. This would be an adventure! For possibly Oriana knew more about Duana Zwolle than she'd told police; possibly she even knew where Duana Zwolle was. Like a mantra the detective's prophetic words had been sounding in Matt's brain for weeks: *People know more than they think they know.*

This truth Matt McBride had been forced to concede, in the testing-ground of the new year.

Matt entered the gallery. A bell tinkled cutely overhead, and a pungent odor of incense assailed his nostrils. Not a good sign. There came Oriana, larger than life, swooping upon her visitor in an iridescent magenta silk tunic and cream-colored wool trousers, her very blond hair stiffly plaited like a giant doll's and her moon face polished to a blinding glow. Her wide, smiling mouth was a luminscent pink, her eyes exotically outlined in black and peacock-blue. Oriana was nearly Matt's height in clattering platform shoes. He felt an instant's purely masculine panic of the kind he hadn't experienced since adolescence: that he would be swallowed up by Woman, sensuous, fleshy, crushed in her perfumy embrace.

Oriana seized his hand in a firm, grasping handshake. " 'Mathias McBride'? *You* were a friend of Duana's?"

Doesn't she believe me? Is it so improbable?

Evasively Matt said, "She knew me as 'Nighthawk.' As a photographer."

" 'Nighthawk'—yes. Yes," Oriana said, nodding vigorously. "I do, too. I mean—your photographs. You work with Sid Krell, don't you? We've met, I think."

"We've met. Briefly."

"In that other world—'Weymouth.' " Oriana's expressive mouth curved ironically. As if, from the perspective of two fellow artists, the affluent upper-middle-class Village of Weymouth was a foreign, not very credible place.

Oriana invited Matt inside, took his coat and offered him a drink— "I'm going to lock up for the day. It has been a damned long day in a damned long season of what the Buddhists call *sangsāra*, the Net of Illusion. Is red wine appropriate?" Oriana positioned the CLOSED sign in a windowpane of the front door. Matt was moving about the lighted gallery space, which was a single rectangular room of about fifteen feet square; here, Oriana's art, pottery and paintings, was for sale. Matt admired the capably wrought pottery, urns and sculpted figures; the large, aggressive paintings on the walls, which close-up were rather more in the style of Rubens than of Rousseau, of fleshy nude females in lush gardens, he liked less. As Nighthawk, he didn't much like color; he certainly didn't like Day-Glo color; as a man who'd had a fair amount of experience with women, he objected that these oversized paintings were a kind of self-portrait of the artist as Woman, Oriana's display of her femaleness forcing voyeurism upon the spectator. Did any man really want to see the bulbous breasts, the rounded belly and coyly shadowed pudendum of a stranger, looming ecstatically at him from a wall? Matt concentrated his attention upon Oriana's pottery, which seemed to him much superior to her paintings. Watching him, Oriana chattered nervously about Weymouth, "mutual friends," Sid Krell—how was he? Oriana's tone was guarded, and Matt's tone, in reply, was rather vague, though polite—"Our relationship is mainly business, these days. But business at Krell Associates, I believe, is very good." Oriana laughed ruefully. "If you have no conscience, if you have no *soul*, yes, probably business can be *very good.*" The implication was that Oriana, who was all conscience, all soul, wasn't a very good businesswoman and ought to be pitied. *Her* products ought to be purchased.

Though Matt was impatient to talk to Oriana about the *missing girl*, he forced himself to take his time; to contemplate Oriana's work as a serious collector might, even to ask to see what other pieces she had in her studio; he knew that Oriana was edgy, and mistrustful of him, for "Mathias McBride" had not been a name or an individual, evidently, spoken of by Duana Zwolle. Of course, that was only logical: *Nighthawk was Duana Zwolle's secret, as Duana Zwolle was Nighthawk's secret.*

After ten minutes deliberation, and admiration, Matt selected two pieces of pottery: a graceful, cylindrical urn in rich earth colors, which resembled an urn of Oriana's on permanent display in the foyer of Krell Associates, which Matt had always liked; and a two-quart casserole dish in glazed clay streaked with red and purple, for Tess. It had been a long time since he'd bought Tess anything on impulse. "God, these are beautiful! May I buy them?" Matt's admiration was genuine, though the prices Oriana was charging were rather steep—$480 for the urn, $210 for the casserole. But it was worth it, to win Oriana's trust.

Matt paid by Visa, and he insisted upon paying the list price. Though Oriana tried to sell the pieces to him at a discount—"One artist to another, Matt! Please." But Matt wouldn't hear of it. He liked the feeling of being generous, charitable; he even liked Oriana, for all her self-dramatizing. She was a good-hearted woman, he believed. And how hard it must be for an independent woman artist trying to support herself with her art.

Even Duana Zwolle, who'd had so much more integrity than Oriana, had had to accept commercial assignments from time to time.

Buying the pieces of pottery was an inspired act. Flushed with pleasure, Oriana set them carefully in cardboard boxes stuffed with excelsior, and kissed Matt wetly on the cheek. "Thank you, 'Nighthawk'! You've redeemed this depressing day. Now, please, sometime soon, I hope I can purchase *you*."

The mistake, Matt would afterward concede, was the red wine.

Oriana switched off lights in the gallery, and led Matt, hand-in-hand, to her cluttered studio at the rear, which opened into a living space of workbenches, floor cushions, scattered pieces of wicker furniture and tall, spiny rubber plants in clay tubs. In this private space there were additional fleshy nudes, some of them very blond but others not recognizably modeled upon the artist; Matt looked quickly about, and was relieved not to see any representation of Duana Zwolle. The canvases ranged in size from fairly small to enormous—the largest, in overly explicit homage to Manet's notorious "Olympia," must have measured five feet by three. There it hung, looming over Matt's shoulder, even as the artist and model, her hair now unplaited and cascading loose about her flushed face, leaned toward him across a table. It was clear that Oriana had begun drinking before Matt arrived. Her manner with him was immediately confidential, even intimate. "There's a reason you've come to me, 'Nighthawk,' I know! Were you in love with her, too?"

"Was I—in love with her? I—"

"*I* was in love with her." Oriana poured more wine into Matt's glass, and into her own. "I mean, I still am. Duana wouldn't have wished me to say so. She wasn't that sort of person. She rarely spoke of emotions. Once she said to me, 'Beauty makes me happy.' It was a sudden confession. She'd been looking at Japanese woodcuts, and the remark sprang from the heart. But she never spoke about people in emotional terms. She might have loved *you*—she might have loved *me*—but she wouldn't have told us. And I know she didn't want to be loved if she couldn't love in return. She was so good, so—spiritual. It's a misused word. It's a cheapened, debased word. I was drawn into using it, in some of the interviews, and I—I regret that, now. Because the Zwolles are angry with me. If not angry, disapproving. Disappointed. D'you know them?—No? They've been devastated by this of course. They've never understood Duana, and there's a sense in which, *I* can certainly sense it, they believe that Duana brought this upon herself, because of her art, because of her life, her aloneness and isolation and what the father calls 'strangeness.' As if 'strangeness' was a sin! Rue, the twin sister, isn't much like Duana; at least, I couldn't see more than a superficial resemblance. She isn't at all religious, for one thing, and Duana was very religious. When I told her I'd been Duana's closest friend for the past three years at least, since Duana moved away from Nicholas Roche and came to New Jersey to live, she said, 'But Duana never mentioned you to me.' As if she was disputing my claim! As if she believed I might be lying! Matt, I helped the Zwolles as best I could, I spent hours with them, I mean days, with them and the Weymouth detectives, I even managed to get Sid to give them money to raise the amount of the reward—but now they've shut me out, they 'disapprove.' The sister thinks I've been 'exploiting' Duana. My God! What I wouldn't give, to have Duana back!" Oriana paused, as a telephone began to ring nearby. Matt hoped she wouldn't answer; he was frankly fascinated by her, the way, warmed by wine, and just possibly attracted by Matt McBride, she spoke so openly, without subterfuge. *One who'd loved Duana Zwolle, too. A bond between strangers.* "Oh, hell. Let it ring. I don't even have the answering service on. It's all *sangsāra*! I've had forty-two years of *sangsāra*! If poor Duana is out of it, maybe that isn't so terribly tragic a thing. She was a mystic, I believe—a true mystic—I mean, she *is* a true mystic. Her art is her 'discipline.' She seemed truly to believe in the purity of the human spirit. And that there are no accidents. People can be 'fated' for one another, before their births. She wasn't a practicing Buddhist, she was involved with the St. Patrick Mission in Newark but she wasn't Catholic, she was the most naturally, instinctively religious person I've ever known—and I think it was this that drew her abductor, or abductors, to her. And that, being Duana, and so lacking in perception of evil, she was susceptible in a way others of us, certainly Oriana, *could not be*."

The first bottle of wine was empty. Oriana, swaying slightly, immediately brought out another. "Here, Oriana, let me open that for you," Matt said, rising from his chair. He was a man who liked to open wine bottles, and he opened them expertly. He'd already removed his warm wool blazer and loosened his tie. Steadying the bottle on the wicker table, Matt's and Oriana's fingers brushed together. Matt asked, "What is, 'The Clear Light of the Void'?—Duana spoke of that sometimes. It's Buddhist, I guess?"

"I suppose. A vision you aspire to. In her collages, she said, if she was working very intensely, for ten, twelve hours at a time, she could break through, she said, of the 'cobweb of self' and enter this realm of 'clear light.' She tried to teach me—

> There is an Unbecome, Unborn, Unmade, Unformed; if there were not this Unbecome, Unborn, Unmade, Unformed, there would be no way out for that which is become, born, made, and formed; but since there is an Unbecome,

Unborn, Unmade, Unformed, there is escape for that which
is become, born, made and formed.' "

Matt said, shivering, "That sounds too final to me."

"Well, to me, too. But I respected—I mean, I respect—Duana's
beliefs. This didn't mean she wasn't an emotional person of course;
it only meant that her emotions ran deep and nothing about Duana
was shallow. There's only one other person I've ever met, a New Jersey
artist in fact, who's what you might call a genuine 'mystic.' 'NAME
UNKNOWN' he calls himself—ever heard of him? Well, you
wouldn't, I suppose. He's a sort of regional William Blake; sweet,
simple, dedicated to art though he isn't, in my opinion, very talented.
Some of us, including Duana, befriended him because he seems so
lonely and so *good*. But what has truly outraged me—"

"Excuse me?" Matt interrupted. "Does this 'NAME UNKNOWN'
have an actual name?"

"Yes, of course. 'Joseph Gavin.' But—"

" 'Joseph *Gavin*'?" The name was familiar to Matt: he'd known a
Gavin family in his family's neighborhood, in Forked River; Gavin
children went to Matt's school.

"—but he isn't a suspect, be assured. Not only is poor NAME
UNKNOWN the very soul of goodness, so boring you practically fall
asleep while he's talking to you, he has an alibi, the detectives told
me. They've checked out everyone who's even a remote possibility for
having abducted Duana. Now what truly outraged me, which is why
I avoid Weymouth as much as I can—are some of the rumors I've
heard there, and those cruel, vicious articles in the tabloid press like
Jersey Citizen, that Duana was involved in drugs, cocaine it's said,
and in 'sexual promiscuity'—whatever the hell that means. Absolute
lies! Slander! Of all people, Duana Zwolle! Duana left New York
because she wanted to get away from that scene, even though she
hadn't been personally involved in it; she never took drugs, and never
drank; except sometimes I'd inveigle her into sharing a little wine
with me, when she came to dinner. Duana worked and exhibited her
art in New Jersey when she might've had a SoHo gallery because such

worldly things meant nothing to her. These rumors, these outright lies, make me *sick*."

Matt listened sympathetically. But he was seeing *Joseph Gavin* in his mind's eye. A hulking, sullen boy two or three years ahead of Matt at Forked River High. Was it the same person, twenty years later? Now an artist—"NAME UNKNOWN"? Matt asked, "This Gavin, where's he live?" Oriana said dismissively, "Somewhere over in Clinton Falls. A mobile home, he calls it. Look, Joseph Gavin isn't a serious suspect, Matt, believe me. He's a child. A virgin—I'm sure! The kind of man who wouldn't know what to do with a naked woman. Joseph is the only artist I've ever met—apart from Duana, I mean— who isn't consumed with envy and jealous of others' success. If you want to find out who took Duana away—assuming that's why you're here, and not just to purchase art—I can tell you, as I've told the police, the names of dozens of other more likely candidates; and maybe it was no one who knew her at all, only just a random, senseless killing—what's called a 'serial killer.' A psychopath."

So Oriana talked. Matt listened to her meandering, passionate words. He believed, as probably the Weymouth detectives had believed, that this woman knew more than she knew; it was necessary to let her talk, and not impede her. Matt noted her expressive hands: the brightly polished yet chipped and uneven nails, the numerous rings on her fingers, the evident strength of her fingers. She was a potter, she kneaded clay. *Oriana herself might have abducted Duana Zwolle. Might have strangled her.* Matt would have liked to take hold of Oriana's hands to comfort her, and to calm her. Nervous people made him nervous. Especially, he reacted to nervous women. There was a sexual undercurrent here, fueled by wine, that Matt was having difficulty seeming not to acknowledge. In the slanted overhead light from a stained glass hanging lamp, Oriana's full, flushed face showed subtle signs of age; there were faint lines bracketing her glamorous mouth and eyes, and shadows like smears beneath her eyes. As if out of habit or custom, Oriana was leaning toward Matt, positioning her shapely body in a way to display its contours to advantage, but there was an air of desperation beneath. Breathily she said, "Duana was in

love with someone, I'm certain. Since last summer. I told the Weymouth detectives I truly had no idea, but I don't think they believed
me. Now I'm wondering, Nighthawk, maybe it was you?" Matt frowned
uncomfortably. Oriana continued, musing aloud as if she hadn't noticed the look in his face, "Whoever it was, he gave her a beautiful
white cashmere shawl for Christmas. At least, it must've been him.
She showed it to me; she was wearing it the last time I saw her, in
the early evening of December 28. I'd dropped by her place, I'd
thought she was planning on traveling to Maine to visit her family,
but she hadn't gone yet, and she was behaving rather secretively. For
Duana, I mean. Probably you know this, it's been in the papers, but
Duana was badly hurt by a man with whom she'd lived for several
years in New York, the painter Nicholas Roche—you've heard of
him? He's famous. I mean, in New York art circles. He's represented
by Leo Castelli; he's all the rage, though less talented, in my opinion,
than poor NAME UNKNOWN himself. Certainly far less talented than
Duana Zwolle from whom he'd stolen many ideas. He'd been in love
with her at first then he began to treat her badly, he's been involved
with cocaine, that's no secret, and finally he drove her away, and she
escaped here. That's when we became friends: Duana seemed so
lonely, and so vulnerable. I wanted to protect her from local predators,
too—like Sid Krell, and certain of his well-to-do friends. The detectives asked my advice as an artist about this ugly, obscene drawing
they found in Duana's loft, on her bed, in the midst of the vandalism,
and I identified it immediately as Roche's style, misogynist caricature
disguised as 'art.' Disgusting!" Oriana deftly drew, on a sheet of paper,
a cartoon of a nude female, grotesquely distorted; genitals like tumors
between her skinny legs. Matt winced, and wished he hadn't seen. "It
was meant to be Duana. So ugly. So vicious. It could only have been
executed by a man who despises and fears women. I told the detectives, 'This is Roche. I know him.' I was terribly upset. I wanted to
tear the drawing into pieces. But it's evidence, of course. They've kept
it secret. No one is supposed to know about it. The detectives said it
meant the crime had been premeditated, and pertained to Duana
Zwolle; it wasn't random or accidental. It was a 'sign' for whoever

found her missing to discover, not for Duana herself. They went to
New York to interview Roche but it turns out the bastard was gone—
he'd been in London. England for several days. Conferring with his
gallery there. So he had an alibi, and a good one. I told police, 'Roche
could have hired someone to do it for him. That would be like him—
he's physically and morally lazy.' I don't think they took me seriously.
Men protect men; male detectives unconsciously identify with male
suspects. And Roche is so glamorous, now he's big-time—"

"Do you have an address for him? 'Nicholas Roche'?"

"He has a studio in SoHo. Greene Street. Look, for God's sake,
Matt, don't show up there and tell him I sent you. He may not be the
one who actually took Duana away, but he's certainly a psychopath.
A few weeks ago he showed up here—literally, here!—in my home!—
and threatened me in his elliptical way. At least, I think that's why
Roche was here. Pretending to be concerned about Duana—'The only
woman I ever really loved, but couldn't live with'—but in fact the
bastard figured out that I, Oriana, must have been the 'art-expert'
who'd identified the drawing and led police to him. I denied it of
course. I don't want Roche killing *me*." Oriana paused, breathing
quickly. Her emotion seemed genuine. But then she couldn't resist
adding, with a sly, simulated fluttering of her eyelids, "Duana never
knew, Nick Roche and I were lovers, briefly. I mean brief-ly. After
they'd broken up of course, and Duana had escaped him. The man is
a *p-i-g*, to be frank."

Matt's disapproval must have shown in his face, for Oriana ex-
claimed, "Oh, don't look so *moral*, Mathias McBride! We're all adults
here." She paused, annoyed and defensive. A warm flush enveloped
her face. "In fact, I happen to know—almost absolutely—Nick Roche
had an affair with Duana's sister, too. The elusive 'Rue.' "

But Matt wasn't interested in Duana's sister. Nor did he want to
inquire too pointedly about Nicholas Roche. "What of Sid Krell?" he
asked Oriana, and Oriana warmed at once, saying vehemently, "Dear
Sid! He might've been a truly vicious human being if he'd had more
imagination and guts. He owns this absurd gun collection—you've
seen it? Expensive shotguns, rifles. A .35-caliber revolver he carries

around with him sometimes. As if he'd need to protect himself! Real tough guy, Sid. But, well—*he* might have hired someone to hurt Duana, too. I doubt he'd have done it himself, he's a fussy, fastidious man. Doesn't like to be touched. When Duana refused his commission he offered her at least $12,000, which was several thousand more than the bastard had offered me, and when he saw he couldn't buy her, he practically stalked her for six, eight months. Don't look so surprised! These aging, wealthy lechers are the *worst*. He telephoned Duana, drove by her place on the river, parked and waited for her to come outside. I told Duana to take him seriously, and to report him to the police, but Duana, being Duana, said she felt sorry for him. 'His vision is clouded. He sees his own reflection in me.' I told her I didn't have the slightest idea what she was saying. I understood *him*, because I understand *vindictive, petty men*. But Duana wouldn't listen. She wasn't Catholic, but over in Newark, at St. Patrick's, she'd go to mass with those people and actually pray for Krell's *soul*. I'd have laughed, if it wasn't so pathetic." Oriana paused, and seemed about to laugh, but the laughter turned to a brief spasm of coughing. She wiped at her eyes, and said, "Sid boasted about harassing Duana to me, as if this was a sign of manhood. A badge of honor. He actually asked advice of me how he could 'hurt that girl so she'd feel it'—as if I might be sympathetic with him! He sent her a mock-gift—a six-hundred-dollar Steuben crystal bird from Tiffany he'd deliberately cracked. Imagine: spending six hundred dollars on meanness! And still the bird was beautiful, a mourning dove, I think. Sid would taunt me, 'Oriana, you must be jealous of Duana Zwolle, she's a superior artist and she's fifteen years younger than you.' As if he could drive a wedge between us in such a way. As if all women are sexual rivals for all men. I told him, 'Sid, go to hell. I value my friendship with Duana over you, any goddamned day.' I told him—"

Matt interrupted, "Do you think Sid might have hired someone to hurt Duana? Seriously?"

Oriana relented, frowning. "I—don't know. I didn't tell the detectives much about Sid so maybe we should change this subject. I've had too much to *drink*." But she lifted her glass another time, and drank.

Matt thought *There's the ex-lover Roche, there's Krell, there's the one who lives in Clinton Falls—Gavin. And how many others, known, and not known.*

For the first time he was beginning to grasp the immensity of a "criminal investigation" as it might be conducted by a detective. Where there was little evidence, where there appeared to be no immediate suspects, how to proceed? He, Matt McBride, had access to relatively little knowledge of the case, and no evidence at all; he was like a blind man stumbling and groping, hit or miss. Yet he felt a prick of excitement. The lure of the forbidden. Possibly, he himself was in danger. He would have to proceed by instinct, and hope for luck.

Oriana, sensing Matt's interest drifting, quickly went on to name other names. These were Weymouth names primarily, some of them known to Matt and some not; names Oriana claimed she'd supplied to the Weymouth detectives—"Under cover of anonymity, of course. I wouldn't want to be *sued*." Matt wondered how serious these names were; possibly, these were men who'd had some involvement with Oriana herself, whom she was hoping to entangle in an embarrassing police investigation. He hesitated to ask her about Duana's diary. *Maybe she doesn't know? Isn't in it?*

Oriana went on to speak of the volunteer work Duana had been doing for the past two years at the St. Patrick Mission in Newark, helping to prepare food for the homeless—"There was a Father Justin she admired, but she didn't say much about him to me, or about the work she did at the Mission. I wanted to accompany her—I intended to, around Christmas—but somehow it never happened. Duana rarely spoke about herself, it seemed to her vanity, I guess." Oriana said that there were graphic artists in Weymouth with whom Duana had worked on projects who claimed it was impossible to get to know her; there was something "uncanny" about her. She seemed lonely, yet unapproachable. Everyone thought it strange that Duana was a perfectionist even in her commercial art, which no one took seriously; as if she believed that, selling her time in exchange for money, she had to work as conscientiously as she worked on her own, private art. "*A*

Garden of Earthly and Unearthly Delights was brilliant work, I think," Oriana said, "even if it was a little rough, and incomplete. It had power, and it had vision. It wasn't what you'd call safe or pretty art— not like mine! It wasn't saleable. Yet two of the collages were sold, from last summer's exhibit: to the State Museum at Trenton, and to the Art Museum at Princeton where the curator has an eye for original, daring new work. The rest were unsold, and were vandalized in her studio. *I* wanted to buy one of the smaller collages, but Duana insisted she'd give it to me when it was completed; but it never did get completed. My God, it makes me sick to think of Duana's art destroyed. Whoever slashed and tore the collages must have felt threatened by them—don't you think?" Oriana shuddered and hugged herself, forcing her breasts tightly between her forearms. She shut her eyes, and for a moment looked genuinely stricken. "When I think of the way Duana's studio looked, and her flat, that she'd furnished with such care—"

"You saw it? You were there?"

"Why do you look so surprised? I was often at Duana's, and she was often here. The detectives brought me over to Mill Row the day after Duana was reported missing, to help them determine what might have been stolen, destroyed or misplaced. I walked on plastic sheeting on the floor. I wasn't allowed to touch anything, of course. I was in a state of shock, I'd been swallowing tranquillizers. The Zwolles hadn't visited Duana for quite a while, and knew less about her life than I did. I could identify broken things. I could give them a sense of Duana's daily life, whom she knew and might be meeting. There were forensics experts there, but it was slow, excruciating work; it took days for them to collect evidence, including casts from tire prints out in the mud, and they never did absolutely determine that a crime had been committed there—I mean, that Duana had been beaten, or raped, or caused to bleed—they never found bloodstains. They found lots of fingerprints, but nothing seems to have come of that, either. The detectives came to the conclusion that Duana probably knew her assailant, she'd let him in, and he'd overpowered her somehow, and may have carried her out, down the stairs and into her car. He might have come on foot, or he might have had an accomplice. But everything was tentative, uncertain. There were times when I screamed at them—'Do something! Find her! Save her!' It was so slow and so methodical and in the meantime hours and days were passing, and Duana was gone, and might still be alive, and waiting for us. That was why I consented to so many interviews. I was frantic to make Duana's situation *known*. How that could be misconstrued as exploitation by her family, and by others, goddamned if I understand."

Matt said, wanting to comfort the stricken woman, "Oriana, you've done what you can. You may have helped."

"But Duana isn't back, is she? It's been twelve weeks."

Oriana indicated a splotched, violated canvas propped against a wall. "That's all that remains of my 'exploration of the metaphysical concept of *suspense*'—a muddle. I've learned that you can't fashion art out of actual emotions as you live them. They're too raw, and somehow ordinary. Even grief is ordinary. Even terror. I've waited for twelve weeks for a sign. A signal. From Duana. In a dream or in a vision. I've never believed in telepathy or ESP but I could believe, now!—I'm that desperate. You'd think that those of us who loved—who love—Duana could at least know *Is she alive or not?* That we would know in our hearts. But even her sister Rue is only just waiting. And in the meantime there's—" in a dramatic gesture Oriana spread her painted nails wide, "—nothing."

Matt wanted to protest. What Nighthawk had been experiencing in this new year couldn't be so easily dismissed as *nothing*.

Oriana lurched from the wicker table. Matt caught her, and she righted herself; went to a Shaker-style bureau against a wall where, murmuring to Matt, "Don't leave yet! I want to show you something," she rummaged through the topmost drawer.

Matt said adamantly, "I'm not going anywhere, Oriana. I'm *here*.'

He hadn't thought of the time since arriving. Since drinking this excellent if rather sweet red wine with Oriana. (Was Tess waiting for him, was he supposed to be having dinner at home tonight? Or had he told Tess he had a business engagement?)

Oriana removed a manila folder from the drawer and took from it a photograph which she handed to Matt ceremoniously. Matt whispered, "My God." It was a remarkable image: Duana Zwolle's face closer to his than he'd ever seen it, only inches from the camera lens and from the viewer: the girl was leaning her left temple against a mirror so that her shadowed face was reflected, not quite symmetrically, in the mirror. A beautiful dreamlike face it was, with thick, defined dark eyebrows, and a mole at her hairline, and cheekbones sharper than Matt recalled. Matt swallowed hard, and stared. He wondered how old Duana was here: nineteen? Oriana was leaning over Matt and watching him closely. "Beautiful, isn't she?"

Matt didn't reply.

Oriana said, in a thrilled voice, "When I first met Duana, I thought she might have Indian blood—east Indian. And that might be, in fact. But there are Portuguese Jewish ancestors in her mother's family, I learned. Those eyes!"

Matt regarded Duana Zwolle's eyes which seemed to be gazing at him.

I am so happy, I could die this hour.

Oriana said, laying a hand on Matt's shoulder, "I feel she is alive, Matt—don't you? And thinking of us."

"Yes." But Matt spoke uncertainly.

"D'you notice something strange, Matt? About the photograph?"

"Yes, as a matter of fact. The faces don't exactly match."

There was no mirror! Duana Zwolle had evidently photographed herself at two separate times, using a stop-time lens. Was that it?

Oriana laughed extravagantly, drawing a provocative forefinger across Matt's knuckles, to the twinned faces. She said, "The faces don't 'exactly match' because even identical twins aren't 'identical.' The photograph invites you to imagine you see a single face mirrored but you're actually seeing two separate faces. Duana and her sister Rue. Ingenious, isn't it?"

Matt stared. "But—which is Duana?"

"Can't you tell? You love her."

Matt looked from one young, dark, exotic face to the other, and could have sworn he'd never seen either before in his life. His face burned with chagrin. And anger, at being the butt of a trick. "Duana is—on the right?"

"You're sure?" Oriana teased.

No, Matt wasn't sure. But he felt a damned fool admitting it.

Oriana said, "Truly, I don't know, either! Duana wouldn't tell me. Her art is filled with games of identity, she thought 'identity' is mere *sangsāra*—a Net of Illusion. When I asked her which of these faces is hers she laughed at me saying, 'Why should it matter? A face is only a face. Skin is skin. Rue and I are nothing alike—or everything alike. A twin is an imaginary construct.' "

"Duana said that? What did she mean?"

It hadn't occurred to him until now that, if he'd been Duana Zwolle's lover, he might have been at a disadvantage in their relationship. He might have been perplexed by Duana Zwolle, and in awe of her greater talent and imagination. He might have been jealous of her. Possessive. While the diary had lulled him into believing that Duana Zwolle's love for Nighthawk was unqualified, as if he were superior to her.

Matt said, "May I have this photograph, Oriana? It would mean so much to me."

"I'm afraid I can't give it up, Matt. But I can have a copy made for you."

"Thank you! I'd appreciate that."

It was time for Matt to leave. He knew, and Oriana knew. Yet when Matt rose from the wicker table, suffused with emotion, too choked to speak, Oriana moved into his half-willing arms with a soft, pleading cry of feminine acquiescence. *Now we have passed beyond words. Now we come together, truly.* Oriana's mouth was damp and searching on Matt's, not so warm as he might have imagined but forceful and demanding. Matt's own mouth felt numbed with wine. A roaring in his ears. Rapidly his hands moved over the woman's body, not to draw her against him but to hold her still. When Oriana slid her strong, supple arms around the small of Matt's back, he felt near-overwhelmed. He'd never embraced a woman of such statuesque proportions and such evident hunger. Oriana was murmuring hyp-

notically, "*You* love her—I know. *I* love her. She's with us now."
Quickly Oriana pulled at Matt who followed her like a blind man,
stumbling into a darkened room off the kitchen. He blundered against
the edge of something—a chest of drawers, a bedside table. A large,
square, oddly low and oddly spongy bed upon which numerous pillows
and cushions had been placed, like boulders. *Do I want this? What
is this?* Oriana's eager mouth sucked at Matt's, her fingers clutched
and tugged at his clothing. Empowered by wine, Matt found himself
kissing the woman in turn, tonguing her, pressing his mouth against
her warm, moist neck, her breasts, her round belly. As if he were
falling from a great height; sinking into sleep; a sensuous, utterly
satisfying sleep; an infantile sleep; a sleep that extinguished his brain
in an ecstasy of oblivion. Was all identity an imaginary construct?
Did it matter who we were, or was all that mattered what we did? Or
what was done through us?

In the confusion of the moment Matt McBride would not think how
strange it was, how ironic, that the *missing girl* should be leading him
to this: a strange woman's bed.

In a delirium Oriana muttered, "Do you love me? Love me? *Love
me?*" Matt had the idea she no longer remembered his name. He lay
with her atop the spongy bed, holding her body in his strong, startled
arms. A draft, like a breath, touched the nape of his neck. *What is
this place? Why am I here?* He was powerfully, sexually aroused as
Oriana kissed and sucked at his chest, tonguing his nipples; yet the
doorway and the lighted room beyond distracted him—as if a shadowy
figure were about to pass by. Out of the corner of his eye he seemed
to be seeing—what? What if he and Oriana weren't alone? This was
the wrong woman he held, her breasts too large, her body, writhing
beneath his, too fleshy. *Now Nighthawk has claimed my soul, & I his.*

Matt pushed away from the woman, panting. Suddenly he was stone
cold sober. "I'm sorry. I can't."

Oriana raised herself on her elbows to stare at him in the half-light.
She too was panting, and her body glistened in patches. In a hurt,
childlike voice she said, "Can't—or won't?"

Matt was on his feet, hurriedly dressing. What a fool! In an instant he'd lost all sexual desire for this woman. And for this place which was no longer romantic but smelled of stale incense, damp bedclothes, yeasty female flesh. *Sorry, sorry, Jesus I'm sorry* he murmured as Oriana began to berate him, hurt and angry and indignant. She chided him in the voice of his long-ago mother who'd banished him from the household more than once as *Satan*! Groping for his clothes, Matt would have liked to switch on a light but such a gesture seemed, in these circumstances, too intrusive; Oriana, naked amid rumpled bedclothes, would have been exposed. Yet even as he hoped to shield the woman she was saying bitterly, " 'Sorry'! Never mind 'sorry'! Get the hell out, 'Nighthawk'! You sorry excuse for a prick."

Like a raging heraldic figure Oriana rose to her knees, long pale hair streaming about her broad face. Something flew past Matt's head and tumbled along the floor—a needlepoint cushion.

Matt McBride fled.

Sick with shame, embarrassment, masculine chagrin—Matt McBride fled.

Outside, in a chill rain, fumbling to unlock his car, Matt was vaguely aware of a vehicle a short distance away, on the opposite side of the narrow street, headlights and taillights off, driving slowly away. A coincidence?

Too late, he realized he'd left the clay urn and casserole dish Oriana had boxed for him inside, on the counter. Beautiful pieces, and expensive. He'd been imagining how Tess would admire them, how grateful she would have been to receive unexpected gifts from Matt. In the early days of their marriage, they were often surprising each other with gifts. Tess was uneasy that Matt didn't love her so much as he once had, and these pieces of Oriana's might have comforted her but Matt couldn't bring himself to risk returning. *Never! Never again.*

Speeding home to Weymouth, sweaty, itchy and deeply ashamed. A woman's harsh angry sobbing in his ears. Already it had become confused in his memory with his wife's sobbing. Which woman?

27 NAME UNKNOWN. His mind was unquiet, he did not know why. He was working very hard. He was earning a paycheck. Every week. This money he would share with the Brough woman and her son who looked to NAME UNKNOWN with such eyes of radiant hope. *I am not your father but will stand in his place.* Yet when the woman touched him sometimes her fingers were like lard, her breath suety & vile & he shoved her from him. *Woman, take care*! But she worshipped him as JOSEPH GAVIN. He had use of her, & believed that use would extend into the future.

His mind was unquiet, he did not know why. The detectives had not returned to question him. Nor did he believe they were spying on him. Yet his heart was heavy. These mornings of late winter, a leaden sky & a smell (it could not be so, he knew) of the decay of the seashore & the Pine Barrens. He yearned to revisit the site of the sacrifice. The snow burial. (By now, the snow would have melted. The shore birds with their sharp cruel beaks would feast.) Along the Batsto River he'd run away as a boy of twelve. There was a rowboat he'd found, & a single oar. The rowboat sloshed with water so he could not really use it. Yet he could play at using it, *it was his boat & he could travel as he wished.* There were Atlantic white cedars, so many thousands & thousands of pines. The cranberry bogs & the farmers he hid from, for they would not have welcomed him maybe. He was from Forked River ten miles out of the Barrens, in their eyes a town boy. He could not explain to them that the Barrens were his home, where he would not be judged. Later, he had brought the girl to Deer Isle. He had not had time to choose a site carefully that first time. He had not known why he brought the girl to the Pine Barrens except he had known it was the right place. As in the late winter of 1993 he had brought M T almost that same place, from Cherry Hill, New Jersey to Deer Isle where she would never be discovered. *Missing to this day.*

M T had been a TV "personality" of local fame. NAME UNKNOWN had shamed himself in adoration of such shallowness, vanity. She had had no true gift to impart. The sacrifice had come to nothing. It was behind him now, rarely did he think of it. Though M T had been the most beautiful in the world's esteem surely.

More vivid to him despite the years intervening was M M for she had been his first sacrifice. How young he had been, and ignorant. Having made no plan beforehand. Trusting to chance. And in the place called Wading which was a crossroads, a general store & gas station he had parked the borrowed van desperate to quench his thirst & purchased two Pepsis from an outdoor vending machine risking being seen. Strange it was when police came to this crossroads as to other small settlements in the Barrens no one in the store or the gas station would recall having seen him, or the van.

You are cloaked in the Invisible. And your NAME UNKNOWN.

A fiery anger touched him, these years later. That bad behavior might be discovered in a girl young as M M (who had been, at age seventeen, the youngest sacrifice as D Z at twenty-six was one of the two oldest). From that day, NAME UNKNOWN had had no illusion. For M M had been an angel in appearance & her smile & in the gift of her pure soprano voice. Yet she had defiled that gift, & could not be allowed to live. Only he knew, & had the courage to act.

As he would discover, her panties too were soiled. He would smell them, in disgust.

He had loved her, yet he knew. There was no choice. SING FOR ME he bade her. (Yet in her terror she could not.) You see, the applause filling the auditorium & the hot sucking kisses of her boyfriend could not save her. The beauty of her voice passed into the strong, capable fingers of NAME UNKNOWN. (That sometimes his own mother would gaze at in wonderment, her Joseph's hands were so big yet shy-seeming in her presence like hairless sleeping creatures.)

And so it was that the voice of M M of which she was not worthy passed into the fingers of the boy then known to the world as Joseph Gavin merely.

For the destiny of NAME UNKNOWN was that of Artist, in the fullness of time.

*   *   *

Yet now it was years later. His mind beat like the surf against the beach, unquiet through the night. He tried to recall the secret history of NAME UNKNOWN which nearly always suffused him with happiness & the certitude & justice of his quest. Yet, the unquiet persisted. *He did not know why. Had the sacrifice been in vain?*

The woman Brough & her son Randy were sick with flu, on TV there were interviews with New Jersey medical workers about the flu, maybe Joseph Gavin was stricken with such but truly he doubted it for it was rare that he got sick, who disciplined himself as he did and ate (mainly fruits & vegetables) sparingly. Yet the new figure born of the sacrifice of D Z failed to catch life in his hands. The sixth figure of THE MARRIAGE OF HEAVEN AND HELL. Of a somewhat lesser height & smaller size than her sisters. Crafted & sculpted of scrap cherrywood from a Clinton Falls lumberyard, tinted wax, copper filings & clay. The face seemed to him one of Purity yet it remained blank, bland. A crude face he realized in this stark morning light. *And the other faces: are they not crude, too?* The actual face of D Z had been soiled as if smudged with a dirty eraser for the female's soul was soiled, yet it had been a face you might stare & stare at while this, the very face of Purity, had no life to it.

Smirking, the detective had asked where did he get his ideas? While the other wearing the blue scarf had walked boldly about peering in all corners seeking evidence. As if NAME UNKNOWN was a simpleminded fool, not knowing how to hide his secret deeds & his secret self. As if NAME UN-KNOWN had not many times in the past twenty-one years played this exciting game with strangers, & won.

I am not he you seek, for he has gone. He has risen, and is gone.

D Z had laughed at him, too. He knew. Not to his face but he had such knowledge. Since the installation of security cameras in so many public places, in 7-Eleven stores, gas stations, food markets & banks, in recent years which NAME UNKNOWN had noticed with his sharp eyes, it had come to seem to him that he, too, possessed the powers of a telephoto camera sometimes; not at all times, but sometimes; and could see, & overhear, persons speaking of NAME UNKNOWN when he was nowhere near, & they believed themselves alone! So D Z, Oriana & others including men too spoke mockingly of him & his art. He knew.

Now D Z might smile at him in mockery. For the bitter fact that NAME UNKNOWN dared not insert those eyes of arresting beauty but had in fear & caution disposed of them (in a Dumpster in town, wrapped like garbage amid stinking pizza trash) & in their place these eyes fashioned out of children's marbles, which looked unreal, glued in wooden sockets. Dead glass. *Dead glass!* And so they smirk at NAME UNKNOWN. In derision behind his back & even sometimes cruelly to his face.

It was a small mean comfort then to gloat to recall Oriana's puffy eyes & her voice that grated against his skin like the fabric of a rough bandage. Believing him her friend! & the friend of the *missing girl!* Her mouth twisting almost crying *Oh Joseph it's a nightmare, it doesn't end. If she is alive she may be suffering. Almost I pray for her to be found. To put an end to this— horror.* He had wished to laugh in the female's ugly face to allow her to realize the POWER OF NAME UNKNOWN. Who seemed in her vision to have little power, someone she might send away unfed like an unwanted dog at the door.

What season was this? Neither winter, nor spring. So the soul of NAME UNKNOWN was undefined. Waking one morning to pelting sleet against the metal roof of the trailer, another morning to harsh blinding sun that in itself seemed somehow to ridicule & mock his beloved figures in the barn. This new year that had begun in a blaze of trumpets was quieted now. As there were no headlines now pertaining to the *missing girl.* And the posters of her face in store windows had become so familiar, no one saw them now & NAME UNKNOWN only glanced at them in passing. He had to work for wages. As a welder in the machine shop. Where the others smiled to see how he tied back his wisps of beard. Wondering at his silence, while they talked & laughed loudly together. Sometimes he shuddered to think how such ignorant jeering eyes might fix upon the sacred figures of THE MARRIAGE OF HEAVEN AND HELL without sympathy or comprehension. *For they are the world, not yet redeemed.* He knew that Jesus Christ had taken upon His shoulders the redemption of that world, but saw now that it was a burden like a great ice-mountain: you could not carry it on your shoulders but would stumble and be crushed beneath it.

For maybe Jesus Christ was mistaken in His heart? Maybe there was no redemption really? In the blinding sun there is emptiness.

Dead glass!

As a hunter stalks his prey at a near distance so he had hunted D Z through the late summer, fall & winter. Until the evening of December 28 when it came to pass. Always he was invisible. Yet there could be a reason for NAME UNKNOWN in Lismore. As NAME UNKNOWN was an artist also. And NAME UNKNOWN was a friend. He might have loved D Z for this female was small-boned & of his temperament. Of few words in company. Shy eyes. Or shy-seeming. On the path above the river where she came sometimes to walk restlessly, he was there in meditation in perfect silence. This was following the opening of D Z's collage exhibit in the Tomato Factory Gallery in Weymouth & NAME UNKNOWN was awaiting a sign of guilt & repentance from her, that she had stolen from NAME UNKNOWN certain ideas & the very title *A Garden of Earthly and Unearthly Delights*. Except for his eyes he was not demanding. *Even then I could forgive her. I have that power.* But she spoke few words, so shyly he could almost not hear. Of the river which is all rivers as this hour of the day is all days from the beginning of Time until now. *It scares me sometimes, this will continue after I am vanished, as if I had never been.* These words were a girl's uttered in surprise & vexation; & NAME UNKNOWN glanced up at her squinting, for such words pierced his heart. As if he had spoken them himself. Yet he could not reply, he had not the words to reply.

Did he wish to love D Z? He did not. For she laughed at him in secret. Her skin a mirror of her soiled soul.

On March 18 a strangeness came upon him. He had a right to know! Telephoned the tabloid *Jersey Citizen* 800-Hot-Line from a pay phone in Newark. Asking what news of the *missing girl?* Why was there little said of her now? Why was there no arrest? Was it true her body had been dredged from the Delaware River and the discovery kept secret? That the act had been perpetrated by the twin sister of D Z in rivalry for a lesbian lover?

Quickly slamming down the receiver before the call might be traced.

*   *   *

Of the six figures of THE MARRIAGE OF HEAVEN AND HELL one that excited him was the second, a dancer. NAME UNKNOWN had known not to weave any of the girl's actual hair into the wiry red-brown hair of the female nor any particles of her freckled flesh; but he had made a powder of burnt fingernail & toenail clippings mixed with clay, & there was a smell of this that pleased his nostrils even after almost seventeen years.

Long ago in Mountainhome, PA. He had been happy. He could not recall the name now, only the initials he had allowed himself to remember—L R. She had a pale skin lightly dusted with freckles. But so pale, at a short distance you could not see. Only by chance he had observed her exercising & practicing her dance routines on a redwood deck of a summerhouse on Mountainhome Lake. In her shabby black leotard, barefoot. Her long fair-brown hair streaked with red. Her breasts were small & compact & her ribcage prominent through the tight black fabric. Her legs were longer than his own, slender with hard muscle. Seeing her he had ached to carve her likeness! His fingers had twitched with their own desire to set the razor-sharp edge of a blade to wood and cut, and cut, and cut! Never had he observed a human body so in motion. So beautiful he fell to his knees slack-jawed in tall grasses. He could not wrench his eyes away for an instant. The thudding beat! beat! of her taped music penetrated the marrow of his bone. How many hours that summer he lay flat on his belly on the roof of an abandoned shed in the next field. There was a screen of scrub trees to hide him. And he was very still not needing to breathe. This was a hilly place in the Poconos Mountains of summer cottages & older dwellings beginning to be sold & razed & in their place expensive summer dwellings. He would learn from TV that L R & her male companion (who was a musician) lived in Philadelphia. They were not married; once he saw the man approach the dancer, & imagining themselves alone boldly they lay on the deck & kissed & tongued each other, & copulated like beasts that appalled his eyes. *How the dancer is Beauty, yet the female filth.*

He was Joseph Gavin at that time renting a cabin outside the village of Mountainhome, PA. He had left Forked River as soon as it was safe for him to leave. The police did not suspect him more than a dozen other men &

boys, he had strong reason to believe. He was twenty-two years old. The *missing girl* had been found in Deer Isle three years before & few talked of her now. He did not think of her now. He quarreled with his family, & left. He would do summer jobs & he would be a welder & make good wages. But that summer he lived alone in a cabin with a rotted roof on a mountainside. He would soon embark upon the first of the nine figures of THE MARRIAGE OF HEAVEN AND HELL but awaited only a vision. AND THIS VISION TO COME SOON.

At the Mountainhome Summer Festival in August he saw her dance! Only that evening did he learn her name, in the printed program. He had not understood that the red-haired dancer was known to others; that she did not dance only on the deck of the summerhouse, but with a troupe of other dancers; that he must share her in adoring her with thousands of others. Alone in his seat amid the audience he sat tense & staring. His eyes ached with angry desire. Like twin flames in their sockets. He knew himself betrayed, as when the man had come to her to lay upon her & twine his limbs with her & copulate in the open air unashamed. For there was a lithe male dancer who lifted her, who embraced her lewdly to the beat of music. Only she riveted his eyes—L R. The most remarkable dance was "The Butterfly" which he would long recall. The music that throbbed like the butterfly's wings. The ecstatic leaps & turns of the dancers. *Her* eager body in a yellow costume showing every muscle, every bone & nipple & the crevices of her groin. Her body that was like living wood smooth-carved & granted life. As he watched, leaning forward in his seat, his long hair sticking to his sweaty neck, his fingers twitched shaping & caressing the wood. *There! She is the one.* Like a vision it came to him. He would perfect her in his art, as he would perfect M M who had been his first sacrifice. Even before applause erupted in the open ampitheatre amid the pines, he had known *I must have her.*

The figure that was The Butterfly, in human form.

Dance for me! he bade her.

But she could not, no more than a sickly or a crippled girl. The terror in her eyes & the stink of her bowels. *The butterfly!*—a cruel jest.

*   *   *

It was true, they would question Joseph Gavin. The Mountainhome sheriff's deputies. Yet they had no special suspicion of him, & no evidence linking Joseph Gavin to the *missing dancer*. As he had made certain.

In exactitude & patience he had taken her one morning. It was very early, not 8 A.M. This was her routine: yoga exercises in the shabby black leotard. And this morning, the man was not there. His car was not there. There was no one but the red-haired dancer. *The butterfly*. Quick as an upright spider he came upon her climbing to the deck & his face masked with a black silk scarf & his hands in rubber gloves & his feet in rubber-soled sneakers two sizes too large. He would not keep her long as some of the others, not more than two hours. She would be buried in a grave to a depth of three feet, in a sinkhole he had discovered in the woods. There was a yearning in him to transport her to Deer Isle but this was not practical, he knew. Only a quarter mile from the gravel road but amid trees, marshy soil. They would not discover the body until twenty-five days later. It was the end of summer, it would be past Labor Day & no reason for Joseph Gavin as for numerous others to remain in Mountainhome. By then, he would be in Delaware. There would be no further evidence linking her body to him. He would not be questioned further. Excitedly he saw on TV news of the discovery of L R after a long search. Slender wrists & ankles bound together by wire, wire sunk deep around the neck, & the long hair not beautiful but limp & dirty in the grave. On TV and in the papers there were photographs only of L R the dancer smiling and lifting her arms as if inviting applause. There were no photographs of a *badly decomposed* body.

Where was L R's talent now? Where, her slender limbs & shining eyes? She was bent, broken. That was the power of NAME UNKNOWN. As a butterfly's wings are broken in an instant. In the grave her shoulders hunched, knees jerked up to her chest, head bowed in a posture of abject prayer.

Now you see! You who believed you might soar beyond the others of us who adore you.

His mind was unquiet, he began to comprehend why.

No visions came to him, nor was there a promise of visions.

In this late winter of the new year that had begun with such triumph.

Slow it was shaping in his mind AS A DUTY, he felt no true appetite for it, that the lewd blond female Oriana who had displayed her body & wept on TV that her friend had been taken, must be taken, too; for NAME UN-KNOWN had cause to believe she had spoken to the police, & he did not trust her. She had not looked NAME UNKNOWN in the eye. She had not fed him. Casting him aside like an unwanted dog unworthy of her female lust.

NAME UNKNOWN waiting for a sign. At the window of his rented barn staring toward the driveway, & the highway beyond. Long minutes passed in this fugue & he was not working, nor thinking; he was not NAME UN-KNOWN in such paralysis but the boy Joseph Gavin some had wished to believe slow-witted. *Will one of them come for me? And shall I know him?*

He would have expected the Weymouth detectives. But the one who came to him had not been foreseen.

28 *Dying, death, disappeared.*

In November of the previous year, one of Davey's third-grade classmates had been killed in a freak accident, a fall down a flight of concrete steps at an amusement park in Florida. Davey had been a close friend of the little boy but, after the boy's death, he'd been strangely indifferent when talking about his friend; this odd, unnerving behavior was reported by the parents of other children who'd been friendly with the dead boy. Tess said, "It's almost as if they blame Mark! They don't want to know him any longer. They're embarrassed by him. They refuse to talk about him." Matt, recalling his father's death, and how he hadn't wanted to talk about it for a long time and had flared up, unreasonably, when anyone, especially women, tried to commiserate with him, said, "Look, these kids are eight years old. They're scared. They know what 'death' is by now, and they don't want to know more. That's the fact. Should we provoke Davey into acknowledging this, and getting him to cry, or should we let the poor kid alone? When he wants to talk, he'll talk. And if he doesn't, that's up to him. Kids that young have to forget. This is what 'nature' does—forgets." Tess said, "That seems so harsh. So cold." To which Matt had no reply.

And a few weeks later there was the *missing girl*.

Matt gritted his teeth, and plunged into an explanation. Telling the boys, "This 'missing girl' everyone is talking about isn't an actual girl, you know. She's a grown woman. She isn't five, like you, Graeme; or eight, like you, Davey. Probably it was someone she knew who took her away, and if you don't know that person, and you sure don't, either of you, he isn't going to take you. O.K.?" This was supremely logical. This was Daddy-wisdom, indeed. But the boys stared at Matt, for all they'd been hearing from Tess and from their teachers was to the contrary: if there was a girl missing, they too could be taken; they had to be extra, extra careful; they must never trust strangers, nor even adults they knew only slightly. *They must be vigilant at all times.* Davey said accusingly, "You told us, Daddy, you had to be mostly old to die, it was something that happened to old people, but that isn't true, Daddy, is it? It can happen right now. It can happen to anybody right *now*."

"Yes, Davey. I suppose. There can always be a fire, or an earthquake. You see it on TV. And Mark fell down hard, concrete steps. But generally the odds are less likely that something bad will happen to you when you're *young*. And you and Graeme are going to be young a long time." Davey mulled over this, doubtfully. Matt tried to speak with authority, yet without that grating confidence he'd so detested in adults when he'd been a child. Davey said, "How old are you and Mommy, Daddy?" Matt, seeing where this was headed, said, "Your Mommy and I are young, still. Not as young as you and Graeme but, for sure, *young*." Davey said, smirking, "But the *missing girl* is younger than you, Daddy! She's twenty-six, it said in the paper. You're a whole lot older than that." Matt said, trying to smile as if this wasn't a low blow, said, "O.K. I'm ten years older. But not, even so, *old*."

At this point, Tess called them for supper. Tess had saved Daddy another time, and the boys ran noisily into the kitchen.

Poor Daddy: appalled by the enormity of the world he was expected to be surveying for his sons. It wasn't just that children require love, every ounce of love you can give them, he'd more or less known that, and that had scared him plenty, too, but beyond that love children require a reliable map of the world provided them by their parents.

And Daddy was having a goddamned difficult time making his own way, with no map and no faith in his ability to find one.

Graeme's voice was earnest, tinged with anxiety. And his breath hot and damp in Daddy's ear.

"Daddy? Where do you go when you *diz-peer?*"

"You mean 'disappear,' Graeme?"

"Yes, Daddy!" the boy shouted. "Where do you *go?*"

Graeme's hazel eyes widened in apprehension. He'd bumped

against Daddy's legs and climbed into Daddy's lap. Five years old and clumsily affectionate as a puppy; loved to take Daddy by surprise climbing into his lap and nuzzling his head against Daddy's shoulder. As he'd done since he'd been a toddler. Now Graeme was getting a little old for such behavior, and Davey sneeringly disapproved. But since the *missing girl*, and all that wasn't being said in his hearing, Graeme had become more anxious, and repetitious in his questions.

"Daddy, where do you *go*?"

"Well. You don't go anywhere exactly. You 'disappear.' " Matt tried to joke, snapping his fingers. Graeme flinched at the sound, but didn't laugh.

"Yes, Daddy, but *where? Where do you go when you disappear?*"

This was a variant of *Where do people go when they die?* which both boys had asked their parents, in turn. First Davey, and then Graeme. Tess told the boys that when a person died, he or she went "to a new place, some people call Heaven"; Matt told them frankly that "wherever people go when they die, it's a mystery to science at the present time." (Matt liked the American optimism of "at the present time.")

Graeme repeated his question and Daddy tried to remember if he'd already answered it. With an effort at earnestness he said, "It isn't always known where people who disappear *go*. If you went upstairs, Graeme, and hid in your closet, that's where you would *go*, but to me down here it's as if you've *disappeared*. See?" But Graeme was shaking his head stubbornly. Before he could ask his question again, Daddy said quickly, "People go all sorts of places! Like—see?" Matt switched off the TV, which no one had been watching, with the remote control. At once the screen went gray, blank.

Graeme giggled, but wasn't satisfied.

"But Daddy: real people, where do they *go*?"

"The TV people are real. They don't *go* anywhere, they stay where they are. But we don't see them."

Graeme was bored by the cheap mysteries of TV, miraculous as they might be. He took the electronic box utterly for granted, and wasn't impressed. "If I disappear, where do I *go*?" He waved toward the window, meaning the outdoors; meaning he wouldn't simply be upstairs in his closet.

Matt sighed, and tried to explain, seriously, that different people, believed to "disappear," go to different places. If you're left behind not knowing where they are, you might conclude that they've *disappeared*—"But they haven't, really."

"Then where are they, Daddy?"

"I told you, Graeme—different places. There's no one place."

Graeme would have sucked at his fingers, pondering this reply, if Daddy hadn't gently removed his fingers from his mouth. To Matt, the reply was supremely logical. And yet . . .

The problem was linguistic. *Disappear* was a single word. It could not reasonably apply to an infinity of events.

Graeme's eyes narrowed in childish dread. His feathery hair floated about his small face giving him a startled, vulnerable look. He was a tiny fledgling, enormous eyes and opened beak demanding to be fed, to be fed, to be fed. His need for Daddy and for Mommy was enormous. Matt could see little of himself in the child, though Graeme's hair was the color Matt's had been in childhood; in adolescence Matt's hair had coarsened and darkened, and by the age of thirty it had turned the curious metallic gray it was now, thick and wiry as a sheep's wool. Matt kissed Graeme, saying, "Graeme, don't worry, O.K.? You're not going to disappear, I promise."

But Graeme nuzzled his head so hard against Daddy's jaw, Daddy winced in pain. "Dad*dy*, I mean you!" he said, reverting to baby-talk. "*You* don't *diz-peer!*"

And all the while, that night as others, Matt was conscious of Tess in another room, listening.

And if he was on the telephone in his study, she might be listening through the door, or on an extension.

Under surveillance in his own house. *You love another woman, Matt, is that it? Please tell me.*

If she asked, he would deny it.

No one. No one living, I swear.

Sometimes at night, on those nights when Matt came upstairs to bed at all, Tess clutched at him, wordless. This was intimacy: the most profound, naked intimacy between a man and a woman. Yet only physical intimacy after all. *Our destinies in a 'cloud of unknowing' braided together before our births. Now Nighthawk has claimed my soul, & I his.* How could Tess, poor Tess, compete with that nocturnal, seductive voice?

How could Matt shut his ears to it, once he'd heard?

Even when Matt made love to Tess, or tried to make love to Tess, his mind seemed to detach itself from the exertions of his body like a soaring hawk. Again he was driving with Duana Zwolle off the highway to their secret place between the cornfields. A windy autumn day, blue sky and high scudding clouds and the rustling of dried cornstalks. He was standing with Duana Zwolle on the bank of the Weymouth River, drawing her white cashmere shawl across her shoulders, looking out with her at the mysterious mist-shrouded river. At last he'd gripped her hand. Her warm, surprisingly strong fingers gripping his. The flash of her dark eyes, her smile. *In the New Year, we will declare ourselves. In the New Year, we will be fearless.*

But there was Tess, and Matt loved Tess. There *was* Tess, in the flesh. And there *was not* Duana Zwolle.

I don't! I don't love another woman.

For, with a part of his mind, Matt McBride understood the madness of his infatuation with the *missing girl*. Even before the diary he'd understood the roots of his morbid attraction. Duana Zwolle was a recrudescence of his old, obsessive infatuation with Marcey Mason as an illness in adulthood may be the recrudescence of a childhood illness or trauma. *I am not in love with a dead girl! I am not in love with a woman I never knew.*

So he would plead.

So he would insist.

For there was Tess, and he lived with Tess; and Duana Zwolle was absent, and it was likely he'd never see her again. *You must be realistic. You are not Nighthawk, you are a separate individual.* He'd come to admire Tess more than ever, since the shock and humiliation of the police search. Since the invasion of their household by strangers. (Had Davey and Graeme ever guessed, that something had happened that day? That something was wrong between Mommy and Daddy?) In Weymouth, among the McBrides' circle, there were rumors—obviously. (Though never outright questions put to Tess or Matt, for Weymouth was too civilized for tactless behavior.) At Krell Associates, Matt McBride wasn't imagining the quizzical looks of his colleagues and their abrupt silences when he approached them talking together; he wasn't imagining Sidney Krell's avoidance of him, an abrupt cessation of invitations for lunch, drinks. (It would come as no surprise that the nomination of the McBrides for membership in the Weymouth Country Club would fade into oblivion.) Nor was Matt imagining the increasing unease between Tess and himself, which he couldn't seem to control.

What is it, Matt? Why won't you talk to me, confide in me? Why is this nightmare happening to us?

No wonder then, when Matt was away, Tess reverted to going through the pockets of his clothing, his bureau and desk drawers, his address book, his calendar. He would notice his old, battered address book facing left, and not right, in the top drawer of his desk, as he always kept it. He would notice the oversized, fussily ornate desk calendar, a Christmas gift from his in-laws, just perceptibly out of place beside his computer. And there was evidence that Tess went into his computer files, and listened to his telephone messages. *But the diary was hidden safely away, in Matt's office. Tess would never see it.*

On the night Matt visited Oriana in Lismore, and was late returning home, his breath smelling of sweet red wine when finally he did arrive past 9 P.M., Tess said only, with an anxious, angry smile, "If you're going to be working late, and having dinner out, you might tell me, you know. Though I don't really expect it of you any longer."

Matt intended to apologize but heard himself say, an edge of belligerence in his voice, "I lose track of time. I have things to think about. I was taking photos along the Weymouth River. I'm sorry."

This was true. After leaving Oriana's, Matt had been too restless to come directly home. He'd considered it a moral triumph that he hadn't given in to the urge to drive along Mill Row; to prowl like a hungry, lovesick ghost about the shuttered residence of the *missing girl*. Instead he'd driven along the river, toward Clinton Falls, parking several times to take photographs; he'd stopped for a single drink at a country tavern, and then returned home. But, stubbornly, he would not explain himself to Tess. It was ironic that, having rejected a woman's sexual pleading, he might be misjudged by his wife as an adulterer.

Matt hesitated on the stairs, and Tess looked at him with brimming eyes, and they embraced suddenly, with a kind of desperation. Tess whispered, "No more, Matt. Don't get into this any deeper. Whatever it is. I'm begging you."

Matt said, "Tess, I won't."

"You promise?"

"I promise."

29

"You're Joseph Gavin?—a sculptor?"

"I am—a sculptor. Who are you?"

Calmly the bearded man stood in the doorway of the battered mobile home on cement blocks. His wormy-pale lips were stretched in a hostile smile. Matt, smiling with the assurance of a successful American junior executive, extended his hand in a direct, friendly gesture—"I'm Mathias McBride. I live over in Weymouth. I collect contemporary American art and I'm an amateur photograher, myself."

The bearded man, staring at Matt, didn't shake his hand. His eyes were flat and luminous like metal, set oddly deep in their sockets. In the harsh morning light his putty-colored skin appeared pitted, the faint scars of old acne. Seen at a distance, Gavin, if that was his name, might be a fey, attractive figure, with shoulder-length silvery hair worn Christ-style, and an airy, floating beard that came to midchest. He was youthful without being young, and his bib-overalls were streaked with paint and clay like a child's soiled playclothes. Seen up close, he seemed subtly disfigured, his face asymmetrical as if it had been squeezed together and released, his narrow chest and shoulders hardened with sinewy muscle, his flowing hair and beard synthetic, bleached as if with acid. His beard in particular aroused Matt's contempt: a pathetic, wispy thing, barely covering the man's weak, receding chin. Matt had a powerful impulse to grab it, and tug.

You son of a bitch. You walking piece of shit. You fucker. Are you the one?

"And so—I was wondering: I've heard a lot about you, and your sculptures, and, as I'm a collector, I'd like very much to see your—"

"Who has told you about me?"

"A very nice woman who's the owner, I think, of the Tomato Factory Gallery. And—others."

Gavin, if that was his name, plucked nervously at his wisps of beard. His eyes were a cobra's eyes, Matt thought. Yet a cobra, too, can be frightened, not only treacherous. It was Matt's task to unfrighten this "suspect." He said, in an appealing voice, the voice of a reasonable, utterly friendly man, "I hope I haven't come to the wrong place? I've been on a buying spree for my 'Americana' collection and I've been commissioned to do a feature on 'New Talent for the New Century' for *American Art*—that's why I have my photographic equipment out in the car. You *are* Joseph Gavin? A sculptor?"

"I am—NAME UNKNOWN."

The wormy-pale lips moved shyly. There was a glint of astonished pride in the eyes. These stiff, ridiculous words—"I am NAME UNKNOWN"—took on a kind of dignity; despite his loathing, Matt had to grant this individual a measure of strength. He still hadn't moved from his tense, slightly crouching posture in the doorway, nor was he about to shake Matt's hand, but he spoke more readily now and seemed to be believing Matt's story. "Yes, I am a sculptor. But my work is not for sale at this time."

"Not for sale? But why?"

"It is—a large work. Not yet completed."

"But may I see it? From what I've been told about the work of NAME UNKNOWN, I'd like to see it, very much."

Matt spoke with naive eagerness. Again came the coppery flash of astonished pride, elation, vindication in the bearded man's eyes. *I knew! I knew I was a genius! All alone, I knew.* Almost, Matt felt sorry for the man. Maybe he was innocent? Hadn't anything to do with Duana Zwolle, no more than Matt himself? Matt felt a moment's dismay, that possibly this "Joseph Gavin" was no abductor, and no killer, only just another loser.

In this America of high-publicity winners, to be a loser is to know yourself contemptible, loathsome. Yet: a murderer?

Seeing Gavin's startled smile, a glimpse of gray, crooked teeth above that receding chin, Matt halfway doubted this guy was capable of planning any violent act, let alone executing it.

"I—I would not wish my figures photographed. Not just now."

"Of course not, Mr.—'NAME UNKNOWN.' I respect your wishes."

Eyes shining, putty-skin flushed with pleasure, the bearded man led Matt to a decaying, weatherworn barn at the rear of the overgrown lot. The men walked on planks sunk deep in mud. It was a windy, late-winter day. A white, glowering light came from all directions. Gavin lived in a scrubby semirural district, at the edge of a crossroads called Clinton Falls and in an area of mobile homes, cheaply built "ranch" houses and crudely renovated old farmhouses. This was a non-affluent area of New Jersey little known to the inhabitants of Weymouth; property values had been depressed here for decades, and developers like Krell Associates were unknown. The fast food franchises, 24-hour gas stations and minimarts along the country highway would have a romantic nocturnal appeal to Nighthawk and his camera; but it was midmorning now, a long way from night.

For hours, Matt had been anticipating this moment. He would be alone with "Joseph Gavin." He, Matt McBride, who knew nothing of police procedure apart from the vague assemblage of techniques and and attitudes he'd picked up from TV and films. He understood that what he was attempting was risky, perhaps futile. *Seeking justice. And maybe revenge.* What if Gavin recognized *him?* He was convinced that the man was from Forked River, and possibly Gavin had seen Matt in Lismore that afternoon. Yet Gavin seemed to trust him. Didn't suspect him.

He wants to believe me. He's desperate.

Led back to the dilapidated barn, taking care not to misstep into the mud, Matt was feeling elated. If Phelan and Ricci could see their man now! Where the Weymouth detectives were agents of the state to whom few people, even the innocent, would wish to speak frankly, and for whom many would feel hostility, he, Matt McBride, was just another civilian.

He could go where police couldn't, and be trusted where they'd never be trusted. That was his advantage, but it was also a risk.

(Not until afterward would Matt consider the profundity of this risk. *He might have killed me and disposed of my body, who'd have known?*)

It hadn't been easy to locate Gavin. Oriana had been vague about where NAME UNKNOWN lived, and Matt had had to make a half-dozen queries in Clinton Falls, identifying himself as an art collector in search of a "local, eccentric, talented sculptor—a man with long hair and beard." Matt saw the expressions in people's faces of sur-prise, bemusement. *They think I'm a fool, a sucker. Good!* A garage mechanic who serviced Gavin's pickup directed Matt to the mobile home on the highway; there was a mailbox at the foot of the drive, but no name was on it. The "mobile home" looked like a large tin capsule, partly screened from the road by a stand of scrubby trees and a McDonald's billboard. Gavin's nearest neighbors were a half-mile away. As Matt drove along the bumpy driveway he had to consider: the crucial difference between civilians and cops is that cops are armed. Gavin's dilapidated rental property came into view. *The scene of the crime. Where the bodies were found.*

Matt hadn't even told anyone where he was headed. How could he? He hadn't known, and he had no business here. When he left the office he'd told his secretary that he was meeting a potential client Fair Hills, he'd be calling in later for his messages.

Now he was saying, with a nervous smile, "You must love it here in the country, Mr.—NAME UNKNOWN? It's quiet, and it's private." He was about to say it was beautiful, but this scrubby rural landscape, with traffic rushing past on the highway, wasn't very beautiful. "You can be—alone with your work."

Gavin didn't reply. As if, embodying genius, he had no patience for social chatter. He swung open a barn door and indicated for Matt to follow him inside. *Do I want to do this? Here goes.* Matt was feeling a visceral, animal alertness; the wariness of an organ-ism that wants simply to survive. A chill, stale, chemical odor made his nostrils pinch. He had to fight a gagging reflex. Here, in the barn, was a smell of something dead, yet more than dead. There was an eerie silence punctuated only by the sound of heavy-duty trucks on the highway. Matt saw that Gavin was glancing sidelong at him, almost shyly, his small cobra-eyes quivering. In his stained bib-overalls, silvery hair straggling about his head, the bearded man resembled a gawky, overgrown boy masquerading as the Messiah, eager for an adult's approval. There was something repulsive and yet touching in this, Matt thought.

"These are—remarkable!" Matt said.

He was staring at five, or was it six, sculpted figures. Humanoid figures. They were meant to be life-sized dolls, or mannequins; female, yet sexless as the trunks of trees, with minimal suggestions of breasts, hips. They might have been executed by a gifted but clumsy child. Though not lifelike they induced in Matt that uneasy sensation he'd often felt, especially as a child, in the presence of a store mannequin. *It's alive. No*! The smallest figure, which was uncompleted, had a naked, plain face and almost comical-looking mismatched glass eyes; her hair, or wig, lay on a bench nearby, a tangle of synthetic brown curls. Was this meant to represent the *missing girl*? Was this, somehow, Duana Zwolle? But the awkward figure bore little resemblance to any individual for, like the others, it was plain, idealized. It had no spark of life, none of that elusive magic that belongs to art; that makes us believe, even in artifice.

"Very interesting. Very . . . original."

Matt was feeling nervous. Something was wrong here. So much effort on the artist's part had been channelled into—what? Outlandish unconvincing humanoid figures. These were crudely fashioned out of pieces of scraps, wood, metal, plastic, molded wax and stained, baked clay. Each had been painstakingly if not very skillfully painted. On several figures paint had begun to blister and peel; the artist hadn't prepared his materials properly. Two of the figures were bald, with smooth, painted, flesh-colored heads; others had been fitted with clumps and strips of hair that ranged from convincing (was this real, human hair?) to obviously artificial. All the figures had been fitted with glass eyes. It was difficult to determine if the figures were meant to be nude, or clothed: their trunk-like bodies were covered in minute Zodiac signs, primitive bird and animal drawings, and small strips of glittering metal.

Matt swallowed hard. The overwhelming impression of the figures, crowded into the dank interior of the cobwebbed, rotting old barn, was one of melancholy captivity.

These are dead women. He has collected them: his brides.

The sculptor said reverently, "These are—*The Marriage of Heaven and Hell*." His voice was hoarse, quavering with emotion. His fingers plucked at his skimpy beard as if it were a living thing that had to be calmed. "Each has a secret name, you see. I may not reveal."

Matt managed to sound buoyant, enthusiastic. An art collector eager to be impressed. "This is unusual work, Mr.—. Unlike anything I've ever seen."

Gavin looked at Matt as if he was a moron.

"Yes. It is. Of course it is—'unlike.' "

Matt tried again, with yet more enthusiasm. "Where do you—get your inspiration?"

Gavin said, "Inspiration is from within. It is a fire that, in some, never burns out. I've been working on these for twenty years. They are incomplete, as you see. And there will be three more."

Three more. Women?

"Twenty years! You must have a—mission."

"A vision. Yes."

Excited, the sculptor picked up a wooden chisel, caressed it against his chest, and set it down again. "My angels. In human form. For the angel may take a human form, sometimes. If you have eyes to see. If you are not blinded by ignorance. 'The Expanding Eyes of Man behold the depths of wonderous worlds'—if we are not cowards, to strike our hammers."

Hammers? Matt saw a claw hammer on a worktable amid a clutter of tools and debris. It was darkly stained.

"Is that Blake? Did you just quote—William Blake?"

The bearded sculptor glanced at Matt, in surprise. For a moment, he almost smiled.

For the next forty minutes Gavin spoke to Matt solemnly of his "vision"; his materials, and his technique; his stoicism about being unheralded at the present time but his confidence that, in the twenty-first century, his work would be universally honored. "It is a matter of continuing, and not losing heart," Gavin said. Here was a shy-seeming, reclusive man coming to life in Matt's presence, starved for sympathy and lonely for a friend. Matt tried to listen. The sensation of nausea came and went, but was alleviated if he managed to tilt his head near a window and inhale fresh, cold air. There was a riddle here, staring him in the face. The ridiculous mannequins with their crude glass eyes, sightless; yet staring him in the face. *Help us! Save us!*

Matt supposed that Phelan and Ricci, his buddies, had been out here, too; they'd seen Gavin's studio, stared at the strange figures, tried not to gag. What had they thought? Had they been suspicious? Oriana had said that they'd questioned "Joseph Gavin" along with other men she'd named, but apparently they hadn't found anything to incriminate him. Still, they must have investigated Gavin's background. They had access to far more information than Matt had.

Maybe Gavin had an alibi for the night of Zwolle's abduction?

Maybe someone was willing to lie for him?

Matt felt an embarrassed sympathy for NAME UNKNOWN even as he could hardly bear to keep looking at the man's work. For here was, simply, bad art; hopeful and ambitious, but bad art; lacking even the wayward, clumsy charm of primitive "outsider" art.

Yet his vanity is such, he wouldn't feel jealousy for another artist— would he? It was hard to imagine NAME UNKNOWN focussing upon Duana Zwolle, or anything apart from THE MARRIAGE OF HEAVEN AND HELL, with the intention of doing harm.

As Gavin spoke, twisting his fingers in his beard, Matt was noticing how dirty he was. Not the flowing hair and beard, which clearly he groomed, but his hands, his fingernails, his neck. The man's body must be covered in grime: holy dirt? His bib-overalls fitted him loosely and were stiff with dirt. Bib-overalls were an affectation Matt McBride particularly loathed. Beneath, Gavin wore a grimy red plaid flannel shirt.

On a windowsill nearby was the yellow leather cap with the visor.

Matt said, interrupting, "Excuse me—you call yourself 'NAME UNKNOWN.' But what *is* your name? I've been told it's 'Joseph—' "

"I have told you: I am NAME UNKNOWN."

"That's not the name you were born with, or your legal name, is it?"

"We are body and soul. Our bodies are 'named,' our souls are not. If you are an artist, you understand."

"I do! I do understand. I'm only just—curious. I've been told that—"

"Who? Who has been telling you?"

"The owners of the galleries I mentioned, and—"

The bearded sculptor confronted Matt with surprising animosity. He was clenching and unclenching his fists, and his flat, metallic eyes gleamed yellow. Through the wisps of beard, Matt could see his weak, receding chin. *I know him!*

"What have they been saying about NAME UNKNOWN? Those females? Ignorant females? They know nothing of NAME UN-KNOWN."

"They—spoke of you very highly. They admire your art. They—"

"They have never seen my art! Not my true art."

"They suggested I seek you out, because—"

Matt found himself involuntarily mimicking the sculptor in his own speech. Adrenaline coursed through his veins, preparing him for a fight; even as he continued to smile, a reasonable, friendly man, an art collector, trying to remain calm. Yet the smells in the barn—paint, chemical, organic rot—were making him sick.

Gavin said, "One of those females was Oriana—yes?"

"Who? 'Oriana'? I'm not sure. I don't think so."

"*She*—is a Judas. Her art is ugly and her bed is a pig's sty. You have discovered—yes?" Gavin laughed contemptuously. He was standing in front of Matt, nearly Matt's height, hands on his hips. Matt was uncomfortably aware of the man's narrow, wiry body; the ropey muscles of his shoulders and upper arms. Gavin was one of those men much stronger and more dangerous than they appear because his appearance was effeminate, but his body, hidden inside his loose clothing, was a man's.

An upright snake. Cobra. Deadly.

Annoyed, Matt said, "No. I have not discovered."

"Yes! You—'McBride' you call yourself—you, too, have discovered."

Goddamned if Matt McBride was going to back down. It may have been, at this point, excited and aroused, he'd forgotten that he was speaking with a man he had reason to suspect of being violent; he'd begun to react as if this was an ordinary confrontation, a man-to-man disagreement. His pride was at stake! "You don't know shit about my private life, 'NAME UNKNOWN,' so drop that crap. And I believe you *are* 'Joseph Gavin'—I guess you've forgotten, we went to school together? Over in Forked River? You were a year or two ahead of me—right?"

The bearded sculptor stared at Matt. He was more surprised than alarmed; it took him a moment to regain his composure.

"No. I have no memory of 'Forked River.' "

"Cut the crap, Gavin. You graduated in '75 or '76—right? You lived close in, in town. I lived—my family lived—a couple of blocks from the beach, on Bayside—"

The bearded sculptor backed off, shaking his head vehemently. "I told you—I have no memory of 'Forked River.' I want you to leave now."

Matt said, "About the time Marcey Mason was killed. You must remember."

Gavin shook his head. No. He did not remember.

"In '76, it was. That fall and winter. Nobody from Forked River would forget."

"Leave, *now*. You have no right."

"Like Duana Zwolle, maybe? Both of them taken away, hidden away, and—what happened to them? Maybe you know about that, 'NAME UNKNOWN'?"

Breathing audibly, Gavin continued to stare at Matt as if he couldn't quite absorb what Matt was saying. His fingers groped about the workbench seeking something—the wood chisel, the claw hammer; Matt noted this, preparing to knock it out of his hand.

But Gavin only stammered, "Leave—*now*! You have no right."

Matt's heart was pounding violently in his chest. He wanted to fight. He was ready.

Instead, Matt managed to compose himself. He backed off, lifting his hands in a gesture to indicate he was leaving. "Maybe I'll see you another time, 'NAME UNKNOWN.' "

He left the sculptor staring after him, plucking at his wispy beard.

30

We will be together I know. This side of the grave. Or the other.

He made a decision then to drive to Forked River. Eighty miles east and south through New Jersey, to the Atlantic Ocean.

In great urgency. In a fever state.

He hadn't intended this—not today! Not this hour. *But he had to know.* Beyond the roar and murmur of heavy traffic on Interstate 287 south to the Garden State Expressway the landscape that should have been familiar to him passed in a blur and the voice of the *missing girl* lifted to him plaintively. *Help me! Help me! If you love me, help me!*

Not in many years had Matt McBride returned to Forked River. Nor to Deer Isle and the Pine Barrens of his boyhood. That part of his life was over. He never thought about it. His father had died. His brothers lived in other states. His mother and retarded sister had moved to Tampa, Florida, where they belonged to the Pentecostal Church of Jesus Christ Crucified. This was the fastest-growing Pentecostal church in Florida, Matt had learned. In his mother's "awakened vision" (as she called it, following a ritual baptism into the Church) Matt McBride was one of Satan's tribe, possibly not an active agent, as her minister supposed, but one of Satan's myriad dupes, performing his wishes unaware. Possibly she believed this of Matt's brothers, as well; Matt didn't know. He wasn't in much communication with his brothers. Matt had listened to his mother's excited accusations a number of times on the telephone, stoic and declining to defend himself. Four times a year he sent a check for a considerable amount of money (which kept rising steadily, with inflation) to the Gulf Isle Retirement Villas, Tampa, Florida, where his mother and sister were "life-residents"; the Villas, which included nursing care facilities, were under the auspices of the Pentecostal Church of Jesus Christ Crucified. Sometimes Matt's mother sent him religious cards thanking him; more often not. Matt didn't expect any response from her, let alone thanks. He was discharging his duty as a son, he supposed. He wasn't a very good son but he didn't feel apologetic. Nor did he feel heroic. He guessed that the Church was surely cheating him, winnowing money from his mentally unstable mother and sister, but what could he do? He'd asked a Tampa lawyer with whom he was doing business to check into the place and the man had reported back to Matt that it looked legitimate; it was newly built, and reasonably clean, and Matt's mother and sister "insisted they were happy. Very happy."

Matt decided to believe the lawyer. He was buying out his responsibility as a son, but damned if he was going to feel guilty. Since his father's death when Matt had been twenty-seven, it was hard to think of himself as anyone's son.

South of Newark, passing South Amboy, the southern tip of Staten Island, Red Bank, the U.S. Navy Depot. Only a few miles inland from the ocean. It was a wild, crazy thing he was doing. *But he had to know.* At Eatontown stopping for gas, needing badly to use a rest room. His stomach had been queasy since the smell of NAME UNKNOWN's barn. The plain naked sorrowful faces of those clumsily sculpted figures, their ridiculous glass eyes. *Help us. Help us. Release us. Don't forsake us!*

God damn, Matt McBride was determined he would forsake no one.

He'd had only a vague idea what he'd meant to do, seeking out "Joseph Gavin" as he had. Only that *he must do it.* Just to see the man's face close up. To hear his voice. Through this "Joseph Gavin" to find a way to the *missing girl.* At the same time, he'd fully intended to return to Krell Associates, afterward. Where he was falling behind in his work, each day a little further behind; on his desk were contracts, documents, printouts Matt McBride needed to expedite, and there were e-mail messages and telephone messages to be returned, and Sid Krell had entrusted him with a major project, drawing up a massive land appraisal contract involving a half-dozen developers, potentially a $25 million deal—and so on. Since his visit with Oriana, however, Matt was having difficulty at Krell Associates. Seeing the old man he felt a spasm of disgust, anger. Each time he had to exchange a few words with the old man he felt an urge to punch Krell in the face. The sick son of a bitch!—harrassing Duana Zwolle as he had; frightening her; wanting 'to hurt that girl so she'd feel it"—an old man's sexual vanity, repulsive! *You bastard, think I don't know?* Between Matt McBride and Sid Krell there was a force-field of tension, though they maintained, in public, amiable enough relations. Matt guessed that Krell suspected that Matt knew of Krell's involvement with Duana Zwolle; as in a funhouse mirror, mirrors reflecting mirrors, distortions multiplied into infinity. What had Krell boasted of himself—he was the fat, dimpled spider at the secret heart of Weymouth.

Yet—and this was the shameful thing—Matt wanted to think that, despite all, Sid Krell favored *him*.

For wasn't Matt McBride (whom Krell sometimes called "Mattie") the fair-haired son of the lot, the junior associate the boss loved and would one day promote to partner?

Since their awkward conversation in early January, Krell had seemed to be avoiding Matt, and Matt understood why, and was becoming slightly anxious. Though he hated Krell, he depended upon him for his livelihood. He made a lot of money, and he and Tess spent a lot of money, living in Weymouth. It wasn't just that, if Krell sacked him, Matt would be out of a job, seeking work in a crazed, competitive field; but the old bastard would put a curse on him, word would spread through New Jersey that Mathias McBride, Jr., was trouble. If Matt was fired, and unemployed, even for a brief period of time, Tess's rich parents, for years waiting like buzzards to intrude in their daughter's marriage, would insist upon "helping out." The thought made Matt cringe.

Washing his hands at a grimy rest room in a gas station outside Eatontown, regarding himself suspiciously in the mirror. His eyes appeared dilated, his skin feverish and blotched. Was this Mathias McBride, Jr.? The day before at Krell Associates, he'd glimpsed Sid

Krell and two junior associates talking earnestly on their way out of the building; they were carrying briefcases, headed for a luncheon meeting at one of Krell's clubs, Matt supposed. (For a panicked moment Matt wondered whether he'd been invited, too, but had forgotten?) Catching sight of Matt, who must have been staring after them, shrewd old Sid Krell grinned and waved in his brisk, brusque way even as he continued walking *H'lo kid, how's it going, busy right now so don't bother me—got it?*

What I should've done was slip into Krell's office. See if that .35-caliber revolver was in his drawer. Something I might've needed, going to see NAME UNKNOWN. Something I might need in the near future.

Like many small towns in this part of south Jersey, Forked River had grown in the past decade but hadn't much prospered. A strip of Rt. 9, out of Lanoka Harbor a few miles away, was being developed— mostly cheap motels catering to tourists who couldn't afford the more expensive motels of Island Beach, on the ocean. Driving into Forked River in the midafternoon, Matt steeled himself for old, aching memories; but mainly felt impatience with slow-moving local traffic. He was in a hurry! On the Garden State, he'd driven as fast as he'd dared.

There was Forked River High, a new addition at the rear and an expanded parking lot, otherwise not much changed since Matt had last seen it, returning for his father's funeral. Nine years ago. This was a landmark of Matt McBride's adolescence, a place once so familiar to him he could have made his way blindfolded through its corridors, downstairs and up. Again he waited for a wave of emotion to sweep over him, but none came. Entering the school by the front door, as he'd never done as a student, Matt didn't take time to look at the glass trophy cases on permanent display in the foyer, on the wall rows of framed photos of the Forked River football teams dating back for decades. Mathias McBride, Jr. had been on the JV team his sophomore year, the varsity team his junior and senior years. Being on the team, wearing the team jersey, had once meant more to him, he would have claimed, than life itself.

But how simple life had been, in those days.

In the front office, Matt introduced himself to a young woman receptionist as a '79 graduate, returned for a visit; could he look through a few yearbooks of previous years? The request might have seemed a little odd but the young woman was obliging, and shortly Matt found himself seated in an adjoining room, on a leather sofa, leafing quickly through the '77 *Forked River Flame*. It wasn't his own photo he was seeking, but that of "Joseph Gavin."

But he didn't find it. In the graduating class there were numerous *G's*, but no *Gavin*.

At the start of the section of graduating seniors, on a page devoted exclusively to her, there was a large photograph of *Marcey Mason*. This would have been the girl's graduating photograph if she'd lived to graduate with her class. Matt felt a stab of emotion, seeing the girl's conventional prettiness, her almost too radiantly smiling face. As an adult he wondered at the appropriateness of the yearbook editors choosing so happy a likeness of the dead girl with which to commemorate her. But maybe all Marcey Mason's photos were happy. Beneath the photo was the stark little caption **In Memorium Our Beloved Marcey 1959–1976**. Around the oval photo was a black border.

Matt stared at the girl. Had NAME UNKNOWN killed her, too?

Matt thumbed through the remainder of the yearbook, not especially curious about finding himself. He'd long ago misplaced his '79 yearbook and felt no sentimentality about the loss. When Marcey Mason had been a senior, he'd been a sophomore. There, *Mathias McBride, Jr.* in Mrs. Farrell's homeroom; and in the second row of the JV football team. Matt had to smile, seeing his young, grinning face. His crewcut made him look like a moron, but an amiable moron. There was a smudge on his forehead that must have been acne.

Matt was struck by the amateur quality of the yearbook. Its glossy pages, quilted hunter-green color, embossed gold letters had once seemed to him the acme of sophistication. How proud he'd been, named to the yearbook photography staff. Now, he couldn't have remembered which photographs among the dozens of photographs in the book had been his.

In the '75 *Forked River Flame*, there was "Joseph Gavin" among the graduating class.

"It's him."

Excited, Matt studied the small oval photograph closely. He was sure this was the man who now called himself NAME UNKNOWN: though in 1975, at the approximate age of eighteen, Gavin had had a sallow, sullen, fattish face. There had been nothing in the slightest ethereal or Christ-like about him. The eyes were sunken and half-closed, his hair was trimmed brutally short. He looked both shy and mean. Beneath his picture there were no lists of activities or sports, only the identifying caption *Joseph Elmore Gavin. Major: Industrial Arts.*

Matt sat with the yearbook in hand, staring for several long minutes at *Joseph Elmore Gavin.* Strange that he could recognize him, when Gavin looked so different now; yet the eyes, the facial bone structure, the very set of the mouth were unmistakable. Gavin's hair had been dark, so he must be bleaching it now. He'd lost weight. His characteristic expression wasn't sullen now, but a childlike look of trust, hope, fatuous idealism. He'd tried to remake himself into a flower child of the Sixties, decades later. Or some bizarre psychological conversion had afflicted him, so that he imagined himself a mystic-artist, like William Blake.

But could a "mystic-artist" abduct and murder young women?

Strange too that Gavin had imagined he could deceive Matt Mc-Bride so easily. As if Matt—or anyone—couldn't have checked on him here in Forked River. As if the name "Joseph Gavin" wasn't known in Clinton Falls and elsewhere.

At least, Matt was certain now: The man he'd sighted on the bank of the Weymouth River, back in October, wearing the yellow leather visor cap, not far from Duana Zwolle's residence—the man he'd seen driving from Oriana's in a battered Ford pickup the first time he'd tried to see her, in January—and the man who called himself NAME UNKNOWN—was Joseph Elmore Gavin who'd graduated from Forked River High School in 1975. He'd been an older classmate of

Marcey Mason. He'd lived in her neighborhood, which hadn't been far from Matt McBride's home.

He! He was the one.

He'd taken her away. He'd tortured and killed her. He'd removed something from her body. (Of which no one would speak.)

And if he'd done this with Marcey Mason, he'd done it with Duana Zwolle.

Matt returned the yearbooks to the receptionist, thanked her politely and before she could engage him in conversation walked out of Forked River High School in a trance. A bell sounded without his awareness. Packs of teenagers were streaming around him, eager to escape. Matt followed them into the parking lot and sat for a while in his car, thinking. His eyes were damp. His brain ached. What should he do with his new knowledge? Was this something the Weymouth detectives already knew? (He'd sent them the anonymous note, after all. He was cautious about getting involved with cops ever again.)

Why not you, McBride? You knew both girls. You could have taken both Marcey Mason and Duana Zwolle, tortured and killed them. Hidden their broken bodies in the Pine Barrens. And now you're haunted by them.

Matt drove slowly, distracted, along the narrow, potholed streets of his old hometown. Thinking he never wanted to set foot in a police station again. Never wanted to be "interviewed" by police officers again. Never the shock and humiliation of a search. His own house, his privacy violated: his wife made to see her husband in a new, altered light. *Never again.*

Gavin might be guilty as hell, yet there would be no arrest, let alone a conviction, without evidence. What the police called "hard evidence"—"physical evidence." Even a confession was inadequate. If you could get the maniac to confess.

If, Matt was thinking, he got hold of a gun, pressed the barrel against Gavin's head, demanded to know what he'd done to Duana Zwolle, if Gavin broke down and confessed. . . . Without evidence, the confession would be worthless.

Yes, but the body of the *missing girl* would be evidence.

But Joseph Gavin would never give it up.

For there was madness in him. That look of radiance, absolute conviction. *For the angel may take a human form sometimes. If you have eyes to see.* Never would Gavin succumb to another's threat, the man's will was inviolable.

So, if Matt killed Gavin, the secret of where Duana Zwolle was, living or dead, would never be revealed.

Turning from South Main onto Harbor Road, and from Harbor onto Bayside; on Bayside, passing the house in which Matt had lived as a boy, now much changed, with buff-brick siding and what looked like a solarium addition at the side; a remodeled garage now joined to the house to expand its cramped space. In the kitchen of that house, now the province of strangers, Matt's mother had once clawed and screamed at him—"*You!* Little Satan."

Matt shivered.

Had there been any truth to it?

Matt waited for emotion to sweep over him. At least a sense of loss, regret. Grief.

Nothing.

He drove along Lebanon Avenue. With emotion now, passing the gray shingleboard corner house of the *missing girl*. This house too had been altered since the late 1970's, converted into small offices like most houses on Lebanon Avenue. Dentist, photographer. Not very prosperous-looking. After Marcey's terrible death, the Mason family moved away from Forked River. Not just the parents, other relatives as well. As if the name "Mason" had been despoiled.

Matt's father had said, furious, "If there's a God, now's His big chance to redeem Himself: catch and punish that girl's killer."

But Marcey Mason's killer had never been caught, still less punished. God remained aloof from Forked River, New Jersey.

There was a summer of Matt McBride pedaling past the Masons' house, rapidly, not slowly, not wanting to be seen; as if he had a purpose pedaling along Lebanon Avenue. Passing the house Matt would glance at it sidelong, almost overcome with excitement. The shades were usually drawn in the front downstairs windows, the grass in the front yard went unmowed. "I could have saved her. If I'd had the chance." It was a comic book scenario, a kid's fantasy, yet painfully real. As real as any emotion of Matt's adult life.

Of course, it was entirely a fantasy. He'd been too young even to know the popular senior. If, a few times, Marcey had smiled at Matt in the school halls and called out, "Hi!" in her radiant soprano voice, her friendliness was nothing more than a phenomenon of the moment, and of Marcey's generous sunny good-girl Christian nature. There were other girls like Marcey, known as "popular"—though the term seems so inadequate, to suggest the luminous power of high school charisma; that sense that, if Marcey Mason, cheerleader and soloist in girls' chorus, beautiful Marcey Mason paused to speak with you, you were raised to another level of significance, like a lottery winner. Of course, this wasn't going to happen. The girl's happy gaze slid through you because you were transparent. You were an asshole to imagine otherwise, right? Matt McBride knew.

But Joseph Gavin possibly hadn't known.

Joe Gavin. That heavyset sullen boy who rarely spoke, and mumbled when he spoke, as if with a speech impediment, scarcely moving his mouth. Never smiled. Had no friends. Even his scornful older brothers dismissed him as "weird." Yet he had a quirky talent for drawing cartoons, mimicking comic strip figures you could recognize. Bored in class, he'd cover sheets of notebook paper he would later tear out, crumple and toss away, as if he valued his own gift lightly. One of the IA—Industrial Arts—majors. (Lots of jokes about industrial "arts.") One of those background people you never much notice in school, in the neighborhood, in life. You would not wish to think what Joe Gavin might be thinking behind that sullen face.

Matt was driving now on Delahunt, a rundown block. He had the idea that the Gavins had lived on this block. That house, with the tilted veranda? Cracked sidewalk? Matt thought, yes. Of course, the family would have moved away, probably. No Gavins there now.

No Joseph Gavin. NAME UNKNOWN.

Matt had to wonder: The police must have suspected Gavin? How had they let him slip through the net?

At the age of fifteen, Matt had been questioned by Forked River police, among a group of high school boys, boys from Marcey's neighborhood. Matt had not been singled out for separate questioning, of course. Afterward he'd joined a search team to look through vacant houses and lots in Forked River, in fields and culverts and desolate areas of the beach. They'd hiked for miles in a freezing November rain led by a male teacher from the high school. They hadn't found Marcey Mason who would not be found for many days but they'd searched until they'd staggered with exhaustion.

Sure I loved her. We all did.

The missing girl.

At the intersection of Ocean Avenue and Main Street was the old redbrick Lutheran church to which Matt's mother had taken him. A shock to see it still stood. And solid-looking, if dour. A sign announcing Sunday School times was prominent near the front door. How many hours Matt had spent captive in that building, trying to block out sermons, Bible verses, the breathy, braying singing of the congregation. It had seemed to him, even as a child, a snare and a delusion. He hadn't had the vocabulary, but he'd had the concept. He hadn't even needed his father's skepticism to feed his own. *You! Little Satan.*

From Oriana he'd learned about the St. Patrick Mission in Newark. Duana Zwolle hadn't been Catholic, yet she'd volunteered her time in the kitchen. She'd donated food, helped to prepare food and ladled it out to homeless men, women, and children. Matt McBride wouldn't have approved, as her lover. Wasn't it risky, a young woman, attractive as Duana Zwolle, in such a place? Though he might have accompanied her, and protected her. As Nighthawk, he might have photographed the church hall lighted for night, the long shuffling lines of the homeless and the needy, and in their midst Duana Zwolle's rapt, radiant face. *Why hadn't I? Why was I such a coward?* At one time it had seemed a possibility that Duana Zwolle's abductor might have been connected with the St. Patrick Mission, though now it seemed unlikely. Matt had planned to drive to Newark to speak with the priest who headed the Mission; he'd even telephoned him the previous day, introducing himself as a "close friend of Duana Zwolle's." Father Justin Carey at the other end of the line said warily that he'd already given information to Weymouth police and to state police several times; his testimony had been taped, and he hadn't anything further to add. He was devastated by Duana's disappearance but knew nothing about it, and didn't want to talk about it. Matt said, "I can understand that, Father Carey. But there might be something you'd think of, talking with me, that you didn't think of with the police. People always know more than they think they know." Father Carey must have been in a communal office of some kind; voices were raised in the background. He told Matt he was very sorry but he didn't believe it would be helpful for them to meet. "We're all praying for Duana here, and we're all still hoping. But it's been hard." This was an ambiguous statement. Matt didn't know how to interpret it. Quietly he said, "For me, too, Father, it's been hard. I loved—love—her. I was her lover, Father." There was a brief silence. Father Carey didn't reply, but the background voices were louder. Matt said, desperately, gripping the receiver tight, "No one knew. I wasn't strong enough to claim her. And now it's too late. I'm afraid it's too late. I—want her back so badly, Father!" The priest said, "You sound troubled, Mr.—is it McBride? I'm not sure what I can do for you, but if you'd like to come see me, I suppose we could talk." Matt said quickly, "I'd like that, Father. Since Duana disappeared, I'm so lonely. I have no one to talk to. I feel that I failed her, her love was a crucial test I failed. I know in my heart that she must be dead by now, but I—can't accept it. My God—" Father Carey said there was no reason to believe that Duana was dead; it was enough that she was missing, and police were investigating her disappearance; things could turn out well after all— "We must only not give up faith." "Yes! We mustn't give up faith," Matt agreed, wiping at his eyes. "I'm not Catholic but—sometimes I wish I was." Father Carey said, "People often tell me that, and I suppose I know what it means. But what does it mean to you, Mr.

McBride?" Matt said, "It means—I wouldn't be so miserable, maybe. I wouldn't be so conflicted. I might have saved her." The priest said sympathetically, "Is that what you think being 'Catholic' means? Yes, you'd better come see me. Tomorrow?" They'd spoken for a while longer but Matt hung up without making a specific appointment. Next morning, it would be "Joseph Gavin" he sought.

He'd been drinking before calling Father Carey, to build up his courage. Maybe that explained it.

And he was drinking now, in the Oceanside Inn on Rt. 9 north of Forked River. *He was drinking now* though he'd fully intended to get back to Weymouth if not in time to return to the office, in time for dinner with his family. *He was drinking now* in one of those roadside taverns you see often in south Jersey, and in the Pine Barrens, wood-frame places with windows covered in aluminum foil to keep out, in summer, the blistering heat of the sun. A dazzle of cheap neon tubing advertising beer and an interior smell of beer, cigarette smoke, men's hair lotion and men's bodies. Matt remembered the Oceanside from high school days. Trying to get served with his buddies. You never brought a girl to a place like this. And entering it now, he was hoping someone would call out—"Matt? Matt McBride? Je-sus! It's *you*?" But no one called out, it was twenty years later.

For the past three months Matt had been carrying with him in the glove compartment of the Acura a few fliers and the poster with Duana Zwolle's photograph on it, and some of these he brought into the tavern to pass around to the bartender and the half-dozen men sitting at the bar. Matt was earnest and matter-of-fact knowing it wasn't likely that anyone in this part of Jersey might recognize the *missing girl*, but he felt compelled to try just the same. The men were immediately sympathetic. They passed the materials around, held them to the light and examined them closely. DUANA ZWOLLE, 26. MISSING SINCE DEC. 28. LISMORE, N.J. $50,000 REWARD FOR INFORMATION LEADING TO HER RETURN. One of the men, stroking his short, trimmed beard, said he might've seen this girl—"Or maybe it was on TV? A while back?" Another said there'd been a girl looking like this

passing through last summer, living in Toms River with some guy, or
guys, bikers; he hadn't seen her in a long time, that he knew. The
bartender, a young, fattish guy with sideburns and tinted glasses worn
even in the dim light, frowned at Duana Zwolle's photo, saying som-
berly, "Hell, there's lots of girls lost like this. My own stepsister, in
fact. They run away, and some sick bastard gets hold of 'em. You
can't tell 'em, though. They hitch rides, like, with truckers. Truckers!
Wind up in some swamp in Florida, and nobody knows who the fuck
they are." The bartender's words hovered in the air. The men may
have perceived that Matt McBride winced. An older man said quickly,
"Wish I could help you, son, but this poor girl don't look like anybody
I've seen. Looks like she's maybe Indian or something? I mean from
India, the actual place." Another man asked, doubtfully, "Where's
'Lismore'? Upstate?" When Matt explained that Lismore was about
thirty-five miles north and west of Newark, about halfway between the
Delaware River and New York City, the men began shaking their
heads as if he'd confronted them with a tricky math problem. North
Jersey was a distant place. One said with a low whistle, "Fifty thou!
Sure wish I could help you, mister." Matt decided to give up. Or
maybe he'd try another place. His hands were trembling. *He was
drinking now* and it was a deliberate decision and he didn't want to
lose control. A couple of the men saw the sick, stricken look in his
face and asked belatedly what connection he had with the *missing
girl* and Matt shrugged and said evasively that he knew her family, it
was a terrible thing and he wanted to help in any way he could. The
bartender, overhearing this, said in an incensed voice, "Like I told
you, mister: these young girls, some of 'em, you can't tell 'em shit. I
realize there's some of 'em it ain't their fault, some sick bastard gets
hold of 'em, but others, it *is*. They invite it. They do whatever the hell
they wanta do and you're left behind, is what I'm saying."

Matt finished his beer and thanked the men and left the bar. They
called after him, without irony—"Good luck!"

Somehow, it was 9:09 P.M.

At a pay phone in the next place Matt stopped, somewhere on Rt.
36 near Sea Girt, he dialed his home number. *He was drinking now*

but he was determined not to be irresponsible. Davey answered on the first ring, asking Daddy where he was, if he was O.K., and Tess took the phone from the boy, her voice quick and anxious. Matt told her apologetically that he'd been held up at a meeting with Sid Krell and some others; he'd meant to call earlier, to explain he'd be missing dinner, but the time had slipped by him. Matt believed he was speaking with genuine regret, but without sounding guilty. Though wanting to plead with this woman, his wife. *I love you, forgive me, let me go.* Tess was oddly quiet. Close by, Davey and Graeme were making a good deal of noise. Wasn't it past their bedtime? Matt could hear "Daddy! Dad-*dy*!" Uneasily Matt asked, "What's wrong, Tess?" and Tess said coldly, "It's funny you should mention Sid, Matt. He's just been here, and he was talking about you. He's just left."

**31** Even in his fever state, desperate to get to Forked River and to know, Matt McBride had brought camera equipment with him.

Nighthawk had brought camera equipment with him.

Guessing beforehand it might be one of his nights.

Jesus, he was excited! As in the old speedy amphetamine nights. *He was drinking now* but it felt natural. An extension of his mood. Well under control. Especially tramping in the fresh cold damp wind that blew westward from the Atlantic, whipping the waves to a frenzy and bringing tears to his eyes, Nighthawk was alert and alive and in control. And happy.

Happiest he's been in a goddamned long time.

Since the photos he'd taken in Lismore, photos of mourning, Nighthawk been on the prowl. This new year hadn't been a good time for him. Lovesick for the *missing girl*. And guilt-sick. And his head ringing not knowing what to do about it, or about his life. He had come to believe that the diary of the *missing girl* was a document of truth. If not the truth of fact, the truth of the heart. The truth of the soul. *Our destinies as in a 'cloud of unknowing' braided together before our births.* Nighthawk had lost Duana Zwolle. Night-hawk would find Duana Zwolle. He would find the *missing girl* if he had to torture Joseph Gavin to make him confess. If he had to kill Joseph Gavin! He believed he was capable of such an act, as Nighthawk.

How petty, how confining and cowardly his day-life. Mathias McBride, Jr.! Krell Associates! It had been a mistake to get married, probably it had been a mistake but he had kids now and he loved them, and he loved their mother, too. He wanted to love them, he wanted to be a good, decent husband and father. *Forgive me, let me go! I can't breathe.*

But it was a fact he couldn't deny: Nighthawk's favorite camera in hand, tramping along the windswept beach at Sea Girt, three-foot foaming-white waves and the glimmering lights of houses and roadside businesses behind him, in the distance—he was able at last to breathe. He took a roll of film, and a second roll of film. And again at Bradley Beach, and Beach Isle. It was late now, he'd lost track of time. Nighthawk felt only contempt for time. A gusty flurried moonlight at Beach Isle, which he hadn't seen in twenty years, or more. Prowling the boardwalk, taking pictures of the shut-up fast food restaurants, saltwater taffy and souvenir shops. There was the tall throne-like empty lifeguard chair, long ago in Forked River Matt McBride had been a lifeguard and he'd liked the feeling, the responsibility and the power and fortunately for him he hadn't had to save anyone from drowning, it came back to him now in a rush as he took photos of the lifeguard chair, the empty beach, piles of debris blown like waterlogged corpses against a plank snow fence. *Prowling the night. No happiness like this.*

As a kid he'd first discovered you could "see" through a camera lens. And what he saw blew his mind. So wild, and so beautiful. You needed freedom for it, though. You needed space, and time. You couldn't be on someone's leash. You couldn't give a damn about disappointing someone. *You couldn't love someone except a woman like yourself.*

It was a continual surprise to Nighthawk that whatever vision he retained in memory would be weak, dull, anemic set beside the negatives he snatched from the night. And the prints he could develop from these negatives. As if the eye saw only surfaces, and the camera saw both surfaces and beneath surfaces. Those hours of Nighthawk "sitting watch" as he came to call it along the Turnpike, in the parking lots of 24-hour gas stations and restaurants, outside bus stations, train depots. Close-ups of waitresses he'd gotten to know, who'd liked and trusted him. Truckers. The graveyard shift of the Hoboken Bakery. Among Nighthawk's early published photos which had drawn a good deal of commentary was a sequence titled "The Searchers": he'd been allowed to follow, at a short distance, a police search party near the

George Washington Bridge, on the New Jersey side, using up rolls of film as a November day occluded with storm clouds waned to dusk. The men's figures in raincoats, the men's obscured faces. There was a police photographer with them and Nighthawk had taken shots of him, too. You could see these men were searching for something— but what? (Eventually, they found what they were looking for, a woman's body washed up against rocks at the shore.) Nighthawk hadn't photographed what these men sought, only their searching. *For we are all searchers. In the night.*

You had to see the world as beautiful, and mysterious. You couldn't judge. It wasn't for Nighthawk to judge.

At Asbury Park he stopped at a 7-Eleven store to get a cup of coffee. Recalling those nights he'd slept in his car and woken at dawn not always knowing where he was. The gritty urban sky, rainwashed pavement. But he didn't want to drift off into sleep in his car tonight, it was hell on his neck. Nighthawk wasn't a kid any longer. He could get home to Weymouth by 2 A.M. and sleep in his own bed but the prospect held little attraction for him. He couldn't confront Tess another time tonight. So maybe a motel? There were lots of cheap motels along this strip. Budget Inn, Day's End. One of those anonymous two-storey stucco places with VACANCY signs in bright neon. Years ago Nighthawk had photographed motels like these and their patrons, along Route 1 outside Jersey City. He'd photographed the rooms. And the women who came with the rooms. Hookers who'd been happy to pose for Nighthawk, as long as he paid them, and he'd always paid them generously.

In the 7-Eleven lot he was sitting at the wheel of his parked car sipping black coffee from a foam cup, and liking it that the coffee was hot enough to burn his mouth, he hated lukewarm coffee, and at that moment he happened to notice a figure hurriedly leaving the store and crossing the lot, a young woman in jeans and an oversized purple canvas jacket, her dark hair whipping in the wind and her face turned toward him for a fleet, teasing moment. *Was it—her? Duana Zwolle?*

Matt stared at the girl as she crossed a littered vacant lot to a pickup or sports utility vehicle parked on a parallel road, its headlights on.

She, too, was carrying a foam cup. Matt's heart had begun to pound violently. In that instant, all his senses came alive. Clumsily he set aside the coffee, spilling some on the front seat of the car, and grabbed for his camera, and was in pursuit.

Yet he was cautious of alarming her. Calling tentatively, "Excuse me? Is it—Duana? Duana Zwolle?"

The girl didn't hear him. Matt followed her to the parked vehicle where someone, a shadowy figure, was waiting. He gripped his camera against his chest; he was utterly dazed, confused. "Excuse me?" he tried again, "—is it—Duana?"

This time, the girl glanced back at him, frowning. In a blur of harsh headlights she was a stranger. A short, thin, wiry woman in her thirties, with a swarthy complexion, sharp features; frightened eyes and an angry mouth. "Get the hell away, mister!" she shouted. "I don't know you." Matt stood staring after her. He stammered, "I'm sorry. I thought—you were someone I know." "Well, I'm not. So fuck off," the woman said, climbing into the vehicle on the passenger's side. The driver backed roughly around, and sped away throwing up gravel in derision.

Nighthawk photographed the rapidly departing vehicle. The red taillights, and the streetlights beyond. The lights of the Asbury Diner. Headlights on the beachfront road that led to Long Branch. He'd come away with a memento of this encounter, and he'd make it an image of tawdry heartbreak and beauty. That was Nighthawk's consolation. That was Nighthawk's gift. The world was *sangsāra*—"Net of Illusion." But illusion was goddamned better than nothing, if that was all you could get.

III

The Reckoning

32 NAME UNKNOWN. Now that his enemies had declared themselves, he felt a newborn strength & certainty of purpose. Of his own suffering face he created a plaster cast of purest white. For the mere fact of him, that was "Joseph Gavin" living in a rundown trailer outside Clinton Falls, New Jersey, was not the truth of him, that was NAME UNKNOWN.

This mask, one of NAME UNKNOWN's most startling creations. A mask of Crucifixion & Beauty. He had not viewed himself as an angel of wrath but seeing the eyes like blind bulbs transfixed from within, and the mouth in its grimace (for he had had to leave a conduit in the plaster, in order to breathe), he saw that it was so.

The face, affixed to a plaster head. And hair of finespun silver and gold to adorn the head & chin.

THE KINGDOM OF WRATH IS WITHIN.

He would depart. Yet not far. He would become yet again INVISIBLE. For God who is the God of Invisible Beings would always bless him, & laugh with him at the ignorance of his enemies.

Where flame walks upright gliding swiftly along the Earth as a shadow no ordinary men dare TOUCH.

Yet unable to take with him at this time the sacred figures. THE MARRIAGE OF HEAVEN AND HELL. For these, he would one day soon return, & trust to INVISIBILITY to cloak him.

He did not recall his enemy's stated name. NAME UNKNOWN was not one to honor names. Which are mere breath, of no substance. Yet he had reason to believe that this enemy was a plainclothes detective like the other two who had come to his trailer weeks before, to persecute NAME UNKNOWN, only yet more deceitful. *I am a collector of contemporary American art.* And he, NAME UNKNOWN, had believed!

If ever he saw this enemy again, out of INVISIBILITY he would strike, to kill. He had his chisel, his hammer & a fine-honed carving knife. Never had he killed a man before, for never had any man aroused the wrath of NAME UNKNOWN to such a degree. And yet there was the wisdom—*A dead body revenges not injuries.*

From his welding jobs he had saved some money, & from the woman he would receive more at his request. The Brough woman who was a nurse's aide in Hopatcong. To this woman NAME UNKNOWN spoke forcefully, eyes blazing in light she cringed before. *You will not betray NAME UNKNOWN, will you? For Judas who betrayed the living Christ hanged himself, & carrion birds feasted on his rank flesh.* With fearful veined eyes & her puffy face quivering in worry this woman looked upon NAME UNKNOWN. For she was only thirty-four years old but would be mistaken for a woman of fifty. For she was heavyset & short of breath; her breath stale with cigarette smoke in disobedience of NAME UNKNOWN she adored & her husband-to-be of whom she was so proud. Claiming she could not help herself, needing cigarettes, which angered him. Which made his fingers twitch in an unspeakable lust to bury themselves in the fatty folds of her neck & SQUEEZE, & SQUEEZE. For such weakness infuriated him who had conquered his own weakness as a youth. Yet there was the woman's son Randy who adored NAME UNKNOWN as his lost father. Slow-witted & diabetic yet one of God's angel-children of simplicity. And when the strange fit came upon him, & he screamed, & kicked, & bit his lips & tongue until they bled, & his eyes rolled up inside his head, it was NAME UNKNOWN who clasped him firmly in his strong embrace speaking soothingly to him, & calming him. If misfortune befell the Brough woman, this boy's soul would be riven.

You will not betray me, Shirley, will you?—gripping the lard-face in his fingers that were the powerful talon-fingers of the sculptor & could rip the face from its bone. And the woman cried *Why would I betray you, Joseph? I love you.* And sobs wracked her bosom, & a spillage of tears from out of her glistening eyes.

Gazed upon her then with sudden eyes of kindness, & the blessing of NAME UNKNOWN that suffused him at such times, unexpected & unwilled as grace. Placating her fear—*I will believe you, then. I will allow you to love me, & I will believe you. And you & the child will come to no injury, so long as this is so. By this covenant NAME UNKNOWN will swear.*

* * *

Before slipping into INVISIBILITY, he purchased from a cousin of the Brough woman a double-barreled .410 shotgun sawed off to assure a wide lethal spread of buckshot up close. Once previous, in Salem, Delaware, NAME UN- KNOWN had been forced to protect himself against his enemies by fashion- ing a booby trap in his residence, which had not gone off. This time, too, he hoped it would not go off, to cause NAME UNKNOWN himself trouble. Yet he had to protect himself. He had no choice. The .410 he loaded with two shells & positioned inside his trailer, tied to a chair & aimed for the front doorway at about the height of a man's torso, & twine so positioned across the trigger and attached to the doorknob, that any opening of the door would cause the shotgun to discharge. Like a cobweb of twine, it was. A trap to catch his enemies.

NAME UNKNOWN was an artist & not a vindictive man. Never had he wished to injure any human being. Yet he hoped the first detective through the door, to take the brunt of the shot in the fullness of his chest, and be blasted nearly in two, would be the detective who had deceived NAME UN- KNOWN with the lie of claiming a desire to see his art; & had then revealed himself as a spy, speaking of Forked River & the first of the sacrifices. *He knows! He must die.*

NAME UNKNOWN then squirmed through a rear window of his trailer, & was gone.

This window was so narrow a space you would swear no full-grown man *but rather a lithe, sinewy snake* had made its way through the opening, to vanish in the wood lot beyond.

33

It was justice he wanted.

Justice, and revenge.

Matt several times returned to Clinton Falls, to Joseph Gavin's mobile home, looking for him. *So it's dangerous. He's the one who should be frightened of me.* In April, a new season, in bright daylight, Matt recklessly drove his white Acura up the mud-rutted lane of Gavin's property and went to knock at the front door of the mobile home. He shook the doorknob, hard.

(Seeing that Gavin's Ford pickup was gone. Guessing no one was home.)

There was a manic energy in this. A compulsiveness. When he was in this state, Tess, and his sons, were wary of him.

To Graeme, Matt tried to explain himself. "When you grow up, you'll want people to be treated fairly. It's what we call 'justice.' Sometimes they're not, and you want to make things right. Somehow." Graeme stared wide-eyed at his Daddy, not knowing if he should laugh, or solemnly repeat what Daddy said.

"Jus-*tice*?"

Matt didn't speak to his sons of revenge.

He brought his camera to Clinton Falls, and shot rolls of film on Gavin's property. Maybe this was trespassing. Maybe it would result in evidence. Nighthawk trusted his gut instinct. Even to lead him into error. (Which might be fruitful error—who knew?)

On his first return visit, after the revelation in Forked River, Matt, seeing that no one was home, stepped onto a concrete block to peer into the front of the trailer: there, only a few feet away, was what appeared to be Joseph Gavin's head, in white, positioned on a table-top. The blank white eyes gazed with mocking impassivity at Matt McBride.

"Jesus!" Matt lost his balance, dropped his camera and almost fell into a pile of rubbish. If he'd landed on his back, he might've cracked his spine or his skull.

What was it? A white plaster head, a death-mask of a face. It was the face of NAME UNKNOWN made by himself. When Matt looked more closely, he saw that the eyes were blank, blind bulbs and the mouth was subtly distended, pursed as if the subject were breathing through a straw. *Because he'd needed to breathe through a straw, through a hole in the plaster.* On top of the head and glued to the chin were fine, glinting threads, maybe fishing line. NAME UNKNOWN's hair and beard.

Matt had to admire the freaky thing. It was ugly, and it was ingenious. *He wants us to believe he's crazy. That will be his defense when he's arrested.*

Nighthawk photographed the head of NAME UNKNOWN through the trailer window. Twenty-four shots. He was fascinated, even as he was repelled and disgusted. The man was his enemy, the man was a killer. Still, Nighthawk couldn't resist.

NAME UNKNOWN: Portrait of a Murderer would be the title of the sequence. That weird ghastly white human head with synthetic glinting hair and beard, blind eyes and a jeering, just perceptibly pursed mouth. A human head, in white plaster, on a tabletop. Viewed through a grimy window and a rust-flecked, cobwebbed screen.

Matt circled the trailer, taking shots. Was it trespassing, prowling around a man's home when he wasn't there? He was hoping Gavin would turn up, to confront him.

He was wondering what he'd say to Gavin, armed with his new knowledge.

I know you. I know what you've done. Murderer!

Matt knew he'd made a mistake, tipping his hand to his enemy. He'd been hot-headed and reckless. No professional would have blundered as Matt had. He'd risked being injured or killed: Gavin might have attacked him with one of those sculpting tools. At the very least, Matt had driven his enemy into hiding. For all he knew, Gavin might be scared away permanently.

At the barn, Matt discovered to his disappointment that both the front and rear doors were padlocked, and the barn's few windows had been boarded up from within. He tried to peer through, but saw little. He wondered if the clumsy doll-figures were still inside; he supposed, yes, they must be, which was why the windows were boarded up. He'd wanted to take pictures of *The Marriage of Heaven and Hell* through a window, with a telephoto lens.

He'd been thinking: maybe the doll-figures contained body parts of actual, murdered women? Their blood, or hair? Maybe Duana Zwolle was one of these, transfigured into NAME UNKNOWN's clumsy art.

The only way to get inside that barn was to smash a door with a battering ram. If police had a search warrant. With a battering ram, you could get into a virtual fortress. But you did need a search warrant, police had to convince a judge they had sufficient evidence.

How could you convince police another man was a murderer, if they suspected *you*?

Matt circled the barn, taking photographs. Even closeups of the shuttered windows. He could envision the female figures inside, forlorn, trapped. Their plain, blank faces and silly glass eyes.

Save us. Don't forsake us.

But it was only the wind in the trees: those faint, melancholy cries.

Matt was beginning to feel spooked. He saw, or seemed to see, movement in the corner of his eye. When he turned—nothing! Only traffic out on the highway, a flock of noisy crows in a field.

Was NAME UNKNOWN watching? If so, he kept his distance.

When Matt was Nighthawk, with his camera in hand, he became acutely sensitive to what you might call *pathos of place*. Plenty of *pathos of place* here. Gavin's shabby trailer on concrete blocks, a rusted gas tank at the rear, litter, mounds of rotted leaves and the debris of winter storm damage. Even the sky looked impoverished above Gavin's property.

In the small town, Matt had made discreet inquiries and learned that the land and trailer belonged to a retired couple now living in Florida, who rented it out and knew little about their tenants.

Joseph Gavin had moved here almost two years ago. No one knew much about him except he was "quiet"—"sort of strange"—"kept to himself."

Matt, prowling the property, was looking for signs of recently dug earth. But the bastard was too smart for that. *If he'd buried Duana Zwolle anywhere, it would be the Pine Barrens.*

The vast, desolate acres of the Barrens. White cedar pines, bleached sand, marshes to the horizon. Where no one would ever find her, if Gavin wasn't made to confess.

Matt had an impulse to break into Gavin's trailer. Kick in the door, smash the plaster head on the table. *But maybe he's booby-trapped it. A bomb or a shotgun inside, rigged to go off if the door is forced.*

It was a sudden, warning thought. Out of nowhere.

Was that what Nighthawk would have done, in NAME UN-KNOWN's place? *A booby trap. To blow my head off.*

Once at the end of March, and twice in early April, Matt made the fifty-eight-mile trip to check out Gavin's trailer, and each time he found no one around, no signs of recent occupancy, no fresh tire marks in the muddy lane. He'd about given up expecting to see anyone, any signs of life. And each time he couldn't resist looking into the trailer window to see the ghastly white head and blank, jeering face of his enemy inside. *Laughing at me. Mocking me. Knowing I'd be back.*

Jules Cliffe had told Matt that the search for Duana Zwolle had entered a "lower voltage" phase and was no longer top priority even among Weymouth police. Matt wasn't surprised: the case had dropped out of the media. Local and state police had followed dozens of leads but these had come to nothing or were stalled; there'd been hundreds of tips from would-be informants, hoping for the $50,000 reward, but none of these, either, had come to anything. Matt was relieved to hear that virtually everyone who'd known Duana Zwolle more than casually had been investigated, as he'd been investigated—but trails led no-where. Matt wanted to tell Cliffe that *he knew who the killer was, even if he couldn't prove it*! But he understood what Cliffe's response would be, and how the lawyer would tell the next person he saw what Matt

McBride had said, and that person would tell several others, word would spread rapidly through Weymouth and vicinity—to what purpose? Matt had learned to keep his mouth shut.

Since the New Year, he'd learned what consequences the most innocent remarks can have, let alone innocent, unpremeditated actions.

Each time Matt returned to Gavin's property he checked the mailbox at the roadside, of course. Appropriately, this battered old box had no name on its sides. The only mail Gavin received were gas and electric bills, and second notices for these bills, and advertising circulars addressed to "tenant." But one afternoon in mid-April, Matt discovered to his surprise that the box was empty.

So Gavin, or someone in his place, had picked up the mail.

So he'll be back. Of course. He can't leave The Marriage of Heaven and Hell behind.

It was then that Matt thought of enlisting the help of the young garage mechanic at the Amoco station up the road, who'd originally told Matt how to find Gavin's trailer. He was a kid in his twenties with a scruffy biker's beard and a gold death's-head stud in his left earlobe who'd indicated clearly to Matt, man-to-man, that he held the man he knew as "Joseph Gavin" in bemused contempt as a local character, a "weirdo" who counted out payment at the garage in small bills and coins—"A faggot-type, like. With that *hair*." Matt told the young man, whose name was Todd, "Look, if you see that Gavin is back, will you call me? My name's McBride. You can leave a message on my answering service if I'm not home."

Todd stared at the four fifty-dollar bills Matt had placed in his greasy hand, which, Matt promised, would be doubled if, or when, Gavin returned, and Matt was notified. The young man's sloe eyes shimmered with surprise and childlike greed. He said, "Mister, for four hundred bucks, I'd tag my old man."

34

He'd touch nothing, Matt promised.

Wouldn't take any photographs. Wouldn't steal any mementos. He'd stay only ten, fifteen minutes. He only just wanted to *see*.

"See what, mister?"

"Where she lived."

"And what's that to you?"

"Everything."

The caretaker of the Mill Row building in which Duana Zwolle had lived was a man in his sixties with a drinker's venous, enlarged nose and bloodhound eyes. He was doubtful at first. He'd needed to be convinced. He was worried, he told Matt McBride, about "desecrating" the memory of the young woman whom he'd known as a "quiet, good girl"—a "reliable tenant"—who hadn't given wild parties or dealt in drugs as the tabloid papers claimed.

Matt listened respectfully to this. He raised his initial offer of $100 to $200. Eventually, he would hand over $250 in cash.

The caretaker said, in a mournful, whining voice, "Well. But I could get fired for this, mister. Maybe sued by the Zwolles. Doing a favor for you, and I don't even know you. All kinds of reporters and TV people were around here begging me to let them in a few weeks ago and I told them 'no way.' That was my orders from the cops and the Zwolle family. Now, it's quieter. Like you see. There's other things in the news. Nobody ever comes by except a few times Miss Zwolle's father, one of her sisters. They've got their own keys. They don't bother me. They own the girl's stuff, y'know, as next-of-kin, and they're keeping up payments on the rent thinking she'll be back. The owner would just as soon clear out the Zwolle loft and repaint and lease it to some new tenant. But the mother, Mrs. Zwolle, won't allow that." The caretaker sighed, shaking his head. "Somebody told me she's sick now, Mrs. Zwolle. In a hospital up in Maine. You know the family?"

"No. I don't know the Zwolle family."

"There's a sister, looks like her. But don't act like her. The father, he took it hard like you'd expect. The mother was just—well, in a state of shock. If it was a daughter of mine—!" Again the caretaker sighed. He'd been observing Matt covertly as if trying to place him. "Were you one of Miss Zwolle's artist-friends, mister? Your face is sort of familiar."

"I—I was a friend. But not a close friend."

"Miss Zwolle didn't have many friends. She was choosy, you could tell. Some days she'd talk to me, and smile and be friendly; other days, she'd look right through me like she was in her own world. That's what an artist is like, I guess. But she must've had one too many friends, y'know? That she let in, that night. *I* never saw who it was."

The old man spoke broodingly, rubbing at his unshaven cheeks.

As if wanting Matt to know *Maybe it was you, mister. But I can't know that, can I.*

They worked it out that Matt would drop by on a weekday around 6 P.M. This was an ideal time when the several shops in the building would be closed, their proprietors and customers gone; yet not so late that activity at that end of the building would draw attention. Most nights, the caretaker checked the premises at that time, and another time around midnight. Since Duana Zwolle's disappearance, security had been stepped up. There were powerful new lights along Mill Row where previously there'd been none. Many of the residents had been negligent about locking doors and windows even at night. Lismore had always been that kind of place. And Duana Zwolle had been one of those people—"Too damned trusting, y'know? Whoever came to get her, he hadn't needed to break in, the police said. She'd let him in. Or, maybe, he just opened the door and *walked in*."

The man's voice quavered lewdly. He was leading Matt up the outside, wooden steps to Duana Zwolle's loft. Matt's heart had begun to pound. He'd been anticipating this moment for weeks. *I haven't been here before—have I?* The red-lacquered door, the very doorknob of that door, looked somehow familiar to him. He felt a moment's vertigo, like a dreamer stumbling on steps or at the threshold of a dream, and waking himself.

Only a few times before in his life had he paid out bribes to be admitted to places otherwise closed to him; but he'd never been taken into a crime scene. He wondered if such a trespass itself was a crime?

The net flung over me, & over you.

Almost, as the caretaker pushed open the door, Matt heard Duana Zwolle's low, throaty voice.

Then they were inside. The caretaker switched on a glaring overhead light and hastily shut the door. He was a stout man, short of breath from the stairs.

Matt said quietly, not at all impolitely, "You can leave now, thank you. I'll shut and lock the door when I'm finished."

The caretaker protested, "Hey, no—I better stay. I could get fired if—"

"Just leave, please. I don't have a camera, and I'm not going to take anything. But I'd like to be alone."

"But, mister—"

"I'd like to be alone."

Seeing Matt's face, the caretaker left, muttering to himself.

Matt's first, unexpected impression of Duana Zwolle's loft was that it more resembled a storage room than a place in which a young woman artist had lived and worked. There was a smell of old, damp stone; the air had a refrigerated, stale quality; there was a skylight in the ceiling, but the walls had been stripped bare and showed myriad patterns of waterstains; the old pine floors were scuffed; carpets had been rolled up and dragged against a wall. Furniture, too, had been pushed aside. Large art books, some of them of very high quality, were piled in stacks on a workbench, and there were stacks of what Matt supposed was collage material everywhere. Scattered across the floor were partly packed cardboard boxes. An antique dressmaker's mirror had been tilted back, and mirrored only the ceiling. There was an aged tin sink; stiff, yellowed photographs glued to pieces of cardboard on the counter. Matt's attention was drawn to the crudely slashed, vandalized remains of the striking collages that had comprised *A Garden of Earthly and Unearthly Delights* at which he'd stared for so long in the Weymouth gallery last summer. These had been laid out on a waist-high workbench and on the surrounding floor, like dissected corpses. Clearly, police investigators had gone through all this material and they, or more likely the Zwolle family, had rearranged it. Matt winced to think how this devastation would look to Duana Zwolle if she ever saw it.

Feeling how his love for her suffused even this violated space.

Quickly Matt walked through the rooms like a man in a dream, switching on lights. Kitchen, bathroom, bedroom. He needed to make sure that the loft was in fact empty. No one hiding. No one waiting.

He was wearing gloves: since he'd become a suspect in a criminal investigation, he'd learned to be cautious.

Catching sight, in a hallway, of paintings, framed photographs and other artworks stacked against the wall, and one of these, he saw to his surprise, was a Nighthawk photograph. He squatted to examine it. Not a print, but a photograph taken from an issue of *New Jersey Life* of perhaps two years before. It was a photograph of which Matt was proud, a lucky shot, stark yet poetic, depicting the industrial hell-haze of Elizabeth, New Jersey: elegantly tall, columnar Con Edison smokestacks rimmed in flame against a smudged night sky, a luridly white, perfectly round moon balanced on one of the smokestacks. Duana Zwolle had framed this photograph carefully, with matting, under glass. Matt was deeply moved. He regretted it wasn't a print, only a magazine page, glossy and thin.

Matt remembered the circumstances of the photograph: he'd been parked on a shoulder of the Turnpike, mesmerized by the unexpected beauty, the dazzle of lights. You knew you should hate this industrial wasteland but, to the camera's eye, it *was* beauty, and it *was* art. The air was so virulent, smelling of something like rotted yeast, Matt couldn't keep the car window down for more than a few minutes.

Preserved now, in this frame. In the residence of the *missing girl* whom Matt McBride had scarcely known.

Matt returned to the front room, Duana Zwolle's studio. It was a cavernous space, unheated, drafty, with a high, waterstained ceiling. There was only one window, fronting the river, and across this were white louver shutters, tightly closed. Matt knew that the Zwolle family had installed these shutters to prevent photographers and TV cameras from violating Duana's space. "And here I am—'Nighthawk.' Forgive me!"

He'd have time to feel guilty, later. To berate himself as a shit. Later.

Trembling with excitement, and a sense of dread, Matt surveyed the wreckage in the studio. The vandalized collages, the overall look of displaced things. A crime scene. Yet everything he saw fascinated him, for these were Duana Zwolle's possessions; in this place, Duana Zwolle had lived her intense, secret life. *I have never been here before. Have I?* Here was a massive book with a torn cover, *Three Thousand Years of Chinese Art.* A battered paperback, *The Tibetan Book of the Dead. Zen Meditations, Classic Japanese Watercolors, Art of Antiquity.* In other piles were *Magritte, Photographs of Edward Weston, Mondrian, Cézanne, Nineteenth-Century American Landscape Painting, Edvard Munch, Classic Italian Art, The Sculpture of Picasso*—the jumbled accumulation of years, of an ambitious art student. This side of Duana Zwolle, unknown to Matt, touched him deeply. He'd never been much of a student of art history, even of photography. Duana would have taught him so much.

It was painful to see the collages in their mutilated condition. Whoever had slashed them—of course, it was NAME UNKNOWN—must have worked quickly, and deliberately. But why take the time? He must have overcome Duana Zwolle, tied her up or knocked her insensible, then set to work destroying the collages with a knife, (or a chisel) he'd possibly brought with him. Probably, he'd destroyed them in front of Duana Zwolle, to inflict maximum pain.

Matt wiped at his eyes. He was beginning to feel sick. This was upsetting to see, and it was upsetting to think about. For months the *missing girl* had been a media phenomenon: her image in newspapers and on TV; her abduction, and this "studio-loft in Lismore" an idea merely. Now, it was real. It was ugly, depressing, and real. For here were the collages, irreparably damaged. Broken puzzles. Puzzles not to be solved. The art of collage is an art of careful selection and juxtaposition but now these meticulously assembled canvases had been reduced to their individual components, or nearly. Matt had a longing to repair some of the most obvious damage, but he wouldn't have known how to begin. The artist had made a pattern out of various materials including aged, sepia-toned photographs she'd probably acquired at local antique shops and flea markets; some of these were of formally posed, dignified corpses in elaborate coffins, their waxen faces peaceful in death, taken in funeral parlors in the early years of the century. Matt wondered what these striking but random images of strangers had meant to Duana Zwolle. Maybe she'd been guided sheerly by instinct, choosing faces that appealed to her. As she'd chosen Nighthawk.

Contemplating the ruins of *A Garden of Earthly and Unearthly Delights*, Matt was reminded of Joseph Gavin's awkward female figures, whose thick bodies were adorned with a confusion of primitive designs and images. *The Marriage of Heaven and Hell*—Gavin had proudly called them. But there was no true comparison between his work and Duana Zwolle's, for Duana's collages had been both profound and witty, beautiful and disturbing, with their own distinctive, idiosyncratic style; while the work of NAME UNKNOWN was mawkish, amateurish.

If I was NAME UNKNOWN, I'd be goddamned jealous, too.

Maybe it was simply that. Jealousy?

The rage of the mediocre artist against the gifted?

Yet why focus upon Duana Zwolle, in that case. For NAME UNKNOWN couldn't fail to be aware of other, numerous contemporary artists living in the New Jersey–New York region, more gifted than he, and far more successful. There had to be another, more specific connection. *He was in love with her, a sick, draining love. To be free of that love, he had to kill her.* She'd been a talented artist, and he'd wanted that talent for himself. There were primitive peoples who'd

eaten the hearts of their enemies, to acquire their strength. And sometimes their brains. Was that the logic of NAME UNKNOWN?

That was why he'd killed Marcey Mason, too. She'd been a pretty,
popular girl of seventeen with a beautiful soprano voice. At least, it
had seemed beautiful, it had seemed "the real thing," at Forked River
High twenty years ago. Joe Gavin, the vocational arts major, sullen,
silent, staring at this golden girl from the shadowy edge of high school
life, had been infatuated with her, and had needed to hurt her. Both
Marcey Mason and Duana Zwolle had sunk deep into Gavin's embittered consciousness unknowingly. He'd been haunted by them and
infuriated by them and he'd kidnapped them, to make them *his*.

Sick bastard! Think I don't know?

Think I don't know you?

Matt was reminded of Nighthawk's old, melancholy yearning years
ago in his twenties. A wanderer, a loner. Prowling the city streets. In
residential neighborhoods catching glimpses, through carelessly
drawn blinds, of domestic lives; seeing human silhouettes, shadows.
How fascinating they'd seemed to him. How mysterious, inaccessible.
Through the lens of his camera they were enhanced. Couples kissing,
touching. On the street, or in passing cars. In doorways. In parks.
Above the river. In rain. In mist. In memory. Nighthawk, a raw-boned
gangling kid, would feel a pang of desire as he took his photographs,
his hundreds of photographs, though in fact, *and he understood this
at the time*, he could have had a domestic, settled life of his own any
time he'd seriously wanted it: a woman who adored him, and married,
erotic, tender love. And children.

But Nighthawk hadn't wanted that life, much. It was the ache of
desire he'd wanted.

The voyeur doesn't want the object of his desire. Only desire.

For desire is the fuel of art. Consummated desire, the enemy of art.

It seemed to Matt probable that, given his nature, Joseph Gavin
must have victimized other young women and girls. He'd created six
of those mannequin figures and he'd said there would be three more.
It had become a deliberate quest. He had to be stopped! But if police

had linked Duana Zwolle's disappearance to other, similar disappearances in this part of the country, in recent years, Matt hadn't heard a word of it.

From Jules Cliffe, with whom Matt was still in contact, he'd learned that New Jersey forensics investigators had yet to establish that any "crime" had occurred in this loft on the evening of December 28, 1997. Cliffe had pointed out to Matt with lawyerly logic that you couldn't prove that Duana Zwolle hadn't simulated an abduction herself. She might have trashed her own art and ransacked her own rooms. Her abandoned car near the Delaware River, and the cashmere shawl stained with her blood, were no more conclusive. For many *missing persons* aren't in fact missing, only absent. "Stranger things have happened," Cliffe told Matt, with satisfaction. "Which is why it's difficult for the state to prosecute for murder without a body, and why it should be difficult." He'd paused, smiling at Matt. As if nudging him in the ribs. *If you killed the girl, Matt McBride, and the body's never recovered—I can get you off, probably. For a fee.*

It was a local rumor that the *missing girl* might have staged her own disappearance. Made it look like an "abduction." She'd done this to take revenge on a lover, maybe. The rumor, repeated by Tess and her friends, had originated with Sid Krell, Matt knew. Though the wily old buzzard had attributed it to other sources.

When in doubt, blame the victim.

Matt was feeling a touch of vertigo. He saw himself as a man squatting at the edge of an abyss. Before him in these ruined collages there was a great drop, and darkness. His sons were anxious to know: *Where do you go, Daddy, when you disappear? When you die?*

Daddy hadn't a clue.

Nor did Daddy know what love was, any longer. A man's love for a woman. He'd thought he knew, but he'd been mistaken.

Tess would angrily dismiss her husband's preoccupation with the *missing girl* as Nighthawk's influence. All that was "strange"—"unhealthy"—"morbid" in Matt. All that Tess disliked and feared.

The converted mill was drafty. Wind blew from the river, and the walls weren't adequately insulated. Duana Zwolle had lived in this rough-hewn setting, this place of Bohemian romance, because she hadn't much money. And she hadn't much money because she had integrity: she'd refused to sell her talent for a steady income.

Unlike Matt who'd been eager, a young married man, to sell what talent he had to the highest bidder.

Matt felt hairs stir at the nape of his neck. Was someone in the room with him? Close behind him, her fingers gently touching him? Consoling him for his failure. Yet somehow still she loved him, she had faith in him. *We will be together I know. This side of the grave or the other.*

Matt had a sudden impulse to remove one of the old photos from the collages and slip it into his pocket. Who would know? Matt, at least, would cherish it. Many of the photos, once part of an intricate mosaic, were no longer attached to the canvas and had been placed arbitrarily on top of it, by the forensics team perhaps. Strangers had sifted through every square inch of the loft. Carpet fibers examined, every surface dusted for fingerprints, footprints. Every square inch of the victim's life scoured.

A sad, torn, sepia-colored photo caught Matt's eye. Two girls of about fourteen in long dresses, dark-haired, dark-eyed, seated together in an old-fashioned swing, matching parasols on their shoulders. These were girls long since grown into adult women, and probably they were no longer living. But how vivid, their eyes! their shy smiles! Neither girl looked much like Duana Zwolle but there was a spiritual kinship among them, Matt believed.

Take it! No one will know.

Duana would have wanted you to take it.

But no, he couldn't. He'd promised the caretaker. Even if no one would miss it, Nighthawk was no thief.

Matt went to the front window and opened the louver shutter just slightly. He supposed he should turn off the overhead light, but he was certain no one was outside. This end of Mill Row was deserted. He was looking out over the Weymouth River and the farther shore which was obscured in mist. Since he'd come into the loft, the sky had rapidly darkened. The wind was rising. He seemed to recall that he'd once stood here, with Duana, in the dark. After lovemaking, and they'd been spent and silent gazing out at the river. Tonight, the river was lightly rippled by wind, blowing against the current; that night, it had been turbulent, waves crashing against the rocky shore. The Weymouth River was only one-third as wide as the Delaware but its current was as rapid, or more rapid. They'd stood with their arms around each other's waist, naked, warm, and Duana had said *The river is so beautiful, like the sky. It scares me sometimes, this will continue after we're gone. As if we've never been.*

These words Matt heard as distinctly as if Duana were beside him now, gazing out at the river.

At the same time, with the lucidity that came to him at such lonely, reckless moments, Matt McBride knew that Duana Zwolle had never said those words. They'd never been together at this window, and they'd never made love. Nighthawk had never touched the young woman, nor had she touched him, though she'd written about their love in her diary. Matt understood this. At least intermittently, he understood. He'd succumbed to a spell. It was love, but it was more than love. Like a man who has been galvanized by religious faith, given a new, vital life, he both knew and did not know that his faith was groundless. He couldn't bear to know. He couldn't bear to give up Duana Zwolle. He believed that, if she were miraculously restored to him, he would leave his family at once and join his life to hers.

This side of the grave. Or the other.

For his marriage with Tess was nearing its end. They were like doomed passengers in a speeding, careening car, a car with no one at the wheel; they could see the impending disaster yet neither would reach for the wheel. There was a gathering tension between them, yet a paralysis. Matt came home late; Tess herself was frequently gone. The boys were at school, or with a babysitter, or, as she'd done twice in the past month, Tess took them for the weekend to their grandparents' sprawling house in Connecticut. Davey and Graeme loved their Grandma and Grandpa who doted upon them, as they doted upon Tess, their beautiful daughter, and their only child. From the start of their marriage, Matt had known he couldn't compete with his in-laws in loving Tess; she was a childlike woman, at times a childish woman, basking in love and attention like one of those rare, exquisite orchids that fade and die under routine care but, with special care, thrive remarkably. *You see, someone knows how to cherish me!* Tess seemed to be announcing to Matt, each time she returned from her parents' home. Matt had said, "Maybe I should be the one to leave for a few days. Maybe you'd be happier." Coolly Tess had replied, "Maybe." But it had ended at that.

Matt quickly closed the louver shutters.

"I should leave. It's time."

But Duana Zwolle's loft held him. He'd been imagining it so long.

He peered into the kitchen at the rear of the studio, a narrow alcove with a single high window looking out upon pine trees; this window hadn't been shuttered like the others, presumably because it was so small. In overhead light the kitchen was all glazed, gleaming surfaces. Matt supposed that Duana Zwolle had laid the earthen-colored tiles by hand. Almost, he could see her lithe, small-boned figure silhouetted against the wall. The kitchen had been spared trashing. Some-one had tidied it up, put things away. There was a light coating of dust over the tile surfaces but the burners of the small electric stove were clean and the aluminum sink was spotless. There were a number of canned goods in the cupboards, but nothing in the squat Pullman refrigerator. Only just that stale, dead odor of a refrigerator whose power has been switched off.

On a wall near the window were several watercolor sketches of the river, unsigned. These were subtle, delicate paintings executed with a few strokes of a brush, Japanese-influenced. Matt studied these, which must have been Duana Zwolle's work, yet very different from the collages. His respect for her talent deepened.

And in the bedroom, seeing an old brass bed with pillows and quilts piled on it, a bed whose mattress, sheets and coverings had been examined by forensics experts for blood traces, for semen and hairs— Matt felt a powerful, choking emotion. It was love, but also protec-tiveness; a yearning to make things right, if only he knew how. He'd come too late in her life. He had to figure that the bed, a charming old bed, had been totally remade with a fresh mattress cover, laundered sheets and blankets, by the Zwolles, in readiness for Duana Zwolle's imminent return. They didn't want to give up hope. Matt wondered what stories they'd been telling themselves—her family. How long these stories could endure before they began to crumble.

This bedroom, very small, was less drafty than the big front room, with attractive stenciled designs on the walls, dark maroon on cream, which Duana Zwolle had surely done herself. There was a junk-shop stained glass chandelier. A Shaker-style bureau. A single small, horizontal window, shuttered like the window in the front room. Here too art books and magazines were stacked on every available surface. All the wall hangings had been removed and were stacked in a corner. Matt recalled that Duana Zwolle's assailant had left behind a crudely executed, obscene drawing on her bed. Oriana had obligingly sketched it for Matt, more provocatively than he'd liked. Female breasts, genitals. A simian face meant to mock the victim's dark skin and small features. If NAME UNKNOWN had left this memento, allegedly in the style of Duana Zwolle's former lover Nicholas Roche, he must have more talent, and be shrewder, than Matt had thought.

Unconsciously, Matt was drawing his gloved fingertips across one of the quilts on the bed. This was a faded, intricately designed quilt composed of squares, triangles and rectangles, starbursts of bright color against a midnight-blue background. An old quilt, softened by numerous launderings. *Nighthawk had purchased this quilt for his lover Duana at an antique shop in the Weymouth Valley. The same place they'd found the funky brass bed.* She'd caused him to cherish things he'd hardly noticed before. She'd caused him to reconsider his life. There she lay curled up beneath the quilt, naked; dark shining hair spread across a pillow, her forehead lightly in sweat after their lovemaking. Her eyes smiled up at him as he leaned over to kiss her. Her lips moved, in a whisper—but Matt couldn't hear. In a mirror on the bureau, part hidden by a pile of books, his anguished face stared out at him, a trapped face. His eyes were sheathed in shadow and there was a sharp crease between his eyebrows. His hair, which needed cutting, was an unnatural shade of metallic silver, thickly whorled as a sheep's, and windblown. Though Matt had shaved that morning, he badly needed a shave now.

Is that me, the man I've become? Jesus.

No woman could ever love him again. He'd become a desperate man. An obsessed man. What had Duana called it—*a hungry ghost.*

On a table at the back of the room were miscellaneous items. One of them, which immediately caught Matt's eye, was a crystal dove, nearly life-sized. Matt lifted it—yes, it was heavy. And expensive. An elegant piece of sculpted glass by Steuben, but disfigured by a worm-like crack that ran through it. This must be Sid Krell's gift to Duana Zwolle. An embittered old man's clumsy attempt at revenge. Matt felt a stab of rage at Krell. Wanting to *hurt that girl so she'd feel it!* Matt had to wonder whether Krell, not Gavin, was responsible for Duana's disappearance. *He* had a more immediate motive. *He* might well have hired someone to hurt her.

"Fucker! I could kill you."

It was at that moment that Matt realized he wasn't alone. A faint creaking of the old floorboards behind him. Hairs stirred at the nape of his neck and he turned to see, in the doorway, staring at him incredulously—Duana Zwolle.

She stammered, "What—are you doing here? Who are you?"

She was white-faced, trembling. She was obviously very excited. In her uplifted right hand was an object Matt believed at first to be a weapon of some kind, then realized was a long-handled flashlight. She meant to use this flashlight as self-protection, or maybe to attack. Her eyes were blackly dilated and her mouth was a startling blood-red, as Matt had never seen it before. And her hair fell only to her shoulders now, thick, dark, wiry and wavy but brushed smooth, and not oily. Her face was fine-chiseled, a beautiful face yet not an exotic face as he'd remembered it, and older and more drawn, her forehead creased in concentration. And her clothes—expensive and stylish, a dark fitted suede jacket over black silken-wool trousers, a copper-colored silk scarf around her neck. As Matt stood rooted to the spot, staring at her, stunned, she repeated, angry, frightened, "I said—what are you doing here? *Who are you?*"

Matt thought, It isn't Duana.

It was her sister—of course. Her twin. Whose name, in the shock of the moment, Matt had totally forgotten.

He said, trying to speak calmly, "I—I was a friend of your sister's. I mean—I am. I'm a friend of Duana's." Matt's heart was pounding violently and he'd broken into a cold, sickly sweat. Quickly he said, "Don't be afraid, I won't hurt you."

"I'm not afraid! Just—get out of here."

"Yes. Certainly."

They were staring at each other. Matt would afterward marvel at Duana's sister's recklessness in confronting him, a stranger, in this isolated place, alone and armed with only a flashlight. In the very place from which her sister had been abducted.

He said, "Jesus, I'm sorry. I didn't mean to scare you. I only just felt I needed to see where Duana lived. I haven't taken anything, and I haven't disturbed anything. I'm sick about what happened. I miss her—very much."

"You 'miss her'! Do you! What d'you think we're feeling—her family? You have no right to intrude. Who let you in here?"

"I—let myself in."

"You broke in? Goddamn you! How dare you! I'm going to call the police."

Matt said quickly, "Hey, no. I'm leaving. I swear, I haven't disturbed anything—you can see for yourself."

As if, in this violated and deranged setting, she could have seen anything of the sort.

Matt continued to apologize. He knew about female emotion, female hysteria. Like a lighted match, it was, not to be brought near flammable material. He was edging away from Duana's sister, hands and fingers spread to indicate he was harmless. Though needing a shave, his weird, whorled hair disheveled, you could see he was a good, decent, sane man—couldn't you? Not a thief, not a rapist or murderer.

Not a madman. He repeated he was a friend, a close friend, of Duana's; a photographer-friend who lived in Weymouth; they'd only just become acquainted the previous summer.

As Matt edged away, Duana's sister was edging aside to let him pass. Again it crossed Matt's mind how incautious this young woman was, seemingly not knowing she was backing toward a corner, so that Matt, who outweighed her by seventy pounds, might easily have shoved her into the corner and overpowered her. For how did she know that he was telling the truth? That he was a friend of her sister's? Not watching where she stepped, the young woman collided with a stack of canvases, knocking several over. She gave a little sob of hurt and anger—"God*damn!*"

Matt said, "Did you hurt yourself?"

"No! Get away. Just *get out*."

"Yes. I will. Please forgive me, I—"

" 'Forgive you'! *Fuck you*."

Matt was so shocked, he simply stared at the furious woman. For here, miraculously yet mockingly restored to him, was the *missing girl* of whom he'd dreamt obsessively for months, only not a girl, and not the Duana Zwolle of memory, but a tense, choked, frustrated individual who clearly wanted to fly at him. Never had he seen a woman's mouth so luridly blood-red, and never had he passed so close to a stranger on the razor-edge of hysteria. She's going to attack me, Matt thought.

Matt tried to placate her, murmuring he was *sorry! sorry*! speaking as evenly as he could under the circumstances, and sincerely, headed for the front door which stood open. *If I can get to that door, I'll be O.K.* In the cavernous front room the overhead light glared down upon a scene of pillage: boxes, shoved-aside furniture and rolled-up carpet, the mutilated collages. Matt understood that Duana's sister was blaming him for this. Her fury enlivened her like an electric current; her mouth was spasming, like an animal's. She couldn't strike out against the person who'd taken her sister but she could strike out against Matt McBride.

In the corner of his eye, Matt saw something lift, and swing, and like a boxer he ducked, and lurched aside, grabbed hold of the woman's wrist and wrenched the flashlight from her surprisingly strong fingers. It fell clattering to the floor. Pieces of glass went flying. Duana's sister drew breath to scream, not in fear but in rage, and Matt wrestled her back against a wall, pinioning her slender but hard-muscled arms, and clamping his hand against her mouth. She struggled wildly, her eyes bulging. Trying to wrench free, turning her head from side to side; trying to free her mouth so she could scream, or sink her teeth into Matt's hand. But Matt, desperate, and canny, held her fast.

Panting he pleaded, "Hey, no. I'm not going to hurt you. I'm a friend, like I said—a friend of your sister's. I only want to help. I want to do what I can. I'm sick, frustrated—like you. I loved Duana. Please believe me."

Still the furious young woman struggled. She tried to bring her knee up into Matt's groin, tried to kick his ankles, bite his hand. But Matt had the advantage of superior strength, and experience: as a father, he'd had years of practice in hugging, and subduing, his sons on those rare occasions when they flew into tantrums. So he held this squirming woman firm, and controlled his temper. In his heart he'd have liked to seize the bitch by her shoulders and shake her back against the wall until her teeth rattled and her eyes rolled up into her head—but he didn't. This was a matter of stamina, stubbornness. He'd outlast her.

They were like a drowning couple, clutching at each other. Both were panting and their faces beaded in sweat. Matt muttered, his face close to hers, "Look—if I let you go, don't scream, O.K.? There's no need." Still her eyes bulged, and she struggled against him, though more weakly. Matt said, "I'm ashamed, and I apologize, and I'll leave here and never come back. O.K.?" At last the woman began to calm, or gave that impression. Perhaps she was only just exhausted. Cautiously Matt removed the flat of his hand from her mouth. Lipstick was smeared on her face, and on his hand; a lurid, blotchy red. And a thin trickle of blood ran from her left nostril. The eerie impulse came to Matt, almost too quick, and too fleeting, to be absorbed, that he'd have liked to lick that blood away; he'd have liked to lick the woman's fevered, sweaty face. He stepped back from her, looking at her searchingly. He was frankly excited, aroused; the woman continued to glare at him, now wiping at her mouth as if the taste of Matt's hand was repugnant to her.

Matt murmured, "Goodnight!" It was like backing off from a wounded, rabid dog.

To Matt's great relief, Duana's sister didn't scream. Only when he was at the door, and glanced back guiltily at her, did she speak, in a low, husky voice like the one he knew, but accusingly. "*You*—I know you. You're in Duana's diary. 'Nighthawk.' Her secret lover."

Matt hurriedly descended the weatherworn wooden stairs, wanting to escape. He was still aroused. Adrenaline illuminated his veins and a hard angry flamelike pulse rang in his head. He would afterward wonder why he hadn't confirmed, or denied, the words Duana's sister had called after him.

He'd had to escape from the woman. He'd wanted her so badly. There was no tenderness in it: he could have torn at her with his teeth. For hours, for days, he would think of nothing else, of no one else. *This time, he didn't even know her name.*

35

" 'Ruellen Zwolle.' She's called 'Rue.' "

"And how long is—'Rue'—staying in Weymouth?"

"A few days, I think. She's going to pack and ship some of her sister's art home to Maine."

"Is she alone?"

"As far as I know, yes. Usually her family is with her, or part of her family, but this time she seems to be alone. It's Mrs. Zwolle we've spoken with most, preparing the fliers and the video, but I understand the poor woman is hospitalized in Maine."

Matt knew he was asking too many questions, but he couldn't resist asking one more. "Where is 'Ruellen Zwolle' staying, do you know?"

"The Zwolles have stayed various places in Weymouth—people have opened their homes to them. Sid Krell, in fact. But this time, Rue is staying, I think, at—"

There was a pause. Matt, grimacing as he held the phone receiver crooked between his ear and his shoulder, checked an impulse to assure the woman he didn't intend to bother Ruellen Zwolle, he'd respect her privacy.

"—well, I'm not sure. It might be the Weymouth Inn, or that bed-and-breakfast with the blue shingles, on Bayard Avenue. This time, she's kept a low profile."

Or possibly you don't want to tell me, is that it?

Matt said, sympathetically, "God. I don't blame her."

Matt had called a Weymouth woman who'd been involved in the local volunteer effort to find Duana Zwolle. He and this woman were on easy, friendly terms, both belonged to the Stony Brook Tennis & Racquet Club, but Matt had to guess she'd heard of his personal involvement in the Duana Zwolle investigation—the diary, the police search and interrogation—and this would account for a certain guardedness in her voice, not entirely masked by her warm social manner. Certainly she liked Matt McBride, everyone who knew Matt McBride liked him, but—there were disturbing rumors he'd been "not himself" lately.

A certain intensity in his manner. His recent separation from his wife.

Still Matt persisted, into the awkward silence, "Well, Linda, thanks! I'm just curious, I guess. This sister of Duana's, her 'identical twin'—she's actually very different from Duana, isn't she?"

Coolly Linda said, "Well. I didn't really know Duana."

"In appearance, I mean. And in behavior."

Linda made no reply this time. Matt could imagine her, a woman of about Tess's age, an attractive, well-bred and poised woman like Tess, stirring uncomfortably. A man's sexual interest is unmistakable, even when elliptical, at second hand.

Matt thanked her again, and hung up the phone. Why did he feel exhilarated? As if, while he'd learned little about Ruellen Zwolle, he'd somehow learned quite a lot?

36

It was true: Matt McBride was separated from his family.

In mid-April he'd moved into a rented condominium in East Weymouth, a fifteen-minute drive from his former home, and a five-minute drive to Krell Associates. A strange, bachelor life. A Nighthawk life. Rarely went anywhere without his camera equipment on the car seat beside him. Sometimes at night, unable to sleep, thinking of the *missing girl*, he cruised the Turnpike beyond Newark, exited onto Route 1 and the desolate thoroughfares of Jersey City, Hoboken, The Oranges. *Where no one knows my face, or my name.*

He was determined not to approach Duana's sister Rue. Though having discovered, within the space of a few phone calls, where she was staying in Weymouth: a newly built, luxurious and impersonal Marriot Inn outside town.

He was determined not to speak with her, not to further alarm her. Though he wanted to apologize. *Look, we must talk. If you think you know me from Duana's diary—we must talk.* He wanted to tell her he believed he knew who had taken her sister; he was the one who knew, not the police; he did not trust the police, and knew they did not trust him. *I don't want to upset you. I don't want to frighten you. The impression you may have of me—from the other evening, and from the diary—may be mistaken. If we could only just talk for a few minutes.*

Would he call her "Rue"—"Ruellen"? The name sounded strange on his lips. It was as beautiful a name as "Duana," and as exotic. But "Duana" was familiar to him now. "Rue" was troubling.

He was determined not to speak with her. Not to force himself upon her. After the shock of the other evening, she'd be justified in calling the police on him. Already she'd threatened to call the police, and Matt had to admit that, in her place, he'd probably have done so. He was starting to forget how he'd pushed her back against the wall, held her pinioned and his hand over her mouth—not to forget it exactly, for his body retained the vivid memory of the woman's struggling, heated body against his, but to discount it, as if the crucial event had been her surprising him in the bedroom, and Matt, in turn, surprising and frightening her. *She must have thought I was the kidnapper. The murderer. Returning to the crime scene, to gloat.* It seemed to him crucial to speak with her simply to explain himself to her. He believed that, if she could know him, if she saw him, for instance, with Davey and Graeme, she would understand his fundamental decency, sincerity. *She would know I'm her ally, not her adversary.*

He heard himself rehearsing—"Rue? Please listen. Don't judge me prematurely."

And—"Rue? It's because I love your sister, I've been acting recklessly. I don't know what has happened to me."

He was determined not to speak with her. Yet in the early evening of the day following their encounter in Lismore, approximately twenty-four hours after the encounter, he found himself telephoning her at the Marriott, from his office at Krell Associates. He was surprised when his request for "Ruellen Zwolle" wasn't met with a denial that any guest of that name was registered there. Instead, the switchboard operator rang her room number. Matt would have believed that the sister of Duana Zwolle would want anonymity in Weymouth *but maybe anonymity isn't the point, getting information about her sister is more important.* At the other end the phone rang, and rang. She wasn't in. Matt was spared. An answering tape switched on, and Matt hesitated before speaking. He didn't want to harass this distraught young woman; he didn't want even to give the impression of harassing her. She was the sister of the *missing girl* and he could only just imagine what the past fifteen weeks had been for her, as for her parents. He was about to identify himself, and say quietly that he was calling her to apologize about the previous evening, when a panicked sense of danger came over him, and he froze.

No! Don't. You will only regret it.

Quickly Matt hung up the phone.

He was excited, shaken. The door to his office was discreetly shut, and most of his coworkers had gone home, but Matt had the feeling, almost, that someone had been in the room with him. Advancing upon him from behind with an upraised weapon, about to bring it down on his bowed, unprotected head.

Subtle as a gossamer-thin thread passing through the eye of a needle came the thought *Maybe she's the one—'Rue.' The one who has killed Duana.*

It was true, the McBrides were separated. "Temporarily," as they told friends.

Tess had taken the boys for Easter weekend to their grandparents in Connecticut, and asked Matt to please move out while they were gone. "It will be so much easier on us all. I'm thinking of Davey and Graeme especially." Matt said, a little stunned, "In a single weekend? *Out?*" He was smiling, as a man might smile who's been punched in the stomach unexpectedly. You didn't want to assume that a punch was meant to hurt just because it hurt. "If you need help, you can ask one of your friends," Tess said. *Women friends* she meant. She threw off Matt's hand when he touched her, she wasn't in a mood to be touched.

These many weeks, the name *Duana Zwolle* had not passed between them.

Instead Tess had discovered, carelessly left in Matt's desk drawer, a sheet of paper with Oriana's telephone number scribbled on it. No name, just the initial "O" and the number with a Lismore code. Tess had immediately called that number, and Oriana had answered. Of course, Tess knew who Oriana was; and she knew the reputation of "Oriana" locally. Tess had identified herself as Matt McBride's wife, and asked Oriana bluntly if she knew her husband, and Oriana responded with equal bluntness saying it was none of Tess's business who knew who—"We're all adults, I hope." Tess must have spoken indignantly, and Oriana must have replied in kind, for after a heated exchange Tess slammed down the receiver. Oriana called her back at once saying that Matt McBride had left "certain purchases" with her, she'd been waiting for him to return and pick them up, and if he didn't intend to pick them up he should send sufficient postage so that she could mail them, and Tess said she'd send postage, which she did, and when the glazed clay urn and casserole dish arrived, though carefully packed, they were in pieces.

These pieces, Tess had dumped across Matt's desk in his home office, onto his chair and onto the carpet. Matt had been shocked to find them; he'd recognized the pieces at once, and assumed that Tess was responsible for the breakage.

Not that it mattered which woman was responsible.

Not that it mattered which woman Tess had discovered, or believed she'd discovered.

For Matt hadn't the energy to defend himself. And, distracted by other thoughts, hadn't the passion.

Tess said, "It's for the best. At least temporarily," and Matt said, "Yes. If you say so." Tess said, "*You* say so, too—don't you?" and Matt said, "Yes. All right." Tess said in angry triumph, "Then, *good.* We'll be back Sunday after eight o'clock, so you can be gone by then." And Matt heard himself agree.

Recalling how, after the debacle of the police search, the zest with which Tess had cleaned the house. Even the attic, and the basement. The satisfaction with which she'd tossed out years of accumulated things—once possessions she'd valued, and now had no use for.

It was Tess who skillfully choreographed *telling the boys.* Which Matt, who was Daddy, most dreaded. *They will see that I don't love them. That I love them, but not enough.* In fact, the boys would be crying too much, when Daddy spoke with them, to see much of anything in his guilty eyes. And whatever they saw, they would have forgiven him. First, Tess spoke with Davey; and then, while Tess spoke with Graeme, Matt spoke with Davey. Then Matt spoke with Graeme. Then Tess and Matt spoke together with Davey and Graeme. This seemed to go on for hours. It was an epic slaughter scene. The boys cried, and Daddy cried, and Tess shouted at him, "Shut up! Liar!" and ran from the room; and Daddy, Davey and Graeme ran after her, and found her sobbing furiously in a corner of the darkened kitchen. Another time Tess threw off Matt's hand, and cried, "I'm the woman! I'm the one who's supposed to break! *Adulterer!*"

But Tess took the boys away as planned, and Matt moved out as planned. And in his swanky new condominium in East Weymouth, in a building composed primarily of single men and women, some of them separated, some divorced, he took solace in his new bachelor life. *Which was so like Nighthawk's old life, before marriage.* He'd begun cruising the Internet, checking out information on *Duana Zwolle, missing girls, missing women, serial killers, unsolved abductions*—it was astonishing how much information was out there in cyberspace, unknown to Matt McBride. And there were the nights he didn't come home after work but cruised the Turnpike, restless and excited, his camera equipment on the seat beside him. He visited taverns, all-night restaurants, bus stations and train depots. Though he knew it wasn't likely he would sight her, he was always looking for the *missing girl.*

Separated from his family, Daddy called home daily when the boys were there to speak with him, and tried to visit them daily, or every other day, if their schedules worked out. (Strange, Matt had never quite realized how complicated children's lives had become in Weymouth. Their socially ambitious mothers were forever arranging parties and "activities" for them after school and on weekends, and this left little time for an estranged dad to be factored in.) He took them out to McDonald's, Pizza Hut, or Burger King, or brought them back to "Daddy's new place" for a few hours. They devoured takeout food and watched videos and then it was time for Matt to drive them back to Tess who was waiting for them and who murmured to Matt only, "Thank you," and "Goodnight." None of it was very real to Matt but he managed capably. Seeming to know beforehand the drill, the very vocabulary, of separation.

Krell came into Matt's office more frequently now, looking just slightly embarrassed, sympathetic. "How's it going, kid?" he'd ask, and before Matt could reply he'd say, "Not too hot, eh, kid?—well, hang in there." Cuffing Matt's shoulder.

Krell was commiserating with Tess, too. The McBrides were like family to him, he said.

Matt's sons, an ache in the heart. Never would he be able to explain himself to them because he himself didn't understand. They wept, they teased, they accused, they clamored—"Why? Daddy, why?" They clung to Daddy's legs, they pushed away from Daddy's hugs and kisses. They squeezed Daddy's fingers until he winced with pain. Recalling how tightly an infant's fingers can squeeze. It was especially upsetting for Daddy to hear his older, now nine-year-old son cry as hard as his younger, five-year-old son, as he hadn't cried in years.

"Daddy, *why*?"

Daddy had to think hard, to remember.

That ache in the heart! He would have liked to explain this to Duana's sister Rue. That he was a good man, a decent man; a man with two small sons who loved him. He believed that Ruellen Zwolle misjudged him, and he felt both the injustice of her judgment and its logic. What had she called contemptuously after him—"*You*—I know you. 'Night-hawk.' "

Her smeared red mouth. Her furious, hurt eyes.

Walking briskly on Main Street in Weymouth, a chilly sunny Saturday morning following Matt's telephone call to the Marriot Inn of the previous day, and Matt McBride was holding each of his sons' hands firmly in his taking them to their swim lessons at the Y, and he glanced up to see—was it Ruellen Zwolle?—in dark glasses, her lustrous dark hair pulled sharply back from her face, and her face pale, strained, except for the vivid red mouth; Matt's impression was that she'd disguised herself not wanting to be recognized as the twin sister of the *missing girl*, or the *missing girl* herself, so long as she was in Weymouth on business, and that business having to do with Duana. She wore a snugly fitted cream-colored jacket, dark tailored trousers, and pale gloves. She carried a hefty shoulder bag and was only just emerging, frowning and distracted, from the Jameson Gallery, where some of Duana Zwolle's earlier work, woodcuts and monotypes, had been displayed. Matt was staring at the young woman, gripping his sons' hands tight. She glanced up at him, and their eyes locked. Matt steeled himself not to utter a word, not unless Rue spoke first, though he began to smile, hesitantly, not at all aggressively, and he saw her stiffen, staring at him and then at Davey and at Graeme, and Matt's heart began to pound absurdly, and he thought *You can't ignore me!* even as he thought *Yes, we should pass by in silence, that's only right.*

They passed each other without speaking. Graeme was chattering excitedly, tugging at Daddy's hand.

He'd seen the way Rue had looked at Davey and Graeme.

You see? I'm a husband and a father. A normal man. A good, decent, well-intentioned man.

I loved your sister. I did not harm your sister.

I would not harm you.

37

NAME UNKNOWN. *I will be consumed from within & by my own terrible heat. The ANGEL OF WRATH abiding in my own burning bones.*

It was no vision that came to him. He had no need. In his fury in exile. Where his enemies had caused him to flee. Where the female had humbled him, as one devouring dirt. He knew it was the slattern female O who had directed the police to him to humiliate him. The plainclothes detective staring & jeering with a pretense of *collecting contemporary American art*. & NAME UNKNOWN had wished to believe, like a child, & had believed. Never so shamed, & in his own eyes above all.

Thus his rage grounded him, & his certainty. For many days in fog & rain-driven exile (in the Pine Barrens above the Mullica River, in the rotted remains of a hunter's cabin he had discovered years before) he made his plan. Yet would not leave the marsh until beyond Easter.

For Easter is the RESURRECTION OF THE DEAD. Easter is the MIRACLE OF MIRACLES. Even in despair NAME UNKNOWN had not ceased to believe.

But he was angry, & would remain so! Causing his back teeth to grind together & to ache in his head like fire. Thinking then *I will be consumed from within & by my own terrible heat*. & not knowing whether such was a curse, or a blessing.

For long hours lying naked full length & arms & legs spread upon the chill, sandy soil above the river. Protruding ribs of his body like rippled ribs of sand. Forty days & forty nights in exile he would envision. & his tongue crawling back into his mouth, to choke him like the very snake of wickedness. Until at last the April sun emerged out of mist & cold to beat into his back, to rouse him to life.

To life, & to vengeance.

It was his fear that in his absence & cunning they would break into the barn, to expose *The Marriage of Heaven and Hell*. The six chaste brides of

NAME UNKNOWN. These they would laugh at, & revile & destroy. Perhaps they would make a conflagration of the art of NAME UNKNOWN.

The female O would direct them. Many times had O denounced & betrayed NAME UNKNOWN while professing to be his friend.

Jo-seph. Jo-seph Ga-vin she would utter the name he was loathe to hear, those syllables jeering in the world's voice. As one might identify a dog. *Oh. Jo-seph. You?*

Upriver from the cabin at the juncture of the Batsto & the Mullica strangely swollen & swift-running & mud-brown in the rains of Jersey spring. There, where the sand roads formed their perfect cross

& there emerged from underbrush the collapsed ruin of the old church, & its tarnished cross that by sunset turned to flame. Her whispered cries drew him. *God have mercy upon you, Joseph! O God have mercy on us both.*

Yet God had had no mercy on her, & on him God had set His fiery hand. To direct in vengeance as NAME UNKNOWN would be instructed. In the fullness of time.

The powder-fine snow of the New Year had long since melted to expose the female's small broken body. You would think *This is a child.* Almost, NAME UNKNOWN wished he had purified it by fire. For nothing would then remain. He had burnt the soiled clothing, & had not wished to burn the rest & now in a spasm of pity NAME UNKNOWN gathered smooth stones & sand in handfuls. The eyeless sockets of the part-rotted head. Skin mummified like leather. Yet long brittle hair coiled & twined about her bones. Squatting above what remained of her panting suddenly & the lust between his legs. This was the fire of which he was sometimes ashamed & sometimes proud. The female taunting him *You? A man? Are you a man?* He had no choice but to prove it was so, again & yet again. His seed exploding into her. Fiery-hot & painful. Not D Z but another before her who had taunted him. J C was the female's name who had shamed him, spat at him even as he grunted squeezing the wire about her throat to choke off her poisonous words & set her body squirming like a snake, & in her death throes he came inside her, & again & again; & now recalled it breathless, the ferocity of such feeling.

J C like the coal-black girl, the runner V J in disgust NAME UNKNOWN had disjointed limb by limb. He had decapitated the jeering head & wrapped it in tarpaulin & buried it deep in an oil drum, in the county dump of Salem, Delaware. Her flesh parts he had scattered & buried deep. Her female part, *uterus*, which was a sac of slimy skin like a chicken's he had kept in a secret place in dry ice wrapped in aluminum foil & at last surrendered for he could not employ it as he had wished in that female's figure in *The Marriage of Heaven and Hell* & so left it in a public place to be found if it would be found, & if not, not. *NAME UNKNOWN did not look back.* Moved from Delaware forever & erased from his memory that ugliness.

Worms of Earth would devour her. She did not merit the cleansing of sacred flame.

Nor had he wished to transport her body to the Pine Barrens to any sacred place for she was not worthy of decent burial. He had not wished to preserve her memory like the others.

D Z was of a higher quality. Her suffering & courage & the wisdom of her eyes he acknowledged. & now her very head he took pity upon. For it was like the head of a child. NAME UNKNOWN had never hurt any child. For a child has not yet tasted of the apple of sin. This head of D Z in fascination he pried loose from the bones of the neck & upper spine & lifted in the sun to contemplate. There were no eyes. Only eye sockets. Yet it seemed to NAME UNKNOWN in the fearfulness of his vision, *the female could see.*

38 He had no intention of approaching Ruellen Zwolle. "I've already upset her enough. No more!"

Matt was ashamed, and he was repentant. It was enough for him to worry about his responsibilities as a husband and father separated from his family. ("Daddy, when are you coming home? Dad-*dy*?" the boys demanded.)

It was enough for him to contemplate what he could do about Joseph Gavin/NAME UNKNOWN.

A night passed, and part of a morning. Matt had slept only intermittently. Sleep came to him in glassy waves, slicing at his eyes. He reached out for—what? whom? *Time is running out. She's still in Weymouth.* Yet Matt refrained from telephoning Ruellen Zwolle, nor did he try to see her, though he knew she'd be leaving Weymouth soon to return to Santa Monica.

Instead, Matt slipped away from Krell Associates in the late morning. (Was the old man watching him? Matt had to risk it.) He dropped by the Jameson Gallery to inquire about "purchasing art" by Duana Zwolle, and was informed that the artist's work was not available at the present time. "The Zwolle family has reclaimed it and is keeping it, they say, until Duana returns." The gallery owner, a fading-blond, petulant woman whom Matt knew socially, though not well, spoke with an air of disapproval.

Matt said, "I see. I'm sorry. But I can understand that decision."

"The Zwolles seem to think that Duana will be back. People have to have faith, I suppose."

"*You* don't think so?"

"I wouldn't know."

"Duana has been missing, how long?—since before New Year's. I hate to say this, I admired her art and her courage and I admired her, so far as I knew her, but—it seems self-evident she must be dead."

The word *dead* struck an ugly note. Matt realized no one had used it, in speaking of Duana Zwolle: only just the word *missing*. But this woman, nervously stroking her slender, freckled forearm, adorned with myriad thin gold bracelets, spoke with a grim relish, looking at Matt. "Duana Zwolle will never be back."

Matt had been turning a black plastic pen embossed with the gallery name, and it snapped in his fingers. "Sorry!"

It was a quiet weekday morning. Matt was the sole visitor to the gallery. The owner seemed eager to talk. Matt asked her about Duana's sister and was informed that Ruellen Zwolle had taken over Duana's estate and was to act as her executor. This, the family had decided. "Essentially, the sister has frozen Duana's work. No more sales, everything returned to the estate. It makes sense, I suppose, but we're not very happy about it, from an economic perspective. With all the publicity, Duana's art could *sell*, for once. I mean, God!—it could *take off*. People buy art for all kinds of reasons and most of them have nothing to do with aesthetics. You're frowning, sure,"— (had Matt been frowning? he hadn't known), "—but that's how the market is. Posthumous success, for an artist, is better than no success, right? Most artists never sell, living or dead."

Again that word: *dead*. Matt felt a stab of sheer hatred.

"How many works of Duana Zwolle's exist?"

" 'Exist'? That depends upon what you mean. We had six monotypes here. The Tomato Factory exhibited the collage-sculptures, and at least two of them sold—which isn't bad, considering their 'difficulty.' The rest were destroyed, I heard." The woman lowered her voice, as if this were confidential. "With a razor."

Matt saw again the slashed, mutilated canvases. He couldn't bring himself to comment.

"You know, they were destroyed . . . don't you? Or hadn't you heard?"

Matt shrugged, noncommittal.

The woman continued, "In all, there are said to be about thirty of Duana Zwolle's works, from various stages in her career, unsold. The Zwolles may intend to keep these if she's—if she doesn't return. The sister seems to be the one making these decisions. However, works of Duana's in private collections can be resold, and I'm betting they'll be on the market soon. We've been making inquiries, here. As I said, Zwolle's quirky kind of art could really take off if a shrewd dealer gets hold of it. A major review in the *New York Times* or the *New Yorker* is all it would take."

Matt nodded sympathetically. "Good luck to you, then."

"In a tragedy like this," the woman said, stroking her bracelets, "you hope for something positive to come of it. For someone."

"This sister? Ruellen Zwolle? I'm wondering if you have an address for her in Santa Monica."

The woman hesitated. You could see that she liked Matt McBride, and she'd been enjoying this conversation, but now, for an instant, she hesitated. "Maybe I should check with her first, before . . ."

But Matt smiled, attractive and well-groomed and exuding that Weymouth confidentiality *You can trust me, of course: I'm someone just like you.* So the woman said, "Well. No problem. Here's a business card of hers—'Zodiac Graphics.' " The woman paused, seeing that she'd pleased her visitor. "*She's* a strange one, too. Just like her sister."

Matt was reasoning: if he missed seeing Ruellen in Weymouth, he would fly to Santa Monica. In some ways that might be preferable. The last thing he wanted was to upset her.

The Internet: the insomniac's solace. That vast depthless uncharted sea in which the lonely, the yearning, the confused, the lost, the hopeful and the desperate are swimming alongside one another, invisible to one another, yet excitedly aware of one another as blind, insensate sea creatures might be aware of one another, if only as faint electronic impulses. The Internet, which, more and more frequently these sleepless spring nights, Matt was cruising; and where he'd made the acquaintance of an erudite individual known only as "Hugo"— self-described connoisseur of "Serial Killers of the Eastern Seaboard, Mid-20th Century Onward." After several wittily intense, enigmatic exchanges, Matt found himself unexpectedly invited to visit Hugo, who lived in Paramus, New Jersey. Even on the computer screen, Hugo's boast had an air of breathless authenticity:

If you want to know HOT ZONE CLASSIFIED SICKO STUFF never released by cops to the public, HUGO is your man!

Matt thought uneasily, Yes. He wanted to know.

Hugo L. Chauncey, as he formally introduced himself, was a wheelchair-bound, fattish young man of about twenty-seven. Nearly bald, with a fringe of fair, fluffy brown hair on a head round as a bowling ball, with a pair of large, pained, staring brown eyes behind thick plastic-rimmed glasses. There was an aura of both middle age and infancy about Hugo; he lived with his widowed mother, as he called her, in a small, asphalt-sided bungalow in a crowded residential neighborhood of similar homes. At the door, Hugo greeted Matt effusively. "Come in, Mathias McBride! Welcome! Just follow me, please." There was no shaking of hands, for which Matt was grateful. He'd stepped into a dim living room smelling of autumn decay like damp leaves, newspapers. And from close by, a strong sizzling smell of cooking with grease. "Ma-a! My friend from the Web-site is here," Hugo bawled. There was no reply, so he cupped his hands to his mouth and called out, louder, "Ma-aaa! My friend has arrived. Don't disturb us, ple-ase."

A muffled reply came from the kitchen. With a jerk of his chin Hugo indicated that Matt should follow him, and began wheeling away energetically. He moved with such animation that his fringe of hair stirred in the breeze. "Through here, Mathias! My quar-ters."

The odor of damp decay increased. Matt, smiling awkwardly, found himself in a bedroom crowded with computer and electronic equipment. On the walls were maps of of the eastern seaboard states cryptically encoded and dotted with colored pins; against the inner wall was a sagging bookcase crammed with hardcover and paperback books, including individual volumes of *Encyclopedia Britannica*. Matt was surprised to see a complete shelf of the tragedies of Aeschylus, Sophocles, Euripides and translations of Homer, Ovid, Catullus, Livy. Mere names to Matt McBride. But impressive names. On a higher

shelf was William Roughhead's *Chronicles of Murder*: that work of
classic amateur criminology Matt had always intended to look into,
but never had. There were numerous more recent books with such
titles as *On Death's Bloody Trail, Sexual Violence in America, Serial
Killers: A History, True Crime Files.* On a worn carpet in the center
of the room was a dining room table, and on this table were Hugo's
computer and printer. One of the *Duana Zwolle: Missing* fliers caught
Matt's eye. And a paperback copy of *Hunting Humans: The Encyclopedia of Serial Killers.*

Through their e-mail exchange Matt had told Hugo of his special
interest in the Duana Zwolle case. He'd described himself as an ad-
mirer of the young artist's work who had not known her personally.

"Let's get started."

Wasting no time, Hugo urged Matt to sit beside him as he wheeled
himself up to the computer terminal. His breath came in eager little
puffs. "Preparatory to your visit, Mathias, I've been doing homework."
Hugo was eager, frowning, owlish; in a red plaid flannel shirt buttoned
to his throat, shapeless dungarees and open sandals worn with white
cotton socks, he reminded Matt of a precociously bright but emotionally
unstable twelve-year-old. Yet Matt felt intimidated by him. He'd have
liked to feel pity, but was nearly overcome by a visceral unease.

At least, he can't be a killer. Poor bastard.

For the next ninety minutes, Matt stared at the screen and listened
to Hugo, enthralled. Like a master magician the young man typed out
commands on the computer keyboard, summoning phenomena out of
the void of cyberspace. "Too bad you don't have time today for a
survey of the field, Mathias! Just my region, the eastern seaboard,
since the fifties, is quite a saga. It isn't often I get to display my
archives. Most of the characters you meet on the Web are just splat-
terpunk kids with no interest in history or psychology, I could tell
right away *you were someone special.*"

Rapidly Hugo clicked, and the screen changed, and changed again,
like a dream veering out of control. Matt said apologetically, "Well—
maybe another time. Today I'm mainly interested in any background
you can give me on the Duana Zwolle case. Abductions of girls and

young woman in the New Jersey region since 1976, beginning with a high school girl named Marcey—"

"—Mason, 1976. South Jersey. Ri-ight?"

Matt looked at Hugo L. Chauncey, astonished. "Yes. That's right. Do you know about her?"

"I know about them all. Some more than others. I don't know a lot about Mason except it's an unsolved case, after twenty-one years." The face of smiling, freckled, radiantly happy Marcey Mason appeared on the screen. Matt winced. It was the familiar media image, one he'd seen, and imagined, hundreds of times, but he couldn't help reacting with shock. Hugo squinted at the screen, saying brightly, " 'Marcey Mason.' Forked River, N.J. Body found in Deer Isle Wildlife Sanctuary, November 18, 1976. Lots of 'leads'—'tips'—possible suspects brought in for questioning—but never any arrest. The m.o.—modus operandi—you're looking for is strangulation with wire, right?"

Matt said uncertainly, "I think so, yes."

"It helps to be as specific as possible. There are so many of these cases—'girls/women missing, bodies found'—just in my region alone, you'd go crazy trying to factor together dozens of names and cases, and for sure you'd be dealing with the work of a number of serial killers. So it would get all confused. We narrow down the m.o. as best we can. Usually, it's distinctive. The guy leaves his signature. See, Marcey Mason was tied up, wrists and ankles, with wire, and strangled with wire, her head practically decapitated; and she was positioned in a place near a nature trail where she'd eventually be found, like an artwork."

"A—what?"

"An artwork. Y'know—work of art. A sculpture, like. The guy intended the body for display. If he hadn't, he would've buried it or burned it or, in the Pine Barrens, he could've sunk it in a swamp and nobody'd ever know. Also, he burned her clothes close by." Hugo was indicating the screen where columns of print were rising as he clicked to scroll with his thumb. Matt was having difficulty listening to this through a roaring in his ears. "You got to figure, this stuff is all deliberate. These killings are like private rituals. The killer's a priest, sort of—takes his time, knows what he's doing even if he doesn't know why he's doing it; it's done in the way it's done 'cause it can't be done any other way, he'd tell you. Like a priest, preparing the eucharist. You Catholic? No? Well, you get my point. A ritual is a weird little thing you do because it's what you *do*. A serial killer doesn't know why he's performing a ritual in just the way he does any more than a Catholic priest has a clue about his ritual and they'd both get emotional if you tried to debate it. It's the opposite of, say, break-ing into somebody's house and robbing them. Or armed robbery. Things can go wrong 'cause the other participants don't know the script. That's improvisation, and it's crude. The serial killer has things planned, usually. Maybe not his first time, but every time following. He won't improvise except as an artist improvises. *He's in control.*"

Hugo spoke with pleasure, all but smacking his lips.

Matt said, "The serial killer is an—artist?"

"A priest and an artist. Sure."

"What kind of artist?"

Hugo shrugged. "An artist whose raw material is other people, obvi-ously. Their bodies, their flesh, blood—whatever. But also their souls."

He pronounced *souls* with an eerie sort of reverence.

Matt said, disgusted, "This sick monster, this psychopath who killed a defenseless girl, Marcey Mason, and maybe others—is an *artist*?"

"Well. Not exactly Grandma Moses. But, yeah. I think so."

Matt was infuriated. He knew, NAME UNKNOWN was in fact an "artist." And how proud NAME UNKNOWN would be if he could overhear this exchange.

But Hugo declined to debate the issue. He sucked at his lips with childish obstinacy. Why bother to convert Mathias McBride to his way of thinking? He was enjoying himself too much, the power in-vested in his arms and fingers as he typed out commands, clicked and summoned images, photographs, columns of data.

Matt said, more evenly, "I suppose there's a way of interpreting almost everything we do as 'art.' Whatever isn't primarily for use. That's a minimal, working definition of art." *And I'm an artist, too, you bastard. I know what I'm talking about.*

But Hugo stubbornly shook his head. He said, with sudden passion,

laying his pudgy hand on his heart, "Whatever speaks of beauty—
even a repugnant beauty—is art. Whatever pierces the heart, makes
the pulses race, shocks us with the profound, ineffable mystery of
*Why are we here? Who are we? What have we to do with one another?
What is our human destiny?*—that, Mathias McBride, is *art*."

Matt stared at Hugo L. Chauncy, appalled. He wanted to think,
This guy is crazy.

Matt thought, He's one of us. He knows.

" 'Art' has always had its enemies in the authority of the state, in
self-appointed moralists and phony religious leaders," Hugo went on
zestfully. "But so what? *We* know."

In dread Matt asked, "We know—what?"

But Hugo, smirking at the screen, suddenly relented. So sure of himself he could afford to grant the opposition some ground. "Hey, sure,
Mathias, I'm possibly exaggerating. I've been flamed on the Web for 'ro-
manticizing'—seeing intentions and designs where others see just
crude dumb chance. I grant there's that trait in me, as in other sufferers
of that mystery-malady known to the trade as 'MS'—for which, Mathias,
you may read 'Much Shit'—being wheelchair bound, since the age of
sixteen, and somewhat restricted as to my mobility. And opportunities."

Matt said, "I see."

Hugo said patiently, "Well, now—maybe you do, and maybe you
don't. No one with legs under him knows what it's like in this chair,
the metaphysics of this chair, 'cause even if you sit in this chair,
friend, you'd only be *sitting* in it; like *resting*. You'd be thinking *how
does it feel to be in this chair permanently*, but if you're in the chair
permanently you don't think that thought. Ri-ight?"

Matt was feeling bullied and resentful. But he had to agree. He
said, "Yes. You're right. I'm sorry."

"Sorry for what?" Hugo chuckled. "Having legs?"

"No, but—"

"—not being in the chair? Like me?"

"No. But I—"

"Then let's change the subject. We aren't going to change our
minds 'cause our minds are *in our bodies* and we sure ain't gonna

change our bodies, but we can change the subject just like this."
Hugo struck more keys, and Matt leaned over to see, with relief, that
the computer screen was still focussed on Marcey Mason. Hugo had
been scrolling through a vast quantity of unedited information, his
eyes narrowed, squinting like a hunter's.

Matt said hesitantly, "What more can you tell me about Marcey
Mason?"

"A lot. Some of it you already know, some might be new. I'll print
it out for you before you leave. For instance, there's a note here that
local cops, in Forked River, wanted to believe the girl was taken by
some stranger passing through, like from Atlantic City; but the New
Jersey cops had reason to believe it was some guy living right in her
neighborhood." Hugo glanced over at Matt, smirking. *Your neighborhood, Mathias. Right?* "There the girl is going home from school like
any ordinary day, says good-bye to her teachers, friends walk with
her, she cuts through an alley or whatever, she 'disappears' in five
minutes—you got to figure, she took a ride with somebody she knew.
Trusted. Makes sense, ri-ight? Guy's got it all planned. It's like he's
eloping with his bride only the bride doesn't know she's a bride or
this guy's her bridegroom, till too late. You could see this as a play
or a movie but he's writing all the script, he's in charge and it isn't
improvised once he gets her alone. In the case of Marcey Mason, he
tortures her sexually—'mutilates' her with a power tool—"

"What? A power tool?"

"Seems so." Hugo, squinting behind his glasses, was scrolling
through the information with the avidity of a child discovering forbidden material. "This information is classified, I mean the cops never
released it publicly but there's access to it out in cyberspace if you
know the way in. See?—'power tool.' That was what the medical examiner thought. He'd used it on her 'genital area'—'lower abdomen."
It isn't original but it's not too common. (If I click on 'power tool' I
don't get much, see? Fresno, CA in the early 1980's and they caught
the guy so the case is closed.) You'd assume the power tool would be
this one's m.o. but so far as Hugo L. Chauncey could discover, he
never did it again. Or if so, it wasn't identified as such. At least, based

on bodies actually found. Of course, there's missing bodies, bodies no one ever discovered, and what he did to them we don't know and probably never will. And maybe this guy isn't even living now—who knows? What we have here is the wire; wire looped around the victim's neck so tight it cuts into the flesh; and, after the victim's death, according to the medical examiner, he removed her vocal cords." Hugo sniggered, continuing to scroll. "A 'botched job,' it says here. So we know he wasn't any medical student or doctor, ri-ight?"

"Vocal cords!"

"That's crucial for the m.o., as I'll demonstrate in a minute—"

Hugo continued to chatter, but Matt was too shocked to hear.

For more than twenty years he'd assumed that the mysterious, unspeakable "body part" removed from Marcey Mason had been genital; that was what everyone believed. Matt stammered, "—Vocal cords? Jesus! But—why?" Hugo kept scrolling and there on the glimmering screen was Marcey Mason another time, a slender-faced, pretty girl, a girl you could see was anxious to please, smiling just a little too hard into the camera, one of how many, thousands, hundreds of thousands, victims, the innocent, the lost, those whom time has swept away like a great tidal wave, or in fact a quite ordinary wave, surf breaking on the beach at Forked River.

Hugo was thinking aloud, speculatively. "The girl was a singer. In high school. Every news article makes that point. So this guy who took her, the Bridegroom we might call him, wanted a memento. He'd heard Marcey Mason sing, it made an impression on him. The cops kept this classified, or tried to."

Matt felt sick. He stared at Marcey Mason's smiling face on the screen, even as Hugo relentlessly scrolled and clicked past. He was thinking he'd never saved her. He'd never come near. It had been a ridiculous adolescent fantasy. Marcey Mason had been terrified, she'd suffered in utter loneliness and died an excruciating death and no one had been able to save her, certainly not Matt McBride.

And Duana Zwolle, too. For all his crazed devotion, for all that he'd ruined his life, Matt McBride hadn't done a thing for Duana Zwolle, either.

Even if I kill Gavin. Kill the bastard. What good will that do.

At last, Hugo had come to the end of the material on Marcey Mason.

Expertly he typed another command. The screen dissolved and shifted. Waiting for the information to come up, Hugo said, "I've been doing a little homework, Mathias. I'm working with an m.o. of 'strangulation, wire'—'clothes burned'—'body part removed.' Of course, most of it leads nowhere. You know the Web. But I came up with at least two more possibilities—brides for our Bridegroom. Ever heard of—" The screen cleared, and a striking young woman in a leotard appeared, in black and white. "—Lucille Rideau? Summer of 1981. She was a dancer from Philadelphia who was abducted and murdered in Mountainhome, PA. The Poconos. The scenario here reminds me a lot of Marcey Mason."

Matt leaned over, staring at the image of a young woman he was sure he'd never seen before. Hugo clicked, and other photographs appeared, some in full color: the lithe, graceful young woman with the long red hair had evidently been a well-known dancer with the Philadelphia Dance Troupe. "I'm afraid I've never heard of Lucille Rideau."

"Another unsolved case. Like Mason, Rideau 'disappeared' one day. From her summer place. Eventually, her body was found only a few miles away, in a wooded area, on a mountainside; she'd been strangled exactly the way Mason had been, same kind of looped wire, which is efficient but doesn't have to be too quick so the guy can register it, maybe make a video. 'Wrists, ankles bound'—'sexual mutilation' (but no power tool this time, at least not identified). Like Mason's her clothes were daubed with gasoline and burned in a sort of funeral pyre near the body. This time, our guy 'attempts to remove' muscle tendons from both her calves, long ropey messes they must've been, each about twelve inches, but again he did a lousy job of it. Real clumsy. He didn't have any surgical instruments, just something like a fish-gutting knife according to the medical examiner."

Faintly Matt said, "Leg tendons—?"

But it made sense. He knew. Lucille Rideau had been a dancer.

Hugo continued to scroll and click along the screen. There would be even more data on Lucille Rideau, owing to her reputation as a dancer in the Philadelphia area. Features in local magazines, numerous stills from her performances, publicity photos. A barrage of headlines. Hugo said patiently, "Like I say, Mathias, our guy wanted a memento. He couldn't have the woman, the dancer, so he takes what he can get. A part of her body that's special."

"Yes. A part of her body that has distinguished her."

"Like the high school soprano—her vocal cords."

Matt was perspiring. He felt sick, but couldn't look away from the fascinating screen. "But—what does he do with these body parts?"

Hugo grinned sidelong at him, and barked with laughter as if Matt were joking. "How the hell do I know, Mathias? I'm not one of these *nuts*."

After Lucille Rideau, Hugo had to make what he called a speculative leap to an abduction in Salem, Delaware, in December of 1987. There was no strangulation by wire, there were no burned clothes. At least, that anyone knew of. But an attractive blond twenty-five-year-old woman named Jennifer Casey had disappeared from a parking lot behind her condominium and was never again seen. No witnesses to the apparent abduction. No ransom note, no phone calls. There was an intensive multistate search—Casey was the niece of an influential state senator—but no trace of the young woman was ever found. Except, five weeks later, a body part turned up in Salem: a human uterus wrapped in aluminum foil, left on the front stoop of a feminist-run medical clinic called WomanSpace.

Matt murmured, "A—uterus?"

Hugo said excitedly, "It was Casey's! They identified it. See, the woman was an abortion-rights organizer. She got interviewed a lot on local TV, led demonstrations. She was one of a group of feminists that presented a bill to the Delaware state legislature. An aggressive female like that, she'd catch your attention, wouldn't she?" As Hugo scrolled, ghostly images of the blond, defiant Jennifer Casey emerged out of the void, seemed to stare directly and reproachfully at the men, and vanished. Rapidly Hugo summarized lengthy columns of print. "Some of the stories suggested that Casey was a lesbian. Her 'partner' was a female resident at a hospital, an Indian from Delhi, though a

U.S. citizen. This woman was a suspect in the case for years. The cops wouldn't let her out of their sight. Then in 1991, on the anniversary of Casey's disappearance, the woman was killed in a car crash in Washington. The commentary was 'suicide.' Technically, the case is still open but the Salem cops are convinced it's closed, and the murderer is dead. But we suspect otherwise, Mathias, don't we?"

Matt rubbed his eyes vigorously with his fingers. You would want to think that this was only a bad dream, a nightmare. Except Matt had never been more fully awake. He said, "This time, though—he gave the body part back. I wonder why?"

Hugo shivered. "Yeah, man. That's *weird*."

Suddenly they were laughing together. Hugo had a loud, gutsy hyena-laugh, Matt's laughter was near-soundless, like choking.

Strange: it was still daylight. A bright, warm April afternoon. Outside children were shouting. Little more than an hour had passed but Matt felt as if he'd been in this claustrophobic, dim-lit room for many hours. He was sickened by all he'd learned, and he had to fight a physical revulsion for the young man in the wheelchair who was "Hugo" on the Web, a lauded amateur-expert on the subject of serial killers, American. Hugo's specialty was the Eastern seaboard since the early Sixties. Matt hadn't any doubt now, this boast was justified.

Hugo said, all but winking at Matt, "I could run a trace on 'uterus, removed'—see where it takes us, eh?"

Matt said quickly, "No, please. Let's stay with what we have."

"Well. Beyond Casey, the trail isn't so clear."

Hugo had located a number of missing women—twenty-two, in fact—but these were women whose bodies had never been discovered, so there was no way of knowing how they'd been killed, with wire or not, or even if they were dead. "Some missing women are, y'know, just *missing*." One was a young woman named Vesna Jones, nineteen, a champion long-distance runner who'd disappeared in March 1991 while jogging at dawn around a reservoir near the branch of the state university at Catonsville, Maryland. "Vesna Jones was black. I wouldn't have said our guy, if this is our guy, would go for a black woman, would you?" Hugo brooded. "But this one did get a lot of local attention. On the Olympic team. He'd have seen her picture in the papers, on TV. She isn't bad-looking. Looks *young*. There was a witness said she thought she saw 'somebody suspicious' around the reservoir—'a Caucasian male with long hair, a headband, weighing maybe one hundred sixty pounds and about five feet ten.' But no one else saw him, and Vesna Jones, too, disappeared without a trace."

Caucasian male, long hair. One hundred sixty pounds. Five feet ten. Seven years ago, that could have been Joseph Gavin.

Hugo located several other women missing in Maryland-Delaware in the early 1990's—"But they don't sound like they'd be of interest to our guy." Then there was the June 1993 abduction of Marie Tompkins in Trenton, New Jersey: another "disappearance" from a parking lot. No witnesses, no trace of the victim. Hugo typed in a command, and the image of a strikingly beautiful, glamorous young woman appeared on the screen—"Tompkins was a Trenton TV newscaster, our guy must've seen her and got interested." Hugo clicked a few more times, bringing up more of Tompkins, and more; Matt had to admit, the woman was highly attractive, with a dazzling smile and long eyelashes. By cosmetic design, or by an accident of bone structure, Marie Tompkins rather resembled the film star Julia Roberts. Hugo was thinking out loud, "Wonder what part of this one our guy 'removed.' The whole face, maybe! You could peel it right off, it'd serve the bitch right."

Matt wasn't sure he'd heard this. "What did you say?"

Hugo was muttering to himself, hunched in his wheelchair scrolling and clicking energetically. He gave off a heated air of yeasty flesh, oily hair and not-clean clothes. Matt shivered with revulsion for his companion even as he was enormously grateful for Hugo's information and generosity. *He means well. He's on my side. The side of justice, decency.* Up floated news articles on Tompkins' disappearance, magazine features and more photos of the *missing girl* which, now, Matt recalled having seen some years ago, though without paying a good deal of attention to them. Now, he felt a pang of sympathy; a sense of what it must have been like, for Tompkins' family. Of the young women he believed to be victims of Joseph Gavin, Marie Tompkins was the only one married, with a child.

Beyond 1993 there wasn't much to interest Matt, Hugo said, until of course December 1997 and the Duana Zwolle disappearance. At once there floated onto the screen the familiar images of the *missing girl*. Matt swallowed hard, staring. He'd been seeing Duana Zwolle's face so frequently, so obsessively, but usually in private, it was a shock now to share the experience with a stranger. Rapidly Hugo scrolled through the data, most of which was repetitive and already known to Matt. Hugo said, "This one's sort of strange-looking, isn't she? Like kind of foreign? But sexy. Dirty-sexy. I bet. An 'artist'—what kind?" On the screen were lurid *Jersey Citizen* tabloid pages, Duana Zwolle's innocent plaintive image juxtaposed with blurred and surely staged photographs of "lesbian drug users"—"crack cocaine ring leaders." There was a faked photo Matt had never seen before, Duana Zwolle's head on a scantily clad, fleshy female straddling a Harley-Davidson—"Lismore Dyke-on-Bike." Matt felt nauseated. The Web made no distinction between one type of information and another. As in an enormous Sargasso Sea, all was one. Hugo, vastly amused, clicked and clicked. He said, "This one's got the worst press, must be 'cause she's an artist, and maybe a lesbian? The body's still missing so we don't know the crucial m.o. That would seem to mean whoever took her doesn't want her to be found. 'Cause if he did, somebody would've found it by now. Assuming it's the Bridegroom—our boy. And I'd bet you one million bucks it *is*. I get a good feeling from this one, don't you, Mathias? Duana Zwolle is—was—some kind of artist, so that fits the victim profile. She's not bad-looking, sort of exotic. Yeah, you could get a real rush from this one. I predict, if Zwolle is ever found, cause of death will be strangulation by wire, and her wrists and ankles bound, and some body part 'removed'—her hands? Maybe her hands? For an artist, hands are important. Or maybe—"

Matt said, more loudly than he intended, "Excuse me. What do you think about—her car being found? Over by the Delaware River? And her shawl with her blood on it?"

"What do I think about—what?"

"Well, this is a little different, isn't it, from the other cases?"

Hugo had to concede, yes it was. "He wanted cops to think she'd driven there herself, maybe committed suicide in the river. But they saw through that, for sure."

"They did? How do you know?"

"The bloody shawl. How'd it get bloody, if she jumped in the river? It was a set-up. Sure, they knew."

Hugo spoke adamantly. He continued clicking and scrolling. Matt wondered at his certainty. He asked, "Do you think police have made a connection with these other abductions? Going back to Marcey Mason—"

Hugo thought so, yes. "It's routine detective work these days. Lots of stuff in the computer, like the 'automated fingerprint i.d. system'—the profiles of victims, known or suspected serial killers, sex offenders, cons, and ex-cons. They'd have caught our pal Bundy years earlier if they'd had the equipment they have now. The Green River guy. Hillside Stranglers. The Golden Age of Serial Killing is maybe over. All it takes now is one fingerprint—one fraction of a fingerprint—and they can nab you. Transmit it from Alaska to New Jersey in thirty seconds. Livy said, in *The History of Rome*, it's always stayed with me—'Diseases must be known before their cures are found; by the same token, appetites come into being before there are laws to limit their exercise.' Now we have laws, and we have DNA and blood work. All kinds of forensics stuff. Some of us can get into their computer files, but it's risky. I know my way into the New Jersey Department of Law Enforcement files and I've found some really fantastic classified stuff, like inadmissible evidence in high-profile cases, for instance illegally obtained photos and in some cases photos of victims the prosecution couldn't use at trial 'cause a judge has tossed them out as 'prejudicial' against the defendant. Photos of little Megan, y'know—raped, strangled etcetera down in Trenton. I could tap into it except I'm getting the vibes you aren't into kiddie stuff, and I can respect that. Anyway—it *exists*, it's *there*, all this stuff. But like I say it's risky to fool around with any cops, and I'd never go near the feds. Most of this stuff I've been showing you is public access. I hope it's been helpful?"

"Yes," Matt said, forcing a smile. "Very helpful, Hugo."

Hugo sat back in his chair, hands clasped behind his head in a philosophical mood. "The profile I'm getting for our guy is, yeah he's an artist but a special, experimental kind. He wouldn't make a living from his art, probably. He's got another line of work—let's say power tools. Uses his hands. Good with his hands. Strong with his hands. As to age, he's pushing forty. As to race, Caucasian for sure. If we draw a circumference around the 'suspected victims' we see that it's a pretty small area. I'd guess he was a kid in south Jersey in 1976 and probably comes from Forked River. Probably went to school with Mason. After that, he's been moving around. Maybe his line of work makes him mobile. He could actually be married—but to a woman with her own kid. He probably fits in O.K. with people—the kind of guy everybody would say, 'Oh, *him*? Oh, no! He wouldn't harm a fly, not *him*!'" Hugo laughed his deep-belly hyena laugh. But Matt couldn't join in.

Matt had been jotting down some of this, with shaky fingers. As if he didn't know it, already.

"You said, on the Web, you knew Duana Zwolle? Or—no, you like her art?" Hugo asked, his eyes shining with curiosity. "What's it like?"

"It's—very special."

"And Duana Zwolle? What's she like?"

"I—did I say I knew her? No."

Hugo gnawed at his lower lip, brooding. "Well. She's number six, at least. Maybe there's more, we don't know. But probably not less. I got a gut instinct for this, once I get started. I predict—" Hugo was peering at Matt sidelong, through nearly shut eyes. Matt was uncomfortably aware of his scrutiny. *He wishes he could think I'm the Bridegroom. That's his thrill for today.* "—he'll take another victim, soon. It's something in the air."

"Jesus. I hope not."

Matt was thinking of Ruellen Zwolle. *It's possible that Gavin knows she's in Weymouth.*

There was Oriana, too.

Hugo continued to speak, clearly enjoying his authority. Matt tried to respond civilly. He was, in fact, deeply grateful to Hugo L. Chauncey. Why then did he feel an almost overwhelming urge to shove the young man out of his wheelchair? Beat at his fat, gleaming face?

Matt said evenly, winding things up, "Hugo, you've been enormously helpful. You've allowed me to see a definite pattern leading to Duana Zwolle's disappearance. She and her predecessors share a trait in common—talent. Visibility. While the killer is nobody—unknown. Maybe he calls himself 'NAME UNKNOWN.' " This odd remark elicited no sign of recognition from the fattish young man who continued to blink at Matt with his faint, smirking smile. Matt said, "You've called this psychopath an artist and maybe he is, but he's a failed artist. A failure. As a human being, and as an artist. He victimizes young women out of envy. Jealousy."

Matt had begun to speak vehemently. Hugo adjusted his glasses to peer at him owlishly. He protested, "No! He loves them, in his secret way. Don't you get it, Mathias? He adores them. He wants to devour them. He wants to *be them*. It's the highest form of love."

"That's ridiculous! That isn't love at all."

Hugo drew himself up to his full height. Stubbornly he said, "*I* think it is. From my position here, I see things other people, so-called 'normal people,' are blind to. And I see this: How do you love when you aren't loved in return? Is your love any less beautiful? Or valuable? How do you elope when your beloved is unwilling? When she has scorned you? *You have to take her by force.* She's reluctant, she refuses, she begins to scream, struggle—*you have to take her by force.* You betray your own passion if you don't. Only eight or ten inches of strong wire—" Hugo made a graceful gesture as if looping a wire noose around an invisible head, squeezing the neck tight and crinkling his face with the effort, "—and the female is yours."

Matt shuddered in disgust. He'd had enough.

He thanked Hugo, and offered to pay him for his services, but Hugo quickly shook his head, surprised as if Matt had insulted him. "Don't you want me to print out some of this stuff? It will take awhile, but—"

"No, thanks. I've taken a few notes. The names, places and dates—that's mainly what I need."

Hugo said eagerly, "I could transmit it via e-mail. No trouble."

"Thanks. But I don't believe I need so much detail."

I can go to the police with this. I can go to Ruellen Zwolle.

Matt was easing toward the door of the airless room, and Hugo was wheeling himself beside him, puffing. Now he all but pleaded, "You could stay for supper, Mathias. We eat kind of early, it wouldn't be long to wait. We could watch videos. I got some you might be interested in. And Ma wouldn't mind, she likes me to have friends. Hey, Ma-a!"

Matt said quickly, "No, thank you! I couldn't."

Hugo said, "It's no trouble, really." At the doorway he bellowed, "Ma-a!" There was a muffled response from the next room. Matt looked down at the flushed, shiny crown of Hugo's round head. The young man's shoulders and arms were muscled but his legs, in wrinkled dungarees, appeared shrunken. A pathetic character Matt didn't want to pity, but by this time Matt was desperate to escape.

"Hugo, thanks! But I have to pick up my sons from school."

What time was it? Past five o'clock. But Hugo wouldn't know better.

Hugo's moist brown eyes registered shock and dismay. "You have—sons?"

"Afraid I do."

At the front door, Matt stooped to shake hands with Hugo. The handshake was exactly as he'd dreaded—a clammy-cool grip, self-conscious yet pleading. Another time Matt politely offered to pay for Hugo's expertise, and another time, now slightly hurt, Hugo demurred. "I don't accept payment for what I provide for *friends*," he said. "I hope we will be friends, Mathias?"

"I'm—sure we will."

"Through the Web, and e-mail? Promise?"

"Yes. I'm sure."

In his car as Matt was about to speed away from the curb, he saw Hugo L. Chauncey's round ghostly face bobbing in a front window of the asphalt-sided bungalow. Those eyes staring wistfully after him.

Did you think I was like you? One of you?

39

NAME UNKNOWN. The ANGEL OF WRATH urged him out of exile. His rage would guide him through the night. On the country highways the headlights of his vehicle blazed like eyes bent upon revenge. *Vengeance is mine* saith the Lord. *Yes, it is time.*

The female had denied him. Had denied him lentil soup & sent him from her doorstep starving.

Her heavy swinging breasts inside her careless clothes. Bare, unfettered & the nipples erect. As she & others of that lesbian sisterhood laughing at NAME UNKNOWN. Sending him away in scorn with his carvings. *Not quite for us.*

In the rear of the rattling pickup beneath a tarpaulin, for it was raining, he carried a three-gallon container of kerosene. He had purchased the kerosene at the crossroads in the Pine Barrens where years ago he had purchased two cans of Pepsi-Cola. Only a youth of nineteen then & not yet come into his VISION. And tonight he had not yet a VISION of what he must do with the kerosene.

Where the flaming fireball must be unleashed.

But NAME UNKNOWN knew humbly to be prepared.

He followed the Weymouth River. He avoided the town of Weymouth with its nighttime traffic & confusing lights. He descended the hill to Lismore. *Joseph*! she had said. Her female-serpent tongue flicking between her lips. *Joseph Gavin. Hel-lo.*

Her voice flat & eyes indifferent upon him. Never would she gaze at him like that again. & never those mincing condescending words.

D Z he had loved & D Z he had honored. But Oriana he did not & would not. She was his Judas.

In the long fast of his exile. In the Pine Barrens. Beneath the livid sky. He had lost all sense of time. He had summoned forth a strange roiling pool of strength as a man even as flesh melted from his bones. In pride he kneaded his ribs through the skin. For Jesus Christ, too, had fasted forty days & forty nights in the wilderness. & had ascended to the right hand of the Father, to be glorified. In death, He had been glorified. In life, the world of Jews & Pharisees had scorned him. But His was the triumph, in death. & to Him it would be granted, the harrowing of Hell.

The female Oriana was his Judas. She it was who had told the police his name. Detectives had sought him out in his very place of residence. & in his workplace. With mocking eyes gazing upon *The Marriage of Heaven and Hell.* They had scorned him asking of him where did he get his ideas & they had lied to him cruelly declaring they wished to purchase his work. *Contemporary American art.* NAME UNKNOWN scorned & mocked & his enemies laughing at him. & the female Oriana at the heart of it. She too was to blame for the hurt to D Z. With her eyes she had challenged NAME UNKNOWN *Are you a man? Call yourself a man?*

It was not yet midnight. A quarter-moon in the sky reflected in the river. He turned up from the river. His vehicle in a low gear. *The Village of Lismore. Founded 1779.* Slowly he drove past the female's residence. The front part of the building was darkened & the CLOSED sign posted in the door. At the rear, however, where the female lived & worked, there was a light burning. He hoped she would be alone. For he would not wish to kill more than required.

Parking the pickup in the lane. Circling to the rear of the low, squat building. Where the sign ORIANA swung gently in the wind. So too his rage beat in his throat. *It is time* saith the Lord. *And more than time.* In the pocket of his denim work jacket, a wire-loop already fashioned. & on his strong hands, rubber gloves. He would use but once & burn & the ashes he would bury deep.

At the back, where it was lighted, he rapped quietly on the narrow door. There were flimsy bamboo blinds, & the female's body beyond. It was decreed, Oriana was alone. This was her fate & her doom for he would have entry, she could not bar him. Another time he rapped against the door, quietly. The power of NAME UNKNOWN was the power of inward stillness. In the windowpane the female face appeared, startled. A moonface smeared & shiny. Her melon breasts hung between her arms.

Why—Joseph. Is it you?

Guardedly she opened the door to him. Because she knew him. She believed she knew him.

Joseph? It's late, what do you want?

He pushed in. He would cease to think. Seeing his face, the female backed off. Clumsy, she struck a chair. With a deft hand, as if it were the hand of another, NAME UNKNOWN shut the door behind him.

The female was speaking his name. *Jo-seph? I said—what d'you want? I'm busy. I'm working late.* Her voice was angry, & then it was frightened. & seeing his face at last she backed off. In her amazed eyes was the knowledge of NAME UNKNOWN that always came too late.

In a loud yet muted voice NAME UNKNOWN cried *I'm hungry! Mom-ma, I'm hungry! You never fed me! You never fed me enough!*

He had no desire for Oriana. Hers was not a talent to be coveted by NAME UNKNOWN. She was not a sacrifice. He would not transport her to the sacred burial place in the Pine Barrens, for she was not worthy. He took no care with her. He felt no thrill, & he felt no sorrow. Her physical being aroused but disgust in him. Her face which was flaccid & oily & the lips drawn back from the teeth in a grimace of terror. Not her sagging belly, not her melon-breasts, not her reddened greasy lips & her eyes popping from their sockets excited him.

There would be no figure of Oriana. The female would have no place in *The Marriage of Heaven and Hell*.

He saw that she had been sculpting, in clay. A commonplace pot with handles like a stout female with hands on her hips, standing eighteen inches high. He did not touch it. On the workbench was a glass half full of an odorless clear liquid. Vodka, he believed. He did not touch this either.

Jo-seph! Jo-seph!

Never again would he hear that name, mincing & mocking in her mouth.

The heavy nude body he dragged from the floor to the sofa & arranged in the posture of the largest of the nude paintings. That painting on the wall, he had always blushed to see & had hated. A pink-flushed body sprawled on the identical sofa. Bushy henna-red pubic hair & belly rounded like a moon & breasts with nipples like the tips of thumbs. Where the painted

Oriana-nude simpered & gazed without shame at the viewer, the dead woman gaped with mouth ajar & damp with spittle, & her pop-eyes clouded. The wire-noose so tight around her throat you could not see it, except the thin seeping blood-necklace. She was a big woman & had put up a struggle like a great cat & NAME UNKNOWN had been patient jerking the noose tighter & tighter & had not slackened when her bowels spilled, for he was prepared for such. It was but Nature, he knew. & his disgust did not cause him to choke. & carefully then he arranged the female on the sofa in a pose of lascivious welcome. He arranged her rosy limbs in mimicry of the painted nude. & spread her fleshy thighs which were still warm.

Switching on a single light in the hall, quietly he made his way to the front of the gallery. To the door where the CLOSED sign had been hung. This sign he removed, & with a felt-tip pen took care to add words, so that the sign he would return to the windowpane was a new sign bearing a new message.

Still wearing the gloves, he washed his hands at the kitchen sink, at the rear. The gloves were of yellow rubber, for dishwashing. He was in no hurry but he did not linger. His breath came quick, & his senses pleasantly alert. As when he had sunk his face into a pool of chill water in the Barrens. The ANGEL OF WRATH had guided him from that hour long ago this very morning to this hour, past midnight. The ANGEL OF WRATH had guided him in this task as in others. Now the rage had burnt out. As a candle burns down, & out. When he left, he took care to close the back door. The lock he took care to secure. At the front of the building in a damp, fresh wind from the river he smiled to see the sign in the front door, & to see it with the eyes of others. As they would see it in the morning, & beyond.

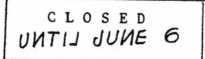

40 The strange, seductive words drummed in his head. Like pelting rain on the roof, the windshield and the hood of his speeding car. In the hypnotic rhythm of the windshield wipers. *How do you love when. You aren't loved in return. How do you love. How do you. Is your love any less beautiful. Betray your own passion if.* Matt shook his head to clear it, not liking the drift of such thoughts.

In the sky, it was dusk. On the expressway, quasi-daylight.

Matt was headed south out of Paramus, New Jersey in a great sea of migrating vehicles. Passing Hackensack which was indistinguishable from Paramus, passing Paterson which was indistinguishable from Hackensack. On Interstate 80 he drove east. Within the hour he would be back in Weymouth, unless there were further traffic slowdowns. With a part of his mind he believed it was urgent that he share the new information he had from Hugo L. Chauncey with Duana Zwolle's sister, if Ruellen was still in Weymouth; yet with another, perhaps more lucid part of his mind he understood that this would be a mistake, he'd be forcing himself upon an emotionally distraught young woman and this would further upset her and would jeopardize any more normal, more natural friendship that might evolve between them.

The first time, with Duana Zwolle, he'd failed. He could not fail a second time, with Ruellen.

He was determined not to seek out Ruellen Zwolle at the Marriott. Not even to telephone her. He had to control himself. Yet the words drummed in his head. The voice of youthful, exuberant wisdom. A brotherly voice. Mocking yet gentle. *How do you love when you aren't loved in return?* It was a reasonable question. It had been formulated rationally. *How do you love when? How do you elope when? When she is unwilling? When she has scorned you? When she refuses?* Matt shook his head, repelled.

You have to take her by force.
Take her by force.
Take her by force.

Yes, all right—he saw the logic. But it was a sick, pathological logic. Not *his*.

From his car phone Matt called his home, that's to say his former home, spoke briefly and politely to Tess, then to Davey and Graeme explaining why he hadn't been able to see them that day but would try to see them tomorrow—"Daddy loves you, O.K.?"

As, seeing the high-rise Marriott Inn emerge out of the traffic haze just outside Weymouth, Matt exited impulsively, and drove into the lot.

Probably, she isn't here.
Probably she's checked out. Returned to Santa Monica.

If that was so, Matt would write to Ruellen Zwolle. He could explain himself more convincingly in a letter; that would be the more civilized, humane approach.

He wasn't thinking at the moment that he should contact the Weymouth detectives whose cards he'd been carrying in his wallet for months. What he'd learned from Hugo L. Chauncey, what he suspected and the man he suspected—Joseph Gavin. (But, as Hugo said, the police must already know most of the information he'd provided Matt. They'd have tapped into the serial killer files as Hugo had, and discovered the connections between cases and victims over the past twenty years. If an amateur like Hugo knew such things, surely police experts would know?) Except Matt hadn't much faith in these police, who'd harassed him and hadn't detained Gavin, allowed the murderer to disappear. And Matt had already sent them an anonymous note. He didn't want to risk further involvement.

In the Marriott, Matt checked at the front desk and was told that, yes, Ms. Ruellen Zwolle was registered there. Matt heard himself ask for her room to be rung. There was no answer, would he like to leave a message? Matt said quickly, "No, thanks. I'll try later."

So she was still in Weymouth.

Somewhere in Weymouth.

In the cocktail lounge off the foyer he saw a slender dark-haired woman seated alone at the bar. An attractive woman about Ruellen Zwolle's age—but not Ruellen Zwolle. Matt's pulse had quickened in that instant, absurdly. *I don't want this. Jesus, I'm not a kid.* The symptoms were obvious, but what to do about it? Matt ordered a drink at the bar, a glass of white wine. Just a single glass. His nerves were shot, but he was under control. He'd been dying for a drink all afternoon. (That session with Hugo L. Chauncey! The stale-smelling room, the glowing computer screen and repellent, profoundly disturbing information Hugo had blithely summoned up with his fingertips. The Bridegroom, he'd called the killer, almost fondly. NAME UN-KNOWN, Matt knew him to be. Six victims, at the least. Six! And the son of a bitch was still free, and would kill again unless stopped.)

People entered the cocktail lounge, couples talking and laughing together. Matt glanced up anxiously. What was this place, why was he here? His home, with his wife and children, was less than five miles away. Yet he had to force himself to recall it, as if that life, and the effort of that life, belonged to another man, in whom Matt no longer had much interest.

He wondered if she was thinking of him, too—Ruellen Zwolle. She'd stared at him in the street the other day, when he'd been walking with Davey and Graeme. That look in her face. Shock, and dismay. *You! You have children.*

She'd read Duana's diary. She'd called him Nighthawk. She believed him to have been her sister's lover.

Matt would have to write to her about that, too. He'd have to be as frank and as truthful as possible. So far as he knew the truth.

He recalled, with a stab of sexual desire, how he'd forced her—Ruellen Zwolle—back against a wall, so swiftly he hadn't known what he was doing, pressing the flat of his hand against her mouth. He'd caused her nose to bleed. He'd wanted to lick the blood with his tongue. *Don't struggle. Don't be afraid. I won't hurt you.*

Except: maybe Matt McBride did want to hurt Ruellen Zwolle? He'd seen the fury in her face, those glaring eyes. She'd certainly wanted to hurt him.

She's afraid of me. But I'm afraid of her, too.

Matt finished his glass of wine and left the cocktail lounge. But he couldn't bring himself to leave the Marriott, just yet. He drifted into the interior, toward the rear. The pool?

Matt would think afterward that he couldn't have known. It hadn't been instinct or even a lucky hunch. Because he'd never heard that Duana Zwolle was a swimmer. Yet, he wasn't surprised to discover Ruellen Zwolle in the pool. He recognized her at once, though she was wearing a black bathing cap, and swimming laps vigorously in a swift, perfectly calibrated Australian crawl. Her forehead was furrowed in thought, her eyes narrowed and her skin olive-pale. She was one of only three adults in the pool, and the only serious swimmer. Matt watched admiringly as the young woman swam from one end of the pool to the other, always staying in her lane, staring straight ahead. There was such fanatic intensity in her gaze, Matt guessed she wasn't seeing anything at all. She would not see him, he hoped. How smooth and beautifully shaped her bare arms and shoulders, though hard-muscled; how strong, her long graceful legs. Her resolute, pursed mouth. He would kiss that mouth, he would force it open to him. *She is Duana returned to me. Yet a more sexual, dangerous Duana.* Matt believed, if he'd never seen Ruellen Zwolle before, he would be struck by her as he was now. He couldn't look away from her. He saw that she was an excellent swimmer though there was a melancholy grimness in her manner that suggested little of play or enjoyment. He couldn't easily imagine her swimming in the company of another, though she could learn to. He ached, suddenly, to be in that pool with her! He'd loved to swim as a kid. He'd loved to dive.

Matt took note of his surroundings, and was relieved to see he wasn't the only clothed, nonswimmer in the pool atrium. There were poolside tables where drinks were served. Children were splashing in a wading pool. Though the air stank of chlorine, and there were glistening puddles on the tile, it was an attractive space, intended to resemble the out-of-doors. There were tropical trees in clay pots and a bright, warm light in imitation of the sun. A soft rock-calypso tape played. Matt stood back from the poolside, dreading being seen. *She'll think I've been following her. Stalking her.*

Yet he lingered. Watching Ruellen Zwolle swimming laps in the Marriot pool. This was where he was, and there must be significance in it. Since the New Year, he'd come to accept his fate. He liked it that, unseen by Ruellen Zwolle, he could protect her; as he had not protected her sister; and she, Ruellen, needn't know he existed. There was a peculiar vividness to the light here, reflected like shattered glass in the choppy aqua water. The rock-calypso Muzak was hypnotic. Matt's mind emptied. He was happy, though to be happy in such circumstances, in a world in which a serial killer tortured and killed young women, was absurd. Yet Matt felt he was in the right place. She'd drawn him here, and he'd come to her, and it was right. He'd penetrated the veil of *sangsāra*—maybe that was it?

"You!—what do you want? Are you following me?"

There was Ruellen Zwolle gasping for breath at the edge of the pool nearest Matt, swiftly and not very gracefully climbing out to confront him. Water streamed from her body. She'd spoken sharply, drawing the attention of others. She'd whipped off her bathing cap and her dark hair sprang disheveled and matted about her face. Her eyes were fierce as icepicks and her mouth twisted as if she'd bitten into something repulsive. Matt came quickly to her, and tried to take hold of her hands, which were clenched like fists, to comfort her. "I didn't mean to startle you. In fact, yes—I've been hoping to speak with you. But I didn't know you were here, I swear."

Ruellen cried, "Don't touch me! I'm afraid of you. Go *away*."

Blinking as if she'd come into a too brightly lit room, she was looking for something to cover herself with. Her one-piece bathing suit, made of a shiny black fabric like satin, clung wetly to her tense body. Matt saw the swell of her breasts, the pale shallow between her breasts, a scattering of tiny freckles on her chest and upper arms. Her thighs were tensely corded with muscle. Her long, narrow, white feet. Matt was dazed by her nearness, and her agitation, the damp, slightly oily smell of her hair, wanting her not to be afraid of him, and not to call attention to the two of them in this public place. He handed her a white terrycloth robe slung across a chair, helped her slip into its awkward, heavy sleeves even as she shrugged from him as if dreading his touch. Matt said in a soft, placating voice, the voice he used to calm his sons when they were emotional, "Hey, I'm sorry. I mean, to surprise you like this. I really didn't intend it. If we could just talk for a few minutes—?"

Ruellen was trying to step into open-toed shoes, and stumbled, and had to lean against Matt's arm to get her balance. Then she was walking quickly away from him, headed for an elevator. Her agitation had drawn attention: a man in a Marriott Inn blazer spoke with her to ask if anything was wrong, and Ruellen Zwolle said vehemently, "No! Just leave me alone." She stepped into the elevator, and Matt joined her just as the door was sliding shut.

The sickening thought came to Matt—*Does she think that I'm the one who has hurt her sister? Nighthawk?*

The elevator was a glass capsule, rapidly rising seventeen floors above the pool, and looking out into a larger atrium space of open walkways and louvered windows. A small elevator, which would scarcely have held three other passengers. Matt was smelling Ruellen Zwolle's hair, and the chlorine, and had to resist the impulse to touch her, she was shivering so. Her face had gone waxen. It was clear she was frightened of him. Matt said, "I'll stay only as long as you want me, I promise. But I need to talk to you about—what has happened to Duana."

Ruellen stammered, "I can't. It's too raw. It makes me crazy. I'm not able to deal with it. Please just leave me alone."

"But it's important that we talk, Ruellen. Can I call you—Ruellen?"

She was angry, and half-sobbing. "No! You can't. You were Duana's lover, *I don't want you.*"

Yet strangely, at the door to her room, which was 1711, as Ruellen fumbled with the card key, she seemed to acquiese to Matt's presence after all. As if they were husband and wife, in an agitated mood, Matt offered to take the card key from her, she slapped at his hand and continued to try to insert it, and at last succeeded—the door unlocked, and Ruellen stepped inside panting, and Matt pushed open the door and stepped inside with her.

He shut the door. He said, "I promise. I won't stay long. I don't want to upset you, but—"

She shoved at him, the palms of her hands against his chest. Her face was furious, contorted as a three-year-old's. Matt thought, amazed *She wants to hurt me. She'd tear my throat with her teeth if she could.* "You were her lover so don't you touch me! You hear?—fuck you! Get the hell away from me or I'll kill you."

Matt laughed, shocked. "Kill *me*? Why? I'm your friend."

"You're not my friend. I don't know who the fuck you are. I don't know you, and I don't trust you. Breaking into Duana's apartment— as if you had the right." Ruellen was panting, still shoving at him; Matt tried to grab hold of her wrists, which were so slender his thumb and fingers fit easily around them. "And following *me*. Spying on *me*. I should report you. They've already investigated you, they said. But they don't know about *this*. They don't know how you've threatened me."

"Ruellen, I haven't threatened you."

"The way you *look at me*. As if *you had the right*. You were Duana's lover—*not mine*."

"I—I wasn't your sister's lover. Not in the way you think."

"You were Duana's lover, she was crazy about you. I've read the diary. I've read the diary a dozen times. 'Nighthawk'—and you didn't come forward, when she—when it happened—did you? The detectives told me. You didn't come to them, they had to go to *you*. If you'd loved my sister, you would have behaved differently."

"I—I did love your sister. But—"

"Damn you! *You can't love me.*"

Another time the agitated woman pushed at Matt. Raked her nails across his face. He'd had enough. He grabbed her, moving his mouth over hers hard enough to stifle her words; gripping her so tightly, wanting to hurt her, they stumbled and swayed together like a wounded couple. It was as if a swoon of oblivion rose about them to encapsulate them. Like a mist, or like the rapidly rising glass elevator, invisibly caging them. But Ruellen struggled, like a panicked animal, and Matt quickly released her.

She backed away from him, pleading. "I—can't. I'm afraid of you. I'm terrified of—all that's happened."

We were sisters, and we were identical twins. Duana never told you about me, I know.

In her place, I wouldn't have told you, either.

It isn't something you tell a lover. That there are two of you, not one. That God made you not-unique.

In the Zwolle family, there's the story that it isn't known which of us was born first, Duana or Ruellen. That's what my parents claimed. They didn't want to seem to favor either of us. Though they loved me more than they loved Duana, I think. Because I was someone known to them, my talent could be plumbed. My soul. I was that shallow, and Duana was deep.

In Duana, a stone could fall, and fall, and fall. You'd never hear it strike bottom.

In Duana, there was mystery. From the start. From the cradle. People are intrigued by mystery, but if they can't solve it, they are frightened by it. They hate it. And people are unnerved by identical twins, in any case. It's true: there is something monstrous about doubling, as about any kind of cloning. Primitive people have destroyed individual twins, sometimes both twins, or made them into deities, which is another kind of destruction.

You want to know: Did we have any psychic connection? After we were grown, we didn't. That was my wish, not Duana's. I, too, was repulsed by twin-ness.

I went to live in California. Where there is only one of me—Ruellen Zwolle. Thousands of miles between us. So I would never risk blundering into a room where my sister might be. I would never risk being exposed—Not-unique!

But when Duana was taken by that madman, and tortured, and killed—yes, there was a psychic connection between us then. A kind of web. A shimmering web. I was in terror of it, I couldn't escape it. Until she died, and I was released, and could breathe again.

I think, yes, I will tell the truth now. To you. Because you were Duana's lover, and even if you didn't really know her, you were loved by her. I'll just say how it was. I'll never tell my parents. My mother is ill now, and if she recovers she won't want to know more than she already knows.

For this is a fact: I was grateful when Duana died, at last. As if we were Siamese twins, joined in our bodies. I didn't want to die with her.

When Duana first disappeared, I flew back East. She'd always been a strange person, guided by her own instinct—it might have been deliberate on her part, to "disappear." But we soon realized she'd been taken. Abducted. Against her will. We came to Weymouth and kept a vigil for her. It was a nightmare time. I had terrible dreams. Even while awake sometimes—hallucinations. Like a whirlpool, like madness. I knew he was torturing my sister, and he would kill her. I could hear her screaming. The screaming was my own. He gouged out her eyes. I know this. He raped her, many times. With something hard, sharp. Finally he killed her. He strangled her. She died choking for breath and I—almost died. Some of this I told the detectives, and maybe they believed me, and maybe they were only just humoring me. I suppose I was emotional—"hysterical." But I know that my sister is dead now, he killed her on the night of December 31. New Year's Eve. It can't have been a coincidence, can it? Where her body is, I don't know. I'm terrified we'll never know. There were hours of her dying and when finally it was over I was unconscious for eighteen hours. My parents thought I'd had a stroke or a cerebral hemorrhage. But I recovered. I'm strong. You know that, don't you?—I'm a strong woman. I'm not weak. I could kill him with my own hands. If I had the opportunity.

Then, I will have my own life again. When her killer has died.

I'll tell you—the thought used to come to me, "Duana might die first." I'd feel a sense of excitement thinking this. It was like an opaque sky opening up. Because as children we'd been so close, and I came to feel I was suffocating. When we were just beginning to talk, Duana and I had a private language. Many twins do. It begins in the crib, and it can continue for years. My parents were fearful of us, our twin-ness. Our secrets. For years, in elementary school, Duana and I had to be together. We'd cry if we were apart. We sensed ourselves empowered somehow. As if we were twice-born in the world. People like twins, at least initially. They like to look at twins. We liked to look at ourselves in the mirror. Duana would draw pictures of the two of us. She'd take photographs of us. A few years ago, when I was back east for the holidays, and Duana was in Maine with us, she asked me if she could take some photographs of us, so I agreed. I didn't really want to, but I agreed. Later, when she sent me some prints, I tore them into pieces. The image was of Duana and me as if we were the same person, a girl resting the side of her face against a mirror except there was no mirror. I was fascinated by the image—I couldn't tell at first which face was Duana's, and which was mine. Then finally I couldn't bear it. I tore every print into pieces.

I loved my mysterious, talented sister. I was proud of her. It was my twin I hated.

When we were eleven, I began to detach myself from Duana. I began to make my own friends. It seemed to happen overnight. And boys began to notice me, too. Because I've always been the more outgoing of the two of us. I've always been more "popular"—if I've wanted to be. Duana was more talented and more intelligent but she never did as well in school as I did. When we were teenagers, I began to hate Duana. I couldn't bear to be touched by her. I didn't want to be near her. She was so quiet, and so special, and so good. We were both art students, but her talent was a genuine talent, and mine was—well, what it is. I told myself I didn't care, but I was bitterly jealous. Once, we were fifteen, I'd said something cruel to Duana and she looked at me with those eyes of hers, which are different from my own eyes, though people swear we look the same; and I lost it, and pinched her arm hard. She only whispered, "Rue, why?" I laughed at her, and ran out of the room. And that night, I saw the bruise, the pinch mark, on my own arm. In the exact place I'd pinched Duana.

After that, I never hurt my sister again. Physically.

Now she's dead. I know she's dead. She's dead, and I survived. But I haven't been the same since she was taken away, and I'm afraid I never will be again. So I want you to leave. Unless—unless you can find the man who did that to her, and destroy him—I can't bear the sight of you. You were her lover, and I can't bear that. I can't bear being touched by you and maybe, for the rest of my life, by any man.

41

When Matt returned home to his empty apartment, there was the phone message he'd been awaiting for weeks.

A nasal voice, not familiar at first. *Hey Mr. McBride? This is Todd over in Clinton Falls? Y'know—the Amoco Station? You asked me to keep an eye out for this guy Gavin? Well, he's back. He stopped just now for gas and he's gonna bring his pickup over in the morning for some work. It's 6 P.M. now.* There was a pause. Then, *Hope you get this message, Mr. McBride, and hope to hear from you. Stay cool!*

Matt replayed the tape. He was smiling, dazed. Couldn't believe his good luck.

He owed the young mechanic two hundred dollars. He'd pay him three hundred. If he survived.

It was fifty-eight miles to Clinton Falls on interstate 78. Clear driving at this hour. Matt passed the darkened Amoco station at 10:12 P.M.

This long, vertiginous day. Like a tall flight of stairs. You can't see the bottom step from the top, and from the bottom step you can't see the top. Maybe Matt wasn't thinking clearly by this time. Maybe he should have gone to the police. (Though he distrusted and feared them.) He should have a better weapon than just a knife to protect himself from a man he knew to be dangerous. A man he knew to be a psychopath, a killer. A man who was cunning, unpredictable and strong, though with his long flowing hair and beard he appeared weak, effeminate.

He shouldn't be going alone. And no one to know where he was headed. At night. Tess had accused him, the last time they'd spoken together at length, of having become increasingly reckless, desperate—"For all I know, suicidal." Matt hadn't wanted to tell her he wasn't suicidal, but murderous. *I don't want to share the bastard with anyone. He's mine.*

Maybe he'd remove Gavin's vocal cords. Maybe that's why he was bringing a knife.

Maybe he'd remove Gavin's leg muscles. Or castrate him.

That was justice, *and what we require is justice.*

As Hugo had explained: a serial killer like Gavin needs to be in control. He plans his killings carefully, his skill isn't in improvising. His victims are young women. Physically weaker than he. And he takes them by surprise.

But Matt would take him by surprise. *And he won't be a match for a man.*

Still, as Matt approached Gavin's driveway along the darkened highway, watching for the mailbox, he was thinking he would have liked to have a gun. Maybe he could have asked Sid Krell for his gun, claiming he needed to protect himself. (But he didn't trust Sid. He couldn't trust anyone.) He had only a knife, and this was a nine-inch stainless steel steak knife he'd purchased at a hardware store when he'd moved into his condominium. Setting up minimal housekeeping for himself. He'd bought the knife knowing it might be the very weapon he would use to protect himself against Joseph Gavin, and possibly it would be the weapon with which he killed Joseph Gavin.

Yet he hadn't bought a hunting knife, or a fishing knife; he hadn't made inquiries about getting a permit for a handgun. Why, he didn't know. And wondering now, the knife with its raw, sharp blade in his jacket pocket—*Can I use it? Can I hurt another person?*

There was Gavin's tilting mailbox, there was the rutted driveway leading back into darkness. From the highway, you couldn't see any sign of human habitation even by daylight, and this was night. Matt drove past the driveway and parked his car in a wooded area a half-mile away. At this hour, there was little traffic on the country highway. There were no nearby neighbors, no lights. Matt took a flashlight from the glove compartment of the Acura and made his way carefully back to Gavin's acre of land through the stubby remains of a cornfield. His heart pounded hard and strong and steady and he believed he was doing the right thing, the necessary thing. If the man was here, he would find him. If the man was here, there was no one but Matt McBride to exact justice. A powerful molten liquid flooded Matt's veins. Vividly he recalled how, a long time ago in Alaska, when he'd been just a naive, lanky kid, a kid out for adventure, he'd taken LSD with friends and he'd been just slightly panicked telling himself *Look, this won't be real, this is a dream, O.K.*? and over several hours he'd hallucinated the Arctic sky blossoming into a kaleidoscope of astonishing colors and shapes like maddened comets and he'd managed, if barely, to keep in mind *This is a dream! This is a dream and can't hurt you*! Yet Matt had known how close he'd come to panic, terror, collapse and psychosis. He'd maintained control like a man walking a tightrope. He hadn't fallen, but he might have. And it was this control he exerted now, crossing the muddy cornfield, and a marshy field, approaching Gavin's trailer and the barn from the side. But he was disappointed—he didn't see any lights. No pickup truck in the driveway, not even behind the trailer or the barn where Gavin might have parked it to hide it from view. *What if he isn't here after all? Where can I find him?*

It was a cold damp spring night. Overhead, clouds like broken chunks of concrete moved across the moon.

Matt cautiously approached the rear of the trailer. A sliver of moonlight was reflected in one of the narrow windows. There were no lights inside, no indication that anyone was there. Matt shone the flashlight sparingly and it seemed to him that nothing had been altered around the trailer since the last time he'd been there, ten days before. Overturned trash containers, a rusty gas tank. Rotted leaves and scattered debris. Matt remembered that Joseph Gavin had a woman friend in the vicinity of Clinton Falls, someone who'd provided an alibi for him for the night of December 28. Maybe he was staying with her.

Or maybe, like Matt, he'd parked somewhere else, not wanting his vehicle to be seen. *Maybe he's inside the trailer watching me right now.*

Matt switched off the flashlight. He stood crouched at a corner of the trailer where no one could have seen him from inside, through any of the windows. He waited. He listened. Leaning his head against the metallic side of the trailer and hearing nothing except his own hard, steady, strong heartbeat.

No one. Not here.

Matt took a circuitous route to get to the barn, avoiding the open space where planks were set down in mud. The barn was slightly uphill and he made his way slowly through underbrush and marshy grass. About fifteen feet from the barn, he seemed to see—a dim light inside? A small square window facing him, boarded-up from the inside, seemed to be emitting, around its edges, a faint glow.

Was Gavin inside? He must be inside. NAME UNKNOWN with his crude mannequins. *The Marriage of Heaven and Hell.*

He misses them. Can't stay away from them. His brides. Six victims. Maybe he's come back to take them away.

Matt's hand was inside his jacket pocket, gripping the knife handle nervously. He was a man who'd been in fights in his younger life and he'd been in some stressful situations but he'd never used a knife even as self-protection. Too late, he was thinking he'd better have brought the tire iron from the trunk of his car. He'd been thinking that righteousness would protect him, like armor?

As every man, though knowing better, thinks *I can't be killed—can I? I can't even be harmed. I am the hero of this story. I am the luminous force for good about which the story tells itself.*

Matt wasn't using his flashlight but he could see by patchy moonlight that the padlock had been removed from this door at the rear of the barn. Cautiously he approached it, and again stood and listened. And again he heard nothing. He leaned to the crack of the door and squinted inside and saw a single naked light bulb burning, in a socket in a beam at a height of about five feet. But no one seemed to be in the barn. Gavin must have been here, and gone away again.

Slowly, his heartbeat in his fingertips, Matt pushed open the door. The hinge creaked faintly. But that was the only sound Matt heard. In the shadows, the mannequin-figures stood expectantly. He should have been prepared to see them, but still it was a mild shock. *Save us! Don't forsake us.* Each was turned toward Matt, yet each seemed isolated from the others, as if unaware of the others. Matt counted only five; what had happened to the sixth? Cautiously he eased into the barn and saw, in an open space amid the clutter, the sixth mannequin, on a crate. NAME UNKNOWN had been working on it recently. The head was no longer bald but covered in dark, tangled hair with a synthetic sheen that fell to the figure's hips. Matt recognized Duana Zwolle instantly.

He switched on his flashlight, requiring more light than the naked bulb could provide, and saw, yes, sickened by the knowledge, and baffled that he hadn't seen it before, that this mawkish, childlike figure, meant to be female, yet sexless, with its shy ducked head and dusky skin was obviously meant to resemble Duana Zwolle.

Save me! Don't forsake me.

The other five figures seemed to be looking on, helpless. Like ungainly dolls they all were, lacking breasts and hips, and their legs oddly thick in proportion to their bodies so that they resembled upright wooden clothespins. *Save us! Save us! Save us!* Their ill-fitting glass eyes glittered wildly. Their mouths were arrested in soundless screams. Matt shone his flashlight boldly into the corners of the barn, confident now that Joseph Gavin wasn't here. The interior was crammed with boxes, crates, farm implements, an old tractor, a harrow, stacks of lumber. Cobwebs festooned every surface and hung in tatters from the thick beams stretching across the width of the ceiling. Matt breathed deeply, smelling dust, grime, rot; and the sharper odor of paint and kerosene. NAME UNKNOWN had been painting the sixth mannequin, but had clearly been having trouble mixing his paints and applying color evenly; he was such an amateur, he'd overlapped brushstrokes so that the mannequin's skin was leaden-beige in places, a darker beige in others, sallow and sickly and mottled. *To die, and at the hands of such a jerk!*

Matt came to stand before the pathetic figure, which seemed to be gazing at him, or toward him, with its mismatched glass eyes. He touched the dull, dead synthetic hair. It wasn't an actual wig, but something Gavin had created. You wouldn't know whether to laugh or feel pity, seeing such a thing. You had to wonder if the eye that had imagined it saw it otherwise than it was. *What does he see? Is this*

how the world looks to him? Almost, amid his disgust, Matt felt a tinge
of pity.

It was then he heard a footfall, and turned to see a rushed, blurred
shape moving at him.

"Devil! *Devil!*"

Gavin leapt at him, out of nowhere. His eyes were narrowed in rage,
and he was swinging something, a hammer? a chisel? at Matt, which
struck him on the upper back of his right shoulder, narrowly missing
his head. The force of the blow sent Matt staggering. He ducked,
turned, in a haze of pain managed to grab Gavin and throw him off
balance. The men fell heavily to the earthen floor, grunting, struggling
together like desperate beasts. They collided with crates, farm implements, one of the mannequin-figures. Gavin continued to curse, "Devil!" Matt managed to get the knife out of his pocket, but couldn't
keep hold of it, as Gavin battered him; the knife slipped from his
fingers and was lost. Then Matt found himself crawling desperate to
escape the blows of a hammer on his unprotected back, kidneys, arms,
grunting with pain trying to shield his head yet somehow he had hold
of a tool of some kind, a chisel, about twelve inches in length, blindly
he turned to use it against his assailant striking Gavin in the cheek,
the chisel's point skidded up into Gavin's left eye, and in a split-
second piercing the eye. Gavin shrieked in animal pain and rage.
Blood streaked his face. Matt held the chisel in both his shaking
hands but hadn't the strength, or the will, to drive the chisel into
Gavin's other eye; and in that moment of hesitation Gavin regained
the advantage, knocking Matt to the ground with a blow on the head,
and blood now gushed from Matt's head, and in a haze of pain he was
crawling again on hands and knees, desperate to save himself, a high-
pitched, furious voice rose behind him—"I am NAME UNKNOWN.
I am NAME UNKNOWN." Suddenly there was a sharp odor of kerosene. A soft explosion, and an eruption of fire. Out of nowhere—
puffs, explosions of fire, and then crackling flames. Matt was astonished to discover his clothes, his hair, sparked by flames. He tried to
push himself to safety as a child might, but where was safety, where

wouldn't the fingers of fire spread, a dark hidden place beneath the tractor, behind the flattened tires, he had the confused idea that there might be water close by, a pool, a dark pond, he could save himself by plunging into it. He was crawling on the earthen floor that tilted and became vertical throwing him off, he was falling, dragged back into the fire which was many fires, kerosene-soaked rags catching fire, clumps of dried hay, Matt was alone in the burning barn, his enemy had staggered to escape and shut the door against him, Matt hadn't the strength to force the door open, had hardly the strength to heave himself to his knees to grasp at the handle, his fingernails clawing at the splintery wood and his thoughts came at him now in explosions of sensation like cartoon balloons, what a wrong, bitter thing this was, that he should die, and Gavin, his enemy, should escape. He believed he would have accepted even this terrible death if his enemy had died with him.

Hearing now the faint, fading cries of the mannequins. *Save us! Save us! Don't forsake us!*

The last thing Matt McBride heard, as the ground seemed to open beneath him, and he fell.

42

NAME UNKNOWN. Dazed & wounded he dragged himself to safety. His eye, his eye!—the Devil-enemy had taken his eye. & hot gushing blood streaking his face, & its taste salty & terrible in his mouth. *Yet he would prevail. He had wrestled with the very Devil, & had escaped with his life.*

Stumbling now through the marshy grass, through underbrush & by clouded moonlight, panting, whimpering with pain, sight remaining only in one eye & that sight blotched & distorted & yet he made his way to the pickup hidden in the derelict lane. & so NAME UNKNOWN slipped from them another time.

NAME UNKNOWN. Who was himself the ANGEL OF WRATH fiery in vengeance.

You will not cage me now. I am escaped from you.

How had it happened, he could not comprehend! His sacred figures destroyed of necessity, & yet cruelly. He would never recover such loss.

Having had no knowledge beforehand, no vision to guide him. How the terrible fiery sword would strike. & his own trembling hands the instrument of ANNIHILATION.

The woman had betrayed him, he believed. The Brough woman.

Yet he had not time to wreak punishment upon her head, & the boy. For NAME UNKNOWN must flee his enemies, that they not mock him & run him to earth, that he devour dirt. *Remains there now but shame & mocking eyes.*

He would escape to the Barrens, & there he would prevail.

Except: bleeding from his eye, & other wounds, & his mind clouded, & *The Marriage of Heaven and Hell* his life's work destroyed. Like a rat run to earth, & what future but to crouch in exile in the tractless swamp. & his enemies might seek him there, with bloodhounds & helicopters, he knew.

For theirs was the power & might of the State, & he but a single man of vision—NAME UNKNOWN.

It is finished, it is done.

& so on the nighttime highway, his vehicle veering & weaving like a wounded beast, & the engine fitful, a VISION came to NAME UNKNOWN who was the ANGEL OF WRATH fiery in his own vengeance & justice.

You need not now continue.

Your earthly life has passed.

Remains there now but shame & mocking eyes.

Remains there now but arrest, & imprisonment.

Remains there now but the cage of death overseen by your enemies.

& the logic of it swept upon him like balm to his throbbing wounds. & the justice of it. NAME UNKNOWN must cleanse himself.

He had no clear knowledge of where he was. Not many miles from Clinton Falls for he had had not strength to drive the pickup, his brain confused & bones of his body broken, & the gash in his face livid with pain. Somewhere in Somerset County near Blawenburg, in a rural landscape not familiar to him, & how many miles & hours he could not endure to the Pine Barrens where he might take refuge, & yet he could not walk there, not in his condition; & the Ford pickup at last shuddered to a stop at the roadside, & the engine would not restart. *Your earthly life has passed.*

& so with a container of kerosene beside him, calmly NAME UNKNOWN poured its contents upon himself, his bloodied clothes & bloodied beard. & the interior of the cab. & calmly seated where he was behind the wheel he took up the matchbox another time, & a single wooden match with shaking fingers he managed to strike.

& the FLAMING SWORD was upon him, in the blazing shape of a figure that was NAME UNKNOWN, & there came an explosion as if from the very Heavens to consume the vehicle that, at daybreak, would yet be smoldering when discovered by a motorist. & sifting through rubble they would discover but the charred, burnt remains of the immortal spirit that was NAME UNKNOWN, but the mere husk & shed skin of mortality.

You will not cage me now. I am escaped from you forever.

Epilogue

Life After Death

Nighthawk. Too stubborn to die.

He'd saved himself, though he'd never remember exactly how.

Must've managed to get the door open. To crawl out. And to crawl fifteen or more feet to safety, lying in shock in marsh grass, in mud-muck. His clothes had been on fire, and his hair. He'd rolled himself screaming in wet grass and mud to save his life. His burnt flesh, lacerated hands and feet.

Too stubborn to die. Just yet.

Anyway, not like that.

Then he was hearing sirens, and the excited shouts of the strangers who would rescue him. They'd come to him from the far side of a vast abyss. Lifting him with care, and the blazing barn only yards away exploding in sparks like fireworks.

Flying then along the deserted interstate eastward toward Weymouth, and Newark where his life would be saved, though he had no knowledge of it, and would not afterward recall.

Only waking one day to understand he had not died. His life had been given back to him and eagerly Matt McBride would seize it, like a prize he didn't deserve but would accept.

Would she come to see him in the hospital?

He waited.

They would graft skin from his buttocks and thighs onto his tender, mutilated face and throat. Here, he'd suffered second-degree burns. On his chest, abdomen and legs he'd suffered first-degree burns which didn't require grafting, yet were painful as scalding steam against flesh. One day these wounds would heal to striated, weirdly smooth and shiny scars a woman might be drawn to touch, even to caress.

There would be something perversely erotic in these scars on Matt's forehead, neck and upper back and shoulders. And an erotic charge in the woman's fingertips. So Matt shuddered, and shut his eyes that suddenly stung with tears. And the woman's breath came quick and panting, and she shut her eyes, too, leaning her face hard against his in a strange, fierce ecstasy.

When did you first know?

When I first saw you.

And I knew, when I first saw you.

In the hospital in Newark, though, Ruellen Zwolle hadn't come to see Matt McBride.

None of the Zwolles had come to see him.

Duana Zwolle's body had been recovered from a desolate area of the Pine Barrens, and identified; and given a funeral and a burial in the young woman's hometown in Maine. But Matt McBride, in misery in the burn ward at Newark Hospital, had known nothing of this.

Later, he would learn that Joseph Gavin (identified in the media as a "local, unsuccessful sculptor who called himself 'NAME UN-KNOWN' ") had killed himself not long after he'd fled the burning barn with Matt inside. On a deserted country road forty miles south of Clinton Falls he'd doused himself and the interior of his Ford pickup with kerosene, struck a match and went up in flames. There were no witnesses to his immolation and identification of his charred remains was circumstantial, since, as Joseph Gavin, he'd seemed to have no dental records. But the next day, Gavin's woman friend Shirley Brough went to Weymouth police to repudiate Gavin, who'd threatened her and her son, she claimed, if she told anyone what she knew of the women he'd boasted of killing. Brough wept saying she "needed to get this sin off my conscience"—informing police where Gavin had said he'd left the body of Duana Zwolle, near the ruins of an abandoned old church at the juncture of the Batsto and Mullica rivers.

Brough told police she thought there might be another body in that area, too. One "going back a few years, before I knew him." A day's search yielded both the partly decomposed remains of Duana Zwolle and a human skeleton to be identified as that of the long-missing

Marie Tompkins, a TV broadcaster who'd disappeared with no trace from Trenton in 1993.

In time, several other unsolved murders and abductions of young women in New Jersey, Pennsylvania, Delaware and Maryland since 1976 would be attributed to Joseph Gavin. And the recent murder of the sculptor-painter Oriana in her Lismore home.

In his hospital bed, Matt watched a TV interview with Shirley Brough. She was a doughy-faced, apologetic woman with small, frightened eyes and a bright lipsticked mouth. Asked why Gavin had murdered Duana Zwolle and Oriana, Brough said she thought it was because "the women had insulted him somehow. He was a proud man." Asked why she'd waited so long to come forward to authorites, Brough began to cry and repeated her claim that Gavin had threatened to kill her and her son both; but also, "He wanted to marry me, and Randy needs a father. He was awful good to Randy and I can appreciate that in a man."

If she chooses to keep her distance from me, then that's that.

I won't pursue her. I'll let her go.

So Matt McBride told himself. Day following day in Newark Hospital.

In his morphine-haze in which pain hovered at a distance only just beyond the perimeters of his cranked-up hospital bed he blinked up eagerly at visitors and stretched his numb rubber lips into a smile of greeting.

They asked him with grave faces how he was and he assured them *not bad! not bad at all!*

"A hell of a lot better than I look, for sure."

The morphine wasn't going to last forever. Even in his floating euphoric hours he knew he'd be brought back down to earth, and fast. Like a helium balloon yanked by its string *down down down*.

He tried to be philosophical about it. His enemy Joseph Gavin had died, and was gone from the earth. The terrible and irrevocable things he'd done were of the past. Matt McBride was living *now*. And Ruellen

Zwolle was living *now*. Even if she kept herself distant from him, and denied the bond between them, this truth could not be altered.

Yet in his nightmares of the burning barn he saw her. It was she, the *missing girl*, he struggled to rescue. *Save me! save me!* she cried as flames engulfed her stricken figure. *Save me! don't forsake me!* as her long thick hair lifted in flames.

It was Matt McBride to whom she cried for help, for there was no one else. Desperately he tried to make his way to her through flames licking at his hands and face, a roaring of fire in his ears.

From these ugly nightmares he would wake to the misery of his burnt, tender skin. He groaned aloud. He clenched his fists and pounded the bedclothes.

Crisp cotton hospital sheets like sandpaper to the touch.

The woman who'd been Matt's wife for nine years came to see him, and brought his sons who were frightened of Daddy, a man with a face they didn't know, and smells about him they didn't know, and his voice hoarse, and cracked, so they had to lean close to his mouth to hear, and it frightened them to lean close because Daddy was changed, and Tess all but chided him—"You expect too much, Matt. You leave our life, yet you haven't *left*." Matt saw that Tess blamed him for not having died in the fire. For how much simpler her life, if her husband had died.

She'd have been a young widow, instead of a not-so-young divorcée. Her pride chafed her like cheap unlined wool against her skin.

Quickly Matt learned not to trust the woman's mouth. "How are you today, Matt?" was a cruel question that meant in code *Are you happy now? Got what you've deserved, yes?*

Matt supposed yes. Yes, that was so.

Seeing that Matt was distracted by someone passing in the corridor, for in his doped-up state he found it difficult to concentrate, Tess said sharply, "She isn't coming! Maybe she's forgotten you."

Matt didn't inquire who was *she*. Tess's glaring eyes suggested she hadn't any actual woman in mind.

For Oriana was dead, and Duana Zwolle was dead. And Tess knew nothing of Abigail, long departed from Matt's life.

And Tess knew nothing of Ruellen Zwolle, Matt was certain.

Matt said slowly, for words literally pained him, "I'm sorry I hurt you, Tess. I never meant—" but Tess deftly intervened, as, on the tennis court, she'd sometimes surprised him by smashing his serve back into his face, "But, Matt, *I'm not hurt.* I'm a happier woman today than I've been in a long, long time." She smiled. She seemed almost to glisten, as with sexual gratification. There was a hint here, or more than a hint: Tess had a lover now.

The boys, wandering about the room, ill-at-ease, seemed not to want to overhear the adults' conversation. Tess was telling Matt how quickly the house sold: "Five hours on the market. *Five hours!* Sid can work miracles, it's as everyone says. *He* says, the house simply sold itself." Tess was moving with the boys into a new town house on the Weymouth River, near the country club. The prospect seemed to liven her heart.

Evidently Sid Krell was Tess's protector now. Her new, devoted friend. Sid Krell who'd become, it almost seemed, a serious individual. He'd stared in horror at Matt in his hospital bed following the first of the skin-graft operations, when most of Matt's flushed face was swathed in bandages, and Matt's eyes were bloodshot and watery. Tubes draining blood curved out of the head bandage like tusks, dripping into twin plastic vials that, when they filled, had to be emptied by nurses; these dangled from Matt's head at about the level of his earlobes. You could see poor Sid's nostrils pinching at the smell. The creases and pouches in his leathery skin tightening. *Mortality. The smell of. God help us.* The old man hadn't wanted to hear about Joseph Gavin, "Name Unknown"; he'd had no questions to put to Matt McBride. In fact, this would be Sid's only visit to the hospital. It was a surprise to Matt, though possibly not a total surprise, that Sid and Tess had become close, how Tess looked to the older, white-haired man for corroboration of even the simplest of remarks, a bright, pretty, dutiful daughter basking in the power of being loved.

If Krell was Tess's lover, good luck to both.

Davey and Graeme were visibly relieved that they didn't have to kiss Daddy good-bye. Not in Daddy's state.

Matt was hurt, that the boys seemed hardly to know him. He'd been feeling such guilt at the breakup of his marriage, it hadn't occurred to him that the boys would not miss him so much as he'd anticipated. "Kids are resilient. Half the kids in Davey's class have divorced parents, it's the way we live now." Tess spoke bravely, with her smile like a knife to the heart. *I don't need you. Not any longer. I've gotten what I needed from you.* She waved good-bye airily with her fingertips. Like the carved figurehead of a ship's prow she seemed to Matt, pushing through choppy yet finally yielding waters.

"Tess, goodnight—"

"Good-bye, Matt! Don't despair."

Don't despair! She was thinking he might be impotent, too.

Santa Monica, California. September 1998.

He would be patient. He was certain of the outcome.

The first time he approached her, having waited on foot outside the small stucco office complex on Pacific Avenue where Zodiac Graphics was located, Ruellen Zwolle went white in the face staring at Matt McBride, and stammering, "No. I—can't. Not just yet. Why are you here! Leave me alone." Quickly she walked away. She didn't look back. Matt stared after her, confused. Was this Ruellen Zwolle's California self? He had not seen her in months and was shocked at the change in her. Her dark, snarled-looking hair had grown long and fell past her shoulders, exactly like her sister's. She was wearing a thin muslin shirt of the kind sold in cheap Indian boutiques in the Santa Monica pedestrian mall, and faded jeans, and her feet were bare in sandals.

Her shock at seeing Matt McBride here in Santa Monica was genuine. Yet it was more fear than anger, and Matt was sorry about that.

Anger, he might overcome, in time. Fear was another matter.

He wondered if she thought of him frequently, as he thought of her. She'd recognized him at once. Though he'd lost fifteen pounds and his hair that had been such a curious metallic-silvery hue was now nearly white, and receding in thick tufts from his forehead; and his burn-scarred jaws were covered by a short, trimmed beard that gave him a look of both dignity and playfulness. He was a battered but still good-looking man, tall, lanky, springy on his feet like a former athlete. And optimistic!

Nighthawk was nothing if not optimistic. He'd come away from death with his life handed back to him.

Matt stood on a sidewalk at the rear of Ruellen Zwolle's office building and as she walked away, he made it a point to remain where he was. In an undertone he called after her, "All right, I understand. I'm sorry, too."

He was hurt, and he was disappointed. But he was sympathetic.

The woman was frightened of Matt, of her feeling for him. There was no question they would be lovers. Sometimes it seemed to Matt they'd already been lovers.

Go away, then. For now. I won't follow you. I promise.

She was driving a dark green Toyota, not a new model. Matt had memorized the license plate number without intending to.

His car was parked close by. But he wasn't going to follow her, he vowed.

Nor was he waiting for her the next day at Zodiac Graphics, as possibly she was expecting. Nor the next day. He would let days, a week pass; he wouldn't pursue her.

He'd allow Ruellen Zwolle, in her thoughts, to pursue him.

For he had no doubt this would happen. The bond between them was so strong.

Like tangled roots of trees, beneath the surface of the earth. So bound together that to extricate one from the other would be to destroy both.

It was in a Venice Beach bookstore that Matt picked up a second-hand copy of a book he'd thought he'd seen in Hugo L. Chauncey's airless, cluttered room. Nietzsche's *Beyond Good and Evil.* An intrigu-

ing title, but what did it mean? The book must have belonged to a
student, it was much annotated and underlined. Matt flipped through
the pages and read, aloud: " 'Ultimately one loves one's desire, not
the desired object.' "

Was this true? Invariably true?

And, if true, did it matter?

After his discharge from the hospital, Matt left Weymouth, New Jersey. He quit his job formally, in writing; he signed over their jointly
owned house to Tess (who did in fact sell it within five hours, for her
asking price of $860,000), and relocated to Santa Monica, California.
Here, he would be a more serious photographer than he'd had time
to be in New Jersey. Though he acquired a job on the staff of the
Santa Monica Weekly, circulation 31,000. It didn't fail to strike him
as ironic that, in his new, regained life, his salary was approximately
one-eleventh of what it had been, with commissions, at Krell Associates.

In their divorce settlement, Matt hadn't contested most of Tess's
demands. He had a vague hope that putting up no opposition might
cause Tess to hate him less passionately, and maybe this was so, and
maybe not. She'd demanded sole custody of their sons, of course, and
Matt hadn't contested this, either. As a gesture of conciliation, Matt
had acquiesced to Tess's allusions to his infidelities though he'd never
asked her who she believed had been his lover: Oriana, or Duana
Zwolle? Or both?

Matt was determined that his marriage be formally ended, before
he took up residence in Santa Monica. Before he approached Ruellen
Zwolle.

In fact, Matt couldn't afford to live in even the more modest sections
of Santa Monica. He'd rented a cheap three-room apartment in a funky
neighborhood in Venice Beach, close by. The place was furnished
and not far from the beach and there was a windowless room he could
use for a darkroom and he was happy there, strangely happy as he'd
rarely been in his expensive, beautiful family home in Weymouth,

New Jersey. Instead of a new-model white Acura, he now drove a 1994 Volkswagen hand-painted steely maroon. With his vivid white hair and beard, with his youthful, flushed face, his T-shirts, sweat-shirts, khaki shorts and trousers and jeans and jogging shoes water-stained from running at the edge of the surf, in wet, hard-packed sand, he became a southern California type. Not young but not middle-aged. Alone much of the time but rarely lonely. In the Volkswagen he cruised nighttime Los Angeles and came to love the smoggy-perfumy air, its acidic taste on the tongue. Of course he took his camera every-where with him. In California, Nighthawk would flourish; Nighthawk would become a serious photographer; Nighthawk's career was just beginning. Matt thought it remarkable that, at the age of thirty-seven, he was being paid to take photographs, at last. Even the boring as-signments, even the repeat assignments, intrigued him. For what's life but boring sometimes, and repetitive, and his mind would flash on the exploding sparks and leaping flames of the burning barn in which Matt McBride had been destined to be burned alive *yet had escaped his fate*, he would never know how. He would never know why. *Except there is no why.*

One day he would explain this to Ruellen Zwolle. They would be lying together, in each other's arms. She would be tracing with rev-erent, deliberate fingers the striated burn-scars on his face, his shoul-ders and back.

There's no why. There's just us.

Now she was aware of him! Seeing him in the corner of her eye, wherever she went. She'd been waiting for him. Since April. She'd known the man would come to her.

Though turning suddenly on the street, accusingly—she felt like a fool, not seeing him.

Peering through the blinds of her windows that were vulnerable to the street, even behind the overgrown bougainvillea shrubs and palm trees.

It was then her fear of the man turned suddenly to anger, even to
rage. She wanted to claw at his face, pound at him with her fists. He
had no right! He didn't know her! He'd been her sister's lover.

Matt was scrupulous about this: he meant to be settled into a life, or
a resemblance of a life, before contacting Ruellen Zwolle. He wanted
an apartment, and a job. He didn't want her to think he was staking
everything on her. He knew she was fragile emotionally, and he was
himself fragile emotionally though he could do a better job of dis-
guising it, than she.

He wouldn't tell her this. How, within forty-eight hours of arriving
in Los Angeles, he'd checked into a motel in Santa Monica and located Zodiac Graphics. He had the idea, which turned out to be cor-
rect, that it was a small business. He called the number and asked
to speak to Ruellen Zwolle and when Ruellen came to the phone and
said, "Yes? Hello?" he choked, and couldn't speak, and fumbled to
put the receiver back on the hook.

Afterward, she'd tell him *I knew then. Even before I knew, I knew.*

On the day Matt purchased the Volkswagen, before he'd even
signed the lease on his apartment, he'd waited at the curb across the
street from Zodiac Graphics from 5 P.M. until 5:55 P.M. when at last
a young woman he believed to be Ruellen Zwolle left the building
and climbed into a dark green Toyota and drove north on Pacific
Avenue and Matt followed her in the Volkswagen beyond Wilshire
Boulevard past high-rise hotels, apartment buildings and restaurants,
at last turning onto a residential street, and from that onto another,
narrower street several blocks inland from the Santa Monica pier. The
street name was Buena Vista. Ruellen Zwolle lived in a small,
Spanish-style stucco bungalow in a neighborhood of similar bunga-
lows, set deep in overgrown lawns of scruffy palms trees and
gorgeously blooming purple and scarlet bougainvillea. There was even
a lopsided wooden picket fence around Ruellen's house.

Matt parked the Volkswagen around the corner and walked past
the house on the opposite side of the street. He tried not to stare too

avidly. His initial impression was confirmed—*the front door was a dark lacquered red*. It hadn't been painted recently and had begun to peel. Which meant that Ruellen Zwolle had painted it independently of having seen Duana's red-lacquered door. This realization made Matt tremble with excitement.

But he didn't linger. He dreaded being seen by Ruellen, or by anyone in the neighborhood, like a man naked in a public place. He wasn't ready yet for Ruellen Zwolle and he knew Ruellen Zwolle wasn't ready for him.

Her pained words echoed in his ears. *I can't bear being touched by you and maybe, for the rest of my life, by any man.*

Her telephone number was unlisted. Yet somehow he had it.

She would never know who'd given it to him. What power he had to enter her life.

Hearing the telephone ring, and ring. Very late at night.

Where she lay sleepless in bed, her eyes moving alertly in the dark. In this house that was her own, a small foursquare stucco bungalow secure as a fortress with bolted doors and windows, an electronically monitored security alarm.

How had Death entered her sister's life. What had been the face of Death except a man's face.

(She'd seen photographs of Joseph Gavin. The meek-seeming mouth inside the feathery beard that hid rage, vindictiveness. The gentle eyes that were in fact mad eyes.)

She knew that Mathias McBride, Jr. was not Joseph Gavin. She knew he'd been responsible for Gavin's exposure, and for Gavin's suicide. She knew. Yet she listened to the telephone ring and she could not lift the receiver. She could not bear to hear his voice.

For, hearing his voice, she would break down. She would break down as she had at Duana's funeral and her heart had grown stony and resolute in the intervening months and she refused to love him, or any man. And so for that reason she would not answer the ringing phone.

She had reason to believe it rang in her absence, too. But there was

never any message from him. Only just silence, as he hung up the
phone. Or, a shock and a disappointment to her, the message was from
someone else.

In early October there was a day, an unexpected hour, she saw him
on the beach north of the Santa Monica pier, at dusk. He had not
been following her.

Though possibly he'd known she sometimes walked on the beach
at this hour of early evening.

A thin, dark young woman in a sweatshirt and paint-stained jeans,
her long, thickly wiry hair tied back in a scarf. A man in his late
thirties with prematurely white hair and a close-trimmed beard wearing wrinkled khaki trousers and jogging shoes and carrying a camera.

This was an hour when there were serious runners and hikers and
still surfers in their sleek black rubber suits, though the air was damp
and chilly and a wind whipped off the ocean and much of the sky was
opaque as concrete. Only at the western edge of the world was the
sky clear as if the setting sun, which was an uncomfortably vivid
glaring-red, a perfectly defined circle, had burnt away clouds at the
horizon.

She was taken by surprise, she smiled at him though her eyes were
frightened. They fell into step together. The wind, it almost seemed,
was urging them together. For an awkward long moment not knowing
what to say, how to begin, until she asked him about the camera, this
was a neutral subject, and a good subject, in which she was in fact
interested, and he could talk about it, his camera, and his work. So
they talked. For an hour hiking north of the pier, in the wind, in the
hard-packed wet sand at the edge of the ocean. He asked her about
her work, too, and she told him, as she'd begun to tell him months
ago, her work that was commercial and in that way freely chosen and
finite and without emotional duress unlike her sister's work that had
arisen from dreams and had involved too much emotion, and there
was a moment when he might have said what was banal and comforting, but did not; and she respected his silence, and was grateful
for it, and was silent herself. By this time the two of them were damp

with spray from the white-capped, breaking surf. It was dark, it was night, and no moonlight. Few other hikers remained. The last of the surfers had gone away. They headed back toward Santa Monica, veering up toward the roadway, walking with difficulty in the drier sand which is like walking with difficulty in a dream in which your will and anxious muscular exertions are not adequate to free you from something like quicksand or glue in which your feet are caught, and they laughed together short of breath in the gusty wind and one of them may have joked about feeling an earthquake tremor, and Matt McBride impulsively touched Ruellen Zwolle's arm and asked would she like to have dinner with him and Ruellen seemed about to say yes but instead drew away as if reflexively, involuntarily; and Matt took hold of her hand, boldly he took hold of both her hands, but her hands were stiff and cold, her hair had slipped partly out of the scarf and was whipping in long strands across her face and his, wiry strands of her hair across his mouth, and quickly he released her, and she murmured good-bye to him and began to run up to the roadway and he didn't follow her but stood in the sand staring after her sick with love and with the realization *It isn't me she's frightened of. It's loving a man. Opening herself to a man. After NAME UNKNOWN.*

The horror and injustice of it swept over him: Even after death, NAME UNKNOWN was still his enemy.

Yet he would come to the little stucco house on Buena Vista.

In November, one rain-lashed evening, invited or simply there and ringing the doorbell of the red-lacquered door. The little stucco house fortified against invasion. But the light above the door was burning. He'd come at last, and would be granted entry.

There she stood barefoot and short of breath as if she'd been running. In a long pale apricot silk tunic and a black ankle-length skirt and her hair that was wavy, wiry, crackling with electricity falling past her shoulders. Damp tendrils at her temples he would have liked to kiss. She laughed nervously. That strange breathless almost inaudible laugh that seemed to startle her. Those dark, shining just slightly shadowed and bruised eyes. The missing girl. Yet she was there taking from him, as if it were the most natural thing in the world, a single long-stemmed deep pink rose. She was alive, and tremulous opening the door to him as if she'd been waiting for the doorbell and must open the door immediately or not open it at all.

A single long-stemmed rose! He hadn't been able to think of anything more original, he said.

It was a strange apology, he was smiling so intensely.

Another time, he would bring her a more personal gift. An ivory silk fringed shawl from an East Asian boutique on Wilshire.

She said, Roses don't have to be original. That's the point of roses, isn't it?

They were in the kitchen. They were laughing, looking at each other and then quickly away. She was fumbling to locate a vase that was both tall and narrow enough for a single rose with a ten-inch stem. Glancing at him she saw the look in his face and the rose slipped from her fingers to fall unnoticed to the tile floor. She was in his arms, or his arms were around her. They held each other tightly as if the ground had begun to tilt. Both were frightened suddenly and overcome by emotion and could not speak. She'd begun to cry as she had vowed she would not. As she hadn't cried since her sister's funeral. Her heart was broken but she was crying in this man's arms, weeping openly and with relief. He was murmuring to her It's O.K., it's going to be O.K. I promise. Outside the brightly lit little kitchen was darkness. Reflections danced in all the windows.

It wasn't clear who the man was. She knew him, yet he was a stranger. Or, he was a stranger, yet she knew him. Over his shoulder, beside his stooped head, in the vertical window above the sink she saw a pale, tear-stained face. Whose?